PRAISE FOR *WARD*

"*Ward* has all the tension and excitement of *Jake*, the first book in this series...The author plays with the readers' emotions and surrounds them in a maze of conflict. *Ward* is joining *Jake* on my shelf of classics."

—*Rendezvous*

"Leigh Greenwood is one of the top writers today of the Western romance...The lead characters are superb and the support cast feel so real that readers will believe they are in the Old west visiting them. Another classy tale by one of the genre's best novelists."

—*Affaire de Coeur*

"Leigh Greenwood captivates readers time and time again! If you enjoyed the *Seven Brides*, you will fall in love with *The Cowboys*!"

—*The Literary Times*

"Leigh Greenwood is synonymous with the best in Americana romance."

—*Romantic Times*

"Few authors write with the fervor of Leigh Greenwood. Once again [Greenwood] has created a tale well worth opening again and again!"

—*Heartland Critiques*

PRAISE FOR *JAKE*

"Reminiscent of an old John Wayne/Maureen O'Hara movie, *Jake* kicks off what is sure to be another popular series from Leigh Greenwood."

—Robin Lee Hatcher, author of
PATTERNS OF LOVE

"Filled with laughter, tenderness, and wonderful family loyalty...Jake is so beautifully rendered that readers will be left feeling as if they have been held in his arms."

—*Romantic Times*

"*Jake* is an exciting, fast-paced Reconstruction Era romance....Readers will definitely want more from this great writer and will want it soon. Leigh Greenwood has another winning series in the works."

—*Affaire de Coeur*

"Exciting and soul searching, *Jake* is bound to win Leigh Greenwood new fans....Only a master craftsman can create so many strong characters and keep them completely individualized. Greenwood's books are bound to become classics."

—*Rendezvous*

"Fun, entertaining and romantic! *Jake* is special—I can't wait for Ward's story!"

—*The Literary Times*

"...unusually perceptive writing with a love story bringing East and West together...."

—*Heartland Critiques*

FEISTY CONVICTION

"I have no intention of letting your brother raise my son."

"Why?"

"Outside of the fact Ramon isn't Tanner's father, he's selfish, spiteful, arrogant and mean. He lacks both honor and honesty. I refuse to allow Tanner to grow up thinking Ramon is the kind of man he ought to become." She waited for a response but he didn't speak. "I'll never forgive you for what you did to me, Ward, but I don't hate you. I couldn't let your brother claim your son."

"But you always wanted Ramon. Marrying him would solve everything."

Would he ever believe anything she said? "I don't want Ramon. I never did. I loved you. Why won't you believe me?"

"How can I after what you did?"

"Ward Dillon, if you dare accuse me of sleeping with Ramon to get a rich husband, I'll shoot you with your own gun."

The Cowboys

WARD

LEIGH GREENWOOD

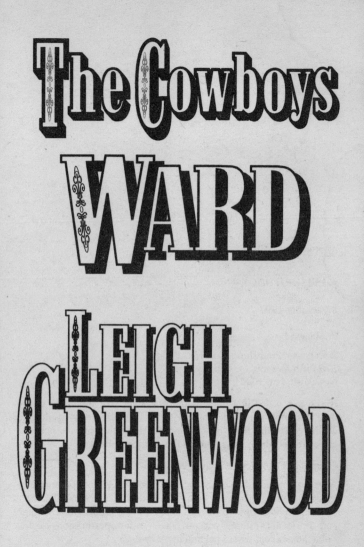

LEISURE BOOKS NEW YORK CITY

To Emma, a friend I still miss.

A LEISURE BOOK®

September 1997

Published by

Dorchester Publishing Co., Inc.
276 Fifth Avenue
New York, NY 10001

Printed in the United States of America.

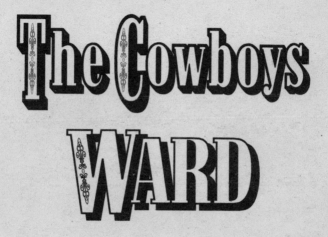

Chapter One

October 1861, San Antonio, Texas

Marina Scott didn't care if she was practically engaged to marry Ramon. She had to get away from his suffocating attention and his mother watching everything she did with cold, hawklike eyes.

Marina sneaked out of her lavishly decorated room during siesta. She sighed in relief when she left the heavy, dark oak furniture for the sunny warmth of the vine-covered balcony that circled the inner courtyard. She skipped down the stairs, darted around the fountain, passed silently through a cool inner hall, and hurried down an oak-lined avenue that led to the stables.

At first she'd been impressed by the huge stone rancho, a testimony to the Dillon wealth. Lately it had begun to feel more like a prison.

She bribed a stableboy to saddle a horse without

telling anyone. He didn't obey her request to choose a "nice, quiet" mount. The animal became more unruly with every step it took. Without warning, it took off through a dry wash and into an area of scattered cedar and mesquite.

Marina knew she shouldn't have come this far from the rancho, especially alone. Gardner Dillon's lands stretched for miles in every direction. His cattle, dozens of which she could see in the brush, numbered more than fifty thousand. Marina wondered what it was like to be so rich.

Marina's family was one of the most influential in San Antonio—her father a hero of two wars, her mother a leader of society—but her father had made several bad business deals. He desperately needed cash to support his tottering empire. Marina Scott's marriage to Ramon Dillon, the younger son of the wealthy rancher, Gardner Dillon, would accomplish that.

Luisa Escalante Dillon, Ramon's mother, had married Gardner for his money and now saw a family connection with the Scotts as the way to achieve her lifelong ambition of attaining leadership in San Antonio society.

It was a perfect marriage for everyone, but Marina had begun to feel like a bird in a cage, a beautiful cage filled with beautiful things, but a cage nevertheless. She should have been flattered by the attention Ramon and his mother showed her. Instead, she was irritated. She needed freedom, room to breath.

The last time she'd felt too cooped up, she'd escaped from school and attended a fiesta escorted by three cowboys. Her mother had fainted; her father had threatened to disown her. Marina had had a wonderful time. The cowboys had made her laugh.

Her horse snorted and sidled to the right. She wasn't a very good horsewoman, and she nearly lost her balance. She clutched nervously at the sidesaddle. Once she was married, she had every intention of learning to ride really well. She'd been kept under tight control all her seventeen years. One advantage of marrying a rancher was all this glorious space in which to roam.

Before she had entirely recovered her balance, a bull burst from the cover of a cedar thicket behind her. Her horse threw up his head, snorted, and broke into a gallop.

Marina pulled back on the reins, but he had the bit between his teeth. There was nothing she could do to stop him. Having driven them off, the bull ended his chase, but the horse didn't slow down. He veered off the trail into the brush. Branches whipped at Marina. Thorns clawed at her skirt. A limb of a live oak nearly swept her from the saddle as the horse raced through another dry wash.

She lost the reins. The only thing she could do was try to stay on until her mount got tired and slowed down. If she fell off, she'd have a very long walk back to the rancho.

Marina spotted a rider in the distance. Holding on with one hand, she waved frantically to him. He waved back. She hoped he realized she was calling for help, not offering a friendly greeting.

Just then her horse jumped a fallen tree. Apparently the rider could tell she was in trouble by the crazy way she rocked in the saddle. He started toward her at a gallop. Now, if she could only hold on until he got there.

For a moment Marina thought her horse would try to outrun the cowboy, but he raced down a wash to intercept her. A powerful arm reached out, grabbed her around the waist, and lifted her out of the saddle. He pulled his horse to a halt, set her down, and hit the ground next to her.

"Are you all right?" a deep voice asked.

Breathless, Marina looked up into gorgeous, deep blue eyes framed by ebony brows and lashes. He towered over her. His skin was browned from the sun, his black hair mostly hidden under his flat-crowned hat. He hadn't shaved in several days, but she found she liked the appearance of roughness. His big jaw, strong chin, and imposing brow, combined with his height, strength, and broad chest completed a picture of the most powerful, overwhelmingly masculine man she'd ever met.

"I'm fine," she managed to stammer. "Now."

The creases of concern relaxed into a smile. His clothes were dusty, and the aromas of sweat and horse were impossible to miss, but so was the aura of raw masculine power. Here, standing before her, was exactly what she'd found missing in every other man she'd met.

Shock caused her legs to go weak and she nearly collapsed. He scooped her up as though she were a featherweight. Her dress would be stained by the moisture in his shirt. He would certainly leave his aroma in her clothes. She didn't care. She could think only of the powerful arms that held her, the rock-ribbed chest she leaned against, the lazy smile that caused something deep inside her to go hot and fluid.

She dragged her mind off his lips. If she didn't, she wouldn't be able to stop herself from touching them.

"What are you doing out here alone?"

He sounded like her parents, critical and disapproving. That destroyed some of her desire to stare mindlessly at him.

"That's none of your business."

"It is when I have to risk my neck to save yours."

His attitude piqued her vanity. As San Antonio's reigning beauty, she was used to being treated with a great deal more deference.

"Let me down. I can take care of myself."

He set her on her feet. "Maybe—as long as you're on foot—but you don't know the first thing about horses."

Marina straightened her clothes. She wished she'd worn something other than this plain dress she'd borrowed from her maid. It didn't show her figure to its best advantage. Her scuffed boots were hidden beneath her skirt, but her hair was in a disgraceful tangle. The cowboy Sir Galahad didn't even pretend to admire her. He probably considered her foolish to ride a horse she couldn't handle. It irritated her that he was right.

"I can do just fine when I'm given a decent mount," she said. "That beast is a rogue."

He laughed. She wasn't tempted to join him. But she couldn't ignore the warmth that spiraled through her body and then pooled in her abdomen at the sound of his deep laughter.

"Any horse is a rogue in the hands of an inexperienced rider."

"I don't ride as well as I wish to," she admitted with a defiant toss of her head, "but living in town I never get any practice. I mean to change that, however. Soon I'll be an excellent horsewoman."

He looked at her, questioning, measuring. "You're quite sure of yourself, aren't you?"

Marina looked him over from boot toe to hat brim.

His boots had seen long service. Tears in his tight pants revealed tantalizing bits of skin. A wide belt circled his slim waist. His shirt stretched to cover his chest. The lowered brim of his hat hid his expression. He was a mighty tempting specimen of the male sex, but he was still just a cowhand.

"Anybody can learn to ride a horse," she said, with a disdainful toss of her head. "Cowboys do it all the time, and everybody knows they're mostly vagrants and misfits."

He didn't like that. Good. Now he knew what it felt like to be belittled. She turned on her heel and started walking toward the rancho.

He followed. "What happened to your horse?"

"He got scared by a bull." She didn't look up, just kept walking.

"What were you doing out here by yourself?"

"Riding."

"Okay, what were you doing riding by yourself?"

"I wanted to be alone."

She couldn't resist peeping over her shoulder to see how he was taking her answers. He seemed perfectly indifferent. She bridled. No man had ever been unaffected by her, certainly not one for whom she felt such a strong attraction. This cowboy wasn't going to be the first.

"Your answers aren't very informative," he said. "I'll have to get you back home. Who are you?"

She cast him an arch look. "I'm not going to tell you."

She walked faster, but he caught up. With those long, powerful legs, she didn't have a hope of getting away from him.

"I can follow you and find out."

"You wouldn't dare."

"Cowboys are vagrants and misfits, remember. We'll do just about anything."

She looked up to see if he was angry and spied a dimple trying to disguise itself.

She grinned. "I shouldn't have said that, but you made me angry."

"Do you always fight back when people make you angry?"

"Usually. It gets me in a lot of trouble."

"I imagine your smile gets you right back out again."

She couldn't resist flashing him her very best. "Not always. My father's practically immune."

"I know what you mean. My mother's like that."

"But you're a man. You can go where you want, do what you please, marry when you like."

"It's not that easy, even for me."

"It's worse for girls."

"Even when they look like you?"

"Looks aren't everything, you know."

"That's not a widely held opinion."

"Well, it's mine." She very carefully turned her gaze to the ground in front of her. "You're very nice looking, especially for a cowboy."

His howl of laughter confused her.

"What's so funny?"

"You."

She wasn't sure she liked that. It didn't sound like a compliment.

"That's not very gallant."

"Gallantry is for society ladies, not a free-spirited little heartbreaker like you."

"You like high-spirited women?"

"Sure. They're much more fun than ladies."

She wasn't sure she liked losing her standing as a

lady. "It gets me into a lot of trouble. Like right now. I should be taking a siesta."

"But then I'd have missed rescuing you."

"Would you have minded that?"

"More than you know."

The heat, the tension Marina had felt when he held her in his arms came rushing back. His was not a mocking smile, not even a friendly one. It was the smile of a man who found the woman at his side very attractive.

Marina found him very attractive, too. She was surprised just how attractive. How was this possible? She was engaged to Ramon Dillon, the handsomest man in Texas and one of the richest. How could this cowboy cause her temperature to rise, her cheeks to feel hot, her blood to sing in her veins?

She could feel this man's presence without even looking up.

"How did you stray onto Dillon land?" he asked.

"I didn't stray. I started on Dillon land."

"Okay, where did you start from on Dillon land?"

"The rancho."

"I've never seen you there." His smile turned brilliant. "I'd have remembered if I had. Do you work in the house or on a nearby ranch?"

Her clothes. He'd taken her for a servant or the daughter of someone who worked for the family. Surprisingly, she decided she liked that. It gave her anonymity, the freedom to act like herself.

She smiled provocatively. "I haven't seen you, either." She couldn't have missed anybody like him.

"I've been on roundup."

"Oh, that explains it."

He suddenly stepped in front of her, smiling down at her like the big, overgrown cowboy he was. Only this cowboy didn't make her laugh. He made her breathless.

"Who are you?"

"Marina Scott. Why do you want to know?" She tried to dart around him, but he caught her in his arms again. Her struggles to break free were half-hearted. They stopped altogether when she saw the warm light in his eyes.

"A man always wants to know the name of the woman who's stolen his heart."

He must be joking. They'd only just met. But her heart lurched in her throat. God help her, she wanted it to be true. She didn't understand what was happening to her. Suddenly she couldn't think. Nothing felt the way it ought to feel, and all because he'd made a joke.

But was it a joke? He was smiling at her, but it wasn't a mocking or teasing smile. It looked like the smile of a man who knew what he liked and meant what he said.

"Don't be nonsensical. It's impossible to lose your heart in less than ten minutes."

"Then why is my chest empty? It couldn't have fallen out." He pretended to look round.

"Now you're teasing me."

"Put your ear to my chest." He held her closer. "Hear anything?"

Only her own heart as it thumped painfully in her chest. She lost all desire to tease or flirt. "Who are you?"

"Ward Dillon. My father owns Rancho del Espada."

His words spilled over her like ice water from a pitcher. She was in the arms of the brother of the man she was engaged to marry.

"Put me down."

"I have a better idea. I'll put you on my horse. On the way to the house you can tell me what you're doing here."

Marina looked at the saddle. "I can't ride astride."

"That's easy." He put her down and swung into the saddle. "Give me your hands."

"Why?"

"Don't question everything. Just give me your hands."

"All right, but I don't see—*eeek!*"

Before she knew what had happened, he'd lifted her off the ground and set her in his lap. She was cradled in his arms, against his chest, her lips practically touching his cheek. She refused to think of what her thighs and legs might be touching. Heat coursed through her entire body. They were intimately close, and there was nothing she could do about it.

"We shouldn't be riding like this," she managed to say.

"It might take hours to find your horse. It would take just as long to get home if I walked."

She couldn't think. She ought to tell him she was engaged to Ramon, but she couldn't frame the words, not with him holding her like this. Why hadn't she known he was Ramon's brother?

"Why haven't I seen you in San Antonio?" she asked.

"I've been in medical school. When I'm home, I help Dad with the ranch."

"You're a doctor?"

"I'm not sure you can say that. I haven't been in practice yet, but I do have a medical degree."

A doctor-cowboy from a wealthy family. Now

wouldn't that surprise her father. But no more than it surprised her. Doctors were supposed to be chubby old men with whiskers, cowboys dirty and a little crude. This man shattered both prejudices at once.

"You're not at all like Ramon," she managed to say.

"I take after my father. He takes after our mother."

"I mean he doesn't work cattle and wear rough clothes."

Ramon was always impeccably dressed, his linen spotless, his clothes free of dust and sweat.

"He's delicate. He nearly died once. After that Mother wouldn't let him out of her sight. We never say anything about it. He doesn't let on, but I know he's ashamed of being sickly."

Marina wasn't sure. She hadn't see Ramon straining to get into the saddle and chase cows. She tried to picture him dressed like Ward, but it was impossible. Ramon was a picture-perfect caballero—all black, white, and silver.

His perfection left her cold.

Not so with Ward. He was a gentleman, too, but with the husk left on. Something about him appealed to the primitive, uncontrollable side of her nature. Like a wild beast prodded into action, it came stampeding to the surface, pushing aside the veneer of sophistication her parents and teachers had worked so hard to give her. She didn't care that she was supposed to marry Ramon. She wanted this man, and she wanted him badly.

Marina's feelings frightened her. She'd been tempted to do some very rash things in her life—had done some of them—but never anything like this. She had to get hold of herself.

She was relieved when several ranch hands rode up, one of them leading her horse. No one seemed to find it unusual to see her firmly settled in Ward's lap.

"Trade you," the man leading her horse said with a broad grin.

"I never found anything but cows in these thickets," another said.

"With your looks, I'm surprised the cow didn't run away," someone teased.

"Would have if he hadn't roped it first."

During this gentle bantering, Ward helped Marina remount her horse. They all rode back together, a cavalcade of seven riders escorting a single woman.

Relieved of the devastating tension of intimate contact with Ward, Marina was soon enjoying herself. Each of the men tried to outdo the others with extravagant compliments. One unstrapped his guitar and sang her a song about a dark-haired Spanish beauty with midnight eyes.

"She's not Spanish," Ward pointed out.

"But she has Spanish eyes," the boy insisted.

Marina had never felt so free. She was disappointed when they reached the rancho. She could feel the girdle of propriety begin squeezing the life out of her. The men melted away, leaving her and Ward to face Luisa Dillon, who waited for them under the live oak trees that shaded the entrance to the house. Marina would have sworn the woman's eyes flashed fire at the sight of them together, but when they drew up and dismounted, she was the same smiling, gracious hostess as always.

"Ward, no one told me you had returned," Luisa said, turning her cheek for a kiss. "I see you found our lost lady."

"Your lost lady?" Ward repeated, looking in confusion from Marina to his mother.

"I'm a guest," Marina explained.

Ward's gaze turned cautious. He kissed his mother's cheek. "Her horse ran away with her."

"My dear, you could have been hurt," Luisa said to Marina in a concerned tone. "You should not have gone out without Ramon."

"I wanted to see something of the ranch," Marina said. "Ramon told me he didn't enjoy riding beyond the avenue."

"That is my fault," Luisa said. "A mother worries. You must go to him. He wants to know whom you plan to invite to the engagement ball."

Marina could feel the impact of Luisa's words on Ward. The air between them froze. Unable to do otherwise, she looked up. The smile had gone from his face. His eyes were as cold as ice.

This was no time for explanations. There was none she could give.

"Where is he?"

"In the salon."

Marina turned to Ward. "Please thank the young man who captured my horse. I'll save you a dance at the fandango tonight for coming to my rescue."

"You must not expect Ward to stay up so late," Luisa said, patting Ward's arm in an affectionate manner. "He must be up early in the morning. There is much to do before he goes into the army."

"You're leaving?" Marina asked, suddenly feeling bereft.

"In two days," Ward said. "I came home only because Dad's too sick to manage the roundup."

He was going to disappear as quickly as he'd appeared. She clasped her hands together to keep from reaching out to hold him back. "I'll pray for your safety."

She turned and ran inside. If he was going, she

21

wanted him to go quickly, disappear before it hurt too much.

Ward entered his room intending to prepare for bed, but the music of the fandango drove thoughts of sleep from his mind. Marina Scott was down there, dancing, smiling into Ramon's eyes, pledging her love, looking forward to becoming Mrs. Ramon Dillon.

He didn't know why he should have been shocked to learn that the most beautiful woman he'd ever seen was engaged to Ramon. It always happened that way. He should have become used to it. He *had* become used to it. It was just that he usually didn't mind it. This time he hated the idea of Ramon winning Marina's heart.

He'd spent the afternoon and evening with his father discussing the ranch, the condition of the range and the herds. Luisa had managed well during his father's illness, but she wasn't as firm as Gardner or Ward in controlling Ramon's spending. Now that Ramon was getting married, it was only natural he would want to increase his expenditures, but the rancho couldn't sustain such extravagance. Ward would have to speak to Ramon before he left.

Which made Ward think of Marina again. Something had sprung up between them the moment he looked into her huge, lustrous black eyes. He wasn't all that experienced with society women, but he could tell when a woman liked him.

That puzzled him. What exactly had she felt when she looked into his eyes? And why did she feel it?

He told himself it was useless to wonder. Whatever she might have felt for him couldn't compare to what she would feel for Ramon. Once a woman saw his brother, she forgot Ward. He was a fool even to think this time would be different.

He made up his mind to go to bed and be out of the house in the morning before anyone woke, but he didn't move. The music reached out to him, drew him, whispered to him. This was the last time he was likely to go to a dance and enjoy himself for a long time. He could sleep during the many dreary months ahead.

Besides, it was unthinkable that he would go away without offering his congratulations and best wishes to his brother and the woman he was to marry. Since he wouldn't be around for the official ball, what better time to do that than tonight? There he wouldn't be in danger of allowing his glance to rest on her lips too long or letting the desire show too plainly in his eyes.

He could seek her out now, say his good-byes in private, but he didn't trust himself not to be bewitched by her smile or the gaiety that danced in her onyx eyes. Jet hair and brows made her skin glow as pale as an ivory madonna. Yet generous red lips lured a pagan response from him. She had felt as fragile in his arms as a doll, slender and weightless. Yet she had rocked his world to its foundations.

No, it was much better to see her in public. There he could say what he needed to say, pretend to feel what he ought to feel. He would have plenty of time to forget her afterwards.

Yet he knew he was only rationalizing. Going to the dance would be the worst mistake he could make. He was going to war. She was getting married. He ought to keep away, leave tonight if necessary.

But he couldn't help himself. He had to go. Casting his fate into the hands of the gods, Ward started to strip.

Chapter Two

The music was wonderful. Ramon was his most charming. The guests were delightful, and Luisa smiled on the whole with an approving gaze. But there was no gaiety in Marina's heart, no lightness in her step, no laughter in her voice. Her willful heart had begun to question the marriage that would make two families happy and secure her own future.

For once she cursed her own waywardness. If there had been any chance her foolish imaginings could become reality, it had died the moment Ward learned she belonged to Ramon. His eyes told her that. His absence this evening confirmed it.

"You're in an unusually solemn mood tonight," Ramon said as they met in the line dance. Usually impatient of these tedious, formal dances, Marina was thankful for them tonight. She could evade conversation for long periods of time.

"I'm a little tired," she said as they circled each other.

"You shouldn't have ridden so far."

"Probably not." They bowed and circled again.

"People will start going home soon. You can sleep late tomorrow."

They separated and she moved to meet her new partner, a portly colonel with big eyes and a bigger paunch. She was responding with only half a mind to his flowery compliments when she saw Ward standing next to one of the carved posts on the balcony that encircled the courtyard.

She missed her step.

She forced herself to face her partner and concentrate on her steps. Ward's presence didn't change anything. She was still destined to be Ramon's wife.

Yet he had come.

What was he doing here? Did he want to see her as much as she wanted to see him? Admitting her fascination with this man frightened and excited her at the same time. Could this mean anything more than a flirtation of a few hours on a soft autumn evening when she was enchanted by the music, the people, the wine, and the excitement of finding herself admired by a man who, with a single glance, had caused her blood to turn to fire, her bones to jelly?

She didn't know, but she felt her step grow light, her mood gay, her pulse tumultuous. She felt a smile spread across her face just in time to dazzle the young man who had replaced the colonel as her partner.

He missed his step.

Marina flushed, averted her eyes, concentrated on not looking in Ward's direction. She scolded herself for being so foolish. She ought to be sensible and do what everyone wanted her to do. But now her resolve was being threatened by a tall, lanky cowboy with sapphire eyes.

She looked up. Ward's glance was so direct, the longing in his eyes so intense, it burned its way though the space that separated them and buried itself in her heart. Marina felt claimed, cut from the herd and branded as his own.

She nearly bumped into her partner. She smiled apologetically at his red-faced embarrassment as he was replaced by a junior officer in splendid uniform.

Marina felt shaken. This was no illusion. His feeling for her was just as strong as hers for him. Yet how could this be? They had just met. They knew nothing about each other. A frisson of fear sent chills through her body. She'd been careless before, even taken chances, but she'd never felt out of control. She'd always known what was happening, known what she wanted to happen.

Now she didn't.

Yet this same feeling of being out of control pulled her onward. All her life she'd been ruled by her parents. When she married Ramon, she'd be ruled by him. And his mother.

Something told her that would never happen with Ward.

But how did she know that? Why did she believe it so firmly?

She looked up. He was still there. She wanted him to come down. He must come down. She had to know if this was real. Suppose she was just imagining it? No, that was impossible. The feeling was too powerful to be imagined.

No dance had ever seemed so long to Marina. She wondered if she dared leave the floor to go to him.

The dance finally ended, but before she could turn around, Ramon had claimed her hand.

"I see your brother came after all," she said as they headed toward a row of chairs set up under the balcony. Her mind searched frantically for some way to get rid of Ramon long enough to go to Ward, to ask, to know.

Ramon looked up, surprised and seemingly pleased. "It must be in your honor. He never comes to dances." Ramon's look and his hold on her hand were possessive. It was all Marina could do to keep from jerking her hand out of the crook of his arm.

"Why is he standing up there?" she asked. "Why doesn't he come down?"

"I don't know."

"Well, call him. Make him come down."

Ramon's look was questioning. "Why are you so anxious for him to come down?"

Afraid she'd spoken too freely, Marina was relieved to see no suspicion in Ramon's eyes. He was too confident to doubt his irresistibility.

"He's your brother. He's going away to war. I must tell him good-bye."

"You saw him this afternoon."

"But he thought I was a servant," she protested.

"They're ready to begin the next dance," Ramon pointed out.

Marina wasn't giving up so easily. "Tell them to wait," she said as she picked up her skirts and ran toward the steps that led to the balcony.

By the time she reached the top, she couldn't hear anything above the fierce pounding of her heart. Yet the moment she found herself face to face with Ward, a swarm of goosebumps prickled her skin.

Ward had dispensed with the loose-fitting black

suit favored by Americans for the tight-fitting pants, bolero jacket, and ruffled white shirt favored by Ramon. The pants clung to his muscled thighs like a second skin. The tiny jacket emphasized the size of his chest, the power in his arms.

"Why didn't you come down?" she asked. Her voice sounded breathless with excitement.

"I like to watch from here."

"But you're missing all the fun, the dancing."

"I don't dance."

She tried to laugh. It sounded like a hiccup. "Don't be ridiculous. Everybody dances." She reached out and took his hand. "Come on. The music's about to start."

He didn't move.

"You can't stay up here now. Everybody's seen you."

He let her lead him down the steps. She was certain he followed because he couldn't let go of her hand. She felt as if they had been holding hands since the beginning of time.

"I didn't know you would be here," Ramon said to his brother when they reached the courtyard.

"I had to pay my respects to you and your future bride," Ward said.

A moment of doubt shook Marina. He didn't appear to be suffering from the frenzy of hope and speculation that tortured her. He spoke with a calm, even voice that betrayed no strained nerves, no tumultuous emotions, no chaotic thoughts. Could she have been mistaken?

"Then you must have this dance," Ramon said.

"You forget Ward does not dance," Luisa said as she floated up to join them. "He said he would never take to the floor when you were present."

"Surely you could try this once," Marina said.

"This is the last dance," Luisa told her. "It is only fitting you dance with your fiancé."

"Then tell them to play one more," Marina said as she pulled Ward toward the dance floor. "You can't send your son to war without one last dance."

"Are you always so disdainful of the rules?" Ward asked as he followed Marina to the part of the court-yard set off for dancing.

"No, but I nearly always want to be."

"It's not a good idea," he said.

"Good ideas are boring."

"But safer."

"Come on, dance," she challenged.

"I told you, I don't dance."

"It's easy. Put your arms around me. I'll show you. Come on. The music won't start until we're ready. Everybody's watching."

It was as if he was reluctant to touch her, and then suddenly made up his mind. He took her firmly in his arms. When the music began, he whirled her off her feet.

"I thought you said you don't dance," she said, recovering from her surprise.

"I don't dance as well as Ramon."

No one danced as well as Ramon. But as Ward guided Marina around the courtyard, she found her-self enveloped by a magical feeling unlike anything she'd ever experienced with her fiancé. She floated, glided, moved effortlessly through the steps, guided by Ward's strong arms. What his movements lacked in grace and fluidity, they made up for in athletic power.

He put her in mind of a wild stallion, running free over the prairie, exulting in his power, confident of his ability to defeat any foe that might face him.

Marina didn't feel defeated. She felt lifted up and borne along with him as though they were one, as though they belonged together.

"Why are you doing this?" he asked.

She understood what he meant. She would always understand.

"I had to know."

"Okay, now you know."

She could tell he spoke to her through a wall of willpower, a determination to do nothing that would dishonor her.

"Is that all you're going to say?" she asked. It couldn't be. There was more. There had to be more.

"What do you want me to say?" he asked.

"There must be something."

"Do you want me to say you're beautiful, that you'll make Ramon a perfect wife?"

Not that. "No. I—"

"Or would you rather I said holding you in my arms is like being in heaven, that if you were marrying any man but my brother, I'd strangle him."

"Would you? I mean, that's against the law."

"Lady, what you're doing to me right now ought to be against the law."

Marina swallowed hard. "Me?"

"You're more dangerous than a wolf in a herd of three-legged calves."

She couldn't tell whether he was kidding her or saying she was driving him crazy. It was terribly important that he not be kidding. Yet what could she say? She was engaged to Ramon. Ward was leaving.

It was too late for words. Maybe it was too late for everything, but his touch told her what his lips would not. His hand at her back, his long fingers wrapped around hers, his body holding her, shielding her, enfolding her, everything about him told her she had reached some place in him no other woman had approached.

She had branded him as surely as he had branded her.

They were alike, kindred souls. She was the flame to his hot coal, the sharp edge of his knife of desire. He was fire, she the fuel. He was wind, she the wide prairie he roamed at will.

She looked up. He was staring at her, his deep blue eyes like glimmering sapphires. The music gradually faded into the distance. The tempo slowed; their bodies drew closer together. Marina sank deeper and deeper into his embrace. The world narrowed until it contained nothing but the two of them. Their lips drew closer together.

They were close, closer, almost touching—

"You were very good, Ward. With a little practice, you could be a creditable dancer."

Ramon's voice shattered their bubble. Marina awoke to find herself surrounded by people applauding them.

"It was Marina," Ward said, gallantly. "Anyone could dance well with her in his arms."

Just then the band broke into a wild rhythm. Flamenco!

"I agree," Ramon said. "I intend to claim the last dance."

Marina fought her way out of the thick fog that still enveloped her. "I couldn't possibly dance the flamenco with you. I have no idea what to do."

"Then watch me," Ramon said proudly. "I'm the best in Texas."

Marina watched as several men and women joined

Ramon, all poised and ready for the dance to begin.

"This is something I *can* do," Ward whispered in her ear as he walked quickly forward and took his place next to a clearly surprised Ramon.

"He has learned this at the campfires from our vaqueros," Luisa said when she came to stand beside Marina. "He is good, but not as good as Ramon."

Luisa was right. Ramon had a grace and precision none of the other dancers could match, but Marina found herself more excited by the rough, virile energy Ward exuded as he danced. The brothers were a stunning pair. Ramon was shorter and almost feline in his perfection. Ward exuded an energy that was primitive in its raw, masculine power.

"See, it is as I told you," Luisa said, pride ringing in her voice. "No one dances as well as Ramon."

Maybe, but Marina preferred Ward's style.

"Ramon does nearly everything better than anyone else," Marina said.

Luisa sighed contentedly. "I am very fortunate to have such a son."

"Two such sons," Marina corrected.

"Yes," Luisa said, smiling sweetly. "Ward has been gone so much I almost forget him."

Marina didn't see how a woman could forget a man like Ward if he'd been gone for twenty years. She certainly wouldn't.

The dance came to an end. Everyone applauded the dancers. Marina noticed a dusky beauty move quickly to give her compliments to Ward. A spear of jealousy pierced her heart. Marina tried to tell herself she had nothing to be jealous of, but the feeling didn't disappear.

She forced herself to smile at Ramon. "You were wonderful, as usual," she said.

He accepted her compliment gracefully. "I enjoy dancing, but I'm tired now. Let's say good night to Ward before we go in."

Marina didn't want to go in. She had no desire to go to bed. "I can't go yet. I haven't had a chance to talk to your brother. I don't know anything about him, where he's going, when he'll be back, what he'll do while he's away." She couldn't let him go yet. She had to hold on just a little bit longer.

"Mother and Ramon can tell you more than enough about me," Ward said, coming up to them in time to hear her remark. "I must go to bed. I have business in San Antonio tomorrow." He took Marina's hand and kissed it. "My very best wishes for a happy marriage."

He was backing away, playing it safe. He was telling her that what might have been would never be.

"Good night, brother. Take care of her. You won't find another one like her."

"I know that," Ramon said, pride of possession resonating in his voice.

Marina wanted to shout that Ramon didn't own her, that she was free to do what she pleased, but Ward had turned, kissed his mother good night, and was climbing the steps.

He was gone.

Was that all there was, a moment when hope soared like mist before an ocean breeze, and then nothing? Was everything gone, discarded, forgotten?

She listened to Ramon and his mother talk about plans for tomorrow. It seemed so pointless when her life had shriveled like a dying leaf. Had she imagined things, seen only what she wanted to see? Ward had spoken to her as he would to any other female, wished her a good night's sleep, good luck for the future. Ordinary. Mundane. Emotionless.

Then why did she feel an almost physical force pulling her to him?

She must forget him, put aside this day, as he had put it aside. She must go on as if they had never met, as if their meeting had been no different from thousands of other meetings.

But Marina didn't know if she could. For one moment, she had caught a glimpse of a half-formed vision of love that liberated rather than imprisoned. It had been snatched away, yet it had forever changed something inside her.

After a night spent pacing her bedchamber, Marina had decided to tell Ramon she couldn't marry him. She came downstairs at dawn to find the house empty and silent. The maid who brought coffee told her Ramon and his mother weren't expected up before ten at the earliest.

It was six o'clock.

Having made up her mind, Marina hated to wait so long. She was afraid her common sense would reassert itself. She knew all the reasons why she should marry Ramon, but she couldn't. That must have been what she was feeling when she'd met Ward.

That was why she was able to fall in love with him.

Marina laughed at herself, but it was a laugh heavily laced with misgivings. How did an engaged woman fall in love with another man at first sight? It was ridiculous. It was impossible. It simply wasn't done.

Yet she'd done it.

The coffee was hot and strong enough to dissolve adobe. Marina diluted it with heavy cream. She had just tasted it again when Ward walked into the breakfast parlor. For a moment the coffee caught in her throat. She managed to swallow just as he turned and saw her.

He had changed back into his work clothes, but the attraction between them was as strong as ever. Stronger. He froze at the sight of her.

Recovering, he moved toward the coffee. "You're up early," he said. "Ramon won't be down for hours."

His voice sounded calm, but his reaction had betrayed him.

"I know. I couldn't sleep."

He poured his coffee. "Excited about your wedding?"

She hadn't intended to tell anybody before she told Ramon, but she couldn't let Ward go on thinking she was going to marry his brother. She lowered her eyes to avoid his gaze. "I'm not going to marry Ramon."

The silence was so deep, she could hear herself breath. She looked up. Ward hadn't moved. His coffee remained untouched.

"When did you decide that?" he asked.

"Last night."

He picked up his coffee and took a drink. He didn't seem to be bothered by its strength. He looked at her across the table. "Why?"

Marina hadn't yet decided what she was going to say to Ramon. She knew that no explanation would satisfy her parents. She would be lucky if she didn't find herself on the street without a penny to her name.

"I prefer not to say," she said, turning away from him. If she married Ramon, she'd be forced to live in the same house with Ward, to see him get married, see another woman have his children. She'd have to face him across the table for the rest of her life.

"You're going to have to tell a lot of people—Ramon, my mother, your parents. I doubt any of them are going to like it. You may as well practice on me."

He had come around the table to stand next to her. He put his hands on her shoulders and forced her to turn until she faced him. "Why don't you want to marry Ramon?"

"Because I don't love him."

It sounded so silly. Her father would shout and make threats. He had already promised to disown her if she didn't marry Ramon. Her mother would weep and cajole. Neither would understand anything so ridiculous as love. Marriage was a business deal made to cement alliances, forge business partnerships, provide a secure future for children, and ensure a continuation of family position in society.

People didn't marry for love. They couldn't afford it.

"That's not a reason I expect your parents to understand."

"No."

She wanted to look away from him, but she couldn't. She couldn't do anything except stare into his eyes.

"Neither will my family."

"You understand, though, don't you?"

It seemed a strange question to ask a man who looked at her without visible emotion. But surely, if the feeling between them meant anything, if she hadn't imagined it entirely, he must feel at least a little of the enchantment, the almost magical feeling that made it impossible for her to think of marrying anyone else.

"Yes, I do."

For a moment she thought he would speak of his

understanding, but he walked back around the table and picked up his coffee. He studied her over his cup.

"Have you given any thought to the possible consequences of your decision?" he asked.

"Not much." She'd been too busy trying to understand her own feelings to consider anything beyond her parents' anger.

"You'll be in disgrace with your own family. My mother and Ramon will hate you."

"I don't care."

"If you marry Ramon, your future will be assured."

He appeared to be drinking his coffee, calmly talking to a woman too silly to understand where her best interests lay. But the vibrations that passed between them whispered another message. It said he was waiting to be sure before he let himself say anything at all.

"I can't marry Ramon," she said. "I tried to want to, but I can't."

"Is loving the man you marry essential?"

It hadn't been before she met Ward. "Of course. Isn't that how you feel?"

"I don't know. Love seems to me a very undependable emotion."

"Don't you believe that love can last?" she asked quietly.

Ward looked just as disturbed by the question as Marina felt.

"Maybe, if that love were strong, well grounded, it could last."

Marina walked around the table until she stood in front of Ward. "Do you believe a man can love a woman like that?"

"I'd like to think so."

"Do you believe you could?"

"I don't know."

"Would you want to try?"

His gaze searched Marina's face. She didn't know what he was looking for, but she hoped he would find it there. She had gambled when she'd decided not to marry Ramon. She was taking an even bigger chance now. She was practically telling Ward she loved him, inviting him to say he loved her, too. It didn't matter that it had happened so fast she could hardly believe it. She *did* believe it. She wanted him to believe it, too.

"For the right woman, I think a man would be willing to take almost any risk."

He looked at her with naked hunger in his eyes. He still held his coffee cup in his hands, but he had forgotten it. His gazed bored into her. Marina wondered what he could see.

"Would you?"

"I think so."

"Have you ever met such a woman?"

"I once thought so."

Each answer seemed to be drawn out of him against his will.

"When?" she asked.

She could hardly stand fencing with him. She had to know what he felt. She had to know if he returned her love. His look became even more intense, but she felt him back away from giving her an answer. She had to reach out, to stop him from withdrawing.

"Yesterday I found someone I could love," she said. "That's why I can't marry Ramon." There, she had said it. Now it was up to him to say he loved her just as madly.

Ward dropped his coffee cup. It shattered on the

tile floor, but he didn't seem to notice. "Are you sure?"

"Yes."

"How do you know?"

He still wouldn't let himself believe she loved him.

"Because from that moment I had no more questions, no more doubt."

He stepped forward. The sound of the cup being ground under his feet didn't slow him. He reached out and touched her cheek with the back of his hand, brushed her parted lips with his fingertips. His eyes were luminous with emotion, feelings she suspected he'd long held tightly inside of himself.

"Can it truly happen so fast?"

"It did for me. The moment I looked into your eyes."

"I thought you must be an angel. You were too beautiful to be real."

She took his hand in hers and pressed it to her cheek. "But I am real."

"Are you sure? I'm not going to wake and find I've been sleeping on a cactus?"

"I'm a little sharp-edged on occasion, but no one ever accused me of being a cactus."

She could see that he was trying to believe their love was possible but he couldn't quite do it.

"I love you, Ward Dillon. I don't know how it happened or why. I can't explain anything about it. I just knew from the moment I looked into your eyes that I would never care for another man as long as I lived."

Still he held back.

"Is that so hard to believe?"

"Yes."

"Why?"

"Because I want it too much."

"Believe it, Ward. You can have everything I am, everything I have to give."

He grabbed her and kissed her hard on the mouth. Then he waited, looking down at her, as though he expected her to slap him. When she didn't, he kissed her again. This time the kiss was filled with fire.

Marina wasn't sure how long they stood kissing without saying a word. It was long enough for him to believe she loved him, long enough for her to believe she'd finally done something right.

"I still can't believe it," he said as he hugged her tightly against him.

"I promise you, every word of it is true."

"People are going to be angry."

"I don't care."

"They're going to try to change your mind."

"They can't."

"I have to leave for the army."

"I'll go with you."

He laughed the kind of wild, uninhibited laugh that was only possible after the tyranny of a long-known fear has been broken.

"You can't. The army baggage train is no place for a lady."

"It won't matter."

And it wouldn't. Nothing would matter ever again as long as she was with him.

The maid entered the breakfast room and exclaimed over the broken cup.

Ignoring the maid, Ward pulled Marina into the hall behind him. With a quick look to make sure no one was about, they ran out the door into the gardens beyond.

An hour later Marina waved good-bye to Ward as he headed toward town. He would be back that evening. They would face Ramon and the rest of the world together.

Chapter Three

But Marina couldn't wait for Ward's return. Neither could she wait any longer for Ramon to come downstairs. It was past noon. The servants had all done their work and retired to the kitchen behind the house to prepare and eat their midday meal. She wasn't hungry. She was anxious to see Ramon and get the confrontation over with. Finally she went upstairs and knocked on his door.

"Who is it?" His voice was muffled.

"Marina. When are you coming down?"

"In a while. I'm still dressing."

"I have to talk to you. May I come in?"

Ramon's manservant opened the door and ushered her in. Ramon sat at his dressing table. He was still in his dressing gown, but he'd been shaved and his hair was groomed to perfection.

The size of his room and its sumptuous decor left Marina open-mouthed. The room was at least twice as large as hers, maybe three times. The walls were covered with stenciled leather. The beams that supported the ceiling had been carved by hand. The bed was big enough for three people to sleep in it without touching and was covered by a vermillion silk brocade bedspread. The hangings were also of silk, fringed with gold tassels. Four enormous wardrobes stood against the wall between windows hung with curtains of deep ruby silk with a peacock pattern woven into them. The floors were parquet and covered with more than a dozen oriental rugs.

Marina had never seen such an ostentatious display of wealth. She decided she didn't like it.

Ramon looked at her closely. "You don't look rested. You must not have slept well."

"I didn't."

He looked gorgeous as usual, perfectly rested.

"Then you shall have your siesta as soon as you've eaten."

"I'm not hungry. I need to talk to you. In private," she added when the servant continued with his work.

"Leave us, Felipe," Ramon said. "I'll ring when we're done."

The man seemed reluctant to go. He finished putting away some clothes and straightened a wrinkle in the bed cover before he finally closed the dressing room door behind him.

Ramon got up and came to her, his hands held out, a welcoming smile on his face. "Now, what is it you want? I hope you've come to tell me I may set the date for our wedding."

Marina allowed him to grasp her hand and kiss her cheek. Then she broke contact and moved away. "I've never seen such a room," she said, reluctant to get to the point now that she was here. She moved to the windows, which were tightly closed against night air that had long since been warmed by the morning sun.

"Mama likes to buy things. Ward never wants anything, so she spoils me."

Marina thought smother was more accurate. "Your view of the river is breathtaking."

"It'll be our room soon," Ramon said, coming toward her, arms outstretched again. "You'll be able to enjoy that view any time you want."

"That's what I wanted to talk to you about."

Ramon's smooth brow furrowed. "You can't mean you don't want to live here after the wedding. There's not another rancho like this in Texas, and one day it will be mine. Naturally I cannot leave."

"I don't expect you to." Marina was tempted to tell him she doubted Ward would be dispossessed so easily, but she bit her tongue. "No, it's not about the ranch."

"Then what could be causing that frown to mar your beautiful face?"

Marina wondered why Ramon's compliments always made her feel as if he were talking to a doll. Yet one look from Ward and she melted into a hot pool of liquid desire.

"I can't marry you," she said, deciding to go right to the core of the issue. "You're handsome and charming, and you've been terribly kind to me, but I don't love you. I tried, but I just don't."

He stood motionless, a stone statue in a red dressing gown, and looked at her as though she were a child babbling nonsense.

"I can't marry you," she repeated when he said nothing.

"But I want you."

"I'm sorry, but I can't marry a man I don't love."

"But you would come to love me. Everybody does."

"No."

He smiled in an appeasing manner. "You are angry," he said, apparently deciding she needed placating. "Someone has upset you. Tell me who it is, and I'll have the culprit sent from here immediately."

"No one has made me angry, Ramon. I simply don't love you. I'd make you a terrible wife."

His smile was beginning to look a tiny bit forced, but he stepped forward and rubbed her cheek with the back of his fingers. "Don't be absurd. You're the most beautiful woman in San Antonio, and I'm the best-looking man. We'll make a perfect couple. Everybody will envy us."

Marina pushed his hand away. "Listen to me, Ramon. Stop acting as if I don't know what I'm talking about. I don't love you. I can't marry you. I'm going to leave first thing in the morning. I want to thank you and your mother for having me here, for the honor of asking me to be your wife. But there will be no engagement."

"You would actually leave?" He clearly didn't believe her.

"Yes. I intend to speak to your mother as soon as I leave here."

An idea struck him. "What happened to change your mind? You didn't feel this way yesterday."

"I hadn't made up my mind."

"But something happened to make it up for you?" He was clearly suspicious.

"Y-yes."

"What?" His gaze narrowed and became angry.

"I met someone I could love. I didn't mean to do

it," she rushed to tell him. "It just happened. I couldn't help it."

"Who?"

"Ward."

She might as well have answered him in Chinese. His expression was blank.

"Who?"

"Ward, your brother. He loves me, too. It happened to both of us at the same time."

"You can't prefer Ward to me. Nobody does." He sounded incredulous, as though he couldn't believe anyone would say such a thing, even in jest. "He acts like a cowhand. He's dirty and smells half the time."

Marina had suspected Ramon might be a little jealous of his older, bigger, stronger brother, but now she realized her mistake. Ramon thought he, himself, was perfect. He wouldn't have been Ward if he could.

"But I do prefer him."

"Why?"

"I don't know. I just do."

She hadn't reduced all her feelings and impressions to words yet, but she knew Ward was a finer, more genuine person than Ramon.

Ramon flashed the smile that had brought San Antonio society to its knees. "You were impressed that he saved you from that loco horse. Young girls like to be rescued. I understand. I forgive you. But he cannot go around rescuing you every day. You will grow tired of his smell. He cannot dance as I can. He cannot turn the compliment or a pretty phrase."

As he talked, Ramon had come closer, put his arms around Marina, moved his face closer to hers until they were practically nose to nose.

"I don't care about all that," she said, struggling unsuccessfully to escape his embrace.

"Of course you do. Every woman loves to be petted and flattered. Ward knows nothing of this."

"He knows enough."

Ramon now had his arms firmly around her.

"He cannot kiss you as I can. When I hold you in my arms, you will forget you ever thought of another man."

He forced his lips down on Marina's mouth. She struggled to push him away, but it was futile. Ramon was stronger than he looked. He was also aroused. She felt the evidence pressed against her.

"Ramon, stop this. You're not—"

"No man can make love to you as I can. I make women weep for joy. After me, they can not bear the thought of any other."

He thrust his hand into her bodice and cupped her breast. Marina struggled to push him away, but he dragged her over to the bed, threw her down upon it.

"You will love me," he said, panting, one hand on her breast, the other under her dress. "You will love only me. For you, Ward will no longer exist."

"Stop it!" Marina cried. "You're not going to change my mind."

She hadn't taken Ramon seriously at first. She figured his feelings were hurt, that as soon as he realized she wasn't responding to his kisses, he'd let her go.

But he didn't. When he reached up and pulled her underwear off, she knew he meant to show her exactly what he could do.

"Ramon, stop!" She screamed as loud as she could.

Someone would hear. Someone would come. They would stop him.

But no one came. No one stopped him from pulling up her skirt and throwing open his robe. No one stopped him from lying down on top of her.

Marina fought with all her strength.

"I like it when women struggle," Ramon said, his voice husky with lust, his eyes heavy with passion. "It excites me."

He struggled to enter her, but Marina fought back, wriggling, twisting, turning every time he tried to part her flesh. She hated the feel of his hands on her.

"You're even more beautiful when you're angry," Ramon said, his breath quick and noisy. "I will have you."

His body was driving, trying to enter her. Marina knew he wouldn't stop. He had gone too far. His eyes glazed over. He finally got her knees apart, his body between them. At the same moment he parted her flesh to enter her, his body jerked and heaved. Marina felt hot liquid spill over her. A moment later, Ramon collapsed on her.

Marina didn't waste time being thankful Ramon hadn't succeeded in raping her. Nearly rigid with fury, she threw him off and scrambled out of the bed. He just lay there, his expression that of a sated devil.

"I hate you," Marina cried. "If I had a pistol, I would kill you. If you ever come near me again, I *will* kill you."

"After you are my wife, you will learn to love me." Ramon spoke the words absentmindedly, like a litany he'd memorized and repeated at appropriate moments.

Marina turned and ran from the room. She had to

have a bath at once. She had to wash every trace of that man from her body.

Marina waited for Ward at the head of the avenue of ancient oaks. She had intended to wait for him in the garden, but once she'd taken her bath and asked the maid to throw the soiled clothes away, she was too nervous. She didn't want to be anywhere near the house. Suppose Ramon should find her and try to renew his suit!

She could have waited in her room, but she was afraid Luisa Dillon might follow her there. She didn't want to have to explain what had happened. She doubted Luisa would believe her. She would probably say Marina had thrown herself at Ramon.

Marina's first thought had been to throw herself into Ward's arms and tell him everything. It would have been wonderfully satisfying to watch him beat Ramon senseless. But that would cause trouble and make it harder for them to leave. She didn't want anything as much as she wanted to put distance between herself and Ramon.

But most important, she feared how Ward might look at her if he knew. Men were strange, territorial creatures. It might not kill his love, but it would certainly change the way he felt about her.

That frightened her. Everything was too new, too fragile. She couldn't take a chance. It wasn't important. Ramon wouldn't say anything; he didn't dare. Ward need never know. It would be better that way.

She had to see Ward before he reached the house. She wanted him to take her away tonight, to marry her immediately.

She was certain he wouldn't want to make such an important decision so quickly, but disaster awaited her whether she went back to the rancho or went home. Her parents would be horrified by her rash behavior. Her only hope for the future lay with Ward.

She breathed a huge sigh of relief when she saw him cantering toward her. She relaxed her fingers. Only then did she see that her nails had dug so deeply into her palms that one had actually drawn blood. She sucked the cut with her mouth until it bled no longer. She didn't want Ward to see. She didn't want him to ask questions she had decided not to answer.

Marina walked out from under a tree when Ward turned into the avenue. His welcoming smile and the immediate quickening of his mount's pace answered her last remaining doubt.

He still loved her.

She threw herself into his arms the moment he dismounted. His kisses washed away the lingering taste of Ramon's lips. His arms tight around her made her feel safe, free of the restraints and pressure that had hung over her for so many years. This was where she wanted to be, where she wanted to stay.

She had come home.

"What are you doing here?" Ward asked as soon as he stopped kissing her.

"I couldn't wait to see you."

"Me either. Are you ready to tell Ramon?"

"I already did."

"What did he say?"

"He didn't believe me." That was true enough. "He was certain I was infatuated because you rescued me. I kept telling him, but I'm not sure he believes me yet."

"I'll take care of that," Ward said. "Mount up. It won't take a minute—"

"I don't want you to talk to Ramon," Marina said, pulling Ward away from the avenue toward the shade. "He won't be convinced any woman could actually prefer you to him until we're married."

"No one ever has before."

"Those girls must have been blind."

"No, just not so giddy as to fall in love in a single afternoon."

She put her arms around his neck and looked up into his eyes. "Do you mind?"

He kissed her on the end of the nose. "I wouldn't have it any other way."

"Would you mind if we got married right away?"

"We'll have to. I'm leaving soon."

"I mean today. Now. Tonight."

His smile faded. His gaze became more intense. "Something has upset you. What was it?"

"I didn't like talking to Ramon. I don't want to face your mother. She'll be just as bad. I can't go home. My parents will be worse."

"I'll be there. I'll face them with you."

"I've been thinking all afternoon of the best way to tell them. There isn't one. They'll scream at us and do everything they can to separate us. It'll be much better if we're already married when we tell them. They'll still scream, but there won't be anything they can do about it."

"I don't like that."

"Please," she begged.

"My father will back us," he pointed out.

"It won't make any difference if the governor of Texas gives us his blessing. My father will lock me up until I agree to marry Ramon."

She had to convince him to marry her tonight. She was certain her father would tear her from Ward's arms. She was also afraid to return to the Rancho del Espada. She couldn't get it out of her mind that no one had come to answer her screams. People must have heard her. Why hadn't somebody come?

"I don't have a change of clothes," Ward said, smiling gently. "Let's go up to the house. If things look as ominous as you fear, I'll think about it."

"I'm not going back to that house," Marina declared. She was desperate. "You go if you have to. I'll wait for you here."

"Marina, this is ridiculous."

"You don't understand what it's like to be a woman and have someone telling you what to do all the time, able to punish you if you don't do exactly what they want."

"I'll protect you."

"You'll try, but you aren't my husband. My parents still own me. Please, Ward, you said you loved me. Why won't you marry me now?"

"I do love you. And I can't wait to marry you, but I—"

"No buts. Take me to San Antonio. Make me your wife."

"Marina!"

"If you don't, I'll go away. You'll never see me again."

"Don't say that."

"I will." She broke away from Ward and ran to her horse. "Help me into the saddle," she ordered as she took hold of the reins.

"Marina, no!"

"I'm going to San Antonio, with or without you."

Ward took her by the shoulders and spun her around. "All right, vixen. I'll marry you tonight, but first thing tomorrow we're telling everybody. No running away this time. Okay?"

Marina threw her arms around his neck and kissed him hard on the mouth.

Luisa Dillon had seen Marina leave the house. Hurrying to an upstairs window, she'd watched her walk to the end of the avenue. Luisa didn't trust Marina, not after the way she'd flirted with Ward last night. The girl was up to something. She had never liked Marina, but Ramon was besotted, insisted he loved her, that he had to marry her. Against her better judgment, Luisa had allowed herself to be persuaded to invite Marina to the Rancho del Espada.

Luisa's Spanish blood turned to fire when she saw Marina throw herself into Ward's arms. Strumpet! Whore! Did she think Ramon was not enough man for her? Confusion momentarily blunted her anger. They were arguing over something, but what? Luisa turned livid when they rode off together. She had no idea what Marina had said, but she was convinced the slut had talked Ward into running off with her.

She rang for a servant. "Find Ramon and send him to my room immediately," she ordered. Rage filled her heart. No woman would make a fool of her son, especially not with Ward. She could not allow it.

"Your precious Marina has run off with Ward," Luisa announced the moment Ramon closed the door.

"I do not believe it," Ramon said.

"Do not tell me what you believe," Luisa raged. "I saw it with my own eyes. She has jilted you for that—that cowboy!"

"She wouldn't do such a thing," Ramon said, his calm only slightly disturbed. "It's impossible."

"And why should what I have seen with my own eyes be impossible?"

"Because I have made love to her. No woman could prefer Ward after that."

"In my house, with that woman! How could you do such a thing?"

"She thought she was in love with Ward because he rescued her. I had to show her she was wrong."

"Was she willing?"

"She said she wasn't, but all women say that."

"And what did she say after your so magical wooing?"

"She said she hated me, but she'll change her mind. No woman can hate me."

"You fool!" Luisa shouted. "Not every woman means yes when she says no. Now she has run off with your brother. I know Ward. He will marry her, and you will be disgraced. Everybody in San Antonio will say she preferred him to you."

"No one would dare."

"Even the stable hands will dare when she comes back here parading him as her husband."

"I won't have her here as Ward's wife."

"Neither will I," Luisa said. "But we cannot simply refuse to let them come back. Your father will not allow it."

"He's sick. What can he do?"

"You try to banish Ward, and you will find out. We have to find a way to make Ward throw her out."

"How can we do that?"

"I think I know a way," Luisa said, suddenly feeling much better. "Tell me everything that happened. Do not leave out a single detail."

* * *

Ward

Ward lay in the bed wide awake. At his side, Marina Scott Dillon lay sleeping soundly. Ward still couldn't believe he was married, that Marina was his wife, that he had made love to her three times before he could leave her alone long enough for her to fall into an exhausted slumber.

Every few minutes he reached out to reassure himself he wasn't dreaming, that she was flesh and blood, not a figment of his imagination. He didn't want to lose her. For the first time in his life, he felt truly, deeply loved.

Ward hadn't had a bad childhood. He was the eldest son of a wealthy rancher. True, his mother tended to shower her affection on his fragile younger brother. But his father loved both his sons equally. Ward had grown up tall and strong, a natural cowhand. He had learned to ride and rope as easily as Ramon learned to dance. By the time he was fifteen, he was doing as much work as his father.

His mother had been disappointed when Ward decided to become a doctor. "I am not pleased you want to leave the management of the ranch to your father," she had said, her eyes bright with anger. "You can see his health is failing."

"Let Ramon learn," Ward had said. "He's sixteen, old enough that you can stop wrapping him in cotton."

"Ramon is too fragile," his mother had replied. "Need I remind you—"

No, she hadn't needed to remind him. He already knew that his mother intended Ramon to become the shining star of San Antonio society.

"You will fail as a doctor," she had said. "A cowboy is all you are. It is all you will ever be."

He'd completed his medical studies with honors

and had been accepted into the army as a surgeon, but none of that seemed to have had any effect on his mother or the people of San Antonio. Ramon was their darling. Anything he wanted, he got. Anyone he wanted, he got. Though Ramon was barely twenty-one, San Antonio society was rife with rumors of ladies, married and unmarried, who'd sacrifice their honor for a few weeks, days, even hours as the object of his affections.

He'd already fought two duels.

Ward thought fighting duels was stupid. If a woman didn't love her husband enough to be faithful to him, he ought to leave her.

No such whirlpools of emotion had disturbed the even tenor of Ward's life. Women generally ignored him. They weren't even aware of his presence when Ramon was around. He didn't mind so much. He wasn't a very sociable man. He liked being by himself. He tended to become silent in the presence of a beautiful woman. It was a marvel to Ward that he hadn't become speechless once he got a good look at Marina.

It was an even greater marvel that Marina had come to the rancho intending marry Ramon and had married Ward instead. Even his father, who had confided to Ward that he thought Ramon soft and over-protected, believed Ramon to be the epitome of what every woman wanted in a man.

That Marina should be offered a chance to marry Ramon, but should turn it down to marry Ward instead . . . well, he just didn't know how it could have happened. Maybe he'd married a crazy woman.

He chuckled softly. They both had to be crazy. Ordinary people didn't fall in love at first sight. And when they did, it was with the worst possible person.

Marina was perfect, wonderful, magical—and she was his.

He wondered if he'd fallen in love because he was going to war and might be killed, because this might his last chance for love.

No. He'd never even thought of falling in love until he saw Marina.

He sighed. He supposed he was having so much trouble getting used to the idea because he'd spent so long believing no woman could prefer him to Ramon. It would take a while to change his pattern of thought. He'd been thinking this way all his life. He'd first set eyes on Marina less than thirty-six hours ago.

Stated that way, it sounded even more incredible. What had he done? He would have to leave for the army tomorrow. They should have faced everybody, told them she wasn't going to marry Ramon, waited until Ward got some leave.

But she hadn't wanted to wait, and he couldn't deny her anything. He supposed that was a good way to begin. Things were going to be mighty tough for the next few years.

He became aware of light pouring into the room. He looked at his pocket watch, which he'd left on the table. Seven twenty-one. Probably earlier than she was used to getting up, but they had a lot to do today. He shook her gently. She moaned softly.

"Wake up," he whispered in her ear. "Time to face the music."

Chapter Four

Ramon and Luisa Dillon were alone in the parlor when Marina and Ward walked in. His mother sat ramrod straight in a high-backed, carved oak chair. Her white skin formed a marked contrast with her black silk dress and black mantilla. Ramon stood at her side, looking more like an adjunct to their mother than a rejected swain. Ward would have preferred his father to be present, but he was too ill to be subjected to a tempestuous scene.

Their reception was nearly the opposite of what Ward had expected.

"Thank goodness, you are safe," Luisa cried, getting up from her chair and hurrying over to Ward. "When you did not come home last night, I worried you had been attacked on the road."

"I didn't carry any money, Mama. I was perfectly safe."

"No rich man is perfectly safe." Turning to Marina,

Luisa was frosty. "I see you are safe as well."

"Yes," Marina answered, standing a little closer to Ward, "perfectly safe."

"Where have you been?" Luisa asked Marina. "I had every man on the rancho out searching half the night—the servants, even the cowhands. *Madre de Dios*, think of what it will do to your reputation if this gets out! I am relieved Ward found you. Where was she, my son?"

"The end of the avenue," Ward said with a laugh. He hugged Marina close. "We didn't come back because we got married last night. We spent our honeymoon in town."

Luisa turned white and clasped her hand to her bosom. With the other hand outstretched, seeking support, she tottered over to her chair. "My cordial," she whispered to Ramon. "Quick, pour me some of my cordial."

"Mother, it's not such a great shock as that. Marina told Ramon she didn't want to marry him. I certainly hadn't planned to get married right now, but we fell in love."

He looked down at Marina. She looked up at him with a gaze of adoration he hoped wouldn't change over the course of the next fifty or a hundred years.

"It seemed we couldn't do anything else," Ward said.

His mother made no reply, only continued sipping her cordial. He'd expected Ramon to say something, but his brother's attention never left their mother.

"Are you all right, mother?" Ward was beginning to be concerned. Even during Ramon's illness, he'd never seen her take more than a sip or two of her cordial. She had finished off her glass and was holding it out to Ramon to refill.

"In a minute," Luisa said, sounding weak and very unlike herself. "Just give me a minute."

They waited in edgy silence while Luisa took two sips from the newly filled glass and settled back into her chair, her glass still firmly in her hand.

"All this is most unexpected," she said, looking at Ward. "I was unaware you two knew each other so well. Marina's mother said nothing of it."

"We didn't. We'd never set eyes on each other until two days ago. We fell in love immediately."

Luisa looked at Ward with a pitying expression. "You poor boy. Was it so overwhelming?"

"Yes, but I'm not a poor boy. I'm very happy."

Luisa's expression grew positively pained. "Whose idea was it to get married so quickly?"

"Mine," Marina said.

"Yours?" The ice in Luisa's tone was unmistakable.

"I wanted to tell everybody," Ward said, "but Marina insisted we get married first."

"Why?"

"Because I didn't want any fuss," Marina said. "If we were already married, there'd be no point in trying to talk us out of it."

Luisa put her hands over her eyes and leaned back in the chair. "I do not know what to say, what to do. If your father were only strong enough . . ."

"I'll tell Dad myself in a few minutes."

Luisa sat up as though she'd been stabbed with a needle. "You will not to say a word to your father! I forbid it!" She collapsed in her chair again. "It would kill him. I know it would."

"Mother, what are you talking about?"

Ward was more amused than upset by his mother's unusual behavior. She had an over-developed sense of the dramatic, but he had never seen it displayed in quite this way. Of course, one son marrying the other son's fiancée wasn't exactly common practice, especially since marriages in wealthy families were usually arranged with great care. He guessed she had a right to be a little over-wrought.

But he wished she wouldn't carry on so. She was upsetting Marina.

"If you had only spoken to me," Luisa moaned, her hand over her eyes once more. "I could have . . ." Her voice trailed off.

"You could have what?"

He was getting irritated now. She was implying things without actually saying anything. He wouldn't tolerate that. "Come on, mother, say what you have to say."

Luisa put her handkerchief to eyes that were suddenly full of tears. "I do not know how to say this, son, except to say it straight out."

Luisa paused dramatically, looking from Ward to Marina, then back to Ward again. "The woman who is now your wife has been intimate with Ramon every day since she came to the rancho. There is every possibility she will present you with your own brother's child."

"That's not true! It's a lie!"

Ward heard Marina's denial as through a wall of cotton. The shock of such an accusation literally stunned him. He couldn't believe Marina would do such a thing. Neither could he imagine why his mother would make such an accusation.

"Who told you such a pack of lies?" Ward demanded.

His mother tried to pretend she wasn't offended, but she wasn't a very good actress. "Ramon did not want to tell me what had transpired between him and Marina, but after you both disappeared and—Ward, do not touch Ramon. Ward! Felipe, come immediately!"

Ward had barreled across the room toward his brother. Ramon dodged his first attack, but there wasn't much room to escape. Ward was on his brother immediately.

"Take it back!" he shouted at Ramon as he banged his brother's head into the thickly carpeted floor. "Tell mother you're a damned liar, or I'll break your neck."

Ward felt hands on him, but he ignored them. He would beat the truth out of Ramon before Felipe could call for help. Suddenly he found himself pulled off Ramon and pinned to the floor. He fought with all his strength, but he was being held by six men.

Marina came running to his side. "Let him up!" she shouted at the men, pushing and hitting as many as she could.

"Stand back," Luisa ordered.

"Not until you let my husband up."

"Ramon, hold her."

Marina tried to evade him, but Ramon took her by the arms and pulled her away. Ward vowed to break Ramon's neck the moment he got to his feet. His mother came to stand over him. She looked angry enough to kill him.

"Do not touch Ramon again!" she said through clenched teeth. "I will not have him hurt for the likes of such a one as her." She gestured furiously at Marina.

"I won't have him lying about my wife," Ward said. "I'll break his neck if he says another word."

"Will you break my neck if *I* say another word?"

"I won't listen, mother. I'll take my wife and go."

"You will listen," Luisa declared. "After that, you will do as you please. Will you leave your brother alone if the men let you up?"

"No." Ward struggled to break free, but it was impossible. He glared at Ramon. For the first time in their lives, Ramon looked frightened of him. Good! The little bastard had better be. One way or the other, when he got free, he was going to beat the truth out of him.

"Tie him," Luisa said.

"Don't you dare!" Marina shouted, but the men paid her no attention. There was a brief pause while someone went to get rope, and then Ward's hands and feet were tied securely.

"Set him in that chair," Luisa ordered. "You may go," she said, once Ward had been propped on a black leather couch. "Now," Luisa said when the door had closed behind the servants, "you will listen to what I have to say."

This was a different woman from the mother he knew. This woman was cold and hard, filled with bitter hatred.

Ward looked at Marina. It was hard to know what she was feeling. Anger, certainly. Fear, too. She was right. They shouldn't have come back. They should have headed straight for Virginia.

"Marina's family proposed this alliance," Luisa said as she seated herself once more. "Ramon was very much in favor of it. He was swept away by Marina's loveliness. I admit she is a very beautiful woman, but she has a reputation for wildness I did not trust.

"Ramon would hear nothing against her, so I invited her for a long visit. I did not invite her parents because I wanted to see what she would do when they were not here to restrain her."

She was only seventeen. Ward could imagine dozens of innocent things she might have done that would have scandalized her parents and their society friends. He wasn't going to be swayed by such tales.

"She was running away when you found her," Luisa said to Ward. "Ramon had just told her he was not so certain he wanted to marry her after all. She was upset, maybe even a little desperate. Her father had let it be known he would disown her if she did not marry Ramon."

"That's not why I ran away," Marina protested. "I was having second thoughts. I wanted to think."

"Did not your father say he would disown you if you did not marry Ramon?" It was impossible not to answer Luisa with her fifty generations of Castilian ancestors reinforcing her demand.

"Yes, but he's always threatening to do that when I get in trouble."

"Like the time you ran away to meet those three cowboys?"

"I didn't run away to meet them," Marina said. "I wanted to go to the fiesta. They offered to escort me."

That didn't change anything. Ward could well imagine she would feel upset and frightened if she thought she was going to be punished for Ramon's refusal to marry her. That had nothing to do with their falling in love. It would have happened anyway. Her spirit was too exuberant, too unfettered to be bound by an empty social contract.

"You should have been on your guard when she flirted with you so openly during the dance," Luisa said.

"It wasn't very prudent, maybe even improper, but

there was nothing really wrong with what she did."

Luisa didn't seem to be worried whether he believed her or not. That bothered Ward more than anything else. Luisa never started an argument she wasn't confident she could win.

"I know you won't believe Ramon in this matter," his mother said, "so I shall have Felipe tell you what he has observed."

That shocked Ward. Felipe had been his father's personal servant until he became so ill he needed a nursing attendant. Why should Felipe lie for Ramon?

"He can't tell you anything," Marina said. "There's nothing to tell."

She was becoming more and more agitated. Ward would never forgive his mother. She might be angry at him for stealing Ramon's bride, but that was no excuse for what she was doing to Marina.

Summoned into the room, Felipe didn't hesitate. He looked Ward in the eye and spoke in a steady, clear voice.

"Miss Scott used to come to Master Ramon's room during siesta," he said. "Master Ramon was a little reluctant at first, seeing she was a guest and all, but Miss Scott said it didn't matter since they were going to be married anyway."

"That's not true," Marina cried. "It's not, Ward. I didn't say any of that."

"Two days ago," Felipe continued, unfazed by Marina's interruption, "after they had . . . afterwards, Master Ramon told her he was having second thoughts. She begged and pleaded, but he said he'd let her know today. She went away very angry."

"He did not!" Marina declared. "If he had, I'd have choked him."

"Not with me waiting in the dressing room," Felipe declared.

"You weren't there!" Marina cried. "And neither was I," she added when she apparently realized what she'd said. "None of this happened. It's all lies."

Ward didn't want to admit to the niggling doubt that had finally made its way through all the boiling anger inside him. He fought it off. He couldn't doubt Marina. She was young enough to have done something foolish, but she was not calculating enough to sleep with Ramon just to make sure he would marry her. She hadn't even wanted to marry him.

"Thousands of women have traded their honor for marriage to a rich man," Luisa said, as though reading Ward's mind. "And there will be thousands more after this."

"I wouldn't do any such thing," Marina protested.

"But you agreed to marry Ramon even though you didn't love him," Luisa observed coldly.

"I . . . he . . . no one said anything about love," Marina whispered.

"I did," Ramon said. "I thought I loved you."

"You don't love anybody but yourself," Marina snapped. "It would never occur to you to think of what would happen to me if you broke off the engagement. Not that he did," she said, turning quickly to Ward. "I broke it."

"Did you tell Ward of your engagement when you met him?" Luisa asked.

"No, but—"

"Continue," Luisa commanded Felipe.

"There was no reason to," Marina said, obviously

determined to finish. "I didn't know I loved Ward yet."

"Yesterday she comes to Master Ramon's room again," Felipe said. "He tells her he has decided not to marry her. She wraps herself around him like a serpent, touching and kissing and tempting until Master Ramon cannot contain himself. Afterwards she says she will tell everybody Master Ramon raped her if he doesn't marry her. I—"

"No! That's not true," Marina cried.

"I step out of the dressing room," Felipe continued remorselessly, "and she knows I know everything. She cannot tell the lie."

"That's not true," Marina said. She was crying now. "I went to his room to tell him I wouldn't marry him, that I was in love with Ward."

Luisa turned her steely gaze on Ward. "When you bedded her, did you have to break her virgin's shield?"

Ward felt as though the blood were turning cold in his veins.

"That's not a true test," Ward said, now trying to convince himself as much as his mother.

"Then maybe you will believe this," his mother said. She rang the bell, and one of the servant girls entered the room bearing an armful of clothes.

Ward turned to Marina, but his question died on his lips. She was staring at the clothes, her face gone dead white, her hand over her mouth. If ever he'd seen a look of defeat, an acceptance of guilt, this was it.

"These are the clothes she wore when she entered Ramon's room yesterday," his mother said. "She discarded them before taking a bath. If you examine them, you'll find—"

"No," Ward said. The idea was revolting.

"He tried to rape me, Ward," Marina said, facing him, tears running down her face. "He said after he made love to me, I would never think of you again."

Rape! Ward's mind reeled. Why hadn't she mentioned that? She hadn't even seemed upset yesterday, only anxious to get married right away. She couldn't be telling the truth now. Something was dreadfully wrong.

"Marina?"

It was a cry for help, a plea to help him find a way to believe her, to help him find something to counterbalance all the evidence that was piling up against her. "How could a woman keep quiet if something like that happened to her?"

"Because it did not happen," Luisa declared. "Ramon does not need to force himself on women. They throw themselves at his feet."

Ward couldn't question that. Women had even tried to seduce him to get into Ramon's bed.

"I didn't want you to know," Marina said. "I thought it would only hurt you."

"She couldn't afford for you to know," his mother said. "She had to marry you quickly, before Ramon spoke. That's why she met you at the road, so you wouldn't come back to the house, so you wouldn't know. I'm surprised she let you come back at all."

She hadn't wanted to. She'd pleaded with Ward to take her straight to Virginia.

"She had to have a husband," Luisa continued. "If not one Dillon, then the other one would do."

Ward felt the last of the warmth flow from his veins, leaving him cold and stiff. He didn't want to move. He didn't even want to breathe. He just wanted to dissolve into nothing. Then maybe this agonizing pain in his heart would go away.

He had been a fool. He should have known no society woman, no woman who'd been instructed since birth in the art of catching a wealthy husband, would fall in love in less than a day. That kind of spontaneous feeling was trained out of them. He'd only believed it because he wanted to.

Why had he been so desperate to believe she loved him? All his life he'd finished second to Ramon. Was this his pathetic attempt to feel that for once he'd finished first?

Ward didn't know. He couldn't think any more. He had to get away, out of this house, away from these people—before he killed somebody.

He looked up at Marina. She was staring at him through eyes wet with tears. Tears stained her face. She was teetering on the edge, waiting for him to announce his verdict, waiting for him to say whether she had succeeded or not.

Could money mean so much to her?

"Untie me," he said. His voice was flat, defeated. Later he would feel the rage, the fury. Now he only felt a desperate desire to get away and suffer his humiliation in private.

"Ward, you've got to believe me," Marina cried. "None of this is true. They're all lying."

"Why, Marina? Why should so many people lie about you? What about the letter, the clothes, your begging to get married without telling anybody, wanting to leave without coming back?"

"Your mother hates me. She's—"

"Are you accusing my mother of having manufactured all this evidence against you, even the words out of your own mouth?"

"You misunderstood. I can explain."

He was too tired. He couldn't stand any more.

"I don't want to hear your explanations. You're my wife, so you're safe from your father. You can stay here. They'll take care of you, but I don't want to see you again. If I die, you'll get my share of the estate. I'll see what I can do to oblige you."

Luisa looked at her son. "You will do nothing foolish," she commanded.

"I've already done that."

"I am sorry, but I could not let you go without knowing. I could not guess what cruel thing she might do some day to break your heart."

"I wish you hadn't, Mother. At least until then I'd have been happy. Now I have nothing."

"Ward!" Marina wailed.

His name was a plea that followed him out of the room, to the stable, and over the miles of road he covered before he paused to buy another horse so he could continue his journey without stopping. He wanted to ride until he couldn't feel anything but the fatigue that gripped his body. He wanted to get so far away from Texas that he could forget he'd ever been there.

Chapter Five

"I can't stay here, Bette," Marina said to her cousin. "The family will disown you, too."

The only daughter of Marina's Aunt Flora, Bette Warren had scandalized the family seven years earlier by marrying a cowboy. Bud Warren's becoming a successful rancher hadn't changed the family's belief that a cowhand wasn't a suitable husband for a Scott.

"They already have," Bette said. "What could be more logical than for the two outcasts to join forces?"

Marina's parents' reaction had been worse than she expected. When he'd learned that she'd been rejected by both Dillon heirs, her father had made good on his promise to disown her. A tearful appeal to her mother had been unavailing. Marina had been turned out without a penny to her name.

The confrontation with her parents had destroyed

the last of Marina's self-esteem. They were her own flesh and blood. They were supposed to love her. If her behavior had estranged her from the mother who gave her birth, what was left for her? Like a wild animal desperately seeking shelter from the pack, she had run blindly to Bette.

"I've become something of an invalid," Bette said. "Your being here will mean that Bud can go back to tending his ranch, and I'll have somebody to keep me company."

"If I stay, I'll work for my keep," Marina said.

"You can manage the household."

"That's not very much."

"That's what I used to think."

Marina didn't have the will to fight any longer. She didn't know what reserve of energy had kept her going this long. Luisa had driven her from the Rancho del Espada only hours after Ward left. Marina had been too numb with shock at his departure, too hurt that he hadn't believed her, too devastated at the collapse of her dreams to put up any resistance. Now she only wanted to find some place safe where she could hide and try to figure out what to do with the rest of her life.

"She tries to hide it," Bud told Marina later, "but Bette worries that she can't take care of me like she wants. I tried to hire someone to help, but she wouldn't let me. But you're family. She'll let you."

So Marina settled in to keep house and be a companion to her cousin. It couldn't be a permanent solution—she didn't want it to be—but it was much better than a penniless seventeen-year-old girl with a ruined reputation had a right to expect.

She still couldn't fully understand how what had seemed so right and perfect could go so wrong. She kept thinking there was something important she had missed, that once she found it she would understand. She had been honest with everyone. She hadn't married for money and position. She hadn't pretended emotions she didn't feel.

She had loved Ward, truly and desperately. He meant more to her than security, pleasing her parents, or the opinion of the world. She had followed her heart and ruined her life. Her mother had warned her about that many times. Now her dire predictions had come true.

It didn't seem right. It didn't seem fair.

But it was the feeling of betrayal that overrode everything else. No one had stood by her, not her family, not Ramon who swore he loved her and wanted to marry her, not her husband.

The devastation was too horrible to cry about. She could only sit huddled in a corner, trying not to breathe too hard for fear her wounds would hurt too much.

But she would endure. She would get better. Then she would decide how to make Ward come back.

Chapter Six

November 15th, 1861, Richmond, Virginia
Dear Mother,

The fighting has been terrible. Lots of casualties, long hours spent trying to put broken bodies back together again. We struggle against the tide of wounded, but they come too fast.

How is Marina? No matter what she did, she's my wife and I'm responsible for her.

I hope father is feeling better. There's a chance the war will end quickly. I hope so. I've seen enough people die to last several lifetimes.

Ward Dillon

December 27th, Rancho del Espada
Dear Ward,

Marina left the house the same day as you. I won't repeat the terrible things she said. She has sought refuge with an equally disgraced cousin.

She sent us papers requesting an annulment. Your father thought it was better to sign them for you rather than risk sending them to you in the middle of the fighting.

Ramon has finally recovered from the shock of her accusations. I never realized the poor boy was so sensitive. He actually stayed at the ranch for nearly two months.

Your father continues in poor health, but we hope he will improve in the spring.

Luisa Escalante Dillon

February 7th, 1862, Gravel Pit Ranch
Mr. Gardner Dillon,

I am writing to tell you that I am carrying Ward's child. As you know, this makes the annulment you requested impossible. Please give me Ward's address so I may write him.

Marina Scott Dillon

February 18th, Rancho del Espada
Miss Marina Scott,

If what you say is true, it is indeed unfortunate. Through the intervention of my family, Ward has been granted an annulment. You are no longer his wife. Neither you nor your child has any claim on him. I suggest you look to your family for a solution to your dilemma.

Luisa Escalante Dillon

March 2nd, Gravel Pit Ranch
Mrs. Luisa Dillon,

How can this be? I didn't sign any papers.

My child is your grandson. I do not want anything for myself, only for my child. It should not be punished for the wrongs of anyone else, real or imagined.

Marina Scott Dillon

March 15, Rancho del Espada

Miss Marina Scott,

My husband would have answered you, but he is too ill to leave his bed. I have communicated with Ward, and here is what he said.

He does not believe your child is his, and he has no intention of recognizing it. Ramon asks me to tell you he will not recognize the child as his, either. If you persist in writing to us, or if you try to destroy my sons' reputations by broadcasting your supposed wrongs, I shall be forced to put it about that you were dallying with one of the cowhands and Ramon would not marry you because of your indiscretions.

Do not bother to write to our family again.

Luisa Escalante Dillon

April 10th, Gravel Pit Ranch

Mrs. Luisa Dillon,

I will not bother your family again. I have ceased to use the Dillon name. However, my child will bear it. Do what you will, I will not give in on that.

Marina Scott

July 28th, Gravel Pit Ranch

Dear Mother and Father,

I'm writing to let you know I've given birth to a beautiful little boy. I've named him Tanner. It wasn't an easy birth. Despite her illness, Bette never left my side. We're both doing well and don't need anything.

Both Bette and her husband have been wonderfully kind, taking me in, giving me a job, seeing that I lack for nothing. I know everybody was angry when she married a cowhand, but she was absolutely right. Bud Warren is a wonderful man.

I tried to be what you wanted, but I suppose I was always a disappointment. I can see why you would be tempted to turn your backs on me, but I can never forgive you for doing it. I could never do such a thing to my child.

However, I accept banishment. I knew I was taking a chance when I fell in love with Ward. I never dreamed it would turn out this way. But it has, and I will bear the consequences without complaint.

Maybe one of my sisters will do better for you than I have. I hope everyone is well.

Marina Scott

February 7th, 1863, Austin

Dear Mama,

You were right to suspect that the man from Austin was a lawyer. Papa did make a new will. You will not like it.

He left Ward $45,000. If it's not claimed within ten years, it reverts to the estate. I told the trustees Ward was away at the war, that I was his brother and would take care of his affairs, but they would not release the money.

But that is not the worst. Papa left half of the estate to Marina's son. It is tied up so that I can't even sell cattle without the trustees' permission.

77

I tried to have our lawyer appointed executor, but they would not agree.

What shall I do next?

Ramon Escalante Dillon

February 13th, Rancho del Espada

Dearest Son,

You are to come home immediately. Put everything in the hands of our lawyer. He will do what he can for us. In the meantime, we will see what we can do. There is more than one way to cheat the dead.

Luisa Escalante Dillon

March 12th, Rancho del Espada

Miss Marina Scott,

I'm writing to tell you Ward Dillon has been reported missing in action and is presumed dead.

Ramon Escalante Dillon

April 3rd, Rancho del Espada

Dearest Brother,

I grieve to tell you that our father passed away in January. Mama would have written you, but she is still too overcome with grief. I am only just now able to put pen to paper to tell you the news. There is no need to come home as the burial was a long time ago.

I do have a piece of news I don't know how to relate. It seems Father was very upset over that business with Marina, more upset than any of us knew. He has left me the rancho, the house in San Antonio, in short, he has left everything to me. He said that you had your profession. You could provide for yourself.

I was grieved to learn this. I am consulting with our lawyer to see what can be done. I hope you are well.

Ramon Escalante Dillon

July 17th, 1884, Warrenton, Virginia

Dearest Mother,

I write this letter from prison. No, I have not been captured by the enemy. I am imprisoned by my own side because I tried to force them to save lives.

The camps are filthy beyond imagination. More men die from disease and infection than are killed in battle. There is a new theory that microscopic organisms called germs carry disease and infection. It is the belief of the doctors who developed this theory that many deaths can be prevented by the simple procedure of washing their hands and instruments before and after all operations.

I tried this with good results but could not get my fellow doctors to adopt the practice. The better my results became, the more angry I got until I attacked several doctors who were the worst offenders.

As a result, they locked me up. Don't worry. They'll let me out as soon as the fighting starts up again. I don't know that I like medicine so much anymore. We kill more than we save. It would be more merciful to shoot them.

I will write again when I'm out.

Ward Dillon

December 25th, Richmond, Virginia
Dear Mother,

The war will be over in a few months. The casualties are terrible. The fighting goes on even though both sides know how it must end.

I'm looking forward to coming home. It seems like such a long time since I've seen you and Ramon.

I know she's no longer my wife, but do you know anything of Marina?

Ward Dillon

January 18th, 1865, Rancho del Espada
Dearest Son,

You asked about Marina, or I would not bother you with such a sordid tale. I hear she has an understanding with a man who is himself married, but I will say no more of that. I hope that once her lover's wife dies—she is gravely ill and not expected to live much longer—she will marry this man and cease trying to defame our good name.

It is my happy duty to tell you Ramon will be married in the spring, and I want nothing to occur that might cause the bride to conceive a distaste for our family. I would dearly love to see you, but I must ask you not to come home at this time. I fear that if you were to do so, Marina would make a scandal. You can have no idea of the extent to which she wishes to be revenged on us.

I am devastated at the brutal way your father treated you in his will, but I take comfort in knowing you have your profession and can make your way quite well.

Write me when you get settled somewhere. I hear they need doctors in California. With all that gold, it should be just the place for a man like you to make his fortune.

I must close. Ramon and his fiancée will be here soon. I must be down to greet them. I look forward to their marriage. I hope the house will soon be full of the sounds of their sons.

Luisa Escalante Dillon

Chapter Seven

Texas Hill County, April, 1868

Ward's gaze swept the hills turned brilliant with color. He drank in the profusion of wildflowers, the rich grass, the soft breeze as it wafted through newly leafed oaks and maples that towered over the flood plain and riverbanks. Hills rose sharply to the west, at a distance to the east. A herd of cattle grazed peacefully in every direction. As he sat coiling his rope, Ward thought for the hundredth time how fortunate he was to have found this haven.

The war years spent trying to piece together young boys and fighting against the blind ignorance of his fellow doctors had given him a cause to occupy his mind and heart while he got over the pain of Marina's betrayal. When the unending work wasn't enough, there was whiskey. Or other women.

The time he'd spent in jail had been the worst.

Then he had had nothing to do but think. He was almost grateful when the last brutal campaign forced the army to let him go back to work.

These days he tried to avoid thinking of the future just as he attempted to ignore the past. The distance of seven years had allowed him to put aside most of the hurt, anger, and devastation of his marriage and its annulment. It was almost as though he'd never been married.

Almost. Try as he might, he couldn't forget the two days that had changed his life forever. He couldn't completely wipe from his mind the memory of Marina's beauty any more than he could completely forget the hurt of her betrayal. She had deceived him from the first and he hadn't seen it, hadn't even suspected.

He'd steered clear of emotional entanglements since then. He couldn't trust his own judgment.

One thing he did hold against Marina. She had made it impossible for him to go home. He had returned to Texas—he couldn't stay away altogether—but he'd been forced to become a nomad.

It was during his wanderings through West Texas that he had stumbled onto an Indian attack and rescued a little girl whose family had been massacred. He and Drew had both found a home on this ranch with Jake Maxwell and his large brood of adopted sons.

He was glad to have found a place where he could be at peace. If he couldn't have a family of his own, it was nice to be able to share Jake's.

The boys came to Ward when they didn't feel they could go to Jake or when they felt they couldn't talk to his wife, Isabelle. Ward was sympathetic to the foibles of this ill-matched group. He could understand their hurt, their loneliness, the feeling that life had shortchanged them. He could help them appreciate how lucky they were to have Jake and Isabelle.

He was also the best cowhand on the place. It was Jake's responsibility to make sure the ranch made money, Isabelle's to see the family was fed and cared for. But when it was a question of cows, they all came to Ward.

Turning his attention back to the herd, Ward noticed two of Jake's boys leave their work and ride toward the ranch house. Ward glanced at Jake, who was directing the round-up, but he was looking away, too.

Ward turned around. Two tall strangers—even at a distance he could tell they were twins—rode toward them with a small boy at their heels. A smile curved Ward's lips as he watched Chet and Luke Attmore approach the strangers like barnyard roosters ready for a fight. He wiped the sweat off his forehead with his sleeve. He decided the next steer could wait to be roped. He had to see this.

Jake was sending five hundred steers to Abilene, Kansas, with the Randolph family herd. Ward assumed these were the Randolph brothers. Though from the way Chet and Luke where squaring up to them, you'd think they were hostile invaders.

Ward saw a chuck wagon in the distance and wondered what it was doing away from the Randolph herd. It would be a while yet before it arrived.

"They look like young wolves protecting their territory, don't they?" Jake said as he rode over to Ward.

The other eight boys had stopped work, too, now. Gradually they gathered around Jake and Ward. None of them seemed happy about the presence of these striking young men. One of the Randolph twins was talking and laughing, but Chet and Luke looked solemn.

"I'd better go say howdy," Jake said. "Somebody's got to make them welcome."

Will, the youngest of the orphans Jake and Isabelle had adopted, came riding up to Ward.

"Are those the men who're taking our cows to Abilene?" He asked.

"Of course they are," another boy, Pete, answered. "Why else would strangers be here?"

"They're big," Will said.

"Jake says all the Randolphs are big," Pete said. "Come on, let's go see what they're saying."

The boys edged closer. Ward followed on his horse.

"Come meet the rest of the boys," Jake was saying. "Of course you're staying for dinner.

"As long as it's good and plentiful, you'll get no argument from me," the huskier of the twins said.

"Just a headache from all his chatter," his brother said.

"You've got to tell me which is which," Jake said, looking from one twin to the other. "George didn't say you were identical."

"I'm Monty," the husky twin said. "That's Hen."

"It's easy to tell us apart," Hen said. "He'll be the one talking."

"Which of your boys are going along?" Monty asked. "George said you had a dozen. Rose would love it. More people to boss around."

"Actually, we have ten boys and one girl. Just three will be going with you," Jake said. "Chet Attmore is my foreman. His brother, Luke, will take care of the horses. Matt Haskins will do the cooking. Is that your chuck wagon?" Jake asked.

"Yeah," Monty answered. "My brother Tyler's driving."

"He's bringing a woman looking for somebody named Ward Dillon," Hen said.

"Me?" Ward asked, stunned. "What does she want?"

"Can't say," Hen said. "She hooked up with George in San Antonio."

Everybody was looking at Ward. "I can't imagine who she is or what she could want," he said.

"I wouldn't worry about it too much," Hen remarked laconically. "She'll be here in a few minutes. Then you'll know."

Ward dismounted and led his horse toward the house while the others headed to the herd, which was being held some distance beyond the barn. He couldn't think of anybody who'd want to see him except maybe the mother or sister of one of the men who'd died in the war. He'd already heard from three mothers and one aunt, each wanting to know how her boy had died, his final words. They wanted to know where their sons had been buried, what kind of service had been said over them, what kind of markers were on their graves.

Ward couldn't say that some of those boys were buried in mass graves, their final resting places unmarked. Nor could he say there wasn't enough of some of them left to bury. He told the women anything he thought might comfort them. He wanted them to go home believing their boys had been treated as tenderly as if they'd laid them to rest themselves.

The wagon pulled into the yard. The boy driving

didn't look the least bit like the Randolph twins. He jumped down. He looked young—fifteen or sixteen probably—the tallest, thinnest kid Ward had ever seen.

"I'm looking for Ward Dillon," the boy said in an accent that owed little to South Texas.

"You found him," Ward said.

"I got a woman here who says she wants to see you."

Ward saw the shadow of a woman inside the wagon. "Tell her to climb down." He might as well get it over quickly. "I'm sure Mrs. Maxwell has a pot of coffee on the stove. If she would like to go inside, just—"

Ward broke off. Shock caused the words to die in his throat. He couldn't be seeing right. His memory must be playing tricks on him. But no, it could be no other—Marina Scott Dillon.

She turned toward him as soon as she reached the ground. "Hello, Ward," she said, her expression perfectly calm, her voice steady, her eyes gazing directly at him.

"What the hell are you doing here?" he demanded, his voice a cracked, broken sound.

"I've come to ask for a divorce."

Seeing Marina climb down out of that wagon was a brutal shock. He'd spent years trying to put her out of his mind, to forget the pain she had caused him. Now she had found and invaded the small part of the world he claimed for himself. What was she doing here? What was she trying to pull this time?

He felt the old hunger for her flame up from ashes he thought had turned cold long ago. Even though she was more beautiful and alluring than ever, it was incredible that he could still feel any kind of desire

for this woman. She showed no sign of being simi-
larly affected.

He felt the old fury begin to rise from deep within
him. With a growing sense of desperation, he struggled to keep it under control. It had taken him seven
brutal years to learn to accept what had happened,
to learn to put it aside. He wasn't about to lose his
hard-won sense of peace now.

"Our marriage was annulled years ago, at your request, remember?"

"I never requested an annulment. You did."

It amazed him that she could lie so calmly, so con-
vincingly, as naturally as she breathed. No wonder
he had fallen into her trap. He might have been older
and more educated that she, but she had a sophistication, a knowledge of the world that couldn't be
taught.

"You may as well go right back to San Antonio.
This whole conversation is pointless unless you tell
me what you really want."

"I want a divorce so I can remarry."

He didn't know why learning she wanted to get
married again should bother him. He'd assumed she
had married her lover years ago. He'd hoped she had.
It would be further insurance that she would never
invade his life again.

"What's stopping you?"

"You."

"I wouldn't stop you even if I could. I don't want
anything to do with you."

"Or I with you, but I have no choice. A month ago
Ramon told me we were still married." Her expression gave no hint of her inner feelings. She could be
glad or furious; Ward couldn't tell.

"What happened to the annulment? Why didn't it go through?"

"I guess because I never signed any papers. Apparently not even your mother's influence and your father's money could get an annulment without my signature." Still her expression did not change.

Ward looked at her long and hard. She looked older, more mature, confident and composed. She showed none of the agitation that made his body feel as though it were held together by badly stretched rawhide bands. She compressed her generous lips into a firm, uncompromising line. He could remember when they were as welcoming as the happiness that used to dance in her eyes. She had been just seventeen, vivacious, enchanting. And he had fallen in love.

"I heard Ramon's wife died. Are you hoping to marry him after all?"

Her eyes grew hard.

"It's no concern of yours whom I marry."

"It is if you intend to marry Ramon."

He could see her struggle to preserve her appearance of complete control, of indifference to him and what he said or felt. It was nice to know she couldn't hide everything. She'd taken his heart and ripped it out of his chest. He was glad he'd been able to puncture her armor, even if it had only been a pinprick.

"I have no desire to marry Ramon," she said, speaking with some effort. "He and your mother threw me out of the house within an hour after you left. I won't repeat the names she called me, but not even the entire Dillon fortune could induce me to set foot in that house again."

Her hatred for his family must be very deep. Now he understood why his mother hadn't wanted him to come home. With lies rolling off her tongue too fast to be counted, there was no telling what kind of scandal Marina could create.

"Who do you want to marry?"

"That's none of your concern."

"It is if I have to give you a divorce to do it."

She lost color. It pleased him to see she could feel something. No shame, however. Her gaze didn't falter.

"His name is Bud Warren. He's a rancher, a widower. His wife died two years ago."

So she was marrying her lover after all. He wondered why she had waited so long. The man might have gotten away.

But this poor rancher probably wasn't any more equipped to withstand her allure than he had been. Marina was still a beautiful woman, capable of lighting a fire in any man. The sharp angles of youth had been softened. Jet-black hair still framed a face of ivory perfection. Her eyes, still huge and black, gazed forthrightly at him from under ebony brows.

"Does he know about you, the things you've done to my family?"

He shouldn't have asked that. It was none of his business, but he couldn't stand the thought of her trapping some other innocent fool the way she'd trapped him.

She held her head high and looked at him with an imperious manner his mother might envy.

"Bud knows everything that happened from the moment my parents proposed my engagement to Ramon until now. I have never lied to anyone."

Ward could hardly believe she would dare make such a statement. She had told lies, pretended what she didn't feel, taken advantage of his naive belief in their love. He'd suffered for seven years because he'd been fool enough to fall in love with a woman who was more cunning than honorable. He'd tried to convince himself he didn't love her, had never loved her, didn't care if she lived or died, to forget the sweetness of her kisses, the bliss he'd found in her arms. Yet, even now, he was tortured by those very memories.

Ward felt years of accumulated bile boiling up to the surface. It was useless to talk with her any longer. Maybe she'd lied to herself so long she'd started to believe her own stories. He didn't know and he didn't care. He just wanted her out of his life. She could lie to half of Texas as long as he never had to set eyes on her again.

Before Ward could open his mouth to tell Marina that he'd give her the divorce or anything else she wanted if she'd promise to never see, speak, or write to him again, the young boy who'd ridden in with the twins came running up.

"They're riding out to see the herd, Mama. Can I go with them?"

Ward's words stuck in this throat. His gaze riveted itself on the child, who stood looking up at his mother with an expectant gaze. He was tall and thin, with Marina's perfect skin. Her son. He had dark hair like his mother. *And like Ramon!*

The shock was numbing. Ramon had never told him Marina had a son. This was his nephew, the son of his wife and brother, the son who should have been his. Seeing the boy was the same as having his failure thrown in his face, of laughing at his longing for a family he couldn't have, the family he should have had with Marina.

"Only if you do everything they say," Marina was telling the boy.

"Okay," the boy said. He headed back at a dead run.

"Your son?" The question was unnecessary, but he needed the sound of his own words to help him believe it.

Marina's color faded. "Yes."

"What's his name?"

"Tanner."

"Does Ramon know?"

"Of course. I told your family as soon as I knew. Fool that I was, I thought it would bring you back. All you said was you didn't believe Tanner was your son."

His son? He still couldn't get over how easily she lied. The words came effortlessly, with the appearance of complete conviction.

"Why should you want me back? You didn't want me. You never wanted me, did you?" he grated out. "It was always Ramon."

"I told you I didn't—"

"Don't treat me like a fool, Marina. Even though you were the mother of his child, you couldn't marry Ramon if you were still married to me. Is that why you waited so long to marry your rancher? Are you hoping to use him to bring Ramon up to the mark?"

"I don't want to marry Ramon. There's nothing between us."

"Do you call that boy nothing?"

Marina's color faded completely. Her skin seemed to be made of parchment. "Tanner is your son."

Ward was so angry, he wanted to choke the life out of her. Her words tore at his soul. He would have given almost anything for that boy to be his.

"You can't think I'm fool enough to believe that. Look at him! He's the spitting image of Ramon."

"You shouldn't be surprised if he bears some resemblance to Ramon. He is your brother."

"My mother says we're as unalike as a thoroughbred and a mustang."

"It's about time you stopped believing everything Luisa Dillon says."

"She's my mother. Of course I believe her."

"Then you'll never know the truth as it is, only as she reshapes it to fit her designs."

She'd insulted him, his brother, and his mother. If she dared to start on his father, he would choke her.

"Look, Ward, I want to get as far away from you and your family as possible. I want a chance to make a decent life for myself, to give Tanner a father."

"If that's what you really want, if you're finally telling the truth for once in your life, you ought to marry the boy's real father."

"I'm already married to his *real* father." She made a gesture of impatience mixed with irritation. "I don't want to talk to you anymore. It does no good. Give me a divorce, and I promise you'll never see me again."

She was promising him exactly what he wanted, but the image of that boy wouldn't let him do it. "No."

"Why?"

"If that boy can't have the right father, at least he can have the right name."

"Your family refused to acknowledge him, Ward. Your mother said she wouldn't recognize a little bastard probably fathered by some cowhand."

His mother wouldn't have said anything so outrageous. He couldn't understand why Marina continued to pile one lie on top of another.

But she had raised a question in his mind. Why

hadn't Ramon written him about Tanner? The boy was a Dillon and ought to be raised as one. It made him wonder, and that made him angry. He turned and strode away. He didn't want to speak to her. He didn't want to see her. He mounted up and rode off. He wouldn't return to the ranch until she had left.

Chapter Eight

Marina watched Ward stalk off, a boiling mass of conflicting emotions inside her. She had been reluctant to make this trip because she knew it wouldn't be easy to meet Ward again, but it had been harder than she had expected. Bud had wanted her to send a lawyer, the same lawyer who'd discovered Ward's whereabouts for her. He'd said there was no need for her to make such a difficult trip. Ramon could be lying, just as he'd lied about Ward being missing in action.

Despite the anger and the bitterness, Marina had to see Ward herself. She still couldn't understand what had gone wrong. She hoped this trip would answer her questions and allow her to put him out of her life forever.

But things weren't going to be easy. Just seeing Ward had given her a severe jolt. He had changed so much. He used to be so open, easygoing, and totally

95

innocent in love. That was what had drawn her attention from his more handsome younger brother. Ramon Dillon swept women off their feet. Many women. Ward didn't believe a woman could prefer him to Ramon. When he finally did believe, he believed with his whole heart.

He was not as handsome as Ramon—few men were—but quite handsome enough to cause an unexpected tug at her heart. He looked older, more tired. Time and the war hadn't dealt gently with him. His hair was not so thick and unruly. His face had lost the softness she remembered. Now his cheekbones stood out under taut skin. His jaw looked as hard as granite. She had noticed the muscles tighten as he clenched his jaw, trying to control the anger inside him, anger that blazed in his eyes.

A few things hadn't changed. His skin was still brown and weathered, his hands work-roughened. His clothes still fitted his muscled body like a glove, causing a flutter in her belly. Marina repressed it. She refused to be attracted to this man ever again.

His eyes still showed the way to his soul, but now they revealed the rage that simmered there. She didn't know the man who'd just left her. He had matured, hardened, turned cold.

"Would you like to come up to the house?"

Marina turned to see a woman in the last weeks of pregnancy standing a short distance away. She appeared to be about the same age as Marina.

"I could offer you something cool."

"Coffee would be fine," Marina said as she walked to meet her.

"I'm Isabelle Maxwell," the woman said, "Jake's wife. I see the men have deserted us for the cows."

Marina felt herself smile as they started toward a house that was much bigger than anything she'd seen leaving the Randolph ranch.

"It looks pretty barren," Isabelle said, indicating the ground surrounding the house. "We just moved in, and I'm under strict orders from Ward to take it easy. Jake won't let me do any work outside the house. He says it's too strenuous, but he doesn't understand how cooking for this army of boys can tire me. I probably won't get around to planting until next year. I don't imagine I'll have much time after the baby comes."

"No," Marina said, remembering how difficult Tanner's first two years had been on her. "But at least you'll have lots of help."

"They're men," Isabelle reminded her. "They'll be more trouble than help."

They laughed, and Marina followed Isabelle into the house. They passed down a wide hall and by four rooms—two sitting rooms, an office, and a dining room—before they reached a huge kitchen, which occupied the whole back of the house. The bright, spacious room raised Marina's spirits, as did the tantalizing aromas of fresh coffee, bread, and apple pie.

"You must be a wonderful cook," Marina said.

Isabelle laughed. "I'm getting better. The first time I cooked breakfast, the beans were so hard they jumped off the plate when Jake tried to stab them with his fork. The bacon looked like charcoal."

Marina glanced at the dining room table through the open door. It seemed to be set for a small army. "You're expecting guests. I wouldn't have come in if I had known."

"Just you and the Randolph boys," Isabelle said.

"But your table is set for more than a dozen people."

Isabelle laughed. "Jake and I have eleven children."

She laughed even harder when Marina's mouth dropped open.

"They're all adopted."

Marina accepted a cup of coffee, still stunned.

"They were orphans," Isabelle explained. "They had nowhere to go."

"You're very brave."

Isabelle laughed again. "Just determined. I was an orphan myself."

Marina drank her coffee. What did you say to a woman who had eleven children and was expecting a baby any minute? It made her dizzy just to think about it.

"I know this is none of my business," Isabelle said, "but do you mean to travel to Abilene with the Randolphs?"

"Heavens, no," Marina said after she'd taken a quick swallow of coffee. "I'm going back to San Antonio. I was only able to persuade Monty to bring me this far by promising he needn't take me a step farther."

"But where do you plan to stay? You must realize we're ten miles from the nearest town."

Marina's stomach knotted. "I didn't know that."

"We'll be happy to see you safely back to San Antonio, but I don't know just when it can be done. Three of the boys are going to Abilene. The rest will be needed when the new herd arrives."

Marina didn't know what to do. She hadn't expected to be stranded in these hills. George Randolph should have warned her, or maybe he thought she'd already made her own plans.

"Maybe the men bringing the new herd could escort you," Isabelle said. "If not, you can stay here until some of the boys are free."

"That's not necessary. I brought a tent. Tanner and I will sleep in it."

"Nonsense. We've got plenty of room, and I'd love some company. My daughter Drew is a little young for companionship."

"You can't have plenty of room, not with so many children."

"The boys sleep in the bunkhouse. Only Ward, Drew, Jake, and I sleep in the house. That leaves three extra bedrooms."

Marina didn't think Ward would stick to his refusal to give her a divorce, but she had to stay to make sure he changed his mind.

"I don't want to be an inconvenience, but I might need to stay for a day or two. I could pay you for—"

"Don't be absurd. If you want to earn my undying gratitude, you can teach me how to make doughnuts. The boys have been asking for them ever since a range cook stopped at our camp last summer and spoiled them for my apple pie forever."

"I can't make them either."

They both laughed, then talked companionably about food for a little while before Isabelle said, "I couldn't help but notice you were talking to Ward. I don't want to ask your business, but I'm curious to know a little about him. He's been here for two years, but all I know is that he used to be a doctor."

"Used to be? Doesn't he practice anymore?"

"He takes scrupulous care of the boys and practically stands over me to make sure I don't do too much. But he insists he doesn't want to be anything but a cowhand."

Marina was shocked. Ward had gone against the wishes of his family in order to study medicine. What could have caused him to turn his back on his chosen profession?

Marina didn't want to tell Isabelle anything about her purpose in coming there, and she didn't feel it was her place to divulge any part of Ward's past. But she couldn't accept this woman's hospitality, possibly upset the household, without telling her something. Besides, it was bound to come out sooner or later. She decided sooner was better.

"Ward and I were married seven years ago," Marina said. "He left me the next day. I hadn't set eyes on him until today. I thought he was dead. I've asked him for a divorce. I doubt he'll want to sleep in the same house with me."

"Ward is a gentleman," Isabelle said. "He'd be the first to insist you stay as long as you need."

Maybe he'd been reared a gentleman, but he hadn't always acted like one.

The moment Ward reached Jake and the others, he wished he'd chosen to ride somewhere else. Despite his attempts to concentrate on what Jake was saying, his gaze and thoughts repeatedly focused on Marina's son.

The boy tried his best to position himself between Hen and Monty. From his adoring gaze, it was easy to tell he idolized the big, handsome, confident Randolph twins.

"It won't be any problem to handle a herd this small," Monty said. "You ought to run 'em in with ours."

"Don't make it too easy on my boys," Jake said.

"Don't worry," Monty said with a chuckle. "Between Salty and me, we'll run 'em ragged."

Chet didn't seem the least bit amused by the prospect of taking orders from this self-assured stranger, but Tanner gazed up at Monty as if he were a Paul Bunyan-sized hero. Ward wondered what could have made Marina bring the boy on such a trip.

He wasn't sure he liked the way the boy idolized Monty. He had nothing against the Randolph boys—they seemed nice enough—but that didn't mean they were suitable role models for an impressionable kid like Tanner.

Ward pulled himself up short. He was wasting his time worrying about the boy. Tanner was Marina's responsibility. If Ramon chose not to help her, well, that was between Ramon and Marina. Ward supposed she had known when she gave herself to Ramon that there was a chance he wouldn't marry her. Now she had a child as a permanent reminder of his rejection.

"Let's get a closer look," Monty said. "Tanner, you'd better stay here with the others."

Monty glanced around, but it was obvious everybody meant to go with them.

"He can stay with me," Ward said.

Tanner's dissatisfaction showed plainly, but he didn't argue.

"You can see everything from here," Ward said, sympathizing with the boy for being left out because he was too young. "They'll just ride through the herd."

Tanner didn't reply. He gazed after the riders, disappointment in his face.

"We've been trail-branding the herd," Ward said. "Have you ever seen that done?"

"I know all about branding cows," Tanner said, with all the scorn of a little boy who knows he's being talked down to.

"Do you live on a ranch?" Jake asked.

"Yes. Uncle Bud has lots of cowboys. But not as many as Mr. Ramon."

"Mr. Ramon?" So Marina hadn't told him who his real father was.

"He comes to see Mama. He wants me to live with him, but Mama won't let me."

Ward didn't understand. Ramon had said he'd had no contact with Marina, but why would Tanner make up something like this? And why should Ramon want Tanner to live with him if he wasn't willing to acknowledge him as his son?

"Do you see him a lot?"

"No. Mama doesn't like Mr. Ramon. Every time he comes, she sends me away because they shout at each other."

Ward couldn't help feeling a hot spot of pleasure that Marina's relationship with Ramon hadn't prospered.

"Where do you live?"

"At the Gravel Pit Ranch. Mama keeps house for Uncle Bud. He wants Mama to marry him. He says I need a daddy, but I already have one."

Ward's confusion grew.

"Mr. Ramon said my daddy died in the war, but I don't believe him. Mama said he was a great hero. Great heros don't die."

"Who told you that?"

"Benjy. His father was a great hero. Everybody thought he was dead. Then one day he just came back. My daddy will come back, too. We'll have the biggest ranch in Texas, even bigger than Mr. Ramon's. My daddy can fight better than Monty and shoot better than Hen. There's nobody as good as my daddy."

Ward didn't know what to say. Tanner wanted a father so badly, he'd created an imaginary parent who could do everything better than anybody else. No wonder Marina was anxious to marry again.

"Mama gets mad whenever I say Daddy's coming back, but I know he will. Mama said he loved me more than anybody else on earth. My daddy wouldn't go away if he loved me that much, would he?"

"No," Ward said, "I guess he wouldn't."

Ward could understand why Marina didn't want to tell Tanner about Ramon, but he was surprised she would go to so much trouble to be sure Tanner thought his father was a wonderful man. Of course, that was much easier when she assigned paternity to a man who was supposed to be dead and unable to complicate her life. Even so, he didn't understand how she could have allowed Tanner to build up such a fantasy.

"Mama said Mr. Ramon got a letter," Tanner said. "It said my daddy was never coming back, but I don't believe it. Benjy's mama got a letter, too."

"Are you sure? You must have been too little to remember."

"Mr. Ramon showed it to me."

Ward was understanding less and less. Why should Ramon say Ward was dead? If so, why change his mind, unless he was trying to keep Marina from marrying Bud Warren? But why would Ramon want to marry Marina now when it was his refusal to marry her seven years ago that had caused all the trouble? And if he did want to marry her, why wasn't he willing to acknowledge Tanner as his son?

And why wouldn't Marina marry Ramon now, when seven years ago she'd disgraced herself over him? Such a marriage would solve all her problems—clear up her reputation, give her wealth and security, provide Tanner with a father and a name.

The more Ward learned, the less things made sense.

The only thing he knew was that he felt strongly drawn to his new-found nephew. Ward had always wanted a family—sons, a wife. He'd been devastated when he learned of his father's death. He'd been hurt when his mother asked him not to come home. Despite a gnawing need to see his family, Ward had stayed away.

"If you stay here a while, we can teach you all about being a cowboy," Ward said.

He didn't know why he'd said that. There was no point in getting to know the boy. It would only make leaving more difficult. Besides, Marina disliked Ward and he distrusted her. He intended to send her back to San Antonio immediately.

"I want to go with Monty," Tanner said. "He's the best cowboy in the whole world."

Ward didn't doubt that the Randolph twins were extremely capable cowmen. But a trail drive was no place for a child.

"I expect your mother will want to return to San Antonio as quickly as possible."

"I don't want to go back," Tanner said.

"I'm sure you'd have fun on the drive for a little while, but soon you'd want to go back home."

"I want to live on a ranch forever," Tanner said.

"Mama said my daddy used to be a cowboy. I want to be a cowboy, too."

So he wanted to be a cowboy like his father. Tanner reminded Ward of himself when he was a boy. He thought the sun rose and set on his father, a big, easygoing Texan.

"I'm sure you will be," Ward said. "Maybe Mr. Ramon would let you live on his ranch. He could teach you about being a cowboy."

"Mama says I can never live with Mr. Ramon. She says he's a snake in the grass."

"Did she tell you that?"

"No. I listened at the door. I didn't have to listen very hard. She shouted it at him."

"Maybe she's waiting until you get a little older. Mamas don't like to lose their boys when they're little."

"Mr. Ramon wants to marry Mama, but she said he was never going to get his hands on me. She said she'd shoot him before she'd let him turn me into the kind of . . . I didn't understand what she said then. It sounded Spanish. I know she meant he was a bad person. Mama told me."

Talking with Tanner had raised several serious questions in Ward's mind. Why had Ramon said Ward was dead? What letter could he have shown the boy? Why had Ramon said he'd never seen Marina? And why did he want to adopt Tanner when he wouldn't acknowledge him as his son?

Ward would have to talk to Marina again. But after all her lies, could he believe anything she said? An even worse thought occurred to him. What if she wasn't lying?

Ward refused even to consider that. The implications were too monstrous.

* * *

Despite having traveled with him for several days, Marina couldn't get used to Monty Randolph's endless chatter.

"You ought to see her hair," he was saying. "It's as red as a sunset in the western sky. And she's just as wild."

"She follows Monty around like a puppy tagging along after its ma," Hen said. "She's the only female I've ever seen him run from."

"You'd run, too," Monty said. "Hell, she's only thirteen. That's not a female. That's a baby."

"I'm twelve," Drew said, taking umbrage, "and I'm no baby."

"And you're not chasing after me."

"I don't chase after boys," Drew said, "especially big, loud showoffs like you."

Much to Drew's embarrassment, everybody laughed. None louder than Monty.

Marina's gaze shifted continually between her son, who was seated between Hen and Monty, and Ward. The similarities were so obvious, anyone could see them. Tanner did have dark hair and a fair complexion, but they came from her, not Ramon. It was Ward's eyes that were the clincher. Marina had never seen anyone with such deep, dark blue eyes as Ward.

Until Tanner was born.

But it was useless to mention it. Ward had closed his mind. She was partly to blame. She should have told him right off about Ramon's attempt to rape her. But she hadn't expected Ramon to tell his mother, or Luisa to tell Ward. Marina had never liked Luisa, but she'd never thought the woman was evil.

Now she knew better.

Marina had to talk to Ward again, but she couldn't make up her mind if it would be better to approach him tonight or wait until the morning. He was so angry that he might not even speak to her. She didn't know why she had allowed herself to forget the depths of the revulsion he felt for her.

Maybe she hadn't wanted to remember. Maybe she didn't want to believe anyone she cared for that much could believe such horrible things about her. The truth was bad enough, but she would never . . .

It did no good to keep dwelling on it. Once she got her divorce, they would never have to see each other again.

She wished she could dispose of Ramon as easily. Ever since his wife died, he'd been trying to convince her to marry him. Ramon refused to believe she didn't love him. Now that her family had disowned her, she could only assume he wanted her because she was the only woman he knew who had ever preferred another man.

He reminded her that Tanner was his heir and ought to be raised on the Rancho del Espada. Ramon's wife had died without giving him a son.

When she refused even to consider marrying him, he said he wanted to adopt Tanner. He even offered to claim paternity. He seemed to be completely unaware of what such a claim would have said about Marina's morals.

She couldn't marry him, not even to give Tanner a name. She hated him for what he'd done to her, to Ward, to Tanner. Marriage to Bud Warren was her best, her only, choice.

"We need to talk."

Marina had been so wrapped up in her own thoughts, she hadn't noticed Ward's approach in the commotion of so many people leaving the table, several of them still talking. He stood above her—tall, slim, silent, his lapis-blue eyes hooded and remote.

Marina felt the physical tug of his presence, felt the warmth spread through her, and it made her angry. She didn't understand how she could be so foolish as to be attracted to a man who hated her.

She indicated the seat next to her.

"Outside." He walked out of the room without waiting for her.

Did he hate her so much that he couldn't stand to be near her for more than a few seconds? She rose. Jake and the Randolphs were talking cows. Some of the boys were clearing and resetting the table so Isabelle could feed the other boys when they came in from watch.

Marina followed Ward outside. Isolation and its distance from San Antonio made Jake's valley seem wild and lonely. Marina wondered how Ward could be happy here. She couldn't understand why he hadn't gone home to the family he loved so dearly.

He walked down the steps and into the yard. He started to walk away from the house the moment Marina reached his side. Was he trying to keep his distance from her or just trying to insure their privacy? He stopped about fifty yards from the house.

"I talked with Tanner."

"He told me."

"He talks too much."

"I know."

"Is that all you're going to say?" he demanded.

"What do you want me to say?" she asked.

"That you'll stop him."

He kept his eyes averted. He obviously couldn't

stand to look at her. Why couldn't she feel equally revolted by him?

"All the boys he knows have fathers," she explained. "He feels deprived. When he's feeling particularly insecure or lonely, he makes up stories. I hope he'll grow out of it when I remarry."

"That's what I wanted to talk to you about."

Surprise caused Marina to stare.

"Tanner says Ramon wants to marry you. Is that true?"

Apparently Tanner had been able to make Ward question his precious family's behavior where she hadn't. Good. She was sorry if it hurt him, but it was time he learned he'd believed cold-blooded liars rather than the woman who'd risked everything to marry him.

"Yes," she said.

"Why?"

She could see the tension in his body. His back seemed to bunch, as if he was preparing for a terrible blow.

"He said he loves me, that he always has. When I refused him, he tried to talk me into letting him adopt Tanner."

"Tanner said Ramon had a paper saying I was dead, that I was killed during the war."

She could hear the tension in his voice, the effort it took to ask that question calmly, as though the answer wouldn't crush him.

"It was a letter. It said you were missing in action and presumed dead. Since it came more than two years before the end of the war, everybody assumed you were dead."

"Where did he get it?"

"I don't know," she answered.

"I don't suppose it matters."

She could tell it mattered very much. He turned to look at her. His face seemed expressionless in the pale, cold moonlight.

"Tanner ought to be raised at Rancho del Espada, even if people don't know he's Ramon's son. He obviously wants a father. Ramon wants to adopt him. Why don't you let him?"

"He's not Ramon's son." Marina felt the heat of anger burning in her cheeks. "He's your son. I refuse to say anything else." It was fruitless to argue with Ward; still, she couldn't stop. "I have no intention of letting your brother raise my son."

"Why?"

"Outside of the fact Ramon *isn't* Tanner's father, he's selfish, spiteful, arrogant, and mean. He lacks both honor and honesty. I refuse to allow Tanner to grow up thinking Ramon is the kind of man he ought to become." She waited for a response, but he didn't speak. "I'll never forgive you for what you did to me, Ward, but I don't hate you. I couldn't let your brother claim your son."

"But you always wanted Ramon. Marrying him would solve everything."

Would he ever believe anything she said? "I don't want Ramon. I never did. I loved you. Why won't you believe me?"

"How can I after what you did?"

"Ward Dillon, if you dare accuse me of sleeping with Ramon to get a rich husband, I'll shoot you with your own gun."

The ghost of a smile flitted across his features. "You always were real feisty." His expression turned bleak again. "How long has Ramon been coming to see you?"

The question surprised her. "Ever since he brought me that letter."

"How many times?"

"Seven."

"You remember so exactly?"

"No. He reminded me."

"He came seven times and still you wouldn't marry him. Why not? No lies or excuses this time. The real reason."

Marina took a deep breath. "I never loved Ramon. I did agree to become engaged to him to please my parents. Unfortunately, I fell in love with you. Ramon tried to rape me, and you deserted me."

"You lied."

"So you chose to believe."

"Your guilt was written all over your face."

"My *hopelessness*. It still is if you'd take the trouble to look."

He turned to face her, his expression as hard as granite. She didn't know why she bothered, why she still cared what he believed. It only hurt her. She wasn't going to tell him again. He could go on believing what he wanted.

"My life is none of your business, Ward. Neither is Tanner's. It hasn't been for seven years, and it's not going to start now. All I want is a divorce. Give it to me, and I'll leave you alone."

"I want Tanner to be raised as a Dillon. I won't have him cheated out of his birthright."

"What you want doesn't matter."

"Then my not giving you a divorce won't matter, either." He turned and stalked off.

Marina was so angry, she was tempted to head straight back to San Antonio. Ward was so used to being a Dillon, to seeing his mother get everything she wanted, that he thought he could do the same with Marina and Tanner. He was in for a surprise this time. Bud's lawyer would find some way to get a divorce, even if she had to cause a scandal.

But she wouldn't do that. The ties that lashed her and Ward together were deeper, stronger, more binding than a few words on a piece of paper. They had been man and wife. They had produced a child.

As she stood alone in the dusk, cooling breezes flowing down from the nearby hills, she finally admitted to herself that she had never let go, never taken his departure as final. Somewhere in the back of her mind, in the depths of her heart, she had always been certain that, given time, he would have acted differently.

Now she wasn't sure. He seemed as angry, as determined as ever. Nevertheless, Marina couldn't turn around and go home. The connection was still there. He had to be willing to stand in front of a judge and say he wanted nothing to do with her. Ever.

She had to hear him with her own ears before she could let go.

Chapter Nine

"Can we go with Monty and Hen?" Tanner asked as he put on his night shirt.

"You know we can't," Marina said. "We have to go back to the Gravel Pit."

Their room was bare of furniture except for a bed, a dressing table, and a chair. Isabelle apologized that she hadn't had time to furnish the house properly. Marina didn't mind the bare walls and floors. She was just glad to have some privacy. Seeing Ward again had left her feelings in an uproar. She brushed her waist-length hair while Tanner crawled into bed. She had already changed into her nightgown.

"I don't want to go back," Tanner said.

"It's our home."

"It's not," Tanner declared angrily.

No matter how kind Bud Warren was to Tanner, no matter how much Tanner liked Bud, home would be the ranch Tanner's father would buy when he came back. Marina had done her best to wean Tanner from his fantasy, but he clung to it.

"My daddy would want me to go with Monty and Hen. He would want me to be a cowboy just like them."

Tanner had fallen into the habit of using his imaginary father to second whatever he wanted to do.

"He might," Marina said, "but he'd never let you go alone."

"I wouldn't be alone. I'd be with Monty."

"Monty isn't your father."

"When my daddy comes back, he'll take me on a cattle drive. He'll take me anywhere I want to go."

"Maybe," Marina said.

She didn't know what to say now that she had found Ward. She couldn't continue trying to convince Tanner that his father was probably dead. But since Ward wanted nothing to do with him, she couldn't tell Tanner his father was alive either.

"We'll have to stay here a few days," Marina said. "Why don't you ask Ward to take you riding? He seems to be a good cowhand. He might be able to teach you as much as Monty could."

"He's not good enough to eat Monty's dust," Tanner said, his voice full of scorn. "He's an old man."

"He's no older than your father would be."

Tanner paused. "How old is daddy?"

"Your father would be thirty-one," Marina said.

"Would he look as old as Ward?"

"He would look almost exactly like Ward."

Tanner looked up at his mother with that innocent, vulnerable look that always made her feel like crying. "Why does Ward look like Mr. Ramon?"

Marina felt her throat tighten. Her hand paused in

brushing her hair. "Maybe he has some Spanish blood in him, too."

"Do you think Mr. Ramon is handsome?"

She started to brush again. "Everybody thinks he's the best-looking man in San Antonio."

"I like Ward better."

Marina stopped and turned toward her son, surprise holding her silent for several moments. "Why do you say that?"

"Don't you think he's handsome?"

She used to. Unfortunately, she still did. "Yes, but—"

"Jake, too. Of course Monty and Hen are the handsomest of all."

Some of the tension eased inside Marina. "You just admire cowboys."

"You said my daddy was the best cowhand on his ranch. I'm going to be just like him."

"Your father would be very proud, but he wanted to do something more with his life."

"I don't want to be a doctor. I wouldn't like cutting people open."

Apparently Ward didn't like it either.

"You don't have to do that."

"That's what Benjy says, and his grandfather is a doctor."

Benjy was Tanner's best friend. His grandfather had served as a doctor in the Mexican War as well as in the War Between the States. He enjoyed telling tales of the gruesome operations he'd performed. Marina suspected Ward's experience had been similar.

"There are all kinds of doctors. Not all of them cut people open. Most just try to make people well."

"I still don't want to be one. Maybe Mr. Maxwell would take me riding with him."

"I imagine he has his hands full running the ranch."

"Okay, I'll ask Ward. But if he's not as good as Monty, I'm coming right back."

"I'm sure he will be."

Tanner slid down under the covers. "We'll see."

Marina finished brushing her hair and blew out the light.

In her eyes, the Randolph twins were mere boys. Not even Jake could inspire more than a moment's appreciation. Yet one look from Ward could start a fire smoldering in her belly.

"What can I call him?" Tanner asked.

"Who?"

"Ward. You never let me call grownups by their first names."

"I don't know. You'll have to ask him."

"Monty says lots of men in Texas don't have last names. He says that's because there's something terrible in their past. Do you think Ward's like that?"

He wants to forget I'm his wife, that you're his son. He wants to forget he was ever a doctor. He wants to turn himself into a dry husk and let the wind blow him where it will.

"Everybody has something they want to forget, but I don't imagine Ward has any terrible secrets," she said. "Ask him what you should call him."

"But what if he wants me to call him Ward?"

"Then that's what you'll call him."

When Ward rode in from his shift as night rider, he found Chet and Jake talking about the drive.

"We can take the herd to Abilene on our own,"

Chet was saying. "We don't need anybody else."

"You've got to pass through Indian territory," Jake said. "We can't afford to lose a herd like we did in New Mexico. We need every cent we can earn to buy up this valley before farmers homestead it. Indians won't bother a herd as big as the Randolphs'."

Knowing the reason for Jake's decision didn't make Chet any happier.

"We're not a big operation," Jake said. "We'll always have to ship as part of a bigger herd."

Ward dismounted. He looped the reins over the corral fence and loosened the saddle cinch. He waited until Chet had gone off before joining Jake. "How are the other boys taking it?" he asked.

Jake smiled, looking relieved. "Most of them are trying to talk me into letting them go along. Buck doesn't mind staying here since I've made him foreman, but Zeke's and Sean's noses are definitely out of joint."

Ward laughed. "They'll forget all about it when the herd arrives."

Jake took the saddle from Ward and put it on top of the fence. Ward removed the saddle blankets and started to rub down the paint.

"Isabelle said you used to be married to Marina."

Ward wasn't pleased everybody seemed to know his business, but in a family this size, nothing remained secret for very long. "I still am."

"Isabelle invited her to stay until she's completed her business with you."

Ward felt tension coil through his chest. He'd hoped Marina would return to San Antonio immediately. He didn't like this resurgence of his old feelings every time he saw her. It made him look for ways to believe her.

Jake spread out the saddle blankets to dry while Ward finished the rubdown. Ward turned his horse into the corral, and the two men stood together in companionable silence as the paint trotted over to join the other horses in the corral.

"It's Isabelle's house."

"It's your home, too."

Ward nodded. He was glad to hear Jake say it. For the first time in years, he had friends and a place he called home. The Broken Circle was as much of a home as any place could be when his family wasn't there.

"I don't know what happened between you two, and I'm not asking you to tell me," Jake said. "But if you're not comfortable with her staying here, she'll have to find some other place."

"I don't imagine Isabelle would like that."

"She didn't." Jake smiled as he gave his head a rueful shake. "The tongue-lashing she gave me had enough salt in it to cure a good-sized ham, but she agrees this is your home. She doesn't want to do anything to make you feel otherwise."

Ward almost felt guilty that he couldn't return the depth of affection Jake and Isabelle obviously felt for him. He liked them more than anybody outside his family—well, maybe not more than Drew. He had a special warm spot for her.

"I don't especially like it," Ward said, "but there's no place else she and the boy can go."

"You sure?"

Odd, Ward thought. His own family had never been nearly so concerned about his feelings.

"You can tell Isabelle I don't mind in the least."

"You'll have to tell her yourself. She thinks I bully you."

Ward grinned. "You do, but I don't mind."

Now it was Jake's turn to grin. "As I'm frequently told, that's a matter of opinion." His expression sobered quickly. "That's a nice boy she's got. Your son?"

Hell! This was the one question Ward didn't want to have to answer.

"So she says."

Jake's look was penetrating. "You don't believe her?"

"I've got my doubts."

"Do you have any idea what a thing like that can do to a kid?"

"I didn't know he existed until today."

"That's all the more reason to consider how he feels," Jake said. "Hell, I went nuts when my ma left us. I'm not telling you what to do, but for the boy's sake, you've got to do something."

Great. Isabelle was taking Marina's side. Now Jake had come down squarely in Tanner's corner. They said this was his home, that he would have a say in everything, yet both of them were doing their best to back him into a corner.

"This is none of your business, Jake. You don't know what happened."

"And I don't want to. I'm just saying, if you *can* do anything about it, you shouldn't leave the boy hanging."

"What about me, Jake? I've been left hanging for seven years. You ever thought about what that has done to me?"

"Isabelle and I have talked about it lots of times. She says you were hurt by love. I say somebody turned on you. Apparently we're both right."

"So what do you think I should do about it?"

"I can't answer that."

"Why not? You've got answers for everybody else."

"No answers, just suggestions. You've got to find your own answers."

"Great. How many days are you giving me?"

"You sound angry."

"You're damned right. I'm mad as hell at Marina for dropping out of the sky and putting me through this all over again. I'm angry at you and Isabelle for assuming it's my fault."

"I didn't say that. If I know anything, it's that nothing is ever one person's fault." Jake backed away from the rail. "It's up to you to make the decision. That woman and her son have feelings."

"What about my feelings?"

"Sometimes you can't afford to give in to your own feelings. You do what's right and learn to live with it."

"Don't give me any of your damned moralizing. I'm not one of your gullible boys."

"It might be better if you were. They're willing to listen. Your mind is closed. Now I'd better be getting to bed." He gave Ward a searching look. "I think I'll lock my door."

"Go to hell!" Ward said and stalked off.

But walking away wasn't the answer. Neither was being angry at Jake and Isabelle. Jake was right, damn him. Ward had to do something.

He firmly believed Ramon was the boy's father, but there was a chance Marina was telling the truth. Only a small chance, but Ward knew he couldn't turn his back on it. Damn, damn, damn! It was happening all over again. He was in the middle between Marina and his family, forced to choose.

He walked past the barn. Below, the valley opened out before him. The dark hulk of the mountains loomed in the distance. Isolated clouds scurried across the sky, occasionally obliterating the moon. A breeze with the feel of frost in it rustled the new green leaves, waved the tall grass.

It was a world of perfect serenity, a dramatic contrast to the turmoil that raged inside him.

He had wanted to believe them both, but he couldn't. He had chosen his family the first time, but now it was clear Ramon had lied over and over again. Why?

Ward was convinced Marina *had* turned her back on Ramon. Tanner wouldn't have lied about that. He was too young to understand why he should. And Marina continued to insist Tanner was Ward's son.

Ward's certainty started to crumble. Tanner did have blue eyes. Ramon's eyes were black, like those of their mother. Gardner had said Ward got his eyes from his Creole grandmother.

What if Tanner were his son? Ward didn't want to let himself even consider the possibility—but what if he were? An indescribable feeling washed through him. His scalp tingled. Small shivers traced the path of every nerve in his body.

What if he had a son!

It was a useless question, as useless as whether he believed Ramon had attempted to rape Marina or whether she had given herself to him willingly. He would never know the truth. The simplest thing was to avoid the questions altogether.

Muttering curses, Ward started toward the corral to saddle a fresh horse. The boys on night duty could always use an extra hand. If things were quiet, they appreciated his company. If they had trouble, they appreciated his help.

Ward appreciated not having to think about questions he couldn't answer.

Chapter Ten

The steers sensed something was about to happen. They moved about restlessly, bellowing, stamping their feet, knocking their horns together. Occasionally one bolted through the herd creating a swirling wave of milling animals behind him. Jake and the boys circled the herd to keep it together. The breath of men and beasts billowed before them in white clouds in the chilly air.

A heavy frost covered the grass. Clouds blocked out the sun and swallowed the tops of the surrounding hills. Mist rose from the ground, obscuring the ranch buildings half a mile away. In thirty minutes, the mist would burn off. Before noon the boys would be sweating.

Even though he wouldn't be going this time, Ward experienced his usual sense of excitement at the beginning of a drive. Huddled in a heavy coat against the morning chill, he considered changing his mind.

Jake had asked if he wanted to go, but Chet didn't need any more supervision. Too much would do more harm than good.

His horse sidestepped restlessly, shaking his head, fighting Ward's tight hold on the reins.

"Whoa, boy. We're not going anywhere."

Ward's horse continued to fight against his inactivity. When he started to buck, Ward decided to let him run. He circled the herd looking for Jake.

Matt and Tyler Randolph had headed out with the chuck wagons before dawn. Sean, Hawk, and Zeke were going along to help Chet drive the steers to meet the Randolphs' main herd. Even though the four boys could easily manage the small herd, Monty had pitched in to help.

"My boys can handle it," Jake was telling Hen when Ward caught up with him.

"Monty can't resist trying to take over," Hen said. "I'll knock him in the head if he gets too obnoxious."

"I'm sure that won't be necessary," Jake said, grinning.

"You don't know Monty." Hen rode toward his twin, who was trying to give the boys different jobs from those Chet had assigned them.

"This ought to be interesting," Jake said.

"Yeah, if you like war," Ward said.

"Maybe I'd better referee," Jake called over his shoulder.

Ward laughed. He watched Drew ride up, her face bright with a delighted grin. "Isabelle made Pete help her this morning," she shouted as she rode past. Ward's grin widened. Drew had won another small victory in her campaign to avoid being treated as a girl.

Tanner followed in Drew's wake. He stopped well

shy of the herd and turned his horse in Ward's direction. His mount, a long-legged thoroughbred, sidled nervously at the closeness of the steers.

Ward felt the tension he'd been ignoring escalate. All the unanswered questions of the previous night came hurtling back. But now he accepted that Tanner could very well be his son. No betrayal could alter that.

Ward had never thought of himself as a father. He had never gotten to be a husband. Now he was looking at a child who could be his own flesh and blood. Extraordinary feelings welled up inside him—wonder that he could have done anything so miraculous as help create another human being, terror that this sensitive child should look to him as an example of how to build his life, sadness that the boy had spent so many years without the love and comfort of a father, anger that he couldn't know for sure, that he couldn't unleash his feelings without fear they would be invalidated by a few words from Marina.

Tanner nudged his nervous chestnut next to Ward's mount. "They're getting ready to leave, aren't they?"

"Yes."

All the children were going with the herd to the edge of Jake's ranch. Chet and Buck had already started the steers moving in a column about six animals wide. Everybody else rode swing except Zeke and Jake, who brought up the rear. Drew had paired herself with Will.

"I wanted to go, but Mama wouldn't let me," Tanner said.

"Maybe when you're older."

"I'm not a baby! I'm six." Tanner's outburst caused his horse to toss its head nervously.

"Pete and Will are older, and Jake won't let them go."

"But he lets them help. Mama said I had to stay far away."

Ward thought Tanner was old enough to ride alongside the herd. If the boy were his son, he'd have some say in how he was raised.

"Come on," Ward said. "We can get a little closer, maybe even haze a steer or two back in line."

Tanner's eyes lit up. "You mean it?"

"Sure." Ward headed off at a fast trot.

"What'll Mama say?" Tanner asked as he nudged his horse alongside Ward's.

"A lot, probably, but we'll already have done it."

Ward didn't know why he was acting this way. He shouldn't let himself be persuaded by a pair of eyes. But only three people in the Dillon family had his grandmother's eyes—his father, himself, and now Tanner. It was becoming increasingly difficult to ignore the probability that Tanner was his son.

He didn't even want to anymore.

"Stay next to me," Ward said as they neared the herd. "You can never tell what longhorns will do."

"Are you going to rope one?" Tanner asked, excited.

"No, we'll just make sure they stay together."

Ward and Tanner became engulfed in the dust stirred up by so many hoofs. Ward put his handkerchief over his nose. Tanner didn't have one, so Ward unfolded his extra handkerchief and gave it to the boy. The smile that lit up Tanner's face caused Ward's heart to turn over. He didn't know what affected him more—that Tanner should smile at him like that or that the boy should be so excited over such a small thing.

He had to talk to Marina. She was too protective. Ward had been allowed to help on the ranch from the time he was able to sit in the saddle.

Ward intentionally provoked a steer into veering out of line so he and Tanner could haze the animal back. The boy's enjoyment was so far out of proportion to what he was doing, Ward couldn't resist doing it again.

"I told you I knew how to be a cowboy," Tanner said to Ward when the steer was back in line.

"So you did. Maybe if you stay long enough, we can work some of the cattle in those hills."

"You mean it?"

"We'll have to talk to your mother first."

Tanner's face fell. "She won't let me go. She says I'll get hurt."

Ward's mother had never objected when his father took him out on the range.

"Can I rope a steer?" Tanner looked up and down the line of animals, clearly hoping one would bolt.

"Maybe we'd better start with calves," Ward said. "Steers can be pretty dangerous, even for a grown man."

"I can do it. I've done it lots of times."

Ward felt certain the boy was exaggerating. He didn't understand why Tanner should have to fabricate stories to make himself seem bigger, more accomplished. Marina loved her son—of that Ward had no doubt—but something was missing. Ward had the guilty feeling it was the lack of a father. Though why it should be so serious in Tanner's case he didn't understand.

"Some other time," Ward said. "We don't rope steers for fun."

Without warning, a steer a little way ahead bolted

from the herd. It darted around a twisted cedar and headed for a drop in the ground that led toward a ravine. Ward's horse was off in a flash. Ward had his rope swinging over his head in nearly the same instant. Just before the steer disappeared into the ravine, the rope snaked through the air and tightened around the steer's hind legs.

The animal fell to the ground. By the time the steer scrambled to his feet, Ward was behind him. The chastened animal allowed himself to be guided back to the herd.

"Golly!" Ward heard Tanner say to Will, who'd come up behind them. "Did you see him do that?"

"He does it all the time," Will said. "Ain't nobody better than Ward with his rope."

"Isn't anyone better," Ward said, correcting Will's grammar. "You'd better not let Isabelle hear you talk like that."

"I always talk better when I'm at the house. If I talked good all the time, everybody'd think I was a sissy."

"I wouldn't," Ward said.

"I wasn't talking about grownups," Will said. He moved away. Ward nudged his horse forward, resuming his place on the flank of the herd while he rewound his rope.

"You aren't even looking," Tanner said.

"Looking at what?" Ward asked.

"Your rope. You coiled it up without even looking."

Ward had coiled his rope thousands of times. Still, he couldn't help taking a little pleasure in Tanner's escalating opinion of him. It made it all that much harder to remember there was only a possibility Tanner was his son. But once he accepted the possibility, he found it more and more difficult to deny the probability.

Why? Ward had known the kid less than twenty-four hours. He was over-protected, created imaginary people, and would be furious if he ever discovered Ward was his father. So why was he so anxious that this boy be his son?

Ward had no idea. He only knew it was so.

"Could you teach me how to do that?"

"What, coil your rope?"

"No, rope a steer's back feet."

"Sure, but I'll need to talk to your mama first."

Tanner's happiness faded. "She'll say no."

"Maybe, but we can ask. Now why don't you take up that rope hanging from your saddle. We can practice a few throws. Not at the steers—I don't want to get them upset—but we'll find something."

Over the next hour Ward discovered roping branches, bushes, and boulders could be a lot more fun than he'd imagined.

"He's terrible," Will muttered to Ward as Tanner recoiled his rope after missing a stump at a canter. "He couldn't lasso a calf unless it ran into his rope."

Ward sent Will about his work before Tanner could overhear. Tanner was so anxious to learn, he didn't have time to realize how bad he was. Ward didn't mind taking the time to explain what he was doing wrong, how to do it right, or to compliment him on his few successes.

"Looks like you've got your work cut out for you," Jake said when he rode by.

Ward felt a faint flush of embarrassment. "Just keeping busy. You don't really need any help with the herd."

Jake grinned knowingly and rode on.

They soon reached the edge of Jake's ranch. Final instructions had barely been given and good-byes uttered when Will shouted, "Race you back to the barn."

Before Jake could say a word, six kids were strung out at a full-out gallop. "You sure Tanner ought to go with them?" Jake asked.

"The only way I'm going to stop him is run him down," Ward replied. "I don't think I can catch his horse."

Ward was certain Marina wouldn't like Tanner racing, but the boy was clearly having the time of his life.

Ward wasn't pleased when he saw Buck turn off the trail and take a shortcut that meant they'd have to jump a narrow ravine. Jake's kids jumped it all the time, but Ward didn't know what Tanner would do. Worse still, the ravine was in full view of the house.

Ward hoped Marina had slept late, couldn't find her shoes, was too busy helping Isabelle to stand around scanning the horizon. His prayers weren't answered. When the house came into view, he could see Marina standing on the front porch, coffee cup in hand, watching the boys as they raced toward the corrals.

He knew the exact instant she spied Tanner in the middle of the mad scramble to be the first to reach the barn. Her body froze, the coffee cup suspended halfway to her mouth. He also knew the exact instant she realized Tanner meant to jump the ravine. She dropped her cup.

Much to Ward's relief, all six riders cleared the ravine without the slightest hesitation. If Tanner noticed his mother, he didn't show it. He was in a neck-and-neck battle with Buck to be the first rider to reach the barn. Moments later an ear-splitting soprano yell told Ward that Tanner had won.

Pride in the boy's riding outweighed any worry about what Marina would say. Tanner might have had the best horse, but he was the youngest kid out there and he was racing over unfamiliar ground. He'd displayed guts, courage, and skill.

"That's quite a boy you've got there," Jake said.

"Yeah, he sure is," Ward said. It was too much trouble to remind Jake that Tanner might not be his son. "Looks like he got better lessons in riding than roping."

"I imagine you can fix that in a short while."

"Yeah. I thought I'd take him out later today and—"

Ward stopped in mid-sentence. He was acting like a proud papa. In less than a day he'd gone from swearing Tanner wasn't his son to wanting him to be so badly, he didn't know if he could stand being told he wasn't.

"That's a good idea," Jake said, "but you're going to have to do some fancy talking first. Here comes his mama. The last female I saw with that kind of fire in her eyes was a longhorn cow about to teach a wolf it was a real bad idea to mess with her calf."

Marina headed toward Ward, ignoring the uneven ground, rocks, and thorns that pulled at her skirt. She was going to kill him. It didn't matter that it was against the law or that she didn't have a gun. She was going to kill him anyway. He should have known better than to let Tanner go off with Will and Drew. They probably raced headlong over dangerous country every day.

But Tanner hadn't been brought up that way. She

had made certain he knew how to ride, but he was too young to go careening about a ranch, even at home with Bud supervising. Let her turn her back for five minutes, and her precious child was galloping across broken country jumping ravines like it was a Sunday afternoon stroll into town.

She'd kill Ward.

He didn't try to avoid her. The minute she charged down the porch steps, he turned his horse toward her.

Marina walked to the edge of the ravine. It didn't look as wide as she had feared, but it was deeper. A chill shook her as she looked at the tangle of rocks and brush that littered the bottom. If Tanner had fallen in, he would have broken his neck. The thought of her only child dead or maimed made her shudder.

"What do you mean letting Tanner jump that ravine?" she demanded even before Ward's horse came to a halt after clearing the ravine. "He could have killed himself. I don't expect you to take responsibility for him, but I figured you'd at least keep an eye on him."

"He won," Ward said as he dismounted. "Did you see that?"

She moved closer. She didn't want him to miss a single word. "Is that all you can see, that he won some senseless race?"

Ward threw up his arms in a mock defensive gesture, grinned, and backed up a step. That he should treat any part of what had happened as a joke made Marina madder than ever.

"I see he's got courage and bottom," Ward said, more seriously. "He didn't hesitate when he saw the others jump that ravine. He's got skill, too. He

131

pushed his horse with hands and knees. He didn't resort to spurs."

"That's beside the point. I—"

"He's got determination. He kept right on driving until he wore Buck's horse down. You ought to be proud of him."

He wasn't listening to her. All he could think of was the dumb race. "What if he had fallen off? What if his horse hadn't jumped that ravine?"

"It's not very wide. Pete and Will jump it all the time."

"Pete and Will aren't my sons," she said with angry gestures that took in Ward, Tanner, and half of Jake's brood. "I'm concerned about Tanner. I know you don't want anything to do with him—"

"I didn't say that," Ward interrupted, the smile wiped from his face. "I don't mind watching out for him. I'll even teach him to use a rope."

Marina hoped she wasn't standing there with her mouth open.

"I don't think that would be a good idea," she said.

"Why not?"

Yes, why? She had traveled all this distance, had swallowed her pride, to ask Ward to give her a divorce so she could provide Tanner with a father. Why didn't she want his real father to have anything to do with him? She looked at the ravine again, the tangled debris at the bottom.

"He's too impressionable right now. He likes you. He'll do anything to keep your attention. Which seems unfair since you refuse to acknowledge him as your son."

"You know I can't—"

He didn't finish his sentence, glanced away, but Marina knew what he was going to say. He wouldn't acknowledge a child he was certain was his brother's son.

"I'm not asking you to, just don't make him like you. Let Bud be the one to teach him to rope and all the other things you men think so important. Bud will adopt him, will give him his name."

Ward had seemed distracted, but now he snapped to attention. "You didn't say anything about Bud adopting him."

"I didn't consider it any of your concern."

"It is if he's my son."

Marina gave him a hard, appraising look. "So now it's if."

"I knew there was a chance," Ward said, his glance sliding away once more. "We did have a honey-moon."

She didn't want to remember that. It was a night that had promised her paradise and landed her in hell.

"Look, Ward, all I want from you is a divorce. If you care about Tanner's future at all, you'll do that for me."

"Suppose I don't think that's best for him?"

Marina swallowed a bitter retort. "You don't want Tanner and you don't want me. The best thing—"

"I never said I didn't want him."

He just stood there, looking straight at her, and made that statement. She could hardly believe it. This ought to be high drama, on a stage full of hot lights, with an audience straining to catch their every word and expression. But here they were, in some valley in the wilds of Texas, standing knee-deep in grass and weeds, on the edge of a ravine, mountains and cows in every direction, the sun threatening to turn it into a beautiful day. It was too absurd for such a prosaic setting.

Her temper burst out of control. "You said you didn't believe he was your son. That sounded pretty much like a rejection to me."

"I was angry then."

"Now you're not?" He looked as stubborn as a goat. "So Tanner is supposed to forget all the years you stayed away, to accept you with open arms."

"I didn't say—"

"What's he going to call you? It can't be Daddy. Or Uncle. Do you mean to pass yourself off as some interested bystander paying him a little attention out of the kindness of your heart?"

"Stop being unreasonable. I only want—"

"You want to indulge yourself, to ease your conscience, to play daddy without having to shoulder the responsibility. Well I won't let you, Ward. I don't care about your conscience or your guilt. I care about my son, and I won't have you playing with his feelings. If you won't leave him alone, I'll leave here today."

"There's nobody to go with you," Ward said. "We have a new herd coming in. It'll take every one of us working from dawn to dusk several days to get them branded."

"Then I'll go on my own. If that's not possible, I'll stay in my room and keep Tanner with me."

She turned and stalked off. It did no good to talk to him. She didn't know why she tried. Ward followed.

"That wouldn't be fair to Tanner."

"It would be more fair than letting him think you had a sincere emotional attachment to him, one that wouldn't shatter at the first moment of doubt," she said over her shoulder, giving him only a glance.

"You aren't going to forgive me for that, are you?"

She turned, faced him. "No." She turned back around.

"I don't suppose I would forgive me, either. It was cowardly."

She had thought the same thing for years, but she'd never expected to hear him admit it. She'd always thought he placed all the blame on her. It was a relief to know he realized he'd behaved badly. But honesty forced her to admit she had to share the blame. She should have told him about Ramon. He ran, but she broke his heart. She was just as guilty as he. No, more. She'd known what danger lay ahead. Ward hadn't.

She lowered her gaze. "We both made mistakes. I just want to put my life together again."

"If you think it's best, I'll stay away from him. But you can't keep him locked up in the house. He'll feel he's being punished."

He seemed earnest, sincere, and all for a boy whose existence he'd wanted to deny yesterday. She couldn't quite take it in, quite believe that his change of heart was genuine. "I'll explain."

"You can't. If you keep him from being with the others, especially Pete and Will, he'll resent it. He'll be angry at you."

"So what do you suggest I do?"

"Talk to Jake."

"And what about you?"

"I can always find something to do on the other side of the ranch."

Damn him! She'd finally been able to get really mad at him, mad enough to forget how attractive he was, and he did something noble. Why did she get this fluttering in her belly, this pounding pulse? Everything between them had died years ago. The attraction, the feeling of sympathy were residue. They meant nothing.

Pounding hooves pulled her from her gloomy thoughts.

"I won, Mama!" Tanner shouted. "Did you see me?"

Chapter Eleven

"Of course I saw you," Marina said, pretending an enthusiasm she didn't feel. He slid from the saddle and she gave him a big hug. "We owe Mrs. Maxwell a new cup. I dropped mine when I saw you jump that ravine."

"Did you see me beat Buck to the barn?" Tanner looked from his mother to Ward and back again. "I did exactly what Bud told me, and it worked. Spitfire won."

Marina remembered smiling indulgently when Bud and Tanner agreed on Spitfire as an appropriate name for the gelding he'd just bought the boy. After seeing how fast the animal could run, she wasn't nearly so pleased with the name or the horse. She would have preferred an aging, swaybacked mare named Dobbin.

Marina put her arm around his shoulder and turned toward the ranch house. "I'm glad you won, but I don't want you doing any more racing. You never know when you might run up on a ravine too big to jump."

"I was following them, Mama," Tanner exclaimed, looking up at his mother, his eyes brighter and his smile more brilliant than she could remember. "Everybody jumped it."

"I'm glad you made it across safely, but I think you ought to come inside for a while. Unsaddle Spitfire and give him a long rest. Maybe this afternoon—"

Tanner stopped; his smile vanished. "Ward's going to teach me to rope. Drew says if Ward doesn't teach me, she will. She said she can't allow anybody as bad as me to stay on her ranch."

Ward grinned. Astonishment held Marina silent. Tanner had always been sensitive to any kind of criticism. She found it incredible that he would cheerfully accept disapproval from a twelve-year-old female.

"Ward has other things he needs to do," Marina said. "You can ask him later. Or maybe Jake will teach you."

"I want Ward." The brightness was gone from Tanner's eyes. "Will says he's the best roper on the ranch, maybe even in all of Texas."

"I'm sure he has work to do."

"I heard Mr. Maxwell say Buck and Zeke were going hunting," Tanner said. "Drew promised to come watch me in case Ward forgot anything."

Marina was caught. If she made him stay inside now, he would be resentful and angry. She had had difficulty controlling him lately. She didn't want to push any limits.

Maybe it wouldn't hurt for Ward to get to know his son a little better. Maybe if he started to like Tanner, he'd be more willing to give her the divorce so the boy could have a normal life.

It might be good for Tanner, too. If he could master a few more skills, maybe he wouldn't feel so in need of an imaginary father. She told herself he wouldn't be around Ward long enough to become too attached to him.

"Okay, but just for the morning." Tanner jumped up to give his mother a hug.

"I'll make sure he doesn't hurt himself," Ward said. "I wasn't going to let him rope anything bigger than a calf anyway."

"Can I really?" Tanner looked as if he'd just been offered the finest present in the world.

Ward smiled and winked at Marina.

"If you can throw a rope anywhere near its head," Drew said, coming up to join them.

Tanner turned on his youthful critic. "I'll bet I can throw as well as you when Ward's done teaching me."

"Ward's good," Drew said, swaggering just like one of the boys, "but I ain't seen him work no miracles lately."

"You let Isabelle hear you talk like that, and it'll be a miracle if she lets you outside for a week," Ward said.

Drew blushed faintly. "Come on, tenderfoot. I'll help you pick out a rope. That thing you've got won't hold a knock-kneed yearling for five seconds."

"It would, too," Tanner said, going off after Drew. "My Uncle Bud gave it to me."

"All show and no substance," Drew said scornfully.

"Are you sure she's a girl?" Marina asked, as she watched the two head toward the barn, sniping at each other.

Ward laughed. "If wanting would do any good, she'd be Chet, Hawk, and Jake all rolled into one."

Marina turned back to Ward. "We're staying only until you agree to the divorce," she said, coming right to the point. "I don't want him missing you after we leave."

"We're only talking about a few days," Ward said. "Not long enough for anything to happen."

"You don't know your son."

"Why do you insist upon calling him my son?"

"Because he is."

"Are you going to tell him?"

"What's the point? You don't want to be a father to him."

"What if I did?"

Marina had had about all the shocks she could stand for one morning. She scrutinized Ward's expression carefully. She could see nothing to make her think he was lying or trying to mislead her.

The attraction between them, seemingly always near the surface now, flared. She thought of being Ward's wife, of making love to him. Their one night together remained vividly in her memory, both as a cherished moment and a painful torment. She would never forget being held in his arms and feeling safe, protected, loved.

But that feeling had vanished beyond all possibility of being reclaimed. It seemed cruel of her mind to continually taunt her with possibilities that didn't exist.

"Why would you do that?" she asked.

"You say the boy needs a father. You say I'm his father. What could be more logical?"

"You've left it a little late. I'm going back to San

Antonio. You're staying here. He can't live in two places."

"He'll know about me if I give you the divorce."

"But you won't be there. He won't have to see you."

"We could tell him now."

"No."

"Why?"

"Because if I did, he'd hate us both."

"Isn't there something I can do to help?" Marina asked. The kitchen smelled wonderfully of beef and onions.

"The potatoes are peeled and the vegetables are on, but you can make the gravy while I start the biscuits."

"I don't know how you feed so many people."

"The boys do a lot of the work," Isabelle answered.

"But you manage so easily," Marina said as she looked through the cabinet for a deep frying pan. "I have trouble with just one."

"Twelve is easier. They expect a lot more when there's only one."

"I'd offer to take over the stove, but you're a much better cook than I am."

"I couldn't be." Isabelle's look was one of disbelief.

"I've managed my cousin's household for years, but I spent most of that time in the sickroom. This is the first time I've been away from the ranch since she died two years ago."

"I couldn't stand not seeing other women at least once in a while."

"It's not so hard when people you've known your whole life stare through you like you're not even there. It's even worse when it's your own mother. I guess that's why I don't care to go into town."

Marina found a pan that suited her. She set it on the stove and dropped some butter in to start heating. Isabelle was up to her elbows in a huge bowl of flour and lard. Marina guessed she planned to make at least four dozen biscuits.

"What about the man you're going to marry?"

"Bud rarely leaves the ranch. If he has guests, it's always men."

"You can't bring Tanner up in a vacuum."

Marina had thought about that more and more recently. She and Ward might have ruined their chances at happiness, but Tanner deserved his. Marrying Bud would help, but there would still be prejudice, thoughtless and cruel remarks for the boy to endure.

"Tanner is part of the reason I'm marrying Bud. He needs a father. He also needs a sponsor. The men who control this world have organized themselves into a kind of secret society—at least it's secret from women. A mother can't introduce her son into it. It takes a man. Disgusting, isn't it?"

Isabelle smiled. "You and Drew ought to get together."

"She must be a remarkable little girl. She has Tanner eating out of her hand, even though she's been criticizing him."

Marina sprinkled a little flour in the pan, but the fat wasn't hot enough yet. She poured buttermilk into Isabelle's bowl until she was told to stop. The sharp, tangy smell tickled her nose.

"Drew will tell you she hates being a girl, but she has a strong mothering instinct. She bullies every one of the boys, and they love her for it."

Isabelle kneaded the dough until she was satisfied with its consistency. She sprinkled flour on the table, pulled off a lump of dough, and started rolling it out. Marina sprinkled flour into the popping fat. She was beginning to feel warm. She noticed beads of perspiration on Isabelle's forehead.

"Have you thought of Ward being the one to usher Tanner into this society you're talking about?"

"Tanner thinks his father's dead. Under the circumstances, I think it best he doesn't know."

Having rolled the dough to the proper thickness, Isabelle cut out biscuits. "Why?"

Marina felt as if she were in a fishbowl with everyone staring at her, criticizing every move she made.

"I know I'm asking too many questions," Isabelle said, apparently not the slightest bit embarrassed. "Aunt Deirdre would have told me I'm being rude and sent me to my room. But being around so many males has taught me to shed polite pretense and get straight to the point. I like Ward. He's kind, understanding, and a gentleman. I should think he'd be the best father for Tanner."

"You've seen a side of him I don't know."

The flour was almost browned. Marina reached for the beef drippings.

"I like Tanner, too," Isabelle continued, apparently determined to have her say. "I know he's your son, but I know something about boys. They need a man they can admire, look up to, depend on."

"I couldn't depend on Ward. Why should he be different with Tanner?"

Isabelle looked surprised. But that didn't stop her from rolling out another lump of dough.

"Have you asked Tanner how he feels?"

"I know Ward better than he does."

"Are you sure?"

Marina paused in stirring the gravy. "What do you mean?"

"I don't know what happened between you two, but are you sure you aren't letting it distort your feelings toward Ward?"

Marina tasted the gravy. It needed salt.

"Of course it colors my feelings. It ruined my life."

"Is it possible your anger is masking another feeling?"

"What do you mean?"

"Why did you come here?"

Bubbles appeared in the thick, brown gravy. Marina added water to thin it. She wanted very much to turn away from Isabelle's gaze. She didn't want anyone to see too deeply into her thoughts and feelings. She didn't want to look at them herself. They were in too much of a tangle.

"You must have loved Ward very much to be so angry at him now."

"The attraction was immediate. I'm afraid it carried us both beyond reason."

She covered the pan of gravy and moved it off the heat. She took two pans of biscuits to put into the oven. The heat hit her like a blast furnace.

"And you don't love him any longer?"

"No."

"Are you sure? You're angry at him for what he did, but I think you're afraid to ask yourself what you truly feel for him now."

Marina was so upset, she let the oven door slam.

"You came here because you wanted to find out something. Do you know what that was?"

"What gives you the right to say these things?" Marina demanded. Looking around for something to do, she uncovered each pot on the stove in succession.

"I haven't any right." Isabelle put her hand to the small of her back to ease the tension. "But I had to throw out everything I'd been taught when I met Jake. If I hadn't, I'd have gone back to Austin and been the most miserable female in Texas."

Marina found a knife and began to slice potatoes.

"Ward left me seven years ago. He never came back."

"You could have gone to him."

"Would you have gone to Jake?"

Isabelle laughed and started to cut biscuits again. "I chased him all the way to Santa Fe. When he balked, I told him to make up his mind before I came after him with a branding iron. I wanted that man, and I meant to have him."

Marina had done almost the same thing with Ward. She still wanted the man she'd fallen in love with. If she were honest, she would have to admit he had had reason to run away. His mother's masterful lies were more believable than the truth.

But if she loved him so much, why hadn't she gone after him? Because she'd been too young and inexperienced to see beyond her own hurt. By the time she'd accepted her share of the blame, she'd been told he was probably dead.

"When I thought Ward was dead, I was sure everything was over," Marina said. "I was wrong. What we had must be brought to a close. I couldn't do that through a letter or a lawyer."

"Be sure of the end you're seeking. Sometimes we can't see what we want until we've lost it."

*   *   *

Ward watched Tanner head up to the house. He'd just spent two hours teaching him about ropes, the differences between rawhide and grass, different knots, how to loop a rope around the saddle horn to get the best hold and prevent the loss of a finger.

He'd lived with Jake's boys for two years, worked with them, done what he could to help them through the awkwardness of their teenage years, but he'd never felt like their father. Not even their big brother. He was just an older friend who could help out with an answer now and then.

It wasn't like that with Tanner.

He had been so preoccupied with his own anger that his feelings for the boy had caught him by surprise. He *wanted* the boy to be his son. He sensed Tanner had a special fondness for him in return. He knew he didn't want Tanner to disappear from his life when Marina returned to San Antonio.

But Marina wasn't going to calmly accept his wanting to be part of Tanner's life. He would probably have to give her the divorce. Maybe it was best. Then they could talk about Tanner without the confusion of their feelings for each other interfering.

Ward had finally admitted to himself that he still had feelings for Marina. His acceptance that she had been telling the truth all those years ago unleashed a flood of emotion. Now every time he saw Marina, a little more of what he'd felt years ago came back. Doubt still remained, but so did the fire he had thought dead so long ago.

"He might not be so bad after a while," Drew said. She peeked at Ward from around the edge of the barn.

"Have you been spying on us?" he asked, relieved to put aside his dilemma for now.

"Of course. How else am I going to find out anything?" She came to stand next to him. She picked up a coiled rope and began to play with it.

"You could ask."

"It never works. People always tell things the way they wish they was."

"Wish they were. You're probably right."

"You always going to correct me?" She threw a loop at nothing in particular, then drew back the rope.

"Probably. I had a very strict tutor. I got a strap across my shoulders if I make the same mistake more than twice."

"Your mama let him do that?"

"It was her order." But the tutor didn't strap Ramon.

"I wouldn't like that." She threw another loop.

"I didn't like it much either."

"You going to strap Tanner if he keeps missing with his rope?"

"Why would I do that?"

"Well, you being his pa and all, I thought you would." She threw a loop at a saddle. It slipped off easily.

"Where'd you hear that?"

Drew avoided his gaze. She threw a loop at a chicken that had escaped the pen. The hen squawked loudly and fluttered off a few feet.

"Listening around corners again, huh?"

Drew nodded.

"You've got to stop that. One of these days you're going to hear something you'll wish you hadn't."

"Well, are you?"

"No."

"Then how's he going to know you're his pa?" She practiced twirling the loop over her head.

"He's not going to know, and you're not going to tell him."

"Why?"

"I can't tell you, but it's extremely important you don't tell anyone, especially Tanner, what you've overheard."

"Why does he think you're dead?" She practiced spinning a loop in front, showing off. She was good and she knew it.

"It was a mistake, a mixup during the war." That wasn't exactly a lie, but it was close enough to make him uneasy.

"Can't you fix it now?"

"It's more complicated than that." She tried jumping through the loop, but it caught on her boot.

"I don't see why. You're married to his mama. All you have to do is live together."

"We don't get along very well."

"My ma and pa shouted at each other all the time. You never shout. Isabelle says you never fall into a fit of passion."

"I did once."

She tried jumping through the loop again. She stepped on it this time. "Don't you think Marina is pretty?" she asked as she hauled in the rope and started to make another loop.

"Yes."

"And you like Tanner."

"Yes."

"Then why—"

"There are things between men and women you don't understand, Drew, things it's not polite to talk about to other people."

"I know. I heard," Drew admitted. She started to spin the loop again. "But I don't know why you care.

148

I can't remember anything that happened that long ago."

Ward wished he could feel the same, wondered why he didn't. Did things that happened so long ago matter? He had thought they did, but now he wondered.

Drew tossed the loop at the chicken, which was stupid enough to wander back within range. This time the silly fowl ran back toward its pen, squawking as if a coyote was after it.

"Is Tanner any better?" she asked.

"Yes. He's a quick learner."

"Good. I like the little varmint."

Ward liked him, too.

Chapter Twelve

The new herd arrived two days later.

"There's not a male on the place who'll be able to think of anything else," Isabelle told Marina. "It'll be dust and heat, bawling cows and shouting men, and the smell of sweat and burning hair. It's awful, but you'd think they'd been handed the greatest treat in the world."

"What does Ward do?" Marina asked.

"He's the best we have with a rope. He'll be in the middle of everything."

"Maybe I shouldn't have let Tanner go."

"You couldn't have kept him here without tying him to the bedpost."

Marina didn't have to be reminded that Tanner was getting more out of control each day. Every time she tried to warn him against becoming too attached to Ward, Tanner got angry with her.

"I like him better than Bud," he'd shouted at her

that morning. "I wish he were going to be my father."

Tanner had rushed outside, and Marina had swallowed her fear and anger. Instead of packing for an immediate departure to San Antonio, she went to find Ward.

Marina had tried to tell herself she never wanted to see Ward again, but that wasn't true. She smiled involuntarily. She still thought he was handsome. If the truth were known—though she had every intention it never would be—she still experienced a strong physical attraction when she was close to him. He might think Tanner looked like Ramon, but she saw more and more of Ward in him with each passing day. She could never find a man who looked like her son unattractive.

Ward wasn't pretty-handsome like Ramon. Ward's chin was strong, but not perfect. His nose was finely chiseled, actually too fine. His jaw was a little too powerful, his brow too broad. Still everything fitted together. Ward's face had character. It looked lived in. It reflected the man.

Who was she kidding? Her attraction to Ward had nothing to do with Tanner. But that was all it was, attraction, not love. She didn't have to be afraid it meant something else. After all, she found Ramon handsome, and she despised him.

Marina hadn't asked where the men were working, but it was impossible to miss. She only had to follow the sounds and the clouds of dust.

The chaos of the branding area was even worse than she had expected. The entire landscape appeared to be in constant motion. The patchwork of colors—black, brown, dun, white, and nearly everything in between—changed like a kaleidoscope.

Every few minutes, Ward would rope a yearling and drag it over to one of two branding crews. Two boys would grab the yearling, throw it to the ground, and pin it down. One of the smaller kids would hand Jake or Buck a branding iron and they would slap it on the side of the downed animal. Then the yearling was released and hazed into a second herd.

It all happened with quick, noisy precision.

The noise was nearly deafening. She would have sworn every one of those thousand yearlings was bawling at once. The ones being roped and branded bawled loudest of all. The men shouted or cut the air with ear-splitting whistles. But the smell was worse. The stench of burning hair and hide nearly caused her to gag.

Only after she got closer did Marina realize the men were notching the calves' ears as well as castrating the males. She thought she would be sick. She focused her attention on Tanner and Drew. They danced around the yearlings with a pot of some tar-like substance they seemed to daub at random on the downed animals.

Her child was involved in this revolting business, and he looked happier than she had ever seen him.

Jake stood up. Night Hawk took his place. He apparently branded the animal to Jake's satisfaction. He notched the ear—fortunately, there was no castration since this was a female calf—and let it up. Pete and Will hazed it to the second herd.

"We sure miss those boys we sent to Abilene," Jake said, coming over to stand with Marina. "Things go a lot faster when they're around. Watch the color of the branding iron," he called out to Hawk. "That's too hot. It'll smear the brand. Thanks for lending us Tanner. He's a great help."

Suddenly Tanner darted into the melee, can and daubing brush in hand. He made a couple of quick daubs, then dashed back to safety.

"What's he doing?" Marina asked, her heart still in her throat.

"Doctoring against screwworms. Blowflies will lay their eggs in any wound. The screwworms that hatch out will nearly ruin a yearling. Tanner and Drew are daubing medicine on any cut or scrape they see."

"Is it dangerous?" It looked that way.

"Not as long as he keeps out of the way until the calf is down. Worst thing that can happen is he'll get kicked."

Marina swallowed. Nothing like this ever happened when Tanner was with Bud.

"He wanted to rope like Ward," Jake said. "I told him he'd have to wait until he was a little bigger."

"Thank you," Marina said, wondering what other dangers Tanner was anxious to expose himself to.

"Don't thank me," Jake said. "When I told him he couldn't rope, he was determined to wrestle them to the ground. Ward convinced him that treating for screwworms was an important job."

Marina wondered what madness had ever made her think it would be okay to bring Tanner here.

"We couldn't do half as much work without Ward doing the roping," Jake was saying. "He can keep everybody busy and then some."

"Ward grew up on a ranch."

"Whoever trained him did a good job."

"Do you like him?" she asked suddenly. "I mean, really like him, admire him, think he'd make a good father?"

"Why are you asking me that?"

"Isabelle says he's changed, that I ought to get to

know the man he is now before I decide what to do about him and Tanner."

"Yes, I like Ward. There isn't anybody I admire more. I asked him to stay because I needed an experienced hand. Now I want him to stay because I don't want to lose a friend."

"And the other?"

"He'd make an excellent father. Ward won't let the boys make excuses for themselves. He makes them face up to things just like I do, but he has his own way of doing it. Tanner sure has taken a shine to him. That ought to tell you something."

It did, but it told her something she didn't want to know.

Without warning, Jake yelled at the boys. "That's not the way to hold that calf." He headed toward them. "If you're not careful, you'll have a gash in your head to prove it."

Marina watched while Jake corrected the boys and got the branding operation going smoothly again. Gradually her attention turned to Ward.

She cast her mind back, trying to remember what about him had first attracted her attention. When she first saw him, a dirty sweaty cowboy in the middle of the trackless Dillon acres, he represented freedom from restraint; release from the proper way of doing things; simple, straightforward emotion. He had no artifice. He didn't like her for anything but herself.

She felt like a real person with him, one allowed to have likes and dislikes, opinions and desires. He focused his whole attention on her. He was never worried about his own looks, never waiting for or expecting her admiration.

She had liked the sincerity in his gaze, the honesty

in his face. She guessed that was why she'd been hurt so deeply when he didn't believe her. She had risked everything by going against her family. He hadn't been ready to risk as much.

As she watched him in the saddle, throwing his rope with unerring accuracy, manipulating horse and calf with well-honed skill, his muscled body easily handling the difficult and exhausting work, she felt a churning deep in her belly, the same feeling that had first told her she was falling in love with the wrong brother.

Marina forced herself to look away. She refused to be seduced a second time. She would talk to him, she would do her best to get to know him, but she would do it for Tanner's sake. She would not remember his kisses, the passion when he made love to her, the comfort of his arms. He was a man like any other. She would treat him that way.

But he wasn't dead. That was an inescapable fact. Tanner would eventually learn that Ward was his father. She needed to know how best to tell Tanner and what kind of relationship to allow between them.

Jake had said they had thirty minutes. Everybody else headed for water and a lie-down in the shade. Ward went back to the house in search of Marina.

He kept telling himself he shouldn't see her, shouldn't talk to her. He told himself he ought to give her the divorce and send her back to San Antonio immediately. He told himself he didn't really care about her, that he only cared about Tanner. He told himself their lives were no longer connected, that the separation had been complete and irrevocable years ago.

He was telling himself lies.

He'd known that the minute she stepped out of that wagon. Tanner merely added another link in a chain that was already unbreakable.

Ward had three things to consider, and he might as well start now. His family had lied. That hurt more than he could say, but it was pointless to keep ignoring facts.

Once he accepted that his family had lied, he had no reason to disbelieve Marina when she said Ramon had tried to rape her. He had never known his brother to do such a thing, but no woman had ever spurned him, especially not a woman Ramon considered his own.

Having accepted Ramon's treachery, he had to remove from his mind any notion that she had betrayed him. He couldn't continue to blame a woman who had herself been betrayed.

And finally there was Tanner. If Marina had never been with Ramon, then Tanner *was* his son!

Ward found Marina down on her knees, digging up the ground next to the porch steps.

"What are you doing?" he asked.

"Rose Randolph sent Isabelle some seeds and plants. She can't bend down to prepare the beds. Everyone else is too busy with the branding, so I'm doing it."

"Here, let me. You shouldn't be doing this."

She looked up at him. "Stay out of the way. You have your work. This is mine."

He watched while she carefully settled a plant in the hole, filled in the dirt, and soaked it with water. It was the last one.

"I need to talk to you."

"Go ahead," she said without looking up. "I can talk while I make rows for the seeds."

If he was going to get answers to any of his questions, he had to start at the beginning. He would rather have had her full attention, but maybe it would be easier if they didn't have to look at each other.

"Why did you come here?" Ward asked.

Marina stilled, but she didn't look up. "Why do you ask? You haven't believed anything I've told you."

"I know, and it wasn't right. If we're going to get things straightened out, we've got to start at the beginning."

Marina looked up. It seemed to be a measuring glance. It told him nothing of what she might be thinking. That was good. He didn't want to know. Not yet.

Apparently satisfied he was sincere, she went back to her digging. "What do you want to know?"

"If you didn't love Ramon, why did you go to the rancho in the first place?"

She sighed, as if some old tension had been released. "Our families decided we ought to marry. Our position was a good match for your money. I was flattered, but I didn't want to get married yet."

"I don't imagine my mother liked that."

"Neither did mine. She decided I was being distracted by the delights of San Antonio, so she sent me to the rancho where I would see no one but Ramon. She hoped I would consent to be married right away."

"Why didn't you?"

She paused in her digging. "I met you and thought I had found all the things missing in Ramon. It happened all at once, like waking up and finding I was in love with a man I'd never seen before."

That was how it had felt to him. He could still remember the shock of knowing she loved him, the hours spent trying to convince himself she was sincere, that he hadn't imagined it all.

"Didn't it frighten you?"

Marina looked up. "Yes, but it intoxicated me as well. I was too young to know the chance I was taking."

"Why didn't you tell your parents about Ramon raping you?"

She attacked the ground with a series of angry stabs of her trowel. "My father would have used it as an excuse to force me to marry him."

"How about my family?"

"Who at the rancho would believe me? Your mother? You?"

They hadn't believed her—none of them.

"If I had chosen to make the accusation public, I would have been ruined. Your mother was angry because I had messed up her plans, but she found it unforgivable that I should prefer you to Ramon. She was determined to punish us both."

"If so, she succeeded better than she hoped."

Marina started making trenches in the soft earth for her seeds. "She despises me, but she hates you. You know that, don't you?"

Ward couldn't accept that. He'd always known his mother preferred Ramon. But hate her own son? No, that was impossible.

"After all that's happened to you, I'm not surprised you feel that way," he said.

"You never could see your family as they really are."

Ward had accepted the fact that they had lied, but he couldn't accept their malice.

"Why did you press me to get married so quickly?" he asked.

Marina reached for a package of seeds, but she didn't begin planting. She looked up at Ward once more. "I was afraid they would keep us apart."

"They couldn't have done that."

Marina ripped open the package and began to distribute the seeds evenly in the rows. "We got married. They still broke us apart, didn't they?"

He couldn't argue that. "Why didn't you tell me what Ramon had done?"

"I didn't see any point. You probably wouldn't have believed me. If you had, it would have hurt you too much. Besides, I hated for you to know Ramon had touched me."

The silence stretched between them. She continued to plant row after row of seeds. He wasn't sure she was going to speak again. Finally, he couldn't wait any longer. "Why didn't you stay at the rancho?"

Her hand shook so the seeds missed the rows. "Your mother threw me out. She called me a whore."

Chapter Thirteen

She waited a moment. When she had regained her calm, she began very deliberately to cover the seeds. "She refused to see me again, except to say you wanted an annulment."

"And you agreed?"

She smoothed the soil with her bare hand. "Until I found I was carrying your child. Your family couldn't deny we had been married, so they put it about that you'd left me when you found out I was going to have another man's baby."

Ward had never felt good about what he'd done. This made him feel far worse.

"I didn't know about Tanner."

She opened another seed packet. "You mother said you didn't believe he was your son. A few days ago you said the same thing."

"You can't produce a six-year-old boy out of thin

air, announce he's my son, and expect me to accept him without question."

She laid the packet aside and looked up at him. "We were married. We shared a bed."

"Ramon had been there before me."

Her eyes blazed brightly with anger. He could have bitten his tongue off. He still had to remind himself that he no longer believed his mother's accusation.

"It was a shock, especially after what I'd been led to believe," he amended.

Some of the fire died down, but the flame was still there. "No more so than learning you've been living in Texas all this time without once trying to see me."

"Acquit me of that."

"I suppose we both have to acquit each other of a great deal."

She turned back to her planting. It was driving him nuts. He pulled her to her feet and took the seeds out of her hand. He wanted to shake her until she lost her aloofness.

"Can we start over?" Maybe that would shake her iron control.

It didn't. Her gaze was as steady as ever. "There's no beginning again for us, Ward. All there ever was ended that day."

"I'm not asking you to try to love me again. I know that's impossible."

But did he? Now that the layers of anger and distrust had been removed, had his feelings changed so very much? He'd never forgotten her, not even when he thought he hated her the most. Now she hardly ever left his thoughts. He wanted to find some way to apologize for what he'd thought, what he'd done. He couldn't change it, but he needed to know she forgave him.

"If we have a son together—" He stumbled over his own words. "Now that we have a son together—"

She shrugged out of his grasp and brushed some loose dirt off her skirt. She picked up a bag and put the unused seeds in with the others.

"That's a matter of fact," she said, finally giving him her full attention, "just as these seeds are a fact. Give me a divorce, and it need never concern you again."

Ward could see no softening in her attitude. She wanted nothing to do with him. She still wanted her divorce.

He became aware of several pairs of running feet. He turned to see Tanner, accompanied by Pete, Will, and Drew, running toward them.

"They're going to turn some of the yearlings loose in the hills," Tanner said, breathlessly, as he came to a halt in front of his mother. "Can I go with them?"

Marina turned to Ward, a question in her eyes.

"We don't just turn the new animals loose. We take them to the part of the ranch that has the most room for them."

"Is it dangerous?" Marina asked.

"Naw," Will said. "Those old yearlings can't wait to get away from here. They'd go by themselves if we'd let 'em."

"But they won't go where we want them," Drew explained, "so we take them."

"Who's going with you?"

"Nobody," Drew said. "We don't need anybody."

"Maybe, but I'm not ready to let Tanner run off without somebody to watch out for him."

"I can do that." Will squared his shoulders, looking so much like Jake, Ward couldn't help smiling.

"And I'll take care of both of them," Drew said, disgust written all over her face.

"You ain't taking care of me," Pete said.

"You didn't hear me offering to, did you?" Drew shot back.

"I had some adult in mind," Marina said.

"We don't need nobody," Drew protested. "Besides, Jake and Ward will be busy with the rest of the branding."

Marina turned to Ward. "Here's your chance. If you're sincere, you go with them."

Ward opened his mouth to tell her he couldn't leave the branding and then closed it again.

"I'll talk to Jake," Ward said. When Tanner started jumping up and down with excitement, he added, "Jake may decide to wait until we've finished branding the whole herd."

"Come on, let's ask him now," Drew said, taking hold of Ward's hand and pulling hard. The boys began pulling and pushing him in the same direction.

"We haven't finished talking," he called back to Marina.

"Yes, we have."

"This one's mine," Pete shouted as he headed after a yearling that broke away and was trying to return to the herd they'd left at the ranch.

"That's two in a row," Will complained.

"You got two before," Drew said.

"That's because you weren't here."

"It doesn't matter," Drew insisted.

"I haven't got any yet," Tanner said.

"You come after me," Drew said.

Ward wondered how he could have been around Will, Pete, and Drew so often without realizing what a rumpus they created. Just then a second yearling broke from the ranks, and Drew was off like a shot.

"She doesn't act much like a girl, does she?" Tanner said to Ward.

"Sometimes," Ward said. "And she gets madder than a trampled rattlesnake if you can't tell when she's being a girl."

Drew drove her yearling back into the herd in less time than it had taken Pete or Will.

"She's fast," Tanner said.

"You say she's faster than me, and I'll bust your lip," Pete threatened.

"You know what Isabelle says about fighting," Ward warned.

"I'll say he fell."

"I'll say he didn't," Will said.

"What are you two arguing about now?" Drew asked as she rode up, the happiness of success spread all over her face.

"They don't need any reason," Ward said. "Just being within sight of each other seems to be enough."

Pete and Will rode a little ahead to get away from Drew.

"The next one is mine," Tanner reminded them.

The boys nodded their agreement.

It looked like Tanner wasn't going to get a chance to chase a yearling. For the next mile the yearlings trotted along without attempting to break away. Then, just as they reached the range Jake had set aside for them, a tall, lanky yearling broke off, running like an antelope.

"Yippee!" Tanner shouted and took off after him. Yearling and boy were both soon out of sight behind a low ridge. Ward didn't have the heart to tell him he could have let it go.

"Nobody but a tenderfoot yells *yippee!*" Drew said in disgust. "Everybody'll know he's from San Antonio."

"I'll tell him," Ward said, trying to hide a grin. "I'm sure he wouldn't want to do anything to embarrass you."

"He's disappeared," Drew said. "You think he got lost?"

"I doubt it," Ward said, "but I'll go after him."

Drew let out a loud "Yee-hah!" that sent the yearlings scattering in all directions. "I'll come with you."

Will and Pete added a few shouts of their own, then came rattling up behind. They followed the tracks in a dry wash that wound down to a dry streambed below. The kids scrambled down ahead of Ward, and in a couple of minutes they were out of sight. He could hear them as they scrambled around the hill, chased into canyons, splashed through a stream. Now that they had a real home, one that was secure, life was one big lark.

Rounding the shoulder of a hill, Ward found a wash that opened up into the valley below. Ward saw Will, Pete, and Drew whipping their horses into a gallop. Farther down below, he saw Tanner approaching a stopped wagon, the escaped yearling apparently forgotten.

Ward didn't know what warned him. Maybe it was the stillness of the mules. Maybe it was the fact that there was no reason for a wagon to be stopped where it was. He spurred his mount into a gallop. He shouted at the kids ahead to stop, but his shouts were drowned out by the sound of galloping hooves. Ward drew his gun and fired over their heads.

Jake's three kids slowed and turned. Tanner didn't. Ward fired again. This time Tanner turned around.

Ward waved his arm, motioning Tanner back. He hoped the boy would understand. If he didn't, he could die.

"What's wrong?" Drew demanded as she galloped up to Ward.

"Jake said we weren't never to shoot off a gun unless it was an emergency," Pete yelled.

"It is," Ward said, driving his horse forward. Tanner was moving forward again. A short distance ahead, he dismounted and started toward the wagon.

"Tanner, don't!" Ward yelled, but the boy kept walking. He reached up, starting to climb into the wagon.

Ward drove his horse right up to the boy. He jumped off, grabbed hold of Tanner, and flung him away from the wagon. They both ended up on the ground.

"Didn't you hear what I said!"

"I was just going to see what was wrong," Tanner said. He looked surprised and a little frightened. "I can hear a baby crying."

"What's wrong?" Drew asked.

"I think they're sick," Ward cautioned. "In fact, I think everybody in that wagon is dead except the baby."

The children backed up involuntarily.

"What caused it?" Drew asked.

"I don't know yet."

"Won't you get sick?"

"There's always a chance," Ward said. "But it's worse for children."

Being careful not to touch anything, Ward looked inside the wagon. The woman was dead. He could tell at a glance. So were two children—a boy and a girl, about three and five. There was no sign of the husband. The woman wouldn't have come out here alone. He backed away from the wagon.

"The man isn't here. Fan out and look for him. He probably headed back toward town. When you find him, come back and tell me. No matter what he says, don't go near him."

"What did they die of?" Drew asked.

"Cholera. We've got to bury these people and burn everything in the wagon."

"What about the baby?" Tanner asked. "You going to burn it?"

The kids snickered.

"No, but it's sick, too. I don't imagine it'll live long. Now get going, all of you."

Ward felt a great weight settle upon him. It was like the war all over again. There was such a great need, and he couldn't do anything about it.

Even if he could, it was too late for this family. He almost wished the baby would die before the children got back. If it didn't, he'd have to do everything he could to save it. That would not only endanger his life, it would endanger the lives of everyone who came near him.

That included Tanner.

Ward didn't have to wait long for the children to return.

"He's dead," Will said.

"Take me to him," Ward said, mounting his horse.

"He was headed back to Cypress Bend," Pete said as they cantered back to where the man had fallen. "He didn't get a half mile."

"He looked awful," Tanner said.

He did look awful. His death had been very painful.

"All of you go back to the ranch," Ward said. "Tell Jake what we've found. Tell him to bring shovels and kerosene to set the wagon afire."

Drew turned and rode off immediately.

"I want to stay with you," Will said.

"There's nothing to do here. I'll bet you can't catch Drew before she reaches the ranch. You know she thinks she's a better rider."

"I can catch her," Pete said, turning and heading back with Will right behind him. "You've got the fastest horse," Ward said to Tanner. "You'd better beat the lot of them, or they'll never let you forget it."

Tanner hesitated only a moment before heading off at a gallop, his honor at stake.

Ward mounted up and headed back to the wagon. He must see what he could do for the baby. He didn't think it would do any good, but he had to try.

Marina insisted upon going with Jake and Buck. If she hadn't, Isabelle would have. She wouldn't have gone if Drew hadn't mentioned the baby. Ward had said it would die soon, but she couldn't stay away if there were the slightest chance it might survive.

She was glad Jake had ordered the kids to stay at home. She doubted they really understood the deadliness of cholera.

She saw the wagon the moment they rounded the shoulder of the hill. Marina didn't see Ward.

Jake checked inside the wagon. "We'll bury them all in one grave. You might as well start digging," he said to Buck. "I'll unhitch the mules."

"Where's Ward?" Buck asked.

"Where's the baby?" Marina asked.

"Maybe with the father," Jake said.

But they didn't see Ward when they reached the spot where the man had fallen.

"I've got to take the mules down to the river for a drink," Jake said. "After that we'll look for Ward."

They didn't need to. They found him and the baby at the river. He'd removed the child's clothes and washed her. He was using his canteen to pour water down her throat. In between attempts to make her drink, he bathed her in cool river water to bring down her temperature.

"She's still alive," he said, looking up at Marina.

Marina looked into the eyes of a different man from the one she'd argued with just an hour ago. All the anger and hardness had disappeared. In its place she saw vulnerability.

It shocked her.

Ward had been the big, strong cowboy who'd walked into her life and rescued her from an arranged marriage. After he left her, he was the cruel, heartless villain who had abandoned his wife to the mercy of vultures. Never once had she seen his hurt; never had she believed he could suffer as much as she suffered.

Now she knew he could, that he had. Knowing that caused her bitterness and anger to slowly melt away.

"Are you sure it's cholera?" Jake asked.

"Yes." Ward squeezed water from his bandanna, letting it run down over the baby's face. "Somebody will have to backtrack them, tell anybody they stayed with about the disease."

"You ought to do that," Marina said. "You're a doctor."

Ward looked at her without expression. "Not anymore."

"You can't empty your head of what you learned," she said. "People need to know what precautions to take, what signs to look for, what to do for the sick."

"There's nothing to do."

"Then why are you pouring water down that baby's throat?"

"She's dehydrated. She needs to take as much liquid as possible."

"Why are you dripping water over her face, bathing her body?"

"To bring down her temperature."

"Then tell them that."

"It won't do any good."

"It might. They'll never know if they don't try."

"She's right," Jake said as he pulled the mules with their dripping muzzles back from the river. "If there's anything to tell, it'll come better from you."

Ward poured some more water into the baby's mouth. She drank, but Ward's expression didn't seem hopeful.

"I'll get back to the wagon," Jake said.

"He ought to be buried with his family," Jake said, motioning to the man, "but don't touch him. Wrap him in the wagon canvas."

"You touched the baby," Marina said.

"I couldn't leave her to die."

She watched as he cradled the child. Somehow she had always known he would be good with children. She had sensed a gentleness in him that seemed incongruent with his ability to rope anything on four legs and throw it to the ground in a matter of seconds. She had guessed his caring, too. She now realized she'd only sensed a tithe of that deep well of concern. He had kept most of it well hidden until this child brought it to light.

She shuddered to think how her supposed betrayal with Ramon must have hurt such an innocent soul. Oh, he hadn't been innocent in every way, but he had been innocent in love. No one in that miserable family had ever loved him.

But he had loved her, had given her everything he had to give, only to have it thrown back in his face. It didn't matter that Ramon had done it for her. It had happened.

A more experienced man might have understood. A more worldly man might not have felt so deeply. A man who could care so much about a baby he'd never seen before couldn't help but be cut to the quick.

She'd spent so long being angry that he couldn't believe in her, she hadn't tried to understand how he might have felt. She couldn't blame him for not coming back. If his mother and the woman he loved could have treated him so, what could he expect from the rest of the world?

No wonder he had closed his heart.

She watched him with the baby, tenderly caring for it though he feared it would die any minute. Maybe he wanted Tanner because he hoped his son could give him the love and acceptance he'd never been able to find anywhere else.

"There were so many of them," he said.

"So many what?" Marina didn't know what he was talking about.

"No matter what we did, they died."

Chapter Fourteen

"It wasn't the guns that killed them as much as disease."

He must be talking about the war.

"Some of them died horribly. Sometimes I gave them chloroform. They said I couldn't do that, but I did it anyway. They wouldn't listen when I told them about germs. They couldn't believe anything they hadn't studied in school. I got so mad, I beat them up. They put me in jail, but they had to let me out when the wounded started coming in again."

She was shocked to know he'd been in jail.

His expression turned angry. "What we did wasn't medicine. We just cut off pieces and threw them aside. Sometimes the mounds were so high you couldn't see over them.

"Many died waiting. More died on the field—unseen, uncomforted, unmourned. We just threw them into a hole and tossed dirt on them, dirt already soaked with their blood.

"They were so young, had come with such high ideals, such hopes. We drew them in with promises of glory, then let them die by the thousands."

Marina's father considered the wars with Mexico great patriotic victories. She had never considered what war could do to a man who lost a part of his soul every time a patient died.

"I said I was a doctor, but I was a liar. We all were. We couldn't do what their families expected, what they deserved."

"You couldn't save everybody," Marina said. "You did what you could. No one expected more than that."

"You didn't see the eyes of the boys I passed over, the boys who understood there was nothing I could do for them. You didn't get the letters from their mothers wanting to know how they died, begging for a trinket to remember them by. Those boys meant everything to their families, and we didn't even have time to wipe their faces clean."

"You can't blame yourself for things you couldn't do anything about."

But obviously he did. Ward was an idealist. When his faith in an ideal died, it killed part of him. Being swept up by the war had presented him with cruel and vivid proof of his limitations. Being faced with her supposed infidelity with his brother had been a different, but equally cruel blow.

"Why don't you let me have the baby?"

Her request seemed to bring him back to the present. She could almost see him square his shoulders for what lay ahead. It made her want to put her arms around him, to hold him close. But she was too afraid of her own weakness. She might start to like it again.

"There's no point in taking a chance on your getting the cholera."

"How is she doing?"

"She's entered the last stage of the disease. She's quiet now. She'll either die or recover. I can't tell which."

There was no question in Marina's mind any longer. She had misjudged Ward. Whatever the reasons for his conduct, a hard, callous heart wasn't one of them.

She remembered the sense of freedom, joy, and just plain fun of that ride to San Antonio, the befuddled Justice of the Peace they virtually forced to marry them, and their wedding night—the down payment on a life she had never believed was possible for her. It was all destroyed by a woman willing to sacrifice one son for the sake of another.

By the same stroke, she'd destroyed Marina as well.

The sound of horses made her look up. Jake and Buck had returned.

"We've burned the bedding and buried the family," Jake said. "How's the baby doing?"

"I don't know."

"Well, you can't sit here until you find out," Jake said. "Bring her back to the house."

"She could infect the boys."

"Not if they stay away from her."

"I brought a tent," Marina said. "We can keep her in that until she's better."

"Maybe you ought to go back and get it. I could stay here with her."

"You've got to ride to Cypress Bend," Jake said.

Ward started to get to his feet, but he couldn't while holding the baby.

"Let me have her," Marina said.

"Are you sure?"

He was asking about more than the disease. He wanted to know whether she could trust again, whether trusting him was important to her.

"If I weren't, I wouldn't have come. Now tell me what to do."

Ward hesitated only a moment. "Keep her warm and dry. Get her to take as much liquid as possible. If she fouls her linen or your clothes, burn them. You're to take a hot bath with strong soap every time you leave the tent. Under no circumstances let anything touch your mouth. We don't know much about cholera, but we do know it's transferred by contaminated liquids."

Marina unfolded one of the blankets she'd brought. Ward placed the baby in her arms. "Hand her up to me when I get in the saddle," she directed.

"If you leave now," Jake told Ward, "you can be back later tonight."

Marina could tell Ward didn't want to be forced back into the role of doctor, but she knew he wouldn't turn his back on his duty.

"Take Buck with you."

"Why did you want Buck to go with Ward?" Marina asked Jake as they watched the two men ride down the valley toward the tiny town several miles away.

"Buck adores Ward. Your husband pulled him through a fever a year ago, wouldn't leave his side until he recovered. Those people aren't going to be happy to see Ward in their town. Buck will make sure nothing happens when he's not looking. That boy's as nice as he can be, but he's got a vengeful streak in him. Harm, even threaten somebody important to him, and watch out."

The residents of Cypress Bend were guilty of wishful thinking when they called it a town. Situated more than sixty miles from San Antonio, it was little more than a cluster of log and wood-frame buildings thrown up in a bend in the Cypress River. Each building faced the only street, gardens and cow lots stretching behind them either down to the river or to the foot of the hill that had caused the river to bend its course.

Ward had been here many times, riding through or stopping for supplies, but he'd never tried to get to know the townspeople. Now he wished he had.

He knew he was in for trouble when he asked the mayor to call the people together. He had waited for Buck to bring the man outside. Ward didn't mean to enter any home until he'd bathed thoroughly.

"What for?" Clyde Pruitt demanded. His wife had followed him to the door. She didn't look any more pleased than her husband.

"We've found a case of cholera, a man and his family traveling up the valley. We wanted to see if anybody here knew where they came from."

"We don't take to strangers," Mr. Pruitt said. "We make them set up outside of town."

"I still need to talk to everybody in town," Ward said. "I'd like to tell them what to look for in case anybody comes down with the cholera."

"We don't want you coming here, frightening everybody with your tales of cholera," Mrs. Pruitt said. "Besides which, we ain't got anybody sick. You

176

can see for yourself, this town is as healthy as a bunch of mustangs."

"Did they come this way?" Ward asked, trying to get back to the reason for the trip. "If nobody saw them, there's nothing to worry about."

"There's already nothing to worry about," Mr. Pruitt said.

Ward had expected resistance, expected they would deny there was any chance their town could be infected. They were frightened of what an epidemic could mean to themselves and their families.

"Who're you to come in here telling us about cholera?" Mrs. Pruitt demanded.

"I'm a doctor," Ward said. "I guess I'm the best one to do it."

"You've been around here for two years, and nobody's ever heard a word about you being a doctor," Mr. Pruitt said. "Why are you telling us now?"

"So you'll believe me when I tell you that family died of cholera."

"We buried four of them," Buck said. "There's only the baby still alive."

"Where is it?" Mr. Pruitt demanded, looking alarmed. "You didn't bring it here, did you?"

"No."

News that an orphaned child had survived altered his wife's attitude. "Clyde, if there's a baby, we've got to do something."

"Let him take care of it. I wouldn't want any harm to come to a child," he told Ward, "but I wouldn't be doing my duty if I let you bring it here. Now I'd be pleased if you'd head back to your ranch."

"You bacon-brained fool!" Buck exploded. "You're sending away the only person who could help you. Can't you see—"

Ward knew it was useless to persist. "It's all right, Buck. We've done what we came to do. If anybody saw that family, they'll know to take precautions."

"But they won't know what precautions to take," Buck protested.

"I don't need anybody to tell me about the cholera." Mrs. Pruitt's words weren't angry now; they were accepting. "I lost my sister and her husband to it two years ago in Brownsville."

"You can leave everything in our hands," Mr. Pruitt said.

"Trusting that gopher-faced coyote is like trusting a mad dog," Buck complained as they headed into the twilight and back to the ranch. "He'll probably dump the first sick person outside town and leave him to take care of himself."

"They're just scared," Ward said. "There's nothing I can do to stop this thing, and they know it."

Marina decided she was the logical person to take care of the baby. Jake and Isabelle had their own family to consider. Ward had too much work to do. Besides, someone had to be responsible for Tanner. She doubted he would listen to anyone besides Ward. She had difficulty keeping him away from the tent—Will and Pete, too—until Isabelle gave Drew the job of standing guard.

The child had lain without moving since Ward placed her in Marina's arms. She had occasionally been able to force some water down her throat, but she didn't know if the baby had swallowed enough to do any good.

Marina was greatly relieved when Ward finally poked his head inside the tent. She saw the anxiety in his eyes change to relief. Holding the lantern up, he examined the baby closely.

"Has she taken any liquid?" he asked.

"Not much."

"Has she passed any?"

"No. Does that mean she's getting better?"

"I hope so. You'd better get to bed. I'll stay with her."

"I've already arranged everything so I can stay with her until she's well."

Ward gave her a hard look. It was impossible to interpret it.

"She's not your responsibility," he said.

"She's not yours, either."

"Yes, she is. I'm the doctor. I can't ignore that."

"Is that what you've been doing?"

"You don't have to ask. You know."

"Why?"

"Because I can't accept being so helpless," Ward exploded. "I can rope any cow in the state of Texas. I can ride, shoot, fight, cuss, and drink, but I can't save even one baby from this terrible disease."

"Maybe you can. Maybe you have."

"I'm practically traveling blind."

"We all do that in one way or another."

"I'm not Tanner. Don't try to make me feel better by spouting childish proverbs."

"It's not childish, and it's not a proverb. It's the truth. Sometimes I think the more important the question, the more blind we are."

"Go to bed, Marina. I'll stay with the baby."

"No. You can check on us during the night if you like, but this is my job. Now go away, or I'll set Drew on you."

Ward scrutinized the baby once more.

"How long before we'll know?" Marina asked.

"I don't know. Sometimes cholera takes just a few hours. Other times it can last a week."

"I'll be here as long as it takes."

Ward started toward the barn the following morning. The baby's condition hadn't changed. Her sunken eyes and cheeks, her bluish lips, gave her a cadaverous look. The dry tongue and drawn, withered skin on hands, face, and feet were further proof the child was badly dehydrated. Ward figured the baby had gone into shock.

No one could do anything now. They could only wait.

But he couldn't stand around knowing every moment could bring the end. Marina was doing everything that could be done.

"I'm okay," Marina had assured him. "I doze now and then. There's no sense in both of us staying here. Isabelle tells me they can't get the branding done without you."

After making certain Marina had everything she needed, he'd washed thoroughly, headed to the house, eaten his breakfast in silence, then started for the barn.

"Where're you going?" Tanner asked, as he ran to catch up with Ward.

"To saddle up. We've got more yearlings to brand."

"Jake said he was going to rope today 'cause of the baby."

Ward didn't slow down. Tanner had to run to keep up. "Your mama's taking care of her."

"Will you teach me to rope like you?"

Ward didn't think he could find the patience to teach anybody anything today. He felt like a coiled spring. If he didn't do something active, physically draining, he was certain he would explode.

"Maybe tomorrow, if we finish branding early enough."

"I want you to teach me now."

"He ain't got time now," Will said coming up on Tanner's heels. "Who's going to rope all the calves if he's messing about trying to get your rope untangled from calves' feet?"

"I don't get my rope tangled up in calves' feet."

"Yes, you do," said Drew coming up a few steps ahead of Pete. "You're awful. Even Pete's better."

"A damned sight better," Pete declared.

"Lay off him," Ward said. "If he'd had as much experience as you three, he'd rope circles around you. And you'd better watch your cussing, Pete. Isabelle will twist your ear right off your head."

"She'll have to catch me first."

"I'll catch you," Drew declared.

"If he runs from Isabelle, Jake'll catch him," Ward said. "Then there'll be hell to pay."

"You're cussing," Pete complained.

"I'm an old geezer. I'm allowed."

"I can't wait 'til I get big," Pete groused.

"It's not so wonderful," Ward said.

Drew looked at him like he was nuts. Maybe he was, but being an adult had been a big disappointment. He'd had more fun when he was six, climbing trees after birds' nests, tying a pair of jingling spurs to the milk cow's tail, never doubting he was loved.

Jake's kids disappeared, probably to get ready to do their jobs, but Tanner followed Ward into the barn.

Ward led his roping horse, Jacko, out of its stall. The short-coupled, lined-back dun wasn't a pretty horse, but he was worth his weight in gold when it came to working cattle.

Ward fitted an ornate black leather-and-silver bridle over Jacko's head and tied him to a post.

"I bet my daddy is better at roping than you. Mama said he was the best ever."

Ward laid the saddle blanket on Jacko's back, making sure to smooth out any folds or creases.

"That's good," Ward said. "It's nice for a boy to have a pa who's good at things."

"I'll ask him to teach me when he comes back," Tanner said. "I'll be better than Pete and Will. Even Drew."

"I'm sure you will," Ward said. He walked over to where a line of saddles rested on a long wooden pole. He chose the one made of black leather and worked with silver. His father had given him that saddle when he was fifteen. He'd thought then that his father must love him very much to give him something so valuable.

He'd learned since to value things differently.

"Drew says you're better than anybody. She says you're better than my father. Are you?"

"Maybe just as good," Ward said. He concentrated on adjusting the saddle on Jacko's back, hoping it would help him ignore the raw emotions churning uncontrolled in the pit of his stomach.

"That's what Jake said."

Having adjusted the saddle to his satisfaction, Ward reached under Jacko, took hold of the cinch strap, and started to buckle it. "Do you and Jake talk about me very often?"

"All the time," Drew said entering the barn. "He keeps harping on you and his pa."

"I do not," Tanner said.

182

"Do, too," Drew shot back. "Jake said he's ready when you are," she said to Ward. "You going to come help me, or are you going to stay here, mooning about roping and your long-gone pa?" she asked Tanner.

"He's not long-gone and I'm not mooning."

"You coulda fooled me. You coming or not?"

"Go on," Ward told Tanner. "Learning how to work a brand is just as important as roping."

Satisfied the cinches were tight, he swung into the saddle. He made a conscious effort to put Tanner and the baby out of his mind. For the next several hours he didn't want to think of anything but roping one yearling calf after another. Maybe if he roped enough of them, his mind would finally grow numb.

Tanner had hardly taken his eyes off Ward for the last hour. Drew's complaints that he was no more help than a crippled steer with two blind eyes—even a sharp jab in the side with the end of a branding iron—failed to divert his attention for more than a few minutes.

Jake had said Ward was attacking his work with fierce energy. Tanner didn't know about that. He did know Ward was roping calves so fast, he kept two branding crews running to keep up with him. Tanner hadn't seen him miss a throw all morning. He'd watched Bud's men lots of times. Nobody had ever done that good.

Jake stood up from a calf he'd just branded. "Take a break!" he shouted to Ward. "You got our tongues hanging out."

"My tongue's not hanging out," Drew declared.

"You're not doing anything but tending the fire,"

Buck snapped, as he jumped away from the newly branded yearling he'd just let up.

"Mine's not either," Will said, but nobody paid him any attention.

Tanner watched as Ward rode his horse over to an oak. He stopped the horse in the shade and slid out of the saddle.

"I never saw anybody rope like that."

"You won't, either," Jake said. "Ward's the best there is, but I think he's outdone himself this morning."

"He throws the rope under them and around their back feet," Tanner said, amazed. "How does he do that?"

"You'll have to ask him. I can't do it," Jake admitted.

"I bet he's as good as my daddy."

Tanner didn't like to admit that, but somehow it didn't bother him so much with Ward.

"Ward's good at anything he does," Jake said. "Sometimes, I think he's too good."

"How can you be too good?" Tanner asked.

"It causes you to have trouble fitting in with people around you," Jake explained. "It makes you unhappy with your limitations."

Tanner didn't understand what Jake was talking about. He thought being the best at everything would be absolutely wonderful. He didn't want to admit he didn't understand, so he just nodded his head.

"You like Ward?" Jake asked.

"Yeah."

Jake smiled. "Good," he said softly. "Very good."

Tanner didn't know what Jake was smiling about, but it made him feel uneasy, as if something was going on that he didn't know about. He'd ask his mother. She'd know. He'd also ask her why she didn't like Ward.

He did. He liked him a lot.

Chapter Fifteen

Ward felt the baby stir in his arms. Her body wasn't clammy or cold; her limbs didn't feel stiff. Still he wouldn't let himself relax. He'd seen too many die when he thought they'd make it.

The ranch was quiet. They had finished the branding last night. Ward had insisted Marina bathe and then go to bed. She had been up for two days. He was sitting on the front porch. He looked down at the baby sleeping in his arms. She was beautiful. He could understand why Marina had become so fond of her.

He wondered what Tanner had been like at the same age. Ward would never have the chance to hold his son like this, to stare down in wonder that something so tiny and helpless could make him love it so much. He could only imagine the fierce protectiveness he would have felt, the worry at every cough or slight change in temperature.

He would never get to spend hours watching Tanner, studying him, getting to know every detail about him. He would never get the chance to watch him grow, to look for changes, to be proud of his first step, his first word.

Most important of all, he would never experience the indescribable happiness of having his child look up and smile in recognition. His little boy would never hold out his arms to be picked up, call him daddy, or cling to him for comfort. No. He'd been denied all of this by the very people who should have wanted it for him more than anybody else in the world.

In that moment he came so close to hating his family, it scared him. He was relieved when Isabelle came out to join him.

"Don't come too close," he warned.

"That baby's going to be fine," Isabelle said, settling herself down in the chair next to Ward. "She wouldn't have lived this long if she weren't."

"It's still too soon to tell for certain."

"You can never tell anything for certain. Instead of worrying about her, you might bend your mind to what you're going to do about Tanner. Marina says he's starting to talk about you more than he does about his imaginary father."

"I've been thinking about little else. Do you have any suggestions?"

Isabelle rocked, a self-satisfied smile on her face. "One or two. But with a little luck, you and Marina might figure them out yourselves."

"Since you know so much, wouldn't it save a lot of time if you just told us what we're supposed to do?"

He hadn't meant to sound sarcastic.

"You're an adult. You get to make up your own mind, no matter how foolish."

"You don't have much confidence in me, do you?"

"I've always had a lot of confidence in you, and I'm getting more each day. Did you notice how pretty that baby is? I think she'll grow up to be a very lovely young woman some day. She has blue eyes just like you. If we can't find her family, you might adopt her."

Startled, Ward looked down into eyes nearly as deep an indigo as his own. He hadn't really looked at the child until now, at least not as a person rather than a patient.

He guessed she was close to six months old. She was gaunt, her eyes sunk into deep sockets, but they were wide open. She regarded him with a steady gaze. Thin, stringy, red-blond hair clung to her head like dry thread. It wouldn't regain its luster until she regained her strength.

"I hadn't thought about finding a home for her," Ward said. "First, we ought to find her some clothes."

The baby was still wrapped in a blanket. All her clothes had been burned.

"We need a name for her as well," Isabelle said.

"I'll let you and Marina do that. I'm no good at that kind of thing."

"Jake and I aren't any better. We still haven't decided on a name for our baby."

"I thought you were going to name it after your aunt."

"What if it's a boy?"

Ward grinned. "Don't you think you've got enough of those already?"

Isabelle smiled in a way that only a woman content with herself could smile. "I hope to have several more in a few years."

Marina came out on the porch. Her hair was still damp from her bath. Ward was relieved she wouldn't have to sit up all night anymore. She looked exhausted.

"She looks fine, doesn't she?" Marina asked Ward.

"Isabelle has already told me she's going to recover."

"Are you certain?"

"Yes, he's sure," Isabelle said. "I don't want to insult you by saying you look terrible, but if you don't get some rest, you soon won't be the most beautiful woman on this ranch."

Marina blushed. "I never thought I was."

"You still are," Isabelle said, "much to my regret."

Tanner came racing around the corner of the house. Ward expected to see Pete, Will, and Drew come tumbling after him, but he was alone.

"Can I ride with you today?" Tanner asked.

Ward looked toward Marina. She looked undecided.

"It's either Ward or the kids," Isabelle said.

"Where are you going?" Marina asked.

"Toward the end of the valley," Ward said, "up into those hills, checking on the new yearlings to see that they're settling in. Jake and the others are doing the same thing."

"They've already gone," Tanner said. "I wanted to go with Will and Pete, but Jake wouldn't let me."

Ward felt a little sorry for Marina. Everything the boy wanted to do seemed to draw him away from her, a sign Tanner was growing up. Ward knew Marina would be the first to want him to grow up strong and independent. But after sacrificing so much for him, it must be very hard to feel him pull away.

"I won't let him jump any ravines or indulge in any races," Ward said.

"That won't be any fun," Tanner complained.

"You want to stay here?" Ward asked.

"No."

"Then don't cause trouble." He winked at Tanner, and the boy smiled in response.

"Come on, Mama," Tanner pleaded. "I won't get into trouble just riding."

"Okay," Marina agreed reluctantly, "but if there's any chasing to be done, let Ward do it. He knows those hills. You don't."

"Here, let me watch the baby," Isabelle said to Ward.

Ward stood up and handed the baby to her, then turned to Marina. "See if you can stop worrying about him long enough to think up a name for her. Now, unless I want Drew tagging along, Tanner and I had better disappear."

Marina managed a tired smile. "When did you start running from little girls?"

"When I picked up Drew. Wait till you've been around her as long as I have."

"They all love her," Isabelle said, "but she is hard on them."

"She's meaner to me than anybody," Tanner said. Ward thought he might actually be proud of that distinction.

"She only approves of Jake because he's her father and Ward because he kept her from being scalped by Indians," Isabelle said. "The rest of the male sex can be dispensed with."

"Come on," Ward said to Tanner. "We're outnumbered."

Tanner grinned proudly and headed off toward the barn doing his best to imitate Ward's walk and stance. Ward had made wisecracks about Will imitating Jake. Now he had to admit it felt great, as if he were at least a foot taller and twice as strong. It was just about the best feeling he'd ever had, almost as good as the day he finally believed Marina loved him.

Ward didn't think anything would ever quite compare to that moment. He'd felt like a different person, as if his life had been entirely made over, free from the limitations he'd struggled against for so long. He couldn't help glancing back at the porch and wondering if it was possible to feel that way again.

If so, Marina was the only one who could do it. He'd been with many women, but none had ever touched the spot in him that Marina found so effortlessly.

Ward put his hand on Tanner's shoulder. He told himself he shouldn't, but he couldn't help himself. Except for the day he'd married Marina, he'd never felt closer to anyone in his life.

Tanner looked up with a smile that went straight to Ward's heart. It wasn't the kind of look a boy gave to a near stranger. It was the kind he gave his father. Ward sensed the love inside Tanner, a love that wasn't afraid to reach out to someone else. It was the kind Ward had wanted from his family all his life, the kind he'd waited for, worked for, hoped for.

And here it was inside this boy, just for the taking.

But Ward didn't have the right to take it.

Marina watched them walk toward the barn together, and a strange feeling came over her. There they went, her two men, together as they should be.

Something inside her budded and flowered when she saw the way Tanner tried to imitate his father, the way Ward rested his hand on the boy's shoulder and drew him close. Unexpected tears came to her eyes, tears so copious they blurred her vision and ran down her cheeks. She brushed them away.

"They make a nice pair, don't they?" Isabelle said.

"Yes," Marina replied, her voice husky with emotion, "they do."

It hit her suddenly, unexpectedly, that terrible sense of loss. All these years she'd concentrated on anger and hurt. Only now did she realize that the real tragedy was not what either of them had done but what they'd missed.

She had missed the boundless love that it was obvious Ward was almost begging to give away. She'd missed the happiness of knowing she was loved for herself and not her family's position, the joy of seeing him come home, of watching his face light up when he saw her. She'd missed the days of being comforted by his presence, the nights of being loved by his body.

She'd missed the supreme joy of seeing her husband with the son she'd borne him of her own body, of her own pain and labor.

She remembered the snubs, the innuendos, the whispers. They didn't mean anything to her now, not when she saw Tanner frisking around Ward like a puppy. Her child had been denied just as much as she, maybe more. But it was more important to him because he couldn't understand. He had no defenses.

All at once it was more than she could take. A sob tore from her.

"What's wrong?" Isabelle asked, worried.

"Nothing," Marina managed to say. "It's just foolish sentiment. I'll be all right in a moment."

But it wasn't all right. She felt overwhelmed, overcome. The tears ran down her cheeks and spilled onto her dress. She turned and ran inside to seek the comfort of her room.

"Can we ride up there?" Tanner asked, pointing to a trail that wound its way up a narrow canyon to a small clearing on the flank of the mountain about a mile distant.

"It'll take the yearlings at least a month to find their way through that maze of canyons and around the ridges."

"Can't we ride a little way up? We haven't done anything but ride over flat, boring trails all day."

Ward didn't want to tell Tanner that many of his days were spent riding over flat, boring trails. The boy wanted excitement, and fat, contented cows weren't providing it. To Tanner, the ride had been little more than a succession of hills, canyons, creeks, and streams, and an occasional white-tailed deer.

"Jake said he needed meat," Tanner reminded him. "You promised you'd look for a deer."

"Hawk will get one," Ward said.

"Jake said with this many people to feed, Isabelle needed at least two."

"Maybe Jake will get one."

"You can't let them both get a deer and us not," Tanner protested.

"I told your mother I wouldn't let you get into trouble."

"How's killing a deer going to get me into trouble?"

Tanner had behaved well all day. They could take a narrow trail across a sharp, high ridge and weave their way through a series of canyons back to the ranch. That was the best place to find a deer.

The climb was long and steep, but it was worth it. If they climbed the ridge behind it, they could see all the way back to the ranch, a full ten miles. Jake hadn't yet bought all of this land, but he intended to.

"Ready to go?" Tanner asked, not dazzled by the view of the valley nearly a thousand feet below.

Ward chuckled to himself. What could he expect? The boy was only six. Marina would have shared his sense of wonder as he looked down on canyons and valleys carved out of solid rock over thousands of years, now lush with green grass and tall, strong trees. It was truly a corner of Eden.

Boulders larger than Jake's house lay scattered about as though flung down by a celestial hand. Others, balanced atop one another, looked as though a single push would send them crashing down into the valley below. Equally impressive mountains of granite branched off in several directions, creating rivers and valleys as though there were nothing to the task.

Ward could never gaze out over this scene without a sense of wonder, a realization of how small and insignificant his problems were. It made him feel better. As long as they were small, surely he could conquer them.

But as much as Ward wanted to prolong the feeling that nothing was impossible, Tanner had already started down the narrow trail to the rocky canyon below. He was determined to find the deer before Ward.

The canyon they entered now was narrow and rocky. Trees offered a canopy overhead protecting them from the sunlight. It was a cool, pleasant trail, but it soon leveled out in a small valley between sharp, high ridges. A cow and a bull were quietly grazing. A calf lay in the grass close by.

Tanner had seen too many cows to be interested in this bovine family. He had deer on his mind.

"There's one!" he shrieked, his face wreathed in excitement.

The doe was more than a thousand feet away, across impassible terrain.

"That's a doe," Ward said. "Besides, I couldn't hit anything that far away."

"Yes, you can," Tanner said, determined not to let this deer escape.

"She probably has a fawn hidden close by."

Ward wanted to linger, but Tanner's every move telegraphed his impatience to find a deer within range. It hit Ward with unexpectedly strong force that it wasn't just the view that was holding him back; it was being with Tanner. He wanted to prolong this afternoon. This was the longest he'd had the boy to himself.

Riding with Tanner, answering his questions, being able to share his joy in learning how to rope, to see his excitement over something as ordinary as spending a day riding over the ranch, to be the person who could bring a shining light of happiness into his eyes—it turned Ward inside out. He felt such an outpouring of love for this boy that he wasn't sure he could contain it.

He couldn't feel this much love for Tanner without feeling something for Marina. She was Tanner's mother, the woman he had once loved so desperately. They'd created this child together.

Tanner made Ward wish for a home, a family, a place where he could love as well as be loved.

He wondered if Marina still felt anything for him.

She'd shown signs that she was no longer angry, but he wanted more than that. Every time he came a step closer to Tanner, he realized just how far he was from Marina, and that he didn't want it to be that way.

"Tanner, slow down," Ward called. "You're making so much noise, you'll scare away every bit of game in the valley."

Tanner's impatience caused him to disappear occasionally around bends and twists in the trail. Ward wasn't worried about his safety, but he was mindful of his promise to Marina not to let the boy out of his sight.

Besides, he didn't want to miss a single minute of this magical day. He was convinced Tanner felt at least a small part of the love Ward felt for him. He saw it in Tanner's eyes when he looked up at him, saw it in the way the boy tried to please him.

It was all the more poignant because Ward saw himself in Tanner. Ward remembered a time when he would have done anything to earn the same love and attention his mother lavished on Ramon. He'd become a top hand, learned how to manage the ranch, worked long hours without complaint, but nothing had changed.

Ward's preoccupation with his own thoughts had caused him to let his horse come to a stop. Tanner was nowhere in sight. Ward snapped the reins, nudged his horse with his heels, and headed down the trail at a trot.

He found Tanner around the first turn in the trail, sitting still on his horse. A hundred feet ahead, the floor of the little canyon widened to several hundred feet. Grazing at the edge of the tree line was a twelve-point white-tailed buck. He didn't seem to be disturbed by Tanner's presence. He kept looking into the trees and sniffing the wind. Ward decided there must be a doe nearby.

Good. As long as the buck's attention was directed elsewhere, maybe he could get close enough to make a sure shot.

"Don't move," Ward cautioned Tanner. "Keep your bridle still. The jingle of metal will scare him off."

Ward tried to quiet the feeling of excitement as he drew his rifle and took aim. Even though they hunted only for food, the boys took pride in trying to bring in the biggest prize. No one at the ranch had even seen a buck like this. He could just hear Drew telling the boys they weren't worth their spurs until they'd brought home a deer with at least a ten-point rack.

Ward squeezed the trigger. The deer leapt straight into the air and bounded toward the woods before plunging to the ground. Letting out an ear-splitting yell, Tanner drove his heels into his horse's sides and took off at a gallop.

Ward shoved his rifle into its scabbard and hurried after Tanner. There was always a chance the buck wasn't dead. A wounded animal that size could be very dangerous to a small, unsuspecting boy.

But even as Ward urged his mount forward, he felt his horse hesitate, throw up its head, and snort loudly. Out of the corner of his eye, Ward glimpsed a flash of tawny color as something ran through the trees along the edge of the valley floor. It wasn't a fawn. It was running toward the kill, not away from it. Even before he could get a clear look, Ward knew what it was.

Tanner and a mountain lion were headed for the same place! Apparently the cat had been stalking the buck and considered it his rightful prize. He meant to get to the kill first and claim it by right of possession.

Tanner hoped to do the same thing.

Ward jerked his rifle out of its holster again and dug his heels into his mount's sides. The smell of lion had spooked the horse. It wanted to flee back over the mountain. Ward forced it forward, but it took both hands to hold the rifle and keep the horse from turning around. He couldn't get a shot.

If he didn't drive the cat away soon, Tanner would be between the mountain lion and the kill. Tanner's horse hadn't seen or smelled the cat.

Unable to aim properly and keep his horse headed forward at the same time, Ward fired into the mountainside.

Neither the cat nor Tanner slowed down.

Ward drove his horse onward. He could only hope Tanner's horse saw or scented the lion before they reached the buck. If not, the lion would most certainly attack. A lion could easily snap the neck of a full-grown horse. He would have no difficulty with a six-year-old boy.

Ward knew the instant Tanner's mount scented the mountain lion. Screaming in fear, the animal jumped sideways through the air in mid-stride. He hit the ground with stiff legs, then whirled to meet the danger head-on.

Unprepared for the sudden change of course, Tanner lost his grip on the reins and his seat in the saddle. He hit the ground rolling. He came to a stop inches from the fallen buck.

In the shadow of the trees, the cat screamed in fury and launched itself into full stride.

Holding tightly to his rifle, Ward threw himself

from the saddle. He landed on his feet and came immediately to a kneeling position, his rifle on his shoulder, desperately trying to get a sight on the lion.

His first shot missed.

Ward had time for one more shot. Even as he squeezed the trigger, the lion left the ground in a leap that was meant to land him squarely atop the kill.

He landed on Tanner instead.

Ward sprang to his feet and ran toward the tangled mass of lion, buck, and boy.

Tanner's horse, screaming in fear, turned and raced down the valley.

Ward was never able to grab on to any of the multitude of thoughts that flashed through his mind in the seconds it took him to reach Tanner. He was only conscious of his overwhelming fear that the lion would spring up and attack the boy before he could get there.

His first sight upon reaching them seemed to confirm his fear. Tanner lay on the ground—still—blood over him, his shirt ripped open by one of the lion's claws. An ugly wound ran from shoulder to elbow. The lion lay still, his open jaws only inches from Tanner's throat.

Ward rushed forward, prepared to shoot the lion again, but he was dead. The second bullet had passed through his heart.

Ward dragged the cat off Tanner. The boy didn't move. Ward prayed the cat hadn't broken his neck. A quick check of his pulse proved the boy was merely unconscious.

Tanner opened his eyes. He looked at the buck, which lay next to him. "Golly, I didn't know he was that big."

Ward wept with relief.

Chapter Sixteen

"Didn't you hear me call you?" Ward asked.

"I guess so," Tanner said.

"Why didn't you stop?"

"I don't know."

The boy was sulky. Ward wasn't sure whether that was the result of knowing he'd done something wrong and not wanting to admit it, the pain from his wound, or both.

"You didn't pay attention when I tried to stop you from approaching that wagon the other day."

"I didn't think there was anything wrong with it."

Just as he hadn't thought there was any danger in approaching an animal that had just been shot. Ward doubted Marina had ever let him near a wild animal, dead or not.

Ward cleaned and bandaged Tanner's cut as best he could. He would cleanse it again when he got back to the ranch. He'd noticed during the war that wounds washed with carbolic festered less frequently. He had no intention of running the danger of gangrene with Tanner's arm.

Ward didn't look forward to facing Marina. He'd told her this would be a harmless ride. Now he was bringing Tanner back with a severe wound, the result of a narrow escape from a mountain lion.

"If your mother ever lets you go off with me again, you've got to make me a promise," Ward said as they started home.

"What?" Tanner looked suspicious.

"If you hear me call, you'll stop in your tracks that instant. No questions, no hesitation."

"Mama's going to be mad, isn't she?"

"I expect she'll be more upset that you're hurt."

"She'll be mad when she hears about the lion."

Ward was certain Tanner was right. Rather than spend so much time trying to keep Tanner away from danger, Marina should have been trying to teach him how to see it coming and avoid it. She couldn't stand guard over him for the rest of his life.

Tanner spoke less and less often as they neared the ranch, then fell completely silent. Ward suspected that his wound was causing him considerable pain. He had seen him wipe tears out of his eyes.

Ward longed to offer him some comfort, but there was nothing he could do to stop the pain. Several times he opened his mouth to offer sympathy but didn't. Tanner was trying very hard to pretend his arm didn't hurt. As long as he thought Ward didn't know how much he hurt, he would remain stoic.

So Ward pointed out things of interest from time to time, identifying plants, rock formations, a new canyon, anything to keep Tanner's mind off his pain.

Despite his best efforts, Tanner started to look rather teary-eyed.

About a mile from the ranch, Ward saw three riders coming toward them. "Unless I miss my guess," he said, "that's the kids coming to see what we've got."

Tanner perked up immediately. "Do you think they got a deer?"

"Maybe, but I bet they didn't get one like ours."

"Have they ever been attacked by a lion?"

"Will got butted by a cow once—Will won't ever do what you tell him—but nothing nearly so dangerous as a mountain lion."

It amused Ward to see Tanner take pride in having been slashed by the big cat. He only wished Marina might be prevailed upon to see it in the same light. He expected she was going to go after his scalp.

"Golly!" Drew gushed, forgetting her blasé manner, when she got a look at the buck tied behind Tanner's saddle. "Where did you find it?"

"I found him," Tanner said.

Will and Pete, who came thundering up right behind Drew, were too moved for words.

"Wait 'til Hawk sees this," Pete said, his eyes bright with glee. "He brought in a buck with nine points, and he thought he'd done something great."

Will could only run his fingers over the buck's rack of horns and make senseless noises.

"We'd have bagged a bigger one if we'd stayed out longer," Drew said, thrown on the defensive on behalf of herself and the absent Night Hawk. "But Hawk was looking for a mountain lion. We found an old kill."

"We found two of them," Ward said.

"We found the lion, too," Tanner said. "Ward killed it."

They all stared at Ward bug-eyed, the buck forgotten.

"Where?" Pete asked.

"How big was it?" Will wanted to know.

"I don't believe you," Drew stated flatly.

"We saw it in that jumble of canyons at the head of the valley," Ward said.

"It was huge," Tanner said, forgetting his assumed role of calm, impassive warrior. "He had teeth this big."

Tanner exaggerated by only a couple of inches.

"Go on," Drew said. "You didn't get close enough to any cat to see its teeth."

Pete and Will were equally skeptical.

"I did, too," Tanner insisted, indignant. "It jumped on me. It made a big hole in my arm. Ward bandaged it up."

For the first time they noticed the bandage that covered Tanner's left arm from shoulder to elbow.

"Go on," Drew said, repeating her favorite phrase, "you probably fell off your horse."

"Yeah, you probably fell off your horse and landed on a cactus," Will echoed.

Pete made no comment. The bundle tied behind Ward's saddle had caught his eye.

"Tell 'em, Ward," Tanner pleaded. "Tell 'em that lion jumped on me and you killed it."

All eyes turned back to Ward.

"Is that it?" Pete asked, pointing to the bundle.

"Is what it?" Ward asked, drawing out the suspense.

"The lion."

"Why don't you look inside?"

"I'm not looking inside," Will said.

"It won't matter, you nitwit," Pete scoffed. "It's dead. It can't hurt you."

"I don't like lions," Will said, "not even dead ones." Will hadn't quite turned ten. There were limits to his courage, even in front of Drew.

"Is that really a lion in there?" Drew asked.

"Open it up and see for yourself," Tanner said, feeling superior again now they believed him.

Pete untied the end of the bundle. But the moment the horses caught the smell of mountain lion, they snorted and plunged in confusion.

"You'd better tie it back up," Ward said. "You can look at it when we get to the house."

"Ugh!" Drew made a face. "Why did you keep the skin?"

"I couldn't leave such a beautiful hide for the varmints to tear to pieces," Ward said. "Maybe Isabelle can use it for a rug."

"She won't want a lion skin in her house," Drew assured him.

"Why not?" Pete asked. "It's dead."

"She just won't," Drew said, secure in her insider's knowledge of what the feminine mind would and would not accept.

"Did it really jump on Tanner?" Will asked Ward.

"Yes," Ward said.

"Did it bite him?"

"No, but he did get a nasty gash on his arm."

"Does it hurt?" Drew asked Tanner.

"It hurts a great deal," Ward said, "but Tanner's too brave to admit it."

The kid deserved some sort of reward for swallowing all those tears.

"It was hiding in the woods. He let out this awful

scream and jumped at me. Ward shot him right in the air. If he hadn't, he'd have eaten me up." Between his excitement and pride over his bravery, Tanner couldn't wait to tell them everything that had happened.

"I'm going to tell Jake," Pete said. He turned his horse and whipped him into a gallop.

"Me, too," Will yelled as he took after Pete.

"Did it really jump on Tanner?" Drew asked. Ward could tell she desperately wanted to join in the race to spread the news, but she considered herself too grownup to indulge in a helter-skelter scramble with Pete and Will. "Did you shoot him in midair?"

"Yes."

"He could have killed Tanner if you had missed."

"He could have killed Tanner if you had missed." Marina used Drew's words without her sense of amazement.

Ward didn't need to be reminded. Even now the horror of what might have happened lingered. He hadn't known there was a lion in that canyon. They didn't find the two kills until later.

Jake and the boys had taken the buck to dress the meat. Since Isabelle had stated categorically that she would not have her home decorated with bits and pieces of dead animals, Ward imagined the boys would hang the horns in the bunkhouse.

Night Hawk had offered to clean and cure the lion skin. Ward was relieved to be rid of that unpleasant job. Trying to explain himself to Marina was more than he could handle at the moment. He would have been happier if she'd let him clean Tanner's arm by himself. Seeing the severity of the wound merely fueled her anger.

"My God!" she exclaimed. "What were you thinking of, letting him near a lion. He could have lost his arm."

"I didn't *let him near a lion,*" Ward said, trying hard to hold on to his temper. "Unfortunately I killed a deer the lion had picked out for his own dinner. He wasn't in a mood to give it up. Tanner couldn't see him because he was under cover of the trees."

That was the wrong thing to say.

"You mean that lion could have killed Tanner before you even knew it was there?"

"I'm always watchful when I'm away from the ranch," Ward said without taking his eyes off the raw flesh of the wound.

"Why didn't Tanner's horse run away when he caught the scent?"

"It did. Unfortunately, it unseated Tanner first."

Another wrong thing to say. Ward couldn't pay attention to what he was doing and think of every word before it came out of his mouth. Right now it was more important that he clean the wound thoroughly than soothe Marina's wrath.

He was proud of the boy, *his son.* It was taking every ounce of courage the boy had to keep from crying. If Marina had offered him sympathy rather than outrage, he would have given in and bawled, even with Drew looking on.

"It doesn't hurt much, Mama," he said. "Ward said he'd wrap it tight and it'd be well in no time."

"If it doesn't get infected."

"It won't," Ward said. He'd failed other people's sons, but he wouldn't fail his own.

"You don't know that."

"I'm a doctor."

"According to Isabelle, you quit being a doctor years ago."

"I haven't forgotten what I know. Besides, you can't expect me to ignore my own . . ." He nearly said *son*. "My responsibilities."

"Tanner is my responsibility, not yours."

"Are you finished?" Drew asked. "Isabelle said I was to take him to her the instant you were done with the bandage. She couldn't leave off making dinner, but she wants Tanner to tell her every word of what happened. Bret said he doesn't care, but he's lying. It was his turn to help in the kitchen today, and he's angry he missed out on everything."

Tanner looked anxious to escape.

"Just keep that arm still," Ward said.

"I want you to go straight to bed," Marina said. "You could get a fever."

"It won't hurt him to stay up a while longer," Ward said. "Isabelle will see he doesn't get over-excited. Run along, you two, and don't exaggerate too much," he said to Tanner.

The boy cast Ward a nervous smile and fled.

"How dare you countermand my orders," Marina said, rigid with fury.

"I didn't exactly countermand them," Ward said. "Being a doctor, I'm qualified to say it wouldn't harm him to stay up."

"Don't think you're going to slip out of this by throwing your medical degree at me," Marina fumed. "I'll have something to say about that later. But right now I'd like to know when you decided you had the right to tell me what was best for Tanner."

"When you told me he was my son."

"You said you didn't believe me."

"I've changed my mind."

207

"Why? I haven't been able to offer you any proof I couldn't offer that first day when you were ready to believe I was a—"

"You needn't go into that," Ward said. "I've changed my mind about a lot of things. Being Tanner's father is just one of them."

"It's a shame you didn't change it before he was born."

"I told you I never knew about him," Ward said.

That took some of the steam out of Marina's wrath. "I keep forgetting."

She was having trouble remembering it after years of thinking otherwise. He understood. He was having the same problem.

"We've strayed away from the point," Marina said. "You promised me nothing would happen to Tanner."

"There's always the chance something will happen," Ward said.

"I'm glad you warned me. I'll be sure to keep Tanner in the house from now on."

"You can't do that. It'd be the same as locking him up."

"I want to get him back to San Antonio in one piece."

Her words nearly caused Ward to panic. He hadn't gotten used to having a son, or to how important Tanner had become to him. Now Marina was threatening to take him back to San Antonio.

"You can't keep him locked away for the rest of his life. The best way to protect him is to teach him what to look for and what to do when he finds it."

"I suppose that's what you were doing today."

"In a way."

"I prefer the way Bud does it."

"I'm his father."

"You're new at the job."

"You could fix that easily enough. Leave him here while you go back to San Antonio and marry your rancher."

The words were out of his mouth before he realized what he was saying, but he knew immediately it was what he wanted. He never wanted to be separated from Tanner again.

"There wouldn't be any point in that since I'm marrying Bud so Tanner will have a father."

The look of chagrin on Marina's face told Ward she had only let that slip because she was too upset to think before she spoke. He felt an unexpected surge of relief. At least that was what he thought it was. It was almost as if he'd been holding his breath for a long time and now he could let it go.

"If you let Tanner stay with me, you won't have to marry anybody unless you want to."

He couldn't tell if she was more angry or embarrassed.

"I'm not letting Tanner stay with you. I can't believe you have the nerve to ask."

"He's my son. I want to be with him."

"Are you ready to explain to him why he's got a father he's never seen?"

"Not yet."

"Not ever, if I have anything to do with it. He's better off with Bud."

"He likes me better."

Tanner hadn't exactly said that, but Ward was certain it was true.

"He's known you less than a week," Marina said. "He's known Bud all his life."

"It doesn't make any difference," he maintained.

"Are you willing to go on pretending you're just a friend?" she asked.

It sounded rather stupid when Marina said it that way, but it didn't feel stupid to Ward. "He needs the company of other boys. This is the perfect place for him."

"The perfect place is with me."

"And a husband you don't love?"

Marina flushed. "That's none of your business."

"It is if it involves my son."

"Forgive me if I don't seem properly sympathetic," she retorted, "but I can't get used to your talking about *your* son. For years Tanner's had only one parent."

"Well, I want him, and I'm willing to do whatever I can to keep him," Ward said firmly.

"You haven't got him to keep. Besides, Tanner needs a father and a mother, not parents separated by seventy-five miles."

"He's already got a father and mother," he pointed out.

"Who're married," she objected.

"We're married."

Marina's gaze narrowed. "Are you saying you'd live with me again just to give Tanner a father?"

"I guess so."

Her gaze seemed to grow harder. "It doesn't bother you that I don't love you and you don't love me?"

Ward's mouth opened and closed, but no words came out. "No," he finally managed to say. It wasn't what he meant to say. It certainly wasn't what he felt. He said what he thought she wanted to hear and hoped for the best.

He didn't get it. Marina dealt him a slap that knocked him sideways and left his ear ringing.

"You're not the man I married," she declared. "He had ideals. He had standards."

Ward touched his stinging cheek. "That man had those standards and ideals knocked out from under him."

"The man I fell in love with would have found a way to put them back again."

"Not all men can do that by themselves. Most of us need some help along the way."

"Don't look for it from me. I think it's best that Tanner and I leave tomorrow."

Ward couldn't let her take Tanner away. He had to do something. Panic led him to say the first thing that came to his mind. "I'll tell Tanner I'm his father. He won't go then."

Ward had thought Marina was angry before. He was wrong. She had been merely irritated. *Now* she was angry. He thought for a moment that she was going to hit him again. She restrained herself, but the fire in her eyes could have singed the hide off a buffalo.

"I'll say you're lying. I'll make up somebody else to be his father. It won't matter who. Your mother has already convinced half of San Antonio I'm a whore."

"You'd do that to keep him?"

"I'll do anything I have to. I'll never give him up, not to you, not to anybody."

That sobered Ward. He realized how foolish he'd been. He wanted Tanner, but he wanted Tanner and Marina—both—together. He wasn't sure it was possible, but he meant to try. He needed time to figure out how to do that. He also needed time for her to stop being so angry with him. Right now she wouldn't believe anything he said.

"Where would you go?" Ward asked.

She eyed him suspiciously. "Cypress Bend. As soon as you agree to the divorce, we'll go back to San Antonio."

"Tanner won't like it."

"Maybe not, but it's a lot better than letting him get attached to you and then making him leave anyway."

"He doesn't have to leave."

"Ward, I don't care how much you think you want him, how much you think he needs you and what he can learn on this ranch. I'm not giving up my child. You think it would be difficult for you to be separated from him, but you've known him only a week. I brought him into this world, nursed him, sat up with him when he was sick, worried about him every hour of every day of his life, and I never resented a minute of it."

"I'm not asking you to give him up."

"I know. You offered to live with me even though you don't love me."

"I didn't mean it that way. But even if I did, is that worse than living with Bud?"

"Yes, a thousand times worse. Can't you see that?"

"No."

"You don't even like me."

"I never said that. I said I thought you'd lied, but I never said I disliked you."

"Don't try telling me that now you've decided I'm telling the truth, you suddenly find you love me."

"For a long time I couldn't feel anything but anger. Now that's gone, but I don't know what I feel."

"I can promise you it won't turn out to be love."

"It was once before. Why couldn't it be again?"

"That was years ago. It happened too fast. It was nothing more than mutual infatuation."

"It was a lot more than that." Ward supposed it was the certainty with which he made that statement that caused Marina's expression to change from aggressive to uncertain. "If it hadn't been, you wouldn't have come here and I wouldn't be reluctant to give you a divorce."

"Why are you so reluctant?"

"I don't want you to leave yet. Maybe never. But too much has happened too fast for me to be certain of my feelings about anything."

"Except Tanner."

"Except Tanner."

"I'm not nearly so confused. I'll talk to Jake. I'd prefer to leave first thing in the morning."

Chapter Seventeen

Marina was relieved to be able to walk away from Ward. Her anger at his being willing to live with her for Tanner's sake had not been proof against his declaration that what they had felt so many years ago was love. Or the implication that his love had survived.

Over the years she'd soothed her hurt by convincing herself they had been mistaken, had confused infatuation with love. She had dismissed her continued attraction to Ward as mere physical appeal, but the surge of emotion within her now left her shaken, unable to insist he was wrong.

He'd only known the truth a few days, yet he'd already sorted through the lies, shed his anger, and uncovered his true feelings.

She hadn't been nearly so quick. She'd foolishly been confusing physical attraction with something much deeper. Knowing Ward believed her and loved

Tanner had peeled back the hard crust on her feelings. She was shocked to find herself responding to Ward much as she had seven years ago.

It frightened her badly. She had to find Jake and make arrangements to move to Cypress Bend. She didn't dare put it off a minute longer.

She found Tanner in the kitchen reveling in being the center of attention.

"Why didn't you see a cat that big?" a skeptical Bret was asking. "I would have."

"He told you he was in the trees," Drew said, as ready now to defend Tanner as she had been to doubt him earlier. "You wouldn't have seen him either. You wouldn't have ridden that far from the ranch."

It hadn't taken Marina long to learn that though Bret was determined no one should slight his courage or ability, he had no liking for ranch life. She'd heard, too, about his rich relatives in Boston.

"Keep stirring the rice," Isabelle cautioned Bret. "If it sticks, you'll have to clean the pot. I think Tanner was very brave. If a mountain lion had jumped on me, I'd still be screaming."

"I couldn't. He knocked me out," Tanner told her, childishly candid. "Ward thought I was dead. He cried when he found out I wasn't."

Marina sank down into a chair next to the worktable. Ward had cried because Tanner was safe! She wouldn't have thought Ward could come to love his son so quickly. But it had to be love. She'd never known him to cry. She felt guilty for taking his son away, but she couldn't give Tanner up. He was all she had.

Ward offered her more. But if he was willing to live with her solely for Tanner's sake, could she trust his declaration of love? She had to get away where she could think.

"Where's Jake?" she asked.

"Helping the boys butcher the deer," Isabelle told her. "I'd wait until he comes in," she said when Marina got up and headed toward the door. "It's not a pleasant sight."

"I supervise the slaughter of beef and pork every fall," Marina said as she headed outside.

But she'd never learned to like it. She was relieved when Jake saw her coming and met her under one of the massive oaks.

"Your boy's quite a hero with the kids," he said. "It takes a powerful lot to keep Drew inside when we're butchering."

Marina returned a weak smile. "He's a lot happier about that than I am."

"You sound like Isabelle."

"I never have understood what attracts men to danger."

"Isabelle says it's downright cussedness. When she gets really riled up, she says it's stupidity." Jake grinned.

"Isabelle's not one to sugarcoat things," Marina agreed.

"She says men have a hard enough time understanding things when she makes it plain as dirt."

Marina knew that Jake sincerely loved his wife and respected her feelings. She'd seen them together too often to doubt that. How could they be so much in love and see the same things from such different angles?

Could it be like that for her and Ward? It didn't seen right, but Jake and Isabelle were proof it could happen. She realized real love was tolerance, acceptance, letting people be who they were meant to be. No changes required. None even wanted. She knew it could work because it worked with Jake's impossible collection of boys.

Raising more questions she couldn't answer wasn't what she had come out here to do.

"It's time for Tanner and me to leave. We've trespassed on your hospitality long enough. I would like to start for Cypress Bend first thing in the morning."

The smile disappeared from Jake's face, the twinkle from his eyes.

"Have you told Isabelle?"

"No. I wanted to talk to you about arrangements first."

"What do you need?"

"Just someone to go with us." She didn't like the idea of riding ten miles through empty country. She didn't understand how Ward could enjoy it.

"Have you spoken to Ward?"

"I've told him I'm leaving."

"Did you ask him to take you?"

"No."

Jake looked uncomfortable. "You put me in an awkward position."

"How?"

"You're Ward's wife. Tanner is his son. You're asking me to help you run away from him. Even if Ward weren't my friend, I don't see how I could do that."

"I'm not running away."

"It comes down to the same thing."

"We could go on our own."

"Do you think Ward would let you? He's your husband."

"Quite frankly, I find it difficult to think of Ward

that way. It's hard to remember a connection of law that has never existed in nature."

"Talk to Ward. If he doesn't want to go, I'll send Buck."

She had expected to find Ward doing almost anything but feeding the baby. It was hard for her to reconcile the Ward who had walked out on her with the man who would take the trouble to learn to feed a child that wasn't even his. She kept imagining how he would have been with Tanner, wondering if he, too, was thinking of how much he'd missed by not knowing his son.

Her irritation with him grew. He kept assaulting her defenses, breaking down her resistance by these sneak attacks of nobility. They were undermining her will to refuse to love him again.

She couldn't think of a way to lead up to her request, so she came right out with it.

"Tanner and I will be leaving for Cypress Bend in the morning. Jake wants to know if you'll be accompanying us or if you'd like one of the boys to show us the way."

"Don't you want to know if I'm going to give you a divorce?"

The question caught her off guard. She'd almost forgotten her original strategy to sever the ties between them. Now that Ward knew he had a son, now that he loved Tanner, now that she knew some of their feeling for each other remained, divorce was no longer the clean, easy, permanent separation of their lives she'd hoped for.

"Would you still marry Bud if you didn't need him to be a father to Tanner?"

She hadn't expected him to ask that, either. "If I

don't, I'll have to leave. I couldn't stay on as his housekeeper after rejecting him. But I have no money, nowhere to go. My family still refuses to see me. Both my sisters married well, one especially so."

"I'll give your situation some thought."

"It's not your business."

"You're my wife, the mother of my son. Of course it is."

Marina couldn't think of herself as Ward's wife. She didn't feel married to him. She barely felt connected to him.

But no sooner had that thought taken shape than she knew it wasn't true. The connection was there, and it was growing stronger. She didn't know it if was something left over from seven years earlier or if it had sprung up in the last few days. She was almost afraid to know.

"You're not responsible for me, Ward. No matter what we decide about Tanner, I'm going to be the one to decide about my own future."

"I expect that. But since it affects me, I want to have my say."

Marina couldn't agree, but she didn't feel up to fighting that battle tonight. She still had to tell Isabelle and Tanner. She didn't expect either conversation to be easy.

"You can't leave yet," Isabelle said. "We're just getting to know each other."

She was teaching a reluctant Drew to crochet. Isabelle admitted it wasn't a terribly useful skill for a rancher's wife, but a crocheted doily here and there helped remind men that a different kind of behavior was expected inside the house than the kind employed wrestling cows.

"You've already got enough people to do for without two more," Marina said.

"Two more hardly makes any difference. No, Drew, not like that. You'll knot your thread. Besides," she said, looking up at Marina, "that's not why I don't want you to go."

"I know what you're going to say. I've thought about it. I'm still thinking about it, but I can't decide here. The pressures are too great."

Drew muttered a curse. Isabelle rapped her knuckles, took the piece of crochet, pulled out the error, and did it correctly. "Now do you see how I did that?"

"Yes," Drew said, "but I don't see why I have to learn how."

"When you have you own home, you'll be glad you did."

Drew didn't look convinced, but she diligently did the figure correctly.

"Are you sure you're not running away from a situation you don't want to face?" Isabelle said, returning her attention to Marina.

Marina sighed. "I don't know why I just don't sit everybody down and explain every last detail of my life. It would save a lot of time."

"I'm sorry," Isabelle said, "but I never was very good at minding my own business. You'd think having landed in the middle of this crowd would have taught me a lesson."

"Everybody's pressing me to make the decision they want me to make, but I can't live my life to please anybody else."

"I must have been unusually clumsy to make you think I was suggesting that," Isabelle said. "I just want you to make certain you know what you're rejecting."

"You were right. He is different from what I thought, but I still don't love him."

But might she be starting to now? She honestly didn't know, but the thought frightened her. She didn't want to love Ward.

"Then I'll say no more. If you want to leave Tanner here for a while, we'll be delighted to have him. As Jake would say, the younger kids have taken quite a shine to him."

Marina smiled. "You wouldn't put it quite that way?"

Isabelle laughed. "If my aunt were alive, she'd turn pale with mortification. But I'm learning. I'll soon be able to sound like a proper cowboy's wife." She stopped once again to correct a mistake in Drew's work. "What are you going to do about the baby?"

Marina had been so upset about her own emotional confusion and Ward's wanting to take Tanner from her, she'd completely forgotten the baby.

"I don't know."

"I'd assumed you wanted to take her with you."

"I did. I mean, I do."

"I could keep her."

"No. You'll soon have a baby of your own."

"You'd better talk to Ward. He's become mighty attached to her, too."

Just what she didn't need, something else for her and Ward to disagree about. Well, she'd work out something. Right now she had to figure out what to do about Tanner.

Telling him was easier than she'd expected. The fact that she didn't tell him the whole truth helped.

"I want to stay here," he protested the minute she broached the subject of leaving.

"This isn't our home, Tanner. We can't stay here any more than Drew and Ward could stay at the Gravel Pit."

"Bud wouldn't care."

"That isn't the point. We're only guests."

Tanner got the same stubborn look she'd seen earlier on Ward's face.

"I don't want to go back to the Gravel Pit. I don't want to be Bud's son. I want to stay here and learn to be a cowboy. Drew said I'm getting better all the time."

Marina had decided to fight just one battle at a time. "We're not going back yet. We're moving to Cypress Bend. Ward is going along to show us the way."

"Is he going to stay with us?"

"I don't know."

"Can I ask him?"

"Not tonight. I just told him we're leaving. He probably hasn't had time to decide. Do you mind if I take the baby with us?"

"What baby?"

"The baby girl whose family died of cholera."

She'd been afraid Tanner might be jealous. "Okay. Ward said I could have the lion skin. Can we take it with us?"

Marina didn't want that skin or anything else that would remind her of how close Tanner had come to being killed.

"It'll probably be weeks, even months, before Hawk's through curing it." Long enough, she hoped, for Tanner to forget about it.

"You won't forget it, will you?"

"No." She wanted to, but she doubted she could. "You'd better get to bed now. I want to leave early in the morning."

* * *

Marina was glad Ward invited Drew to ride with them. Her presence helped dissipate some of the tension. It also kept Marina and Ward from discussing the issues that still hung between them.

It was a beautiful ride. Though it was a bright spring day, the altitude kept the air cool and dry. The sky was a brilliant robin's-egg blue. Tiny puff clouds hung suspended overhead. The broad, flat valley was carpeted with thick grass that touched the horse's bellies, and flowers of every color. Acres of rich blue, miles of red and yellow. The hum of bees seeking nectar thrummed on the edge of her senses. Butterflies filled the air—yellow ones, white ones, big black ones with blue markings.

Marina felt that they were the only people in the world, that this enchanted valley was theirs alone.

Up ahead Tanner was busy counting the white-tailed deer that grazed in the valley singly and in small herds. Drew, accustomed to the presence of deer, was more interested in the condition of Jake's cows.

"We should have brought more of the yearlings down here," she called back to Ward. "There's plenty of grass."

"We can't watch them as well down here."

"Surely you don't have rustlers," Marina said.

"You find cattle thieves wherever you find cattle," Ward said. "Jake's still buying the land along the creek between his house and the mountains. Soon he hopes to start buying the land down to the river. Once he does that, we can run cattle all up and down two valleys. It'll give us double the land we've got now."

"Why does he want so much? And why does he

have to buy it? Bud doesn't own half the land he uses."

"Jake lost his first ranch to farmers who homesteaded land he didn't own. He's going to make sure that doesn't happen again. He figures if he buys enough land, there'll be room for the boys to have ranches if they want."

"Does he expect to provide for every one of those boys?"

"If he can."

"What about his own children?"

"They are his children as much as the one that's coming."

Marina felt rebuked. She was fond of the little girl she carried in her arms, but she didn't feel half of the love for her that she felt for Tanner.

They reached Cypress Bend after a tiring but uneventful journey. Mrs. Pruitt wasn't happy to see Ward again, but her disposition took a turn for the better when she learned Marina was looking for a room.

"I've got exactly what you're looking for," she said, bustling Marina inside before she could ask if there were other rooms in town. "You're lucky it's available. I had a man here all last week. Left just yesterday."

Marina followed demurely.

"Glad to see the back of him. He thought just because he was from San Antonio, I wanted to spend all my time catering to his every whim. Mind you, I'm not one to turn away good money, but I'm not a maid. I said I'd do what I could, but if he wanted a personal servant, he'd best advertise for one."

Marina could easily imagine Mrs. Pruitt telling the governor of Texas to scrape his boots.

"You planning to keep that baby with you?"

"Naturally." Marina wondered if she'd be thrown out if it cried.

"Then you'll be needing a crib. I've got one up in the attic. I'll get my husband to bring it down. Mind you, it'll cost you extra."

"Of course."

Marina would have liked to find something wrong with the room, but it was perfect. Two beds, a spacious wardrobe, a corner for the crib, chairs, a table, and space to move around. She was almost afraid to ask the charge.

"It's fifty cents a day. Meals are extra."

"I'll take it."

"How long do you mean to stay?"

How long *did* she mean to stay? What was she staying for?

"I'm not certain. A couple of days at least."

"I'll put on fresh sheets. Did you lose the baby's clothes? What's her name?"

"I don't know. She's the child we found in that wagon Ward told you about, the family who died of cholera."

Mrs. Pruitt peered closely. "She doesn't look sick to me."

"She's perfectly healthy, but we had to burn everything in the wagon."

"Poor thing," Mrs. Pruitt cooed. "You leave it to me. The minute the ladies know there's a motherless baby around, you'll have enough clothes for two or three babies. Both those boys belong to you and your husband?"

It seemed the whole world was determined to make her Ward's wife. It would have made things a lot easier if she had felt the same.

225

"The younger boy is mine. Mr. Dillon works on a ranch up the valley. The other boy belongs to Jake Maxwell." She didn't figure Drew would appreciate strangers knowing she was a girl.

"He's the one who calls himself a doctor, isn't he?" Mrs. Pruitt asked, nodding at Ward.

"He's a very fine surgeon."

"We don't have any disease."

"I'm sure he'll be relieved to know that."

"Well, you go get your things," Mrs. Pruitt said. "I'll have fresh sheets on the beds before you get back."

"Is there somewhere Mr. Dillon can change a bandage?" Marina asked.

"I'll show him to the kitchen. By the way, what do you want me to call you?"

She almost said Miss Scott. But that would have been just as bad as saying Mrs. Dillon. "Marina will be just fine. My son's name is Tanner."

"We'll have to think of a name for the baby."

"I'd appreciate any suggestions you might have," Marina said. "Now, if you would show me to the kitchen."

Tanner's wound looked good. It was still raw and red, but it didn't show any signs of infection.

"Make sure to keep it clean," Ward said. "Wrap it in fresh bandages. Don't use anything that hasn't been boiled first."

"Mercy, who has time to boil bandages?" Mrs. Pruitt asked.

"Anybody who wants to avoid infection," Ward snapped. "And make sure to wash your hands first."

"What does that do?" Mrs. Pruitt asked, bristling.

"It gets rid of germs."

"What are germs? I never heard of such a thing."

"They're small, invisible organisms that carry disease."

Mrs. Pruitt's expression turned severe, disapproving, and more than a little angry. "I don't believe in things I can't see."

"You can see them, but you need a microscope," Ward countered.

It was obvious Ward had gone beyond Mrs. Pruitt's experience. She wasn't willing to trust in what she didn't know, but she wasn't willing to discount it either. Marina thought that spoke rather well for her intelligence.

"I'll be sure to wash everything," Marina said.

"I'll be back tomorrow to check on Tanner," Ward told her.

"That's not necessary," Marina assured him.

"I'll be back."

"He sure is a rude man," Mrs. Pruitt said after Ward and Drew left.

Marina found herself saying, "He's under a lot of strain right now. He's usually quite sweet-tempered."

"It'll take some doing to convince me," Mrs. Pruitt said. "Boiled bandages, indeed."

"If you can't do it, I'll do it myself," Marina said, pointing to the soiled bandages.

"It'll cost extra."

Marina felt her temper begin to rise. "Just make certain they're absolutely clean."

She'd never heard of boiling bandages either. But if Ward thought it would safeguard Tanner, she'd boil them herself if necessary. She was certain Ward would never take any chances with Tanner's life.

"When is Ward coming back?" Tanner asked. He'd started asking less than an hour after Ward had left

227

the day before. Marina calculated he'd asked the same question at least a dozen times since. She'd counted five times in the last two hours.

"He didn't say, but probably not before midday."

Most of yesterday had been taken up with settling into the room, making arrangements for meals, and talking to nearly every woman in Cypress Bend. True to Mrs. Pruitt's prediction, Marina had more clothes than she could use. She wondered if Isabelle would want some of them if her baby was a girl.

She'd also been given far more names for the baby than she could possibly remember. She got the usual biblical suggestions of Mary, Elizabeth, and Rebecca. She was amused by the folksy Coramae, Birdie, and Floretha. She drew the line at Argonia, Zilpha, and Belsadie.

She settled on Dale. She wasn't sure why. No one seemed to like it, especially Mrs. Pruitt.

"It sounds like a boy's name."

"I know two women named Dale. That's why I thought of it. Besides, we found her in a valley, which is another word for dale."

"I don't hold with naming babies after creeks and such. Might as well call her 'Mountain' or 'Tree' if you're going to do that."

"I can always change my mind," Marina said. "It's just a thought."

Tanner hadn't cared what they called the baby. He still didn't this morning. He could think only of Ward's coming.

Marina didn't want to see Ward. Separation hadn't helped to clarify her feelings. Try as she might, she couldn't forget that Ward had left, that he hadn't believed her. She doubted she could ever entirely forgive him for that.

But her feelings were far from dead. In fact, if their past could be wiped out, she was certain she'd tumble as heedlessly in love with him as she had seven years before. Sometimes it was all she could do not to touch him, not to ask him to hold her for just a minute. Seven years was a long time to go without the comfort of a man's touch.

But the past couldn't be wiped out. And Marina had vowed never to fall heedlessly in love again.

Chapter Eighteen

Marina felt no relief from her confusion when Ward finally arrived. She got no chance to speak with him. Tanner talked nonstop. When he stopped for breath, Mrs. Pruitt jumped in.

"Does it still hurt?" Ward asked Tanner when he'd unwrapped the bandage. The redness was gone, but the flesh was still raw.

"Only when I roll over in bed," Tanner said. "It doesn't hurt to ride."

"Have you been riding?"

"I told him it wasn't a good idea," Mrs. Pruitt said. "He doesn't know his way about. If he was to get hurt with that arm, he might not be able to take care of himself."

"Joe Olwell told me about some falls a few miles from town," Tanner said, speaking of his new friend. "He says there are big, huge rocks in the middle of the river. He says you can walk all the way to the other side. I want to see it. Will you take me?"

"As long as your mother agrees," Ward said without looking up from his work.

"People say those falls are mighty pretty," Mrs. Pruitt said, "but I won't go there myself. Where you find water, you find snakes."

Tanner looked at Marina. She would rather Tanner stayed in their room, but it was useless to suggest it. He was bursting with energy. If he didn't work some of it off, he would drive her crazy. It was time she got back to the Gravel Pit.

But the moment she thought that, she realized it was no solution.

"You should ask Ward if he has time," Marina said. "After all, he had to take time away from his work to come see about your arm."

"Do you?" Tanner asked.

Marina knew Ward's answer before he gave it.

"Sure, but I can't stay too late. I have to get back before dark or Isabelle won't feed me."

Tanner started telling Ward everything he'd heard about the falls. It took Marina only a few minutes to realize Tanner was more interested in being with Ward than he was in seeing the falls. He was doing everything in his power to make Ward like him. If it hadn't been so sweet, it would have been pathetic. If she didn't separate them soon, she would be in for big trouble.

Going back to Ward would change all of that. She had to admit she was tempted to consider the idea. It would solve so many problems, the most important being that Tanner would have his real father and a name no one could take from him. She had once felt those benefits were important enough to marry Bud, whom she didn't love. Weren't they worth staying married to the man who was already her husband?

She wondered if Ward realized that accepting her and Tanner would mean going against his family, possibly being ostracized by them. They might have lied to him, but he still wanted their love.

This was a battle he still had to fight. She didn't know if he could win it.

But as she watched him carefully bandage Tanner's arm, all the time talking to him, answering his questions, never once showing impatience, she was tempted to believe he might. Every day confirmed that Ward had turned into the man she had seen in him when they'd married.

But she didn't want to become emotionally involved with him again. No matter what she did in the future, she was going to be ruled by her head, not her heart.

"Mama says she is going to call the baby Dale," Tanner said.

"That sounds like a good name to me," Ward said.

"It's not a proper name for a girl," Mrs. Pruitt said. "She ought to be called something sensible like Abigail or Eunice or Gertie."

Ward looked over his shoulder at Marina and made a face that almost caused her to burst out laughing.

Living with Ward might not be so bad if he smiled like that more often. He was ready to step up to his responsibilities to Tanner. But what about her? Could she live with him, work closely with him day after day, with the same kind of easygoing friendship that existed between her and Bud?

She knew immediately she couldn't. She couldn't explain why, not even to herself. She just knew it would be impossible. For both of them, she suspected.

"You had any cases of unexplained sickness?" Ward asked Mrs. Pruitt as he put the last pin in Tanner's bandage.

"None at all," Mrs. Pruitt replied.

"Why don't you ask around just to make sure."

Mrs. Pruitt looked offended that her opinion wasn't enough to satisfy Ward. "If you insist."

She stalked out of the room.

"If I'm to get Tanner to the falls and back in time to get home for supper, I'd better be going," Ward said as he led them outside.

Marina was surprised to see Will waiting with the horses.

"Jake said I had to bring him," Ward explained. "He said he had a lot of work, and if I wasn't going to help him, I could at least take Will. It takes one person watching full-time to keep Will out of trouble. Jake figured this would about make things even."

"It's Drew and Pete's fault," Will protested.

"Sometimes, but you cause more than your share. Now go help Tanner saddle his horse. I've got a few questions to ask his mother."

Marina felt her pulses race. She told herself he would only ask her again to give him Tanner, but she knew she was fooling herself. He was going to talk about their living together as man and wife.

"How is Dale doing?"

"Who?"

"The baby. You said you'd named her Dale."

"Oh." She felt like a fool. "I haven't had time to get used to the name yet. Besides, it was just an idea. Do you have any suggestions? You're the one who saved her life."

"Anybody could have done what I did."

"No, they couldn't, not even if they'd known what to do, which they wouldn't. I'm going to tell her that as soon as she's old enough to understand."

"Do you mean to keep her then?"

"I don't know. We've got to look for her family. Do you think there's any chance we'll find them?"

"No. We should have looked through the wagon before we burned it, but I never thought she'd live. You could give her up for adoption."

"If anybody is going to adopt her, I will."

"Then you'd better not ask for a divorce. The court won't give her to you if you're not married."

"Are you going to use that as part of your argument that we live together?"

"No. Her family could turn up at any time. If they took her from you after you'd had her two or three years, you'd be heartbroken."

"How do you know what I'd be?"

"I may have fallen in love with you overnight, but I wasn't a complete fool. You take your commitments and responsibilities very seriously. I have a great respect for your integrity."

"Even though I was ready to marry Bud, a man I didn't love?"

"I'm sure he knows how you feel about him. You've probably told him yourself."

"How do you know?"

"The same way I know you refused to take charity from anybody, that you refused to marry Ramon though it would have solved all your problems, that you came here yourself rather than sending someone else. It's the same reason you use your maiden name but insist Tanner be called Dillon."

Mrs. Pruitt stuck her head outside the door. "You'd

better go check on those boys. They could have sad-
dled a dozen horses by now."

"They'll be here any minute now," Ward said. "She
doesn't know Will," he told Marina. "We'll be lucky
if he stops talking long enough to remember to
tighten the cinch."

Mrs. Pruitt went back inside. Apparently Ward's
lack of faith in her ability to evaluate the health of
the townspeople still irritated her.

"What are you going to do now?" Ward asked.

"I don't know. What would you do if I agreed to
live with you?"

"I haven't decided."

"I know you've given it some thought," she said.
"We were impetuous seven years ago, but you're different now."

"How do you know?"

"You don't trust anybody, Ward, not even yourself.
You look behind every post to make sure there's no
bogeyman ready to jump out."

"Several already have."

"Stop trying to avoid answering my question.
What would you do?"

"That depends on you."

"Okay, tell me my options."

"We could stay at the ranch. I could continue to
work there."

"We couldn't go on living in Isabelle's house."

"We could build our own house."

"With what?"

"I have some money."

"How much?"

"Enough."

"You're not going to tell me?"

"No."

"That's not a good sign. A husband and wife shouldn't keep secrets from each other."

"That depends on how close the husband and wife are."

That statement led Marina firmly in a direction she had no intention of going. "What other options do we have?"

"We could move to San Antonio."

"You realize nobody would speak to me."

"I wouldn't care."

"I would. I have no intention of living with you just so I can bring Tanner up as a social outcast. I can do that by myself."

"We could move back to Rancho del Espada."

"I refuse to live in the same house as Ramon, even if your mother would let me through the door."

"They'll probably stay in San Antonio most of the time."

"You'll have to think of something else. Since you say you have some money, have you considered buying the ranch from Ramon?"

Marina realized she had allowed herself to talk as though she had already decided she was going to live with Ward. Unless she was mistaken, Ward had made that assumption as well.

"Not that I've decided what I'm going to do," she added. "But once Tanner knows you're his father, there'll be no going back."

"There's no going back now," Ward said. "He's got to know. The only question is when and how to tell him."

Marina felt a spurt of anger at Ward. Like so many men, he saw only that he had a son. It seemed the apex of a man's ambition was to have a woman and a son. Only a few could understand the difference between that and having a wife and family. Before she committed her son and herself to this man, she had to be certain he knew the difference.

Tanner and Will finally reappeared. Tanner was already in the saddle.

"Joe's father helped me up," Tanner announced. "He said I was a brave boy to be riding with my arm all wrapped up like a papoose. What's a papoose?"

"It's an Indian baby all wrapped up in blankets to keep it warm," Ward said. "Why don't you come with us?" he asked Marina.

The question startled Marina. Her response upset her even more. She wanted to go, but she was afraid. Ward was being too perfect, and she was too vulnerable.

"I can't leave Dale."

"I'll take care of her for you," Mrs. Pruitt offered, sticking her head out the door again.

"I couldn't take advantage of you."

"Nonsense. That baby's no trouble at all."

"Come on, Mama," Tanner begged.

"I promise not to start any arguments," Ward said. "If I do, you can push me into the river."

Marina let herself be persuaded. In no time at all, she was mounted on a horse and headed to some falls she had no desire to see.

"I hope you know the way," Ward said to Tanner. "If Will tells Drew you got us lost, she'll never let you forget it."

Marina watched them riding side by side, Tanner as happy as she'd ever seen him. She felt a severe pang. This was what Tanner and his father ought to be doing. She would give almost anything to make it last.

But she was one side of this triangle. She couldn't

just throw herself in as part of the bargain because she was Tanner's mother. She had to be wanted for herself. Maybe that was why she'd agreed to come along. She needed to find out if Ward really did want her or just her son.

A few miles outside of Cypress Bend, the terrain changed abruptly from a lush valley with wooded slopes to nearly desert conditions. Twisted, gnarled oaks supplanted towering cypress and maples. Grassy meadows gave way to rocky hills and deep canyons overgrown with thorny shrubs, cactus, and grass that sprang in bunches from rocks instead of soil.

But not even the changing landscape could detract from Marina's pleasure in the ride. She had told herself she was going to enjoy this outing. She wouldn't worry about the future or fret over the past. This was for the moment, and this moment was better than any she'd had in a long time.

The rougher the terrain, the more often Tanner wanted to venture off the trail.

"Don't worry about him," Ward advised her. "Will's with him."

"You said Will was constantly getting into trouble."

"He always gets out again. That boy has an instinct for survival."

Marina was unable to adopt Ward's casual attitude toward Tanner, but she couldn't tell herself it was carelessness. Ward cared more about that boy than about himself. But men had a code of behavior all their own. Marina had never thought much about it before. Now that she realized Ward intended to teach it to her son, she would pay more attention.

Still, she had faith in Ward.

The land became even more rough as they approached the river. Taller trees camouflaged crevasses cut deep into the rock by rainwater over millions of years. The trail led to a small overlook. Two hundred feet below, the river flowed over a wide shelf of rock only to disappear in a jumble of giant boulders. A hundred yards beyond, the banks narrowed and the river resumed its journey as a quiet, tree-shaded, meandering stream.

"We have to leave the horses here and go the rest of the way on foot," Ward said.

"I didn't come prepared for rock climbing," Marina said.

"You can't stop now, Mama," Tanner pleaded.

"Drew wouldn't stop," Will said. "She'd race you to the bottom."

"Drew's a little girl," Marina said. "I'm not."

"Isabella wouldn't stop, either. She's not afraid of no canyon."

Thus shamed, Marina had no choice but to declare, "I'll make it to the bottom before any of you."

Ward, grinning so broadly she wanted to smack him, said, "I'll give you a hand."

Taking the challenge seriously, the boys started to scramble down.

"Tanner, don't—"

Ward put his hand over her mouth. She turned her startled gaze in his direction.

"Nobody worries about anybody else today, okay?"

"I can't help it. I'm his mother."

"And you always will be, so stop worrying about it."

Marina couldn't follow that logic, but she decided it wasn't worth it. The boys were scrambling over the rocks, having the time of their lives.

"Here, take my hand and I'll help you down."

Marina hadn't planned on physical contact. Neither had she planned on the rush of heat that surged through her when Ward took her hand. It made her think of that time so many years ago when he'd hoisted her effortlessly into the saddle. She thought, too, of the feel of his hard body as it leaned against her own, the jumble of emotions and sensations that nearly swamped her.

They threatened to do it again when he put his hands around her waist and lifted her down from a rock. Even the briefest look told her he would have to do this many times before they reached the bottom.

"Maybe I'd better stay up here," she said.

"Afraid?"

"A little." Let him figure out what she was afraid of.

But he knew. "I'm not."

He continued to help her over rocks, down from boulders, along treacherous parts of the trail. By the time they reached the river, Marina was overheated in just about every way possible.

"We beat you," the boys chorused.

"So you did," Marina conceded. "I guess I'm not as fast as I used to be." She suddenly started to run across the wide expanse of smooth, flat rock that covered the river bed. "Bet I can beat you to the other side."

The boys tried to keep up with her, but their boots weren't nearly so comfortable for running as her shoes. They began to fall back before they'd made it halfway across.

"Come on," she teased. "You're not going to let a girl beat you, are you?"

"Drew does it all the time," Will said.

Tanner tried to keep up, but he couldn't. Just as Marina was about to celebrate her success, Ward sprinted past her like she was standing still.

"Oh, no you don't," she cried and took after him, but it was a hopeless chase. Ward was kneeling, drinking from one of several springs in the river, when she reached him.

"You just had to beat me, didn't you?"

Ward looked up and grinned, water dripping from his chin. "I had to defend the honor of the male sex. I couldn't be beaten by a girl."

Marina laughed. "How did you do it? I was sure you'd be a broken-down wreck by now."

"An old Mexican on Dad's ranch taught me to run on my toes. It's the heels that kill you."

"Can we climb down to the sand?" Will asked. Marina looked to where he pointed. An area of pure white sand beckoned. But between them and the sand was a jumble of huge boulders, some nearly as big as a barn.

"Sure," Ward said. "I wish we'd thought to bring a lunch. We could have picnicked in the shade on that island in the middle of the river."

"We can come back tomorrow," Tanner said.

"You don't even know if you can get over those boulders," Marina said.

"Sure we can," Will said. "I climb boulders all the time."

Marina started to tell Tanner to be careful but decided against it. He was having too much fun. She didn't want to spoil it.

"Look, Mama," Tanner called. "There's little fishes down there."

Pools of water had collected at the base of several

boulders. Tiny fish, less than an inch long, darted about in the shady depths. The boys clambered from one rock to the next, calling out their finds to each other, each trying to beat the other to the sand.

Marina was enjoying herself almost as much as Tanner. She didn't reject Ward's offer to help her across the field of boulders. By the time they reached the sand, her temperature was up again. The river crossed the sandbar in several channels. The boys raced from one to the other. When they couldn't jump across one, they took their boots off and waded.

The sun, reflected off the white sand, had become hot. "I'd give anything to be able to sit in the shade," Marina said, indicating the island in the river Ward had mentioned earlier.

"Let's go."

"We can't. The river's between us."

Ward sat down in the sand and took off his boots, stuffed his socks inside, and handed them to Marina.

"Here, hold these."

Before she had time to ask what he intended to do, he swept her up in his arms and waded into the water. It came up to his thighs.

"You're crazy," Marina exclaimed when he set her down on the island, safe and dry.

"It's not half as bad as crossing a river with a herd of longhorns. You're much easier to handle."

Marina sputtered, then burst out laughing. "That's the first time I've been compared to a cow. And it had better be the last."

"I said you were better."

"That's the only reason your boots aren't floating downstream this very minute."

She sat in the shade while Ward stretched out in

the sun to let his clothes dry. In a few minutes he closed his eyes. She watched as the boys played in the water along the shore. Before long they were just as wet as Ward. She looked over at him, so long and strong, dozing peacefully as if he hadn't a care in the world. She smiled when butterflies landed on him, when a bee checked to see if he might be a source of pollen. A dragonfly tried to settle on his nose. He woke up and shooed it away.

She laughed, and he sat up. He looked at her and smiled lazily. "Sorry. Too many sleepless nights." He looked to where the boys were chasing each other through the rough grass along the riverbank. "Find your boots, boys. It's time to head back."

"How are you going to get back without getting wet?" Marina asked as the boys pleaded from a distance to stay just a little longer.

"We're bound to find some debris from the winter's floods if we walk downstream."

Sure enough, a tree had obligingly caught itself between two large rocks. They crossed without mishap. The boys complained all the way to the top. But by the time they reached the horses, Marina could tell they were tired.

The ride back was quiet. They all seemed to feel the weight of the problems that awaited them in Cypress Bend. They had forgotten for a little while, but they couldn't escape forever.

For Marina, the day had demonstrated that she and Ward could be friends. She still didn't know if he wanted her as much as he wanted Tanner, but she did know they could be comfortable together. That was essential if she was to seriously consider going back to him.

"The boys and I will take care of the horses," Ward said when they reached town.

"I enjoyed it," Marina said. "I'm glad you asked me."

"I'm glad you came."

She left him with the boys, no more clear in her mind what she wanted to do than before.

"So he's your husband."

Mrs. Pruitt was waiting in the doorway.

"I overheard you this morning," she explained. "I wasn't meaning to listen, but I didn't stop once I knew what you were talking about."

"You can't tell anybody. Tanner doesn't know."

"A woman's place is with her husband, especially when she's got a boy to think of."

Marina was beginning to feel nobody but Bud had the slightest interest in what she wanted or what she felt. All they could see was that Tanner needed a father and that she ought to marry some man to give him one. Well, she'd managed to raise him so far by herself. If push came to shove, she could keep on doing it.

"I agree with you, but my husband and I were separated the day after our wedding. We hadn't set eyes on each other until a week ago."

Marina decided that trying to explain to Mrs. Pruitt was a mistake. She could see the woman's mind whirling, wondering just what kind of mischief a single woman could have gotten up to in all that time.

"You're lucky he's willing to take you back after such a time."

"I'm not sure I'm willing to take *him* back," Marina retorted. "I've done pretty well on my own."

"No woman should live separate from her husband."

"Would it make any difference if he was missing in the war?"

"Then naturally you'd go home to your family."

"In other words, you believe it takes a man in the house to keep a woman respectable."

"Certainly."

"Then you've got too fine an opinion of men, and too poor an opinion of women. If I get married again—or rather, choose to live with my husband—it'll be because I want to, not because I need him. I've already proved I don't."

"I never thought I'd live to hear a respectable woman say such a thing."

"I probably wouldn't if I'd had the life of an ordinary woman."

"There are those who would say you were a hussy. They'd say you'd never say such a thing if you weren't so pretty you knew you could attract a man any time you wanted one."

"People are welcome to their opinions as long as they don't voice them in my presence. Besides, men are a lot of trouble. More women ought to consider them a luxury rather than a necessity."

"Maybe that's how you truly feel—though I can't imagine a decent woman saying such a thing—but he's a necessity to that boy."

Marina couldn't argue that. Tanner hadn't mentioned his imaginary father in days.

"I'd better go see if Dale is awake. I haven't been able to get her on a regular feeding schedule yet."

"You're more worried about a baby that's none of your kin than you are about your own son."

"No, Mrs. Pruitt, I'm worried about all three of us."

"Worrying is a man's job. You ought to be fixing his supper and taking care of his babies."

"That's what I started out to do, but then things changed."

"Then change them back."

Tanner's noisy arrival put an end to the conversation.

"Have Ward and Will left?" she asked him.

Tanner nodded. "I asked Ward if we could go back to the falls tomorrow. Joe promised to show us where to find some caves with bats in them."

Marina's skin crawled at the thought of being in a cave with bats. "Tanner, you've got to stop asking Ward to do things."

"Why?"

"He has his own work to do," she explained.

"He doesn't mind. He said so," Tanner protested.

"He can't keep doing it forever," she said.

"He likes taking me places," Tanner claimed. "He said he'd take me anyplace I wanted to go."

Marina doubted Ward had said exactly that.

"That's impossible. We have to go back to San Antonio. Ward has to stay here."

She had known Tanner wasn't going to take the news well, but she wasn't prepared for his angry outburst.

"I don't want to go back to San Antonio. I want to stay here."

"We can't."

"Ward would let us. I know he would."

"That isn't Ward's ranch. It belongs to Jake and Isabelle. They already have a house full of children. There's no room for three more people, even if I wanted to stay."

"I don't want Bud to be my father. I want Ward. Why can't you marry him?"

"Did he ask you to tell me that?" she demanded.

"No. Why don't you like him? Everybody else does. Drew says she likes him even better than Jake," Tanner said.

"What would you do if your real father came back?"

She hadn't meant to ask that question. She hadn't even meant to hint at the possibility until she was certain of what she was going to do about Ward's offer.

Tanner's excitement faded, but he grew calmer. He avoided his mother's gaze. "He's not coming back. I know he's dead. Benjy's father came back a long time ago. Drew said I was a little fool for not believing he's dead. I didn't want to be the only one without a father. If I said he was doing something secret, then I could be just like everybody else."

Marina had missed her family when they'd turned their backs on her, but she'd been older than Tanner, and too busy trying to support herself and her child to feel the full weight of her loss.

Apparently, having Bud hadn't spared Tanner any of the sense of loss. She couldn't understand the depth of his pain, but she could feel it, empathize with it.

"There's always the possibility," Marina said. "Records got lost during the war. People don't always know—"

"He's dead," Tanner shouted, angrily. "He's not coming back. Not ever."

"But if he did—"

"You just don't want Ward to like me," Tanner

burst out. "You don't want me to stay here and be a cowboy like Ward."

"You can't, not right now. Maybe a little later—after Isabelle has her baby—she'll ask us to come back. If she does—"

"I'm not going back to the Gravel Pit," Tanner shouted. "I'm going to stay with Ward. He wants me to stay. He said so."

"Tanner—"

But the boy wasn't listening. He flung open the door and raced down the stairs. She heard the door slam behind him.

"You slam that door again," Mrs. Pruitt said, thrusting her head out the kitchen window, "and you'll spend the rest of the afternoon outside."

Tanner didn't stop. He raced around the corner of the house and out of sight. Marina put the empty bottle on the table and put the baby on her shoulder, patting her back. As she leaned out the window to see where Tanner had gone, Dale rewarded her with an enormous burp. Marina started to put the baby in her crib and go after Tanner, but decided to let him clam down before she tried talking to him again.

Five minutes later she wished she hadn't. Tanner rode by headed toward the ranch.

Chapter Nineteen

Normally Will would have been so much trouble, Ward wouldn't have had time to think of anything beyond getting him home in one piece. Today, for some reason, the boy was on his best behavior. He rode alongside Ward on their ride home in companionable silence. If Ward hadn't been so preoccupied with his own troubles, he'd have worried that Will was planning something truly dangerous.

Things couldn't go on as they were. Though Marina knew the anger that lay between them had been caused by clever lies, she still couldn't forget what had happened. Or forgive Ward.

It wasn't the same with Ward. All his doubts had disappeared. Now when he looked at Marina, he saw a beautiful, strong, vital woman, the kind of woman any man would be proud to marry. Each day he became more anxious to convince her that he loved her, that he wanted to be her husband and lover, not just Tanner's father. They had lost so many years, wasted so much love, he couldn't stand the thought of waiting any longer. He searched for any chance to take advantage of her weakening resistance.

Ward still remembered the afternoon he'd fallen in love with her. She was beautiful, vital, full of fun, too young to know how recklessly she loved, exactly the kind of woman to appeal to a man who thought love had passed him by. She had knocked him off his feet.

But they weren't the same innocent couple now that they had been then. She had become self-reliant and cautious, a woman who had no intention of letting herself be hurt again by love. Yet Ward knew her willingness to love, her desire to be loved, was still there. He only had to find a way to dispel the fear that held her back.

Each time he saw Marina, the need to hold her, kiss her, make love to her grew stronger. He had told himself he'd come to Cypress Bend to check Tanner's wound. He knew he'd come to see Marina as well. He didn't want her just for Tanner's sake. He wanted her to want him, to want to be with him.

Was his timing bad!

"Do you think Tanner's father is coming back?" Will asked.

Ward snapped out of his reverie. "Why do you ask?"

"That's all he talked about when he first got here. Drew says Tanner's father is dead. But Drew thinks anybody she can't see is dead."

"Did Tanner say anything about his father today?"

"No. He wants you to be his father. He told me. Are you going to?"

"His mother and I have talked about it." Ward

would rather have kept this to himself, but it didn't seem possible.

"Will you leave the ranch?"

"We haven't decided."

"Tanner wants to stay. He wants to be a cowboy like you. I told him you were a doctor. He said you weren't. Are you a doctor?"

Leave it to Will to poke needles into all the sensitive spots.

"I was trained as one."

"Drew says you like being a cowboy better than doctoring."

"I do." And he did, but for the wrong reasons.

The thud of a horse's hooves on the soft loam of the meadow caused them to turn in their saddles.

"It's Tanner," Will said. "Maybe somebody's sick. Then you can be a doctor again."

Ward had a feeling it wouldn't be as easy as that. His fears were confirmed as soon as he saw Tanner's expression. The boy was crying. Tears spilled down his cheeks to be dashed away by the wind.

"Whoa!" Ward called as he and Will moved out of the way to keep from being run over.

Ward spurred his horse forward, reaching Tanner just as the boy managed to slow his horse sufficiently to turn around.

"What's wrong?" Ward asked. "Has anything happened to your mother or Dale?"

"I'm not going back to San Antonio," Tanner sobbed. "I don't want Bud to be my father. I want to be a cowboy like you."

Ward didn't know what had set Tanner off, but he could tell the boy was too upset to explain.

"I thought you were a cowboy," Will said. "You said you lived on a ranch."

"I mean a real cowboy," Tanner said, still looking at Ward. "You can teach me. You promised."

"I said I'd help you as long as you were at the ranch," Ward said. "I never promised you could stay there forever. You have to go with your mother."

"But she's going back to San Antonio," Tanner wailed.

"Does your mother know where you are?"

Tanner had stopped crying. He looked a little guilty. "I don't know."

"Did you tell her?"

"No."

"What happened?"

"I said I didn't want to go back to San Antonio. She said I had to go anyway, so I ran away."

"We'll have to go back," Ward said. "Your mother will worry herself sick."

"No, I won't go back!"

"Of course you will. You can't run away from your mother."

"Isabelle would beat me if I ran away," Will said. "Mama never beats me."

"Isabelle hasn't beaten me, either," Will admitted, "but Jake would beat me for putting Isabelle in a state as well as being stupid enough to run away."

"I'm not stupid," Tanner said.

"You are if you run away. Then you'd be an orphan. I was an orphan for a long time, and I didn't like it."

"Was it stupid to run away?" Tanner asked Ward. Ward nodded.

"But I don't want to go back to San Antonio."

"I don't want you to go either, but just because you go doesn't mean you can't come back here again."

"Do you think I will?" Tanner asked plaintively.

"You'll have to ask your mother," Ward counseled.

"Will you come with me?" Tanner asked.

"Why do you want me to go back with you?"

"I'm afraid."

"No, you're not." Ward had every intention of going back, but he needed to know why Tanner had run away.

Tanner hung his head. "If you talk to Mama real nice, maybe she'll like you instead of Bud. Then you can be my daddy."

Ward's heart beat faster. From the moment he first began to accept that Tanner might be his son, this was what he'd wanted, what he'd worked for. Now he had it, but at what price? He couldn't let Tanner's love for him come between Tanner and his mother. He wanted their love to bind them together, make them a family, not tear them apart.

"I thought you said your real father was coming home."

Tanner looked up. His tears started again. "He's dead. I didn't want him to be, but I know he is."

Ward almost wished he hadn't asked.

"You could have two daddies," Will said. "That's what I'd do. I never want to leave Jake and Isabelle."

Ward knew he and Marina had to come to some decision soon. Taking their time to make up their minds might be easier for them, but it was only making it more difficult for Tanner.

"We'll talk to your mother and see what she wants to do."

"Can I stay with you?"

"We'll see. But whatever happens, you're not to run away again. Only cowards run away."

Ward wondered why he wasn't blushing from

shame. He was a grown man, and he'd been running away for years.

"I'm not a coward."

"I know you're not. You just didn't understand what you were supposed to do. If you want something, ask. If you don't want to do something, say so."

"But what if Mama makes me do it anyway?" Tanner asked.

"We can't always do what we want," Ward said. "Sometimes we have to stay and try to work things out."

"That's what Jake told Zeke when he threatened to run away last year," Will said. "He said things might not be too good right then, but they'd be a whole lot worse if Zeke ran away."

"Exactly," Ward said. He was relieved to see they were approaching Cypress Bend. It didn't surprise him to see Marina riding toward them. When she saw them, she stopped and waited.

Tanner hung back. "Will you talk to her?"

"No. This is something you have to do."

"She'll be mad at me."

"Probably, but she loves you very much. She'll be glad you're safe. Will and I will wait here."

Ward wanted to go with Tanner. It hurt to deny the look of entreaty in the boy's eyes. But Ward owed this to Marina. She had been Tanner's only parent for seven years. It wouldn't be right to undermine her position now. She would never respect Ward if he did that. Never love him either.

"Is she going to beat him?" Will asked.

"I don't think so."

"Do you think Jake would beat me if I ran away?"

"Not if you were as upset as Tanner. He'd want to

fix what was wrong so you wouldn't want to run away again."

It took Will a moment to digest that. "Tanner doesn't really want to run away. He wants to stay with you."

"He must stay with his mother."

"You two could get married, like Isabelle and Jake."

It seemed the solution to their dilemma was so obvious, even the children had thought of it.

"It takes a little more than that for a man and woman to marry."

"What?"

Ward doubted Will knew what he was asking. He wasn't even certain the boy would listen to the answer. He simply loved asking questions.

Besides, Ward didn't want to answer Will. As long as no one knew he was Tanner's father, he couldn't say much without creating false impressions that would be difficult to straighten out later.

"I think you ought to ask Isabelle."

Fortunately, before Will could ask why he should ask Isabelle, Tanner and Marina started toward them. Tanner didn't look happy, but he seemed calmer.

Marina, however, seemed upset enough for both of them.

"Will, why don't you and Tanner go water your horses," Marina said.

"We already watered them," Will said.

"Then give them some hay."

"Jake says not to feed a horse when you've got to ride him."

"Then rub them down. Braid their manes if you like. I have to talk to Ward."

"Jake says any self-respecting horse would rather be shot than have its mane braided."

"Why don't you and Tanner have a race," Ward said. "See which of you can make it to that big cottonwood we saw on the way to the falls."

Ward knew Marina was really upset when Tanner and Will set out at a gallop and she didn't give them more than a quick glance to make certain they didn't run anybody down.

"This can't go on," she said.

"I agree."

"He ran away from me."

"I know."

"Thank you for bringing him back."

"You didn't think I'd do anything else, did you?"

"I hardly know what I think any longer. Ever since he met you, Tanner hasn't been acting like himself. What did you do to him? He's never acted like this about Bud."

"I didn't do anything but like him back."

"Bud likes him, and he knows him better than you. Why should he want to be with you so badly that he would run away from me?"

"Maybe he can sense how much I love him."

Marina didn't look convinced.

"We have to tell him who I am. He thinks his father is dead. He wants me to take his place."

"He told me," Marina said.

"We have to tell him," Ward insisted.

"I know," she admitted.

"When?"

Marina bit her lower lip. "I don't know. For years I wracked my brain trying to find a way to convince him you were gone for good. Now I've got to turn around and convince him you're here."

"It might be easier if he knew he was going to live with both of us."

"Easier for Tanner, easier for you, but what about me?" she demanded. "Do you think it'll be easy for me to live with a man who walked out on me?"

"Things happened, words were spoken, that can never be changed, that can never be forgiven," he said softly. "They simply have to be forgotten."

"Do you think I can forget you had no faith in me, that your mother branded me a whore, that my family turned their backs on me, that people I'd known my whole life crossed the street to keep from having to speak to me?"

"I'm doing everything I can to forget what my brother did to you."

Marina looked at him in disbelief. "Can you?"

"If I don't, I'll want to kill him. I'd much rather love you."

Marina's look changed to one of fright. "I don't want you to love me. I don't want to love you."

"I know, but I intend to change your mind."

"Ward, don't do this to me."

"Do what?"

"Make me feel guilty for not loving you."

"I'm not."

"Yes, you are. You're forgetting what Ramon did. You want to love me, to be a father to Tanner. I'm the only obstacle in the way of a perfect solution to this horrible mess. You don't have to be so good. Nobody's going to give you a sainthood."

Ward smiled. If she only knew how far he was from wanting to be a saint. The thoughts filling his mind would have gotten him thrown out of even the most liberal fraternity of holy men.

"One thing about being a cowboy, you get plenty

of time to think. I didn't know it seven years ago, but I was so desperate for my family to love me, I threw away my real chance for love. I don't mean to do that again. If forgetting about what Ramon did will give me a second chance, I think I'm getting off cheap."

"I can't be so noble."

She sounded tired and defeated, but Ward knew it was only a reaction to the shock of Tanner's running away. She felt safe now. She could admit weakness. It made him feel good. Whether she knew it or not, she had begun to trust him.

After trust, maybe she could learn to love.

"I can't decide now," she said. "I know I should, but I can't."

"Then we must tell Tanner."

Her anger flared again. "What makes you think you have the right to barge in here and start issuing ultimatums?"

"I didn't create this mess, Marina. I'm just as much a victim as you. But I refuse to give in. Or give up."

"You think I'm giving up?"

"No, but whether we decide to live together or not, we have to tell Tanner. If we don't, somebody will."

"I'll tell him, but I've got to decide how to do it without upsetting him."

Their conversation was interrupted by Tanner and Will rounding a corner in town and heading for them at a mad gallop.

"I won!" Tanner shouted as he shot past, going too fast to stop next to Ward and Marina. "I beat him by a mile."

"It's not fair," Will complained. "Not even Jake could beat that horse." Being the more accomplished horseman, Will had pulled his mount to a stop beside

Ward. A cloud of dust flew from under the horse's hooves.

"Maybe we can have a race at the ranch," Ward said. "We'll let Jake choose the horses so they'll be equal."

"Yeah," Will said.

Tanner, who'd turned around and reached the group, didn't look so excited about the idea.

"Come on, Will. We'd better get home soon or we won't get dinner."

"You could stay here," Tanner said. "Mrs. Pruitt would feed you."

"We'd better let Ward go," Marina said. "We've taken up too much of his time."

"Ward doesn't mind, do you?" Tanner asked.

"I'll be back tomorrow," he said to Marina. "Maybe we can think of something by then."

No one was more surprised than Ward when Tanner burst into the ranch house that night just as everyone was getting ready to go to bed.

"Archie Johon's got the cholera," he announced excitedly. "Mama said we had to leave right away."

Marina, carrying Dale, followed. "I hope you don't mind my bringing the children here," she said to Isabelle. "I couldn't let them stay in Cypress Bend."

"Of course not," Isabelle said. "You can stay here as long as you want."

"I want you to keep them for me. Ward and I have to go back."

Ward felt that hated sense of helplessness sweep over him. "I can only help if they'll let me. Even then I won't be able to save everybody."

"It's worth it, even if you only save one."

Ward knew Marina was right. He would have to

convince himself it wasn't the ones who died but the ones who lived that mattered.

"Let me get my medical bag."

"Where is it?" Drew asked. "I've never seen it."

"I keep it packed away. I've only had it out once since the war ended."

"When you took the bullet out of Jake?"

Ward nodded.

Chapter Twenty

"You must boil every drop of water you put in your mouth," Ward announced. "There's a lot we don't know about cholera, but we do know it's transferred by contaminated water."

It was well after midnight. People were sleepy and cranky. The meager light given out by kerosene lanterns and candles cast eerie shadows across careworn faces. Most of the children had come in their bedclothes. Everyone had gathered in the saloon, a large rectangular building with bare walls and a dirt floor. In the face of danger, the women had dropped their objection to stepping across the threshold. Ward saw frightened, angry faces staring at him from every corner of the room. They didn't know him and they didn't want him there. But in their fear and ignorance, they were forced to turn to him.

For the first time in his medical career, Ward didn't feel powerless. He could help these people if he could only convince them to listen, to believe him, to do what he asked.

Like the rest of the women, Mrs. Pruitt seemed ready to depend on him entirely. However, as Ward soon found out, that didn't mean she was ready to accept his orders without thoroughly examining each one.

"We'll spend half our day standing over the stove and the wash pot," she complained.

"Would you rather have cholera?" Ward asked. Marina's wince told him he was being too rough on inflamed sensibilities, but he had no patience with silly objections when people's lives were at stake.

"Wash everything you use," Ward continued. "Pots, pans, dishes, clothes, bedding. Especially yourselves. The worst outbreaks of cholera in the army occurred in camps that were filthy."

"Our town's not filthy!" Mrs. Pruitt stated, her complexion turning a ruddy color.

"I know that," Ward replied. "I'm just trying to say cholera is spread through dirt and contaminated water."

"It'll use up a year's supply of wood," one of the men objected.

"Would you rather use it to boil clothes or build coffins?"

They might be surrounded by huge trees, but it took a lot of work to reduce one to usable firewood. With land to be plowed and spring planting to be done, the men could ill afford the time.

But Ward held firm. He was certain some of the men hadn't bathed in a month. From the looks of the children, water hadn't touched their bodies since the last time they went swimming in the river.

"How is all this washing and boiling going to stop

the cholera?" asked one woman. She was skeptical but clearly willing to be convinced.

"It kills germs that spread the disease. You can't see them," Ward said, aware that he might be undermining his own orders, "but they're there."

"I ain't believing in nothing I can't see," one man stated.

"Have you ever been sick?" Ward asked him.

"I had the influenza two winters back."

"Did you see what gave you the influenza?"

"Well, no, but—"

"You won't see what gives you cholera, typhus, yellow fever, or dysentery," Ward said, "but you'll die just the same."

The man was silenced, but he didn't look convinced.

"I know some of what I'm saying may be hard to believe, but you must understand that if the cholera gets a hold on this community, nearly all of you will be dead within a week. I'm not going to tell you I know how to cure it. I don't."

"That makes you no different from the rest of us," one man said.

"Not at all," Marina said, answering before Ward. "Dr. Dillon spent three years studying medicine at the University of Virginia. He spent four years serving as a surgeon during the war. He knows more than all of us together."

Ward wasn't certain whether he was more surprised at being called "Dr. Dillon" or at Marina's spirited defense of his medical abilities.

"Cholera is here," Ward said. "I can't change that, but I do know how to keep it from spreading. Stay away from people who're ill unless you're caring for them. It's especially important that you burn any soiled clothes and bedding."

"We can't burn our beds and clothes!" several people protested. "You might as well ask us to burn our houses down over our heads."

"If you die, that's exactly what I'll do."

"Why won't you be getting the cholera?" a woman asked.

"If I don't exercise all the precautions I just outlined, I can get it just as easily as you or anyone else."

"Then what are you doing here?"

"He came to help," Marina said. "He knew as soon as he found that family dead of cholera that there was a danger somebody here would get it."

"What family?" several asked at once.

"We found a wagon up the valley," Ward said. "Everybody was dead but the baby."

"What happened to it?"

"She's perfectly healthy now," Marina said, "thanks to Dr. Dillon."

"Why didn't we know about this family?" someone asked.

"I came into town that same day, but your mayor and his wife assured me nobody was sick."

"There wasn't," Mrs. Pruitt said, her usual forcefulness having deserted her. "I didn't see no sense in getting everybody riled up."

"Well, Archie Johon's sick now," someone said. "It was his place they stopped at."

"Yeah, I remember now," another added. "Right nice-looking family. Couldn't figure out what they was doing going up the valley. Didn't look like a rancher to me."

"Do you know their name?" Ward asked.

"Don't recall they said."

"Well if anybody remembers, tell me or my—Mrs. Dillon," Ward said after stumbling. He didn't know what Marina was going to say to his announcing they had the same name, but he figured they both had more important things to worry about right now.

"Now all of you go home. Stay there unless it's necessary to leave. If anybody gets sick, report it to me or Mrs. Pruitt immediately. Remember, wash everything you use, especially your hands if they're anywhere near food."

"It's a lot of tomfoolery, if you ask me," one man said as they started to file out.

"What do we do for a body who gets sick?" a woman asked.

Everybody stopped and turned back to Ward.

"If they've got a fever, keep them cool. If they're clammy cold, keep them warm. Most important of all, try to get liquids down them."

"How're we going to do that when they're delirious?" one asked.

"Pour it down their throats if you have to. Put a little sugar and salt in it."

"How much?"

"About a teaspoon of salt and a tablespoon of sugar in a gallon of water."

"That would make me throw up," one man objected.

"If you get the cholera, you'll swallow every bit of it, Penton Belknap," his wife informed him promptly. "Or I'll choke you trying. I've no hankering to bring up eleven children by myself, not with me swelling up with the twelfth this very minute."

But Ward could tell most of the people didn't believe in his invisible germs. He would need to give them something they could understand before they'd follow his advice. And he needed every family's co-operation if he was to stop the cholera.

"You'd better show me how to get to Archie Johon's," Ward said.

"I'll show you," Clyde Pruitt volunteered.

"I'm coming, too," Marina said.

"Why don't you stay here and help the women get started with their washing and boiling."

"Mrs. Pruitt can do that. Mr. Johon's wife and family will need my help more than anybody here."

By the time they reached the Johons' cabin, one of his children had come down with cholera. The first thing Ward did upon entering the filthy household was to order the rest of the children outside and down to the river to wash.

"Even river water is better than sleeping in their own dirt," he said, disgusted by what he saw.

Archie suffered from painful cramps in his stomach. A whiff of chloroform from a bottle Ward kept in his medical bag eased his pain.

"As soon as Marina can get some water boiled, I want you to see how much you can get down him," Ward told Mrs. Johon.

"What about Katie?" the nearly hysterical woman asked.

The child had fallen ill after her father, but the disease seemed to have a firmer grip on her.

"Keep her warm, and see if you can get any liquids down her."

Ward hauled the bedding used by the other four children outside. "You can sleep under those trees," he told them as they dried off.

A little girl whimpered for her mother.

"You'll have to care for her tonight," Ward told her

oldest brother. "Your mother has all she can do to take care of your father and little sister."

"Do you think the other children will get the cholera?" Marina asked.

"Once it's in a family, it nearly always hits everybody."

"Do you think the little girl and her father will get better?"

"I don't know."

It was like the war all over again, but this time nobody was going to stop him from using everything he knew. Ward set to work doing what he could to help Mrs. Johon with her husband and Katie. Marina began cleaning the kitchen. It would be a long night for both of them.

Cholera struck the youngest boy about an hour before dawn. One by one, the rest of the children came down with it before noon.

"The poor woman will go crazy if she loses her whole family," Marina said to Ward as they struggled unsuccessfully to get the children to keep liquid down.

"If she doesn't fall sick herself before nightfall," Ward said without ceasing his efforts to force liquid into the oldest boy. He and his father seemed to be the least desperately ill.

Mrs. Johon had gotten nearly a quart of liquid down her husband since midnight. If he could keep it down, Ward was hopeful he would recover. An occasional scream from Katie caused Ward to cringe, but he didn't go inside the house. Her mother was doing all that could be done for her. He had to concentrate on the rest of her children.

"I can't stand to see these poor children in such

Leigh Greenwood

pain," Marina said, her eyes red from crying. She sat between a girl of about five and a boy of about four, bathing their foreheads and bodies to keep them cool, giving them water to drink, and praying their bodies could retain it.

"I can't do anything more to stop the pain," Ward said, going back to the middle boy, a six-year-old named Damron. He seemed in the least pain, but Ward feared he was in the most serious condition. Nothing Ward did helped him keep water down.

Mrs. Pruitt came to check on them three times during the day. She kept well away from the cabin each time, but she proudly reported there was no sign of cholera anywhere else in the town. Ward could tell when she approached the house for the fourth time that something was different.

"Elinor Olwell's boy has come down with the cholera," she announced. "She wants you to come right away."

"What are his symptoms?" Ward asked as he laid Damron back down on his pallet. The child didn't move or utter a sound. He just lay there, staring at Ward out of vacant eyes.

"Elinor said it came on him all of a sudden. One minute he was all right, the next he was falling down sick. He's got terrible pains in his arms and legs. He can't have a quart of liquid left in him."

"I'll come right away," Ward said. "Do you know if he had any contact with these children?"

"He's great friends with little Damron," Mrs. Pruitt said. "They play together all the time."

Ward had been afraid of something like that. Most likely the children from the wagon had given cholera to the Johon children. From there it had passed to Elinor Olwell's boy. But at least now he had something to work with. If he could break the chain, he could save most of the people in the village.

By the time Ward had washed and changed his clothes, Elinor Olwell was nearly hysterical. Her husband, white as a sheet, stood by their son's bedside.

"He's their only child," Mrs. Pruitt had informed Ward when he handed her his clothes to boil. "It will kill her if he dies."

"How long has he been like that?" Ward asked when he saw the boy. The cramping was so bad that even a whiff of chloroform didn't completely ease the pain.

"It started less than an hour ago," Elinor said between sobs. "Once I knew the Johon boys had got the cholera, I asked him most particular how he was feeling. Joe plays with their Damron all the time."

Ward told her exactly what to do.

"I already tried getting him to drink. He just throws it up again."

"Keep trying. It's the only thing I know to do for him."

Following the trail of friendships among the children of Cypress Bend, Ward went to every house in the town. He explained how the dead family had given the cholera to the Johon children and how Damron Johon had given it to little Joe Olwell, how their own child could have contracted the disease from one of these children.

Once again he stressed cleanliness, boiling water, cleaning everything that came into contact with food or water, constant washing of hands. He also repeated the treatment for anyone stricken with the disease.

This time the people believed him, so much so that some were afraid of contracting the disease from him. Most would only speak to him through closed doors. All were frightened.

"You're exhausted," Ward said to Marina when he returned to the Johons' house after dark. "You need some sleep."

"I can't. Little Katie just died."

Ward felt the familiar weight on his chest, but he couldn't let himself give in to it now. There would be plenty of time later. Right now he had to get Marina to bed. She'd been up for thirty-six hours. If she became too exhausted, she'd be more susceptible to cholera herself.

"I'll stay. You go back to Mrs. Pruitt's."

Marina tried to get up from her position between the two children, but she couldn't get to her feet. Ward helped her up. "I should have sent you to bed hours ago."

"What's going to happen to the other children?" Marina asked.

"I don't know. But you won't help them by collapsing. Get some rest. There may be more cases tomorrow."

"You've got to rest, too. You've been up just as long as I have."

"I will. I want to see what I can do for Mrs. Johon."

The woman sat rocking her dead child, kissing her forehead, bathing her face with her tears. Even though Ward was afraid this might cause Mrs. Johon to get the cholera, he didn't have the heart to tell her to stop. Marina did it.

Gently she took the child from her mother's arms and laid her on her bed. "Ward will take care of her," she said. "You must rest. Your other children will need you even more now."

Marina led her to the bedroom and talked her into

lying down for just a few minutes. "One of us will stay with your children and husband. We'll call you if anything happens."

Mrs. Johon lay down, but Ward doubted she would get much sleep. He could hear her sobbing softly. Marina wrapped the child in a sheet and carried her to the woodshed. Ward carried the soiled bedding outside, poured kerosene on it, and set it ablaze.

"We'll have to bury the child as soon as possible," he said to Marina.

"Can't we wait to see if her family will get well enough to attend her funeral?"

"Even if they recover, they won't be able to get out of bed for weeks."

Marina stumbled. Ward reached out to steady her. She leaned against him for support. Tired as he was, he felt his body tighten with desire. She felt soft against him. Need made quiescent by years of anger sprang up with sharp, nerve-shattering intensity. He felt a stampeding desire to hold her tightly and kiss her hungrily until he exhausted his remaining strength.

He restrained himself. When he kissed Marina— and he certainly meant to kiss her—he wanted her to understand exactly what it meant.

As he put his arm around her to lead her out of the house, he asked himself if he knew exactly what it meant. Less than two weeks ago he'd have sworn he hated her. His head wasn't working too well just now, but he knew that had never been true.

"I can make it the rest of the way on my own," she said when they were outside.

"It won't take long for me to walk you home."

"You can't leave Mrs. Johon. You'd never forgive

271

yourself if anything happened while you were gone."

"I'd never forgive myself if anything happened to you."

He wasn't sure the thought had crystallized in his mind before he spoke. But he knew he meant it. She had become a permanent part of his life, and not merely as Tanner's mother.

"Don't say that," Marina said. "I don't want you to feel that way."

"Why?"

"I loved you once, and it ruined my life. Please don't make me fall in love with you again."

"Could I?"

"When I came here I was certain I could hardly stand the sight of you long enough to ask for a divorce. Nothing worked out the way I expected."

"Do you love me, even a little?"

"No . . . I don't know. I'm going to bed now, and I'm not going to think of you or of me."

"Make sure you wash carefully. Tell Mrs. Pruitt to boil your clothes before she washes them."

Marina nodded and moved off into the night. Ward stood watching her as she walked with steps slowed by exhaustion, steps made awkward by muscles cramped from sitting with the children for so long.

He hadn't known much about Marina when he married her except that she was a beautiful woman and he loved her. But she was much more than that now. She was a strong woman, not one likely to throw up her hands in despair when faced with difficulties, not anxious to give up her independence. She was going to have a say in everything that concerned her and her family.

That wasn't the kind of wife some men wanted, but

it sounded great to Ward. Life could impose some heavy burdens. It might be considered selfish by some, a weakness by others, but he liked the idea of having a partner to help lighten the load.

If anything should happen to him, he wouldn't have to worry about Tanner. She'd done a fine job rearing that boy under very trying circumstances. He liked the idea that she wasn't a young girl anymore. Angles had become curves; lines had acquired a seductive give; slimness had matured into a lush fullness. Innocence had acquired wisdom, impulsiveness become tempered by patience.

She had become a woman, fully mature and in her prime. Men far less susceptible than Ward would have had their thinking and feelings derailed by her.

An anguished wail from one of the children recalled Ward to the terrible ordeal that still lay before him. He shouldn't be thinking of Marina now. As long as anyone was sick, he needed to concentrate on trying to keep his patients alive. Maybe he could learn something that would help other victims of this horrible disease. It was a chance he couldn't ignore, no matter how much strain it put on him.

He could stand anything as long as nothing happened to Marina.

Marina began to wonder if she had the strength to make it back to her room. She probably shouldn't have stopped at the Olwell home. According to his father, Joe was suffering even more than before. His mother was too hysterical to talk. She just sat at the boy's bedside crying without stopping.

Marina had left after giving Mrs. Olwell what encouragement she could. If she had stayed longer, she would have broken down and cried herself.

As she trudged the short distance to the Pruitt house, she marveled at what had happened because of her decision to ask Ward for a divorce in person. She doubted she could marry Bud now. She would have to find a way to tell Tanner that Ward was his father. To top it all, she found herself in the middle of a cholera outbreak. She could come down with the disease. She might even die because of her decision to help these people.

Much to her surprise, that didn't upset her as much as the realization that she was falling in love with Ward all over again. Dying would put an end to her problems. Loving Ward would only add to them.

She could still feel his arm around her. She hadn't been so tired that she couldn't respond to the strong arm supporting her, keeping her balanced while her cramped muscles loosened enough to resume their normal functioning. Her heart had raced. She could have put that down to fatigue if her brain hadn't felt as if it, too, was about to spin out of control. She couldn't deny it. She responded to Ward's touch the same way she had seven years ago.

Then again, maybe not. Maybe nothing was the way it had been seven years ago.

She had been seventeen, the oldest and prettiest girl in a family cursed with only girls. From the time she was ten she'd been told she must marry to help restore the family's fading wealth.

Then she'd met Ward, and everything changed.

She had accused Ward of being in love with love, but she'd been equally carried away by their passion.

She'd been too young to understand that people didn't like having their plans overturned, that young men of fragile ego didn't like having their suits rejected, that some men weren't ready to trust a woman they'd known only two days over the families they'd known all their lives.

No, she wasn't the same young woman, yet she still loved him.

Mrs. Pruitt met her at the door. "The doctor said I wasn't to let you near a bed until I'd stripped and bathed you."

Marina couldn't help smiling. Ward wasn't about to give up trying to take care of her even when he wasn't around.

"Come on through to the kitchen. I've got a tub of water all ready."

Marina was too tired to protest. If they wanted to treat her like a little girl, that was fine with her. As a matter of fact, she didn't mind someone else making the decisions. At least the unimportant ones. She was too tired to protest.

She let Mrs. Pruitt strip off the clothes she'd worn for nearly two days. Mrs. Pruitt immediately put the clothes into a pot of boiling water she had on the stove.

"The doctor said these was to go straight from your back into the water. He said I wasn't to take any chances after you being with those children all day."

It amused Marina to hear Mrs. Pruitt now quoting Ward at every turn, as though he were an unimpeachable authority.

Marina sank gratefully into the tub of hot water. She felt her stiff, tired muscles begin to relax.

"I heard that little Katie Johon died," Mrs. Pruitt said as she started to wash Marina's back. "Are the rest of them going to die as well?"

"It's too soon to tell."

"They always was a poor family, but they're nice enough. Do you think it was the dirt that did it?"

"They probably picked it up from those people in the wagon."

"They was dirty, too. I noticed it when they came here asking directions." She scrubbed a bit in silence. "I sure hope Elinor's little Joe pulls through. She and big Joe waited nearly ten years for that boy. It would kill 'em to lose him now."

"If anybody can save him, Ward will."

"You have a mighty lot of faith in that man to be so down on him as a husband."

Marina hadn't thought of that when she first heard about the cholera. She'd turned to Ward automatically. She guessed she did have a lot of confidence in him. Everybody else did. It just seemed to rub off on her.

"Ward was one of the top students in his medical class. If anybody knows what to do, he does."

Marina was finding it harder and harder to think. Fatigue invaded her brain like the incoming tide, seeking out and filling every corner. Mrs. Pruitt continued to talk, but her voice sounded farther and farther away.

"People are so scared they're not coming out unless they have to. Lester closed his hardware store. Lagrande closed the mercantile. I heard they're even thinking of closing the saloon. You know things are bad when they do that. People always want a drink when there's trouble. Leastways the men do. Ladies might, too, but they have to get theirs on the sly. Doesn't seem right, but that's the way of the world."

Marina could have told her a lot of things didn't seem right, but she was too tired to think of them just then. She'd tell her tomorrow.

Chapter Twenty-one

Ward's hair was damp, but he didn't have the energy to dry it. He'd left Mrs. Pruitt sputtering with embarrassment as he stumbled up the stairs wearing nothing but one of her husband's nightshirts. If he hadn't been so tired, he might have had the energy to laugh. He had to give her credit. She hadn't complained about having to heat water or leave the kitchen while he bathed.

"I'll have these clothes in boiling water in a jiffy," she'd said. Then she fixed him with a baleful eye. "Where are you going to sleep?" she asked.

"Tanner's bed," he replied without giving it a thought.

"His bed's in his mother's room."

Now he understood the reason for the severity of her glare.

"I know she's your wife, but she doesn't want you just now. Why is none of my business, but I'll not have a man taking advantage of a woman in my house."

Ward summoned the energy for a reassuring smile. "I'm far too exhausted to take advantage of anyone, even a woman as beautiful as Marina."

Mrs. Pruitt's expression didn't relax.

"I want to convince her to come back to me. I can't think of anything more likely to do just the opposite."

Mrs. Pruitt's frown transformed itself into a smile just as her husband entered the kitchen.

"How are the Johon children?" Mr. Pruitt asked.

"Their father's better, but the other children are still in danger," Ward answered.

"And little Joe Olwell?" his wife asked.

"I wouldn't like to say. Have you heard of any more cases?" he asked Mr. Pruitt.

"No."

"It's early yet," Ward said.

He'd made it upstairs fully expecting to collapse into bed the moment he could reach it. The sight of Marina peacefully sleeping stopped him.

The morning light streamed through the window, piercing parts of the room like arrows while leaving other parts in heavy gloom. Dust particles swam like tiny fish in shafts of light, on air currents stirred to life by the warmth of the sun. One of those shafts struck the pillow only inches from Marina's face. Ward moved the curtain so the light wouldn't wake her.

He'd always thought her beautiful, but she transcended beauty now. Her worries momentarily forgotten, she looked like an angel—serene and utterly perfect. He drew near the bed. He wanted to touch her, yet he knew he didn't have the right.

But something inside him refused to recognize

rules, refused to acknowledge rights, refused to be governed by any code of behavior but his own desire. It drew him steadily forward until he reached her bed.

Marina lay on her back, her head to one side. The warmth of the spring morning had caused her to let the covers slide to the floor. He picked them up and laid them on the foot of the bed. He felt guilty, as though he had invaded her privacy, but he didn't turn away. He couldn't.

She was too beautiful.

The thin cotton of her nightgown did nothing to disguise the shape and outline of her body. His own body stiffened with desire. For the moment, fatigue and the need to lose himself in sleep lost their hold on him.

He couldn't stop himself. His hand moved out and hovered over her arm, which lay slim and white across her abdomen. Her breasts shaped her gown into soft mounds that invited his touch. He lowered his hand until his fingertips brushed the soft fabric of her gown. He itched to caress the nipple he could see though the fabric.

He moved his hand away. It skimmed over her shoulder, whispered by her cheek, and settled in the rich, black hair that covered the pillow.

But that wasn't enough. He had to have more. He couldn't sleep until he had more.

Ward leaned forward until he could feel the soft warmth of Marina's breath on his skin. He allowed himself the merest silken touch of her lips. They felt warm, soft, welcoming.

Danger lay down this path. But the need inside him pushed him forward, beyond what he knew Marina would allow, beyond what he knew was safe.

He kissed her gently, lingeringly, sweetly. It was like the kiss of a young boy who was timid, almost too nervous to breathe, frightened he wouldn't do it right, afraid he might be rejected, certain he wasn't worthy, yet unable to draw back.

Her lips were like nectar.

Marina stirred in her sleep. Ward froze.

She'd be furious if she woke and found him kissing her. She wouldn't accept any excuse.

But he couldn't back away. Not just yet. One taste of her lips was too little—too much. The danger didn't matter. He had to kiss her again.

He tried to merely brush her lips. He tried to pull away after one kiss. But he had reached a point where he was unable to control his desire for her. His kiss deepened; he hungered for more, for everything. His free hand cupped her face, bringing her to him in a full, hot kiss.

Marina started to come awake, slowly fighting her way out of the deep sleep, the utter exhaustion, that held her captive.

What she did next was completely unexpected. She reached up, put her arm around his neck, and drew him down to her. He was certain she was too groggy to know what she was doing, but he didn't draw back. He would hold her in his arms while he could.

Memory of the first time he'd kissed her came flooding back—the tenderness, the sweetness, the elation, the feeling of euphoria that something so incredibly wonderful could be happening to him.

He felt like that now.

He sank to the bed, put his free arm around Marina, and kissed her hard. She clung to him with none of the hesitation or animosity she'd shown toward him from the minute she arrived at the ranch. She pressed her breasts against his chest, opened her mouth to receive his tongue.

She seemed as hungry for him as he was for her. For a moment longer they clung to each other.

Then Marina came fully awake.

Shock and anger showed in her eyes and expression. She pushed him away. "What do you think you're doing?"

"Kissing my wife."

Marina took hold of the sheet, pulled it up under her chin, and moved away from Ward. He guessed that knowing she'd kissed him willingly, even if she had been half asleep, made her even more angry.

"I may be your wife in law but not in any other way. You have no right to force yourself on me."

"I tried to stop, but I couldn't. You were lying there, so serene, so beautiful—so close. I couldn't help myself. I didn't want to."

Marina seemed shaken, but she was not a woman to be swayed by a moment's passion—his or her own.

"I told you I didn't love you. If I decide to live with you, it will be for Tanner's sake and nothing else."

"You can't do that."

"What do you mean?" She almost looked afraid to ask the question. She gripped the sheet more tightly.

"I love you. I want you to be my wife in earnest. I couldn't live with you, see you every day, have you within reach, and never be allowed to touch you, kiss you, or make love to you."

Ward had hoped Marina would be happy that he loved her. At the very least he expected some sign of relief. Her look of alarm hurt.

Was his mother right? Was he so unworthy of love

that just the thought frightened Marina? Living with Jake's boys, being valued and appreciated, had helped him rebuild his self-esteem. Tanner's obvious liking had given it another boost.

But if Marina didn't feel capable of loving him, all the rest didn't add up to much.

"I don't want to love you, Ward. I don't want to love anybody."

"Why?"

"I fell in love once, and it ruined my life. I don't mean to let it happen again."

"Are you afraid of love, or is it just me you can't stand?" He wasn't sure he was ready for her answer, but it was a question he had to ask.

"You're a fine man, Ward. You deserve to be loved. But I don't want to lose control of my life ever again, not because of you, Bud, or anyone else."

He could almost feel the chains fall away. It wasn't his fault.

"This time we won't have anyone but ourselves and our son to consider."

"You think you know what you want. Tanner thinks he knows what he wants, but I don't know what I want. You want more than I'm ready to give."

"You're frightened. I promise—"

"This isn't the time to discuss this. I'm tired. You must be dead on your feet. Go to sleep. We can talk when this is all over."

"I want to talk about it now."

"I don't. We'll say things we don't mean, make promises we can't keep. If you persist, I'll leave."

"You have nowhere to go."

"I'll go downstairs. I'll leave any room I happen to be in the moment you enter it. I'll refuse to speak to you, to look at you, unless it has to do with the cholera."

He knew she meant it. He might have recovered from the hurt and anger caused by what had happened so many years ago, but she hadn't. His pain had been of a white-hot intensity, but the worst of it had been over years ago. She had endured years of humiliation not so easily forgotten.

"I love you, Marina. I want to know you better, to love you more. I want to know my son better, to love him more. I will do whatever I must so we can live as a family."

He took her by the arms and kissed her hard on the mouth. For a moment he thought she would relax in his embrace, but her body stiffened and she pulled away from him. He released her.

"Don't do that again," she said.

"I don't know that I can help myself."

Marina looked at him with an expression he couldn't name. He thought it contained more fear than anything else. He was too tired to think. He could hardly stand. He turned and walked over to the bed across the room.

"Wake me in two hours."

He lay down and went immediately to sleep.

Marina didn't move. Even if she hadn't been exhausted, she didn't think she would have had the strength. She had been fighting the notion that Ward could have fallen in love with her again. She truly believed he only thought he was in love because he wanted Tanner.

Now she wasn't so sure. A person could say all kinds of things and not mean them. But a person's body didn't lie. Ward's kiss, his hands, even his eyes and the tone of his voice, had told her things she wouldn't have believed if they'd been put into words.

But that wasn't what bothered her. Marina had felt herself respond to him in a way she hadn't responded to any man, ever, except when she fell in love with Ward the first time. It scared her.

Try as she might, she couldn't deny a growing attraction that was no longer merely physical. It had grown up despite her determination that it wouldn't. She was afraid it was too much like what she had felt for Ward so long ago. She'd behaved foolishly then. Her heart had said she was in love, and nothing else had mattered.

Now a lot of things mattered. She didn't want to be that much in love ever again. Just as important— maybe more so, if she was brutally honest with herself—she wanted to be loved for herself, not for her son.

The cold spot just under her heart seemed to expand and spread throughout her body. That would be worse than not being loved at all.

Marina threw the covers back and reached for her robe. Weariness still consumed her, but she couldn't stay in bed. She looked over at Ward. The poor man was exhausted. She had no intention of waking him in two hours. She could canvass the village to see if there were any new cases of cholera. The townspeople already knew what to do. Ward would be of more use to them rested and wide awake.

She put on a dress she had borrowed from Mrs. Pruitt. In a move she now recognized as vanity, she'd brought only her best clothes. Now everything she wore had to be boiled. She couldn't afford to ruin any more clothes than necessary.

She washed her face, brushed her teeth, combed

her hair and tied it into a knot at the base of her neck. But even as she turned to leave the room, she found herself wanting one last look at Ward.

He was such a handsome man. She couldn't understand why no one in his family was able to see that in a slightly rough and raw way he was better looking than Ramon. There was nothing soft or pretty about Ward. There was nothing perfect or unblemished. His skin was brown and weathered from being out in the wind and sun. His body was lean and hard from working from dawn to dusk.

He was so strong, his grip on her had felt like a vise. He was raw power, unadorned, unpolished.

Ward himself wasn't even aware of it. He never had been. Why did he think Tanner was so drawn to him? He was everything the boy wanted to be. It stood out plain for all to see.

Clyde Pruitt's nightshirt didn't cover much more than the essentials. His legs were exposed from mid-thigh down.

There was something terribly erotic about the sight of a nightshirt that ended nearly a foot above the knee. She couldn't explain it because she'd never experienced anything like it before, but she knew its effect was dangerous.

She reached over and pulled the sheet up over him.

That only replaced one kind of tension with another. He looked so tired, so worried, she wanted to hug his head to her breast and assure him things would be fine.

Marina turned quickly and forced herself to leave the room. She was getting sentimental. Ward was a grown man, strong enough to take care of himself. The last thing she needed was to develop an emotional dependence on him. She still had to decide if she could be his wife, but she must make that decision based on clear, rational thought, not heedless emotion. Certainly not sentiment. That would lead to disaster.

Her own troubles were sent tumbling out of her mind when she saw Mrs. Pruitt standing at the bottom of the stairs, wringing her hands.

"Three more have come down with the cholera," she told Marina. "One of them is Clyde."

Marina didn't know there was such a thing as a mild case of cholera, but it soon became apparent that Clyde Pruitt was a very fortunate man. Not only did he suffer less than anyone else from the debilitating loss of body fluids, he stopped losing fluids after a few hours. He was even able to keep down the jars of salt-sugar water his wife made him drink one right after the other.

"Thank the Lord you were here," she said to Marina as she hauled more of her husband's clothes and bed linens to the boiling wash pot in the back yard. "I never would have known what to do."

"It was Ward," Marina said. "I wouldn't have known any more than you."

Marina made a quick survey of the village sick, but she spent most of her day helping Mrs. Pruitt so she could devote all of her attention to her husband. It fell to her to take the clothes in off the line. It gave her an odd feeling to handle Ward's clothes, to fold his undergarments. It was a kind of intimacy, a familiarity that caused her body to react in ways she never expected. It startled her to realize her breasts were growing more sensitive. Every movement involved in folding the clothes sent a twinge through her.

It stunned her when the feeling moved to her abdomen. It was as bad as when Ward held her against his body. She didn't want this to happen. She refused to allow it. She quickly folded the last of the clothing and put it in the basket out of sight.

At least once every hour someone came to the house demanding that Ward be waked immediately. They were already doing everything Ward had told them to do, but they wanted him to assure them their loved ones would get well. Marina told them Ward would see them the moment he woke up. They weren't pleased, but they went away. They were willing to have Ward come into their homes, but no one was willing to step inside the Pruitt household once it became known that Clyde had the cholera.

"You'd think he was going to infect them," Mrs. Pruitt said, angry that people should shy away from her husband.

Marina knew she would have been even more angry if they'd attempted to enter her house.

But standing guard over Ward's rest provided only a temporary respite from the tensions that bedeviled Marina. She decided she'd fix his breakfast to distract herself from her worrying thoughts.

"It's a good thing you got your boy away from here when you did," Mrs. Pruitt said. "If he'd had much time to play with any of the boys from the village, he might have come down with the cholera, too."

The notion so startled Marina, she nearly cut herself with the knife she was using to slice the sausage. Tanner had played with Joe Olwell. Even now he could be falling ill. She calmed herself with the knowledge that Isabelle would let her know at once if anything happened to Tanner.

"He's a nice boy," Mrs. Pruitt said. "He's going to

look like his father when he grows up. You'd better tell him."

Marina put the sausage slices into the hot grease and reached for the eggs. Some fried potatoes remained from her own breakfast. That, along with hot bread, jam, and coffee ought to be enough.

"We plan to," Marina said. Pressure continued to come from all corners. "I'd better wake Ward. He's going to be angry I let him sleep this long."

"It's been less than eight hours and him up for the best part of two days."

"He'll still be angry."

"Maybe you'd better let me go."

"No. You stay with your husband. I can deal with Ward."

But could she? She couldn't even fix his breakfast without stirring up all kinds of feelings she didn't know if she could handle.

"You worried about your mother?"

Isabelle had followed Tanner to the bench under one of the huge oaks that shaded the house and corral.

"Yes."

Ward had told him to stay away from Cypress Bend because the cholera was dangerous. It didn't seem anything could happen to his mama as long as he could see her, but now she that was gone, he didn't feel so sure.

He remembered her fright when she'd heard about the cholera. He'd felt it when she bundled him and Dale away as quickly as possible. Then she and Ward had both disappeared, leaving Tanner worried and upset. He was still upset. He needed assurances from his mother and Ward that everything was going to be all right. Jake **and** Isabelle were good to him, but it wasn't the same.

"When is Mama coming back?"

"I don't know. Do you miss her?"

He nodded. "She's never left me before."

He didn't want Isabelle to think he was a baby, but he was scared.

"She didn't want to leave you," Isabelle said, "but she felt she had to help the people in Cypress Bend."

"Is she going to die?"

"Of course not. What makes you ask that?"

"I heard Buck tell Sean people who got the cholera grabbed their stomachs and keeled over dead. Is my mama going to get the cholera?"

"Ward wouldn't have let her go if he thought she'd get sick."

"Buck said Ward could get the cholera, too. He said if he did, he was going to kill everybody in that damned town."

"Ward knows how to keep from getting the cholera. He's a doctor. He feels he has to help take care of the people who are sick. Your mother, too."

"Why can't somebody else do it?"

"Ward's the only doctor."

"Mama's not a doctor."

"No, but she cares about people. That's why she took care of the baby."

"I like Dale. I don't like those people."

"That's because you don't know them."

Tanner was certain that wouldn't make any difference. He wouldn't like anybody who caused his mother to get sick.

Drew came outside. "Are you mooning about your mama again?"

Tanner liked Drew a lot, but there were times when he wished she weren't so mean.

"I'm not mooning," he said. "I was just wondering when she was coming back."

"You won't know until you see her, so there's no point wasting time thinking about it."

Tanner almost said something mean, but he remembered that Drew's parents had been killed by Indians. Maybe she only acted tough because she missed them and knew they would never come back.

"It's all right for him to miss his mother," Isabelle said to Drew. "I'd hope you'd miss me if I were gone."

"Sure I would," Drew agreed rather perfunctorily, "but I wouldn't sit around mooning about it. You want to help me check on the horses?"

Tanner knew nobody had to check on the horses. It was just Drew's way of saying she was sorry. She was awfully mean for a girl, but she was nice, too.

"Sure. Ward said a man should never leave the care of his horse to somebody else, or he might soon find himself with a mighty poor mount."

"I take good care of all the horses," Drew said, taking his remark as a personal insult. "The first person says I don't gets a sock in the nose."

"Everybody knows that," Isabelle said, smiling.

Tanner didn't understand why Isabelle was always smiling at Drew when the girl made everybody else frown. Even Jake threatened to turn her across his knee at least once a day.

"Well, come on if you're coming," Drew said. "I got to get done and get to bed. I want to be in the saddle before the rest of this crew hits the ground."

Tanner got to his feet and followed Drew. He glanced back at Isabelle. He'd rather stay with her, but Drew would accuse him of mooning again.

"Come on, slow poke." Drew started to run. "Beat you to the barn."

Tanner knew he couldn't possibly beat her, but he had to try. Ward had told him it was okay for a cowboy to get beat. It just wasn't okay for him not to try. Even more than Drew, Tanner wanted Ward to approve of him.

Chapter Twenty-two

They buried Katie and Damron Johon together. The boy had died shortly before noon. Mrs. Johon, hysterical over the loss of her children, was finally persuaded to stay home.

The men of the town dug the grave, but no one would touch the children. Ward and Marina carried them through the village to the newly marked-off cemetery. They were the first children to be buried there.

There was no minister in the village. Clyde Pruitt had presided over all civil and religious occasions. It was left to Ward to say the words that would send these children into eternity.

"Dear Lord, it's with heavy hearts that we hand these dear children into Your care. I don't pretend to understand why they've been taken or why they should have suffered so before they could leave this earth, but help us all to believe they have been taken into the safe keeping of Your eternal love. Comfort them as You will comfort those who loved them so well and will miss them more than words can tell. Amen."

Marina turned away before they began to fill the grave. She couldn't bear to see them throw dirt over the children. She kept thinking of how she would feel if Tanner lay in one of those graves.

It would break her heart.

Her heart bled for Mrs. Johon, who must struggle to save the rest of her family while she tried to reconcile herself to her loss. Marina couldn't have done it. Tanner was all she had in the world. If she were to lose him, she would . . . well, she didn't think she could stand it.

That made her think of Ward. What did he have? How would he stand the loss? His family didn't want him. He lived with Jake and Isabelle, but in ways too subtle to be named, he kept his distance from them.

Marina thought it would have been easier to be an orphan. They could start over again without any strings. For her and Ward, the wound caused by their families' rejection stayed open, always bleeding, always painful. She could understand his pain because she suffered from it as well. But they had the cure within their grasp. They had Tanner.

They could have each other.

"I hate it when children die," Mrs. Pruitt said as she and Marina returned to the house together. "I feel like I could have saved each one of them if they'd just been mine."

"Nobody could have saved those children."

"I know it's nonsensical. It's just that Clyde and I wanted children and never had any. That kind of fail-

ure can make a woman queer in the head sometimes."

"There's nothing wrong with you." Marina could
tell Mrs. Pruitt wanted to say something but was reluctant.

Finally Mrs. Pruitt asked, "Have you made up your
mind what you're going to do with Dale?"

"I'll have to try to find her family. If I can't—"

Mrs. Pruitt grabbed Marina's arm and pulled so
hard, she spun in her tracks. "Can we have her?" she
asked. "Clyde and me? We always wanted kids, but
we didn't have any. I made up my mind to be content, but this is like an act of providence. She'd want
for nothing. We're not rich, but you won't find anybody who'd love her more than us."

The intensity of the emotion in Mrs. Pruitt's face
stunned Marina. She didn't know it was possible for
anyone to want something so badly.

"I'd thought I might adopt her."

"You've already got a little boy, and you and your
husband can have more children. From the look in
his eyes, he's just waiting for you to say the word."

Marina felt herself blush.

"It won't be for me to decide," Marina said. "A
judge will have to make the final decision."

"But it'll help if you recommend us. You found her.
You saved her. He'll listen to you."

"I don't know. I'll think about it."

Mrs. Pruitt seemed to collapse inwardly. "I had to
ask," she said. "You understand that, don't you? I had
to ask."

"I understand."

Mrs. Pruitt didn't mention Dale again, but Marina
could tell from her somber demeanor, the way she
moved about the house without her usual energy,

that she had counted heavily on getting the child.

Ward's return helped ease the tension. Marina had already washed, but he made her wash again.

"It's impossible to be too thorough when you've handled a cholera victim," he said.

Marina's skin was dry and chafed from all the washing. She knew his must be in worse condition. He washed and changed clothes every time he left a patient. Poor Mrs. Pruitt had had to enlist the help of several neighbors to keep his clothes boiled, washed, and dried.

"I can't say I believe in these mysterious little critters of yours," Mrs. Pruitt said when Ward checked on her husband, "but you must be doing something right."

"He sure is," Mr. Pruitt said. He still couldn't leave his bed, but he was clearly on the road to recovery. He credited Ward with his being alive.

"I don't know a thing about curing the cholera," Ward said, "just about keeping it from spreading."

But the people of the town had other ideas. They'd been through epidemics before. They knew they'd been extremely lucky. Even as they battled to keep the victims alive, they showered Ward with praise. Some said they were witnessing a miracle.

"It's all the doctor's doing," Mrs. Awalt said. She was one of the women who helped with the washing. "Until this is over, nobody in my house is eating anything that hasn't been boiled, not even if I have to cook the vegetables into mush and every bit of meat into a stew."

Marina smiled at Ward's discomfiture and was angry at the same time. He looked utterly unused to praise, uncomfortable even. She knew he'd never received anything but complaints in that miserable home of his.

But things really were going better. Ward told Marina he was hopeful there would be no new cases. That was why, when Marina came down to breakfast the next morning, she was surprised that Mrs. Pruitt seemed alarmed.

"Something's happened to the doctor. Nobody can find him."

Ward had always thought there was something soothing about flowing water. As he sat on the bank of the river, watching the water eddy around the roots of the giant cypress, a feeling of calm settled over him. For the first time since he'd been in Cypress Bend, he felt some of the tension at the back of his neck begin to ease.

For the first time in several days he was alone.

The long hours of solitude were one of the things he liked best about working for Jake. He guessed he liked people well enough, but he preferred the wide open spaces of the range, the solitude, the quiet of the night beneath a canopy of stars. A man could get in touch with himself, could listen to the quiet voices inside without their being drowned out by the noises of civilization pressing in around him.

His mother was right. He was more suited to working on a ranch than living in society. He understood cows better than people. Liked them better on occasion.

But right now he wasn't escaping the people. He was escaping their praise, their unending thanks. Their praise only made him more aware of his limitations. He did know a few things, but there was so much he didn't know, so much he couldn't do. They expected more of him now than he could give, as if being perfect once obligated him to be perfect again.

He didn't want to try to be perfect. He couldn't, and he didn't want anybody expecting it.

An impulse grabbed at him. At first he ignored it. It was too ridiculous, too silly. But it came over him so strongly that he couldn't shake it off. Why not? What did it matter? With a grin on his face and a lightness in his heart, he jumped up, stripped off his clothes, and jumped into the river. It felt absolutely wonderful. He hadn't gone swimming in deep water for years. It had been even longer since he'd gone swimming without his clothes.

It made him feel like a boy again. Almost as if he were doing something forbidden. Certainly something forbidden to a grown man. A doctor. Something Ramon would never have been allowed to do. That made it nearly irresistible. He suddenly laughed out loud. Thank God he wasn't Ramon. Even better, he didn't want to be.

Suddenly the weight of years of struggle, of failure, of heartache, fell away. He didn't envy Ramon. Much to his shock, Ward realized he was better off than his brother. He had a wife, a son, friends, people who needed and trusted him. He could do something. He was somebody. He wasn't perfect, but he wasn't an ornament. He had a function, a place. He belonged.

The feeling of relief was wonderful. It was like being released from jail after spending his whole life in a tiny cell with a single window showing him what he could never have, what he could never be.

Ward splashed about in the water like a kid. Fish darted away, eluding his efforts to catch them. A turtle sunning itself on a rock looked resentful of the wave of water Ward sent over his rock. He slipped into the water in search of a more peaceful spot. Even the birds in the trees above protested the disruption of their morning quiet.

Ward didn't care. Birds, turtles and fish could rest tomorrow. Today they were witness to his rebirth. He wouldn't let any of them ignore such a momentous event. This was his moment. He couldn't share it with anyone else because no one would know what it meant to him. Not even Marina.

Using powerful strokes, he started to swim upstream. After days of being confined inside, it felt good to stretch his muscles. The water was invigorating. The sun filtered through the branches of the cypress, warming his back as he swam upriver. The water was clear enough to see the fish that darted away at the appearance of this strange being in their watery world. Ward chuckled and tried to catch them. When his hand scraped against a rock, he turned around and headed back downriver. He was going to swim back and forth until all the tension left his body.

Then he would figure out how he was going to make Marina fall in love with him again.

Marina could hardly believe her eyes. Ward was swimming in the river, without any clothes. She would never have imagined he would do such a thing, not even knowing that the townspeople still kept to their own homes for fear of cholera. It wasn't like him. It simply wasn't something he would do.

Yet there he was, apparently having the time of his life. He looked more relaxed and happy than she could remember ever seeing him. She nearly laughed aloud when he splashed a big male turkey who was trying to impress a turkey hen. The big gobbler squawked in protest and took his courtship out to the meadow.

Marina felt guilty spying on him. She knew she ought to go straight back to the house, but she didn't. He was as naked as the day he was born. She couldn't move an inch.

If anyone had asked her, Marina would have said she couldn't possibly be attracted by a naked male body. Men were coarse creatures, often dirty, usually untidy. To ask them to bathe was akin to asking them to admit they were virgins. The cowboys she knew took pride in being salty in the least complimentary sense of the world.

Ward was a cowboy. He liked doing all the things other cowboys did, so why did she suddenly feel as if she could look at him for an hour and still not get enough?

She had already seen his legs. She knew she liked their look of length and power. All those years of gripping a horse with his knees had built strong thighs. The muscles moved easily under his skin as he swam. His calves swelled with more muscles.

It would have been impossible to ignore his back, shoulders, or arms. The work that built his muscles kept him lean, his skin taut. Muscles surged and retreated across his back with each stroke, his shoulders rising and falling with each arm's knifelike entry into the water. She had never associated muscles with body movement. The correlation fascinated her. The show of strength gave her a strange feeling in her belly.

That feeling turned warm and began to spread throughout her body as her eyes were drawn to the rounded curve of his buttocks. Marina tried to look away. She tried to concentrate on his feet, even the ripples that fanned the surface as he passed. She was certain no well-brought-up woman would stare at a man's behind, much less enjoy doing it. But she couldn't look away.

The heat spread through her body until she felt uncomfortably hot. The unusual feeling in her belly spread to her limbs, making it impossible for her to move. She didn't know exactly what it was about Ward's buttocks that mesmerized her so. It could have been the rise and swell as he kicked with each rhythmic stroke. It could have been the rounded curve of firmly muscled flesh that made her want to reach out and squeeze. It could have been the shock at realizing she found his body attractive, knowing she could have it for her very own.

All she had to do was say yes.

A gasp escaped Marina. Ward had turned over on his back. He was directly in front of her. There was nothing about him she couldn't see with extreme clarity and in great detail.

The sound of her shocked intake of breath had made Ward aware of her presence. He stopped swimming, and his body disappeared below the surface of the water. He turned toward the bank. He looked surprised to see her but not shocked. Marina was shocked and mortified to be found staring at him like a common strumpet.

"Is anything wrong?" he asked as he started toward the bank.

She couldn't answer, could only shake her head. He was standing up, nearly half of his body visible. Each step brought him closer, raised more of his body out of the water.

He looked impressive standing half out of the water. He looked like one of those paintings she used to read about in school when the nuns weren't looking, all pagan and wild. She'd never pictured Ward like that. It made him seem like someone totally different. Someone exciting. Someone dangerous.

"Why did you come looking for me?" Ward asked.

Marina backed up. She realized she was standing between Ward and his clothes.

The water only came to his knees now. Then he was out of the river, standing before her as though it were the most natural thing in the world.

Marina couldn't move. She couldn't breathe. She might as well have been turned to stone. A shiver passed through her from head to toe, restoring her ability to move. She averted her eyes.

"You'd better put your clothes on. Someone might come along."

"No one will come as long as the quarantine is in effect."

"It would still be a good idea to get dressed. You might catch a chill."

She couldn't catch a chill. She felt as if she had a fever.

"You don't have to turn away. There's a tree between us now."

She still didn't turn around, but not because she was afraid of anything she would see. She remembered every detail. She doubted she would ever forget any of them.

Marina reminded herself that she was an adult woman, that she was not a virgin, that she had borne a son, that she had been around men all her life. It made no difference. Seeing Ward swimming in the river was like seeing a man for the first time in her life. The sight shocked her; it also excited her in a manner that was new to her.

Her entire body ached with a kind of physical longing she'd never experienced before. She felt her muscles tense and relax; she felt shivers of desire run through her like the ripples over the water, on and on.

"You can turn around now."

She didn't think she could. She wasn't sure she could ever move again. Her strength seemed to have gone.

"Is something wrong?"

She felt his hands on her shoulders and stiffened; her swift intake of breath revealed the chaos of her mind and emotions.

"No."

"Then why don't you turn around?"

She couldn't. He turned her until she faced him. He wasn't wearing a shirt. He was naked from the waist up.

"You said you were dressed."

She hoped the unsteadiness of her voice didn't tell him how unsettled she was at the closeness of his naked flesh.

"I dripped all over my shirt when I came out of the water. I spread it over a bush. The sun will dry it in a few minutes."

She wasn't sure she could survive a few more minutes. She'd never expected the sight of his body to have this kind of effect on her. She hadn't been prepared. Everything was utterly beyond her control before she even sensed danger.

She wanted to reach out and touch him. He was so close. It would be so easy. Her hand moved, actually lifted toward his chest. She managed to move it to her face, as though she were brushing away an insect.

"I ought to go. Mrs. Pruitt was worried when she couldn't find you."

"Wait a minute. My shirt will be dry soon."

Why couldn't she move? Why wouldn't her mind work? Why was she letting herself be borne along on currents of physical sensation that buffeted her about like driftwood in a raging stream?

She looked away. "I ought to go."

He took her face in his hands and forced her to look at him. "Why? Are you afraid of me?"

"No." That was what she meant to say, but no sound came out. She shook her head and looked away.

"Then look at me."

She didn't want to, but he turned her head until she had to either close her eyes or look him full in the face.

"Don't turn away from me. I'm your husband."

"Not really."

"We could change that."

"It would take a long time."

"I thought we'd already begun."

They had. If not, her anger toward him wouldn't have turned to admiration, and she wouldn't be feeling so muddled and helpless. He pulled her toward him. Instinctively she reached out to keep him at a safe distance, and her hands came into full contact with his bare chest.

Marina had thought she was beyond any further shock, but she was wrong. She might as well have placed her hands on a hot stove. She tried to draw back, but she couldn't. Ward had drawn her even closer, catching her hands between their bodies. If she moved her hands, there would be nothing to keep their bodies from touching.

Marina wondered how long a person could live without drawing breath. She wondered if you passed out or if you just died quietly with your eyes open. She expected to find out. No effort of will could draw air into her lungs.

"You can't keep running away. Sooner or later you're going to have to decide whether or not you can live with me."

Some catch was released, and she gulped air. "We don't have to touch to live in the same house," she said, knowing it would be impossible to do anything else.

"I'd have to touch you."

"You're touching me now."

"Not like this," he said and caressed her cheek with the back of his hand. "Not like this at all."

"How?"

It was a stupid question. She didn't want to know the answer.

Ward brushed her lips with his fingertips. They felt rough and calloused.

"I'd want to touch your lips all the time."

"You couldn't do that when you're on a horse half the day."

He continued to rub her lips with his fingertips. Then he pressed them against her mouth until she parted her lips ever so slightly. He slipped his finger inside. Her jaw relaxed and her mouth opened. She didn't do it intentionally. It just happened. Ward slipped his finger between her teeth. It felt rough against her tongue. It tasted warm.

"I don't have to be on a horse so much."

She couldn't answer him. Her lips closed around his finger. Her teeth closed down on the fingernail ever so slightly.

Ward grinned. "I don't have to be on a horse at all."

She bit down a little harder, but his grin widened. He leaned forward until his lips touched her earlobe. Marina shivered from top to bottom as his tongue traced the shell of her ear. Involuntarily she bit down even harder. Ward responded by thrusting his tongue into her ear.

Marina's whole body seemed to grow limp, and she released the pressure on Ward's fingertip.

He responded by taking her earlobe between his teeth and nibbling gently.

Marina moaned softly and sagged against Ward's body. She felt his arousal hard against her abdomen. She tensed and pulled back.

Ward didn't release her earlobe. She didn't release his fingertip. Ward nuzzled her neck. Marina's lips closed tightly around his fingertip. She began to suck gently on Ward's finger. It was a simple action that didn't take much thought. She didn't have much to give. Ward's attentions to her earlobe and the side of her neck were turning her insides to mush. Her bones didn't seem to be doing their job either. She expected to end up in a puddle at his feet.

No one had ever attempted to seduce Marina like this. She had never had the opportunity to discover what such a seduction could do to her body, to her senses. For a split second she wondered where Ward had learned to do this. He hadn't known seven years ago.

But that thought was rendered meaningless by the mind-numbing sensations that rocketed through her body. And he wasn't doing anything but kissing and nuzzling her neck. And her ear. And the hair at the back of her neck. And the top of her shoulder. Such a small part of her, but it set the rest of her body aflame.

"We've got to stop," she mumbled.

"Why?"

He slipped her dress off her shoulder and covered her heated skin with kisses that felt like brands. She let her head fall back. He laid a line of searing kisses along her collarbone. She would wear them like a necklace.

Her attempts to keep distance between them failed utterly. She sagged against him. He held her close. He groaned when she moved against his erection. She moaned when her sensitive nipples rubbed against his chest.

"You've got patients to see."

"I'll see them later," he said as his lips deserted her neck and found her mouth.

Marina yielded. She couldn't stop herself. She wasn't even sure she wanted to stop. It felt incredibly good to be in a man's arms. She'd never let Bud hold her like this. She had been determined she would never allow emotion to sway her.

But this wasn't emotion. It was something altogether new. This was something much more elemental, much more powerful, something impossible to deny.

It had ignited a need in her that was so powerful, it frightened her. She didn't want to desire anybody this much. But even as these thoughts fought their way to the surface of her conscious mind, she found her mouth yielding to the invasion of his insistent tongue. Her own tongue responded, engaging in a sensuous dance—darting, whirling, wrapping itself around Ward's tongue, sucking it into her mouth, endeavoring to hold it prisoner.

"Are you trying to influence my decision?" she murmured breathlessly.

"Am I succeeding?"

"No." She didn't really lie, not entirely. At the moment, her brain was incapable of deciding anything.

Ward continued to kiss her; he pulled her to him. His hands played across her back and down her sides. She moaned softly when he touched her breasts.

Ward backed her up against a tree. She was relieved to have something to lean against. She felt unable to stand on her own. Her entire body was in an uproar. Ward's attentions to her breasts had released feelings within her that hadn't been tapped in years, some never at all.

His knee moved between her legs, and explosions rocketed through her. Her lips, her breasts, her belly, each seemed to be competing for her attention, competing for the right to overwhelm her body with sensations. She tried to hold out, but her resistance collapsed completely.

She didn't object when he pulled down the yoke of her dress and covered the tops of her breasts with hot kisses. Neither did she resist when his hand moved down her side, cupped her buttocks, and pulled her hard against him.

She wanted to, but she couldn't.

The heat radiating from his body poured into her, sapping her energy faster than the heat of an August sun. She had to hold onto him to keep from sliding right out of his arms. But that only caused her to press harder against him. Which caused even more heat to course through her body.

Ward's knee rose between her legs, gently rubbing against the inside of her thigh. The rough bark of the cypress tree dug painfully into her back, but Marina didn't care. Compared to what was happening with the rest of her body, she hardly noticed. Liquid heat poured through her belly in a succession of waves until she could feel her body become heavy and moist.

"We shouldn't do this." She felt she shouldn't, but she wanted it. She'd never wanted anything more.

She experienced a moment of panic when Ward lifted her dress. The feel of his hand on the warm flesh inside her thigh both shocked and excited her. She drew air into her lungs in a long, hissing breath. Her body tensed. Her knees closed tight.

"Relax," Ward said. "You know I wouldn't do anything to hurt you."

She wasn't afraid of him. She never had been. She was afraid of herself.

She managed to force herself to relax and let her breath go. But when Ward's hand moved between her legs, she tensed again. She gasped and the air became locked inside her lungs.

"Open for me," he whispered in her ear. His tongue darted in and out of her ear. It was just as though someone had turned a key. All the resistance went out of her body. She slumped against the tree and the breath escaped her lungs in a single whoosh.

Ward's fingers entered her. The sensation of moist heat grew more intense. He probed more deeply, found a nub so sensitive that Marina gasped and her body turned as rigid as iron. Ward was still teasing her ear with his tongue, with the gentle breath from his nostrils, with his teeth. She felt enveloped, surrounded, virtually consumed. She held on more tightly. It was the only way she could keep from falling down.

Ward had begun to massage her with tiny, spine-tingling strokes. Marina felt the pressure build in her body. But this was unlike any pressure she'd ever felt. It seemed to come from deep within her. It seemed to be in every part of her. It radiated out from her belly and then flowed back. It left nothing untouched.

Even as she felt the pressure continue to build, she felt the muscles in her thighs relax, making Ward's invasion easier. She hadn't done it because she wished to help him. It had happened because she couldn't help herself.

In a very short time Marina felt the tension begin to reach an uncomfortable level. Her limbs began to tremble. She writhed in Ward's arms, whipping her ear away from Ward's ministrations, driving the rough bark deeper into her tender skin.

"What are you doing?" she managed to ask. She hadn't known her body could feel this way. She felt completely out of control. She was frightened by feeling so helpless at the same time that she was exhilarated by the sudden sense of freedom.

"I hope I'm giving you pleasure," Ward whispered against the side of her mouth.

"You're torturing me," Marina answered.

"Give in," Ward whispered. "Let it take you with it."

Marina didn't know how she could do anything else. The waves grew stronger and stronger. She felt her entire body throb as each surge pulsed through her. She tried to hold on to Ward, but her muscles wouldn't respond. She felt herself grow weaker as the surges grew stronger. She gradually lost her hold on Ward's neck and collapsed against the tree.

Marina could hardly breath. She wanted to ask

him to stop; she wanted to ask him to rush ahead. Most of all she wanted to be released from the coils of this sweet agony.

Suddenly the strongest wave of all gripped her like a vice. Her body tensed; she held her breath. The coil tightened around her until she was certain she would suffocate. Then, just as suddenly, it let go, and she soared free. The tension flowed from her like streams of hot liquid.

With a groan of total release, Marina slumped into Ward's arms.

Chapter Twenty-three

The days that followed were slow torture for Marina. By day she and Ward helped care for the people of the village. They washed, boiled, burned, and gave advice on sanitation. Ward began checking every well in town to make certain the water was uncontaminated.

Even though there was a sense of relief, even of victory, in the village, Ward kept strict watch on each household where cholera had struck. Marina and Mrs. Awalt organized the healthy households into providing support for the bereaved and food for those unable to provide their own.

In the evening, after they had bathed themselves thoroughly and boiled their clothes, they were left to themselves. Mr. Pruitt was convalescing. Mrs. Pruitt didn't leave his side unless it was necessary.

Marina would have preferred time alone to attempt to order her thoughts, but she didn't get it.

With Mrs. Pruitt busy elsewhere, Ward kept up his assault on Marina's sagging resistance. He found a hundred reasons during the day to touch her or stand so close that their bodies brushed against each other. Moving away did no good. He simply moved closer. "Leave me alone," she told him, but it didn't work.

"I can't do my job and keep my distance," he said.

But he also insisted on kissing her. He didn't corner her or lie in wait for her. He simply walked up to her, put his hand under her chin, tilted her head up, and kissed her.

"How does this come under *doing your job?*"

He grinned. He did that more often these days. She found it nearly irresistible.

"It helps keep my spirits up," he replied. "Besides, it's an investment in the future."

She wasn't sure exactly how to take that. She told herself Ward didn't know exactly what he meant by it, either. But a suspicion began to grow in her mind that Ward knew exactly what he was doing. And why. And unless she wanted to find herself forced to make a decision she wasn't ready to make, she'd better know exactly what she wanted from Ward and what she was prepared to give him in return.

No one took sick during the fourth day. Even better than that, several sick people showed definite signs of improvement. Joe Olwell was doing so well, his mother cried from thankfulness at least once every hour. No one could get her to leave his bedside. When she wasn't washing him or feeding him, she sat staring at him. Her husband swore she never closed her eyes.

Marina didn't know how she did it.

The three remaining Johon children were still very

sick, but they showed signs of responding to their mother's care. Archie Johon had recovered so well that he wanted to get up. Ward had to keep reminding him that it was essential he remain in bed for at least another two weeks. He had seen too many soldiers suffer heart attacks from trying to get up too soon. Archie remained obstinate, but his wife told him she had lost too much of her family. She didn't intend to lose any more.

A couple who lived down the river died. They had refused to take any of the precautions Ward urged on them. A man driving a wagon bringing supplies found them. He burned the cabin down over them.

When the fifth and sixth day passed without any new cases of cholera, Marina wanted to announce the danger was over, but Ward wouldn't let her.

"I hope the worst is past," he said, "but I've seen it come back. We need to wait to make sure all the wells are safe."

Every day now someone built a fire to burn contaminated beds and linens. Marina decided half the town must be sleeping on the floor. Many people still held out that they didn't believe in Ward's invisible germs, but they continued to boil, clean, and wash. It irritated Marina that in the face of his success they still refused to believe him, but Ward said he didn't care as long as they continued to take all the necessary precautions.

On the morning of the eighth day, Clyde Pruitt came to the table for breakfast. He moved slowly, but he looked remarkably healthy. Ward and Mrs. Pruitt helped him to his seat. Mrs. Pruitt fussed over him every step of the way.

"I don't know why you had to get up," she said. "I

could have taken your breakfast to you, just like I've been doing for the last week."

"I'm tired of staring at those four walls," Clyde complained. "I needed to be up and about."

"You may be up, but you'll not be getting about," his wife declared. "Lean on the doctor. I don't want you wearing yourself down and getting a heart attack."

"I'm not getting no heart attack," Clyde said, letting himself be eased into his usual seat at the table.

"You were sure you weren't getting the cholera either," his wife reminded him.

"I hope the coffee's hot," Clyde said, retreating from an argument he couldn't win.

Ward smiled at Marina in a way that implied he and she shared a secret. Marina felt herself smile in return. She also felt a shiver run through her. It was another of Ward's attempts to out maneuver her until she had no alternative but to accept him on his terms.

She was determined to hold out, but she was finding it harder and harder each day.

"Everyone in town seems to be on the mend," Ward said. "If there aren't any new cases before tomorrow morning, I think Marina and I will return to the ranch."

Clyde and his wife put up a torrent of protests.

"You can't go yet," Mrs. Pruitt stated. "People aren't well."

"They don't need me to get well," Ward said.

"Someone else could get sick," Mrs. Pruitt said, not willing to give up.

"If so, I'll come back," Ward assured them. "But it's been a week. I think everyone's safe."

"We was hoping you'd agree to move here," Clyde said. "This town needs a doctor."

Marina's gaze flew to Ward. They hadn't talked about it, but she knew he still didn't want to be a doctor.

"Thank you," Ward said, reacting more calmly than Marina had expected, "but I couldn't do that. You don't have enough people here, and you're all extremely healthy. I could starve to death waiting for someone to get sick."

"We got seventeen families," Clyde said.

"I'll be happy to lend a hand if anybody gets sick or hurt," Ward said, "but I can't stay here. I have a family of my own that needs me."

Marina felt her pulse quicken. She didn't know whether he meant Jake and Isabelle's family or her and Tanner. Maybe he meant both. There were still a lot of things she had to decide before she went back to the ranch.

If she went back.

"There'll be more people moving here soon," Mrs. Pruitt said. "Why, you have no idea how big this town can grow."

"It'll never be large," Ward said. "There's nothing up river except mountains. It's too far from San Antonio. This is cattle country. It won't ever be anything else."

"But—"

"Leave the man alone, Jerrine," her husband said. "He may not be right about this town, but he's got a right to do what he wants. After all, we weren't too gentle with him when he came to warn us. He can't have much good feeling for us."

"I've got plenty of good feeling toward all of you,"

315

Ward assured him, "but I have to go back. There're people that need me more than you."

Marina had no doubt he was talking about Tanner. She wondered if he included her in that statement. More importantly, did she include herself?

She didn't know that she wanted to. She didn't know that she could.

"Well, don't make yourself a stranger," Clyde said. "I don't know what you know that nobody else does, but Jerrine and I lived through a cholera epidemic when we was young. Nearbout everybody that took sick died."

"I just used what other people have discovered," Ward said.

"And some ideas of his own," Marina added. She didn't mind modesty, but she wasn't about to let Ward take no credit.

Ward smiled warmly at her.

"Well, it's true," she said, feeling a little flushed at the look he gave her. "Besides, not all the doctors have accepted the new findings. You told me so yourself."

"It's always hard to know what to do about new ideas," Ward said.

"That's where the really good doctors come to the forefront," Marina said. "It takes a special kind of understanding to be able to separate real knowledge from unfounded theories."

She was proud of Ward's accomplishments. She wanted him to know that, to be proud of them himself. She wanted him to regain enough confidence in himself so he could go back to being the doctor he was trained to be. It didn't matter whether he practiced in Cypress Bend or somewhere else.

"Well, a good doctor doesn't neglect his patients," Ward said, getting to his feet.

"You telling everybody you won't be coming back?" Clyde asked.

"Yes."

"They won't like it. Elinor Olwell swears you're an angel sent from heaven to save her Joe."

"Then I'd better get out of town before she discovers I lost my wings a long time ago."

"Can you talk him into staying?" Mrs. Pruitt asked Marina when Ward had gone.

"I have no influence on him, no right to any. We still haven't worked out things between us."

"You could stay here," Mrs. Pruitt said, "you and your little boy. He'd never go far away then."

Yes, regardless of what they decided, Marina believed Ward would never be far away from Tanner again. The question in her mind was whether she had an equally strong desire to be close to him. She must, or she couldn't go back to him.

Ward felt better than he had in a long time. He'd been right about the cholera. He couldn't defeat it, but he knew how to fight it. He intended to write a paper about his experiences and get it published in as many medical journals as possible. Many doctors would discount his observations, but he didn't care. A few would listen. It would be worth it for them.

"Morning, doctor. You checking more wells today?"

It was Lois Engels. Her family had been spared. But rather than hide in her house, she and her husband had spent nearly all their time helping families that had been stricken.

"All the wells are fine."

"Elinor's having a hard time keeping little Joe in bed. Maybe you can drop in and have a word with him."

"Sure."

"Don't forget to drop your clothes in my wash pot. Jerrine's still too worried about Clyde." She nodded good-bye and went on her way.

People like Lois Engels made Ward want to consider staying in Cypress Bend, but he had more pressing decisions to make first. As uncharitable as it might sound, the good people of Cypress Bend were way down on his list of priorities. Marina and Tanner came first.

He felt something inside him tense. If they were going back to the ranch tomorrow, Marina had to make a few decisions tonight. Ward wasn't sure they would be the decisions he wanted her to make.

They were alone in the bedroom. They had made all the preparations for their departure the following morning. Everyone had said good-bye. There was no reason for Marina to postpone her talk with Ward. There was nothing else to do, no one to interrupt them.

But Ward didn't give her a chance to say anything. She had hardly closed the door before she was in his arms. He didn't ask. He didn't even give her a warning. He simply took her in his arms and kissed her thoroughly. She finally pulled out of his embrace breathless.

"What was that for?"

"Me."

"Do you always grab women when they're not looking?"

"Only if I expect resistance."

"You must encounter if often."

"Only from you."

That was a distracting bit of news. It had never occurred to her that just because she had been celibate since the night Ward walked out on her, he might not have been.

It occurred to her now. She didn't like the thought.

"I suppose you put it to the test often enough."

"Mmmmm."

What did that mean? She hadn't seen him in seven years. He could have been with hundreds of women. The idea repulsed her. How dare he be unfaithful with hundreds of women while he was still her husband!

She reminded herself that Ward had been told their marriage had been annulled. It wasn't a matter of his being unfaithful, just acting like any other man. When they wanted a woman, they went out and found one. There was nothing unusual about that. It was normal. It was expected.

But knowing that didn't make Marina feel any different. She'd thought he was probably dead, but she had never been unfaithful. She hadn't even wanted to be. Why couldn't he have felt the same way?

She tried to pull away, but he wouldn't release her.

"Let me go," she said, pushing against him. "I don't want to be another in a succession of women in your arms."

"What did I say to make you think something like that?"

"That nobody else had offered resistance. Did you get a regular, or was it a different woman each night? You were gone seven years. That could have been a lot of women."

"Not the last two years. I've been living on the

ranch. It would have been a bad example for the boys."

She turned rigid. "But during the war—no one there cared what you did."

"No."

"Did you go into town or did they come out to camp?"

"Both."

She pushed harder, but he still wouldn't let her go.

"How many were there?" she asked.

"Hundreds. Maybe thousands. I don't know. I never tried to keep count."

An open admission that he'd used other women to satisfy his appetites wouldn't have surprised her, but this cavalier assertion that it was too much trouble to keep track of the number stunned her. Not even Ramon—

She tried to move out of his embrace, but his arms remained locked around her.

"Let me go!" she protested. "I refuse to stand here letting myself by kissed by some conscienceless libertine."

"I'm not a libertine."

"You stand here, tell me you've been with so many women you didn't bother to count them, and you say you're not a libertine!"

Ward grinned. She felt like slapping him. He was proud of himself.

"True, they came to camp, and true there were hundreds of them in town, but I had nothing to do with them."

She stopped fighting him. "What do you mean?"

"Exactly what I said."

"Maybe not thousands, or even hundreds, but there must have been some. Men have needs."

"What needs?"

"You know. Everybody knows."

He was grinning at her again, only this time his grin was predatory. He looked as if he was about to gobble her up in one gulp. "I don't know. Tell me."

She couldn't, not even if she had been able to think of the words.

"Don't women have needs, too?" he said.

She couldn't deny it, not since that afternoon at the river. "Not like men. We don't need hundreds of partners."

His expression suddenly turned serious. "How many men did you entertain?"

"None!" She would have slapped him if she could have gotten her arms loose. "How dare you ask me such a question?"

"But you thought I would chase so many women I couldn't keep track of them?"

"I didn't think it. You were the one who said there were hundreds and thousands. I thought . . . It seemed awfully . . . I know men aren't the same as women. Besides, you thought you weren't married. You had no reason not to chase hundreds of women, maybe thou—"

Ward put his fingers over her lips. "At first I found a woman whenever I could. But it didn't take me long to realize I was only trying to forget you."

Marina stopped struggling. She wanted very badly to believe him, but she didn't know if she could. She didn't know why it mattered so much. She had never stopped thinking of him. Even when she gave in and agreed to marry Bud, she'd had to struggle to put Ward out of her mind. "You thought of me sometimes?"

Ward kissed the side of her mouth. "I thought of you a lot."

"Why?"

"I loved you. I married you. I left you. That was quite a lot to think about, enough to fill up more than seven years."

She moved his face until she could look in his eyes. "But you hated me."

He kissed her again. "Even then I thought about you."

"Me, too." She'd been able to admit that to herself, but she couldn't believe she'd just admitted it to Ward. A feeling of being too exposed, too vulnerable, caused her to add, "I was raising your son."

But was that the only reason? He was kissing her again, confusing her thinking, causing her to want to stop thinking altogether.

Ward pulled back far enough to look at her. "You're beautiful," he murmured as he brushed her lips with his fingertips, "even more beautiful than you were then."

Marina didn't believe it. It had been a long time since she'd had the time to take care of herself or the money to spend on clothes, but she wouldn't stop Ward if he wanted to think she had grown more beautiful. She liked that. It made her feel beautiful.

She had thought of him all those years. Even without Tanner, she had felt married to him.

Ward had begun to kiss her eyelids. Marina didn't know why she found it so comfortable in Ward's arms when Bud's touch had always caused her to pull away. Bud was the stable, dependable man who loved her even though she didn't love him. Ward had left her, yet she liked being held in his arms far better. She liked his kisses even more.

Bud would never have done anything as foolish as kiss her eyelids. Marina offered no resistance to Ward's lips. The foolishness of it made it all that much more wonderful.

"Why are you doing this?" she asked.

"Because I want to."

He was nuzzling her ear. It made it very difficult to concentrate. But it was important to her to know whether he cared for her for herself or only because she was Tanner's mother.

"Are you sure you aren't doing this just because of Tanner?"

"Who's Tanner?"

She knew he was joking, but it pleased her. "He's your son, the boy you intend to have no matter what."

"I want his mother just as much."

"Are you sure?"

"Let me show you."

He took her mouth in a hard, hungry kiss. Marina was surprised to find an equally hard, insistent response inside herself. She didn't understand it, but she had made up her mind not to question anything and to experience everything. Well, nearly everything. Tomorrow she'd try to decide what it all meant.

"Do you believe me now?"

"A little bit."

"Do you need more convincing?"

"It couldn't hurt."

She felt like a flirt, a tease, but she didn't care. She was twenty-four years old. People had shunned her, whispered about her, brazenly pointed to her when she had dared go out in public. That whole time she'd had to hold everything in, contain her feelings, sometimes not even admit they existed, for fear they would overwhelm her.

She hadn't dared ask for love. After a while she had convinced herself she didn't want it.

Now she knew that wasn't so. She wanted love—she wanted it desperately—but she was afraid of it. She could live without it. But she didn't think she could stand to find it and then lose it again.

She let herself relax into Ward's embrace, put her arms around him and let her body lean against him. His strength felt absolutely wonderful. She felt something inside her begin to relax. She knew almost immediately that it was the steely determination that had carried her through these last seven years.

She fought to hold onto it, but it continued to grow softer. She told herself she couldn't grow weak, she couldn't afford to depend on Ward or anyone else to protect her. But that something inside wouldn't listen. It told her Ward was here now. She could relax. He would take care of everything. She held him a little tighter, luxuriated a little more in the warmth of his closeness.

"Are you convinced now?" Ward asked.

He traced the outline of her ear with the tip of his tongue. Shivers ran all through Marina until she was certain she couldn't stand up by herself.

"Mmmmm."

She was finding it increasingly difficult to decide, or to care about deciding.

"I'll see if I can be a little more convincing," Ward said.

Chapter Twenty-four

Ward undid the buttons that held the collar of Marina's dress tight around her neck. The kisses he placed on the side of her neck and the hollow of her throat were more than sufficient to end her faint-hearted protests. Her legs grew weak. It took all the concentration she could muster just to remain on her feet.

"You smell good," Ward murmured, "all warm and soft."

She wondered rather vaguely how one could detect the aroma of warm and soft. Then she remembered snuggling Tanner when he was a baby. Maybe it was possible. Anyway, she liked the thought.

It occurred to her that she didn't know how Ward smelled. He felt strong and warm, solid and comforting, but how did he smell?

He smelled strongly of Mrs. Pruitt's plain soap. He'd washed so much in the last week, there wasn't a bit of Ward smell left. She made a note to remember to check again after they got back to the ranch.

So she had made up her mind to go back. She hadn't known that until just now.

"Am I convincing you?" he asked. He undid enough buttons to expose the top of her breasts.

"You've got my attention," she managed to say.

Ward chuckled and led her over to the bed. Marina was relieved to sink down on its softness. She lay back and gave herself up to Ward's attentions.

He lay down beside her. He pulled the dress off her shoulders. "Has anybody ever told you what beautiful shoulders you have?" he asked as he dropped kiss after kiss on her hot skin. "All white and soft."

"Nobody's seen them but you."

He stopped long enough to look up at her.

"Well, maybe Tanner, but I don't think he was impressed."

Marina had never attempted to categorize men's smiles, but she had no trouble labeling the grin that spread over Ward's face as pure proprietary pleasure.

"I'll teach him better," Ward said.

Marina liked the idea of Ward teaching their son to appreciate women. She liked even better Ward's demonstration of his own appreciation. She let herself lie back and luxuriate in it. It seemed she'd spent her whole life without male appreciation.

Marina felt as limp as a boiled cabbage. She didn't think she could have moved if she'd wanted to, but she didn't want to. Ward was kissing the inside of her arm. She'd never imagined a man would do such a thing. She'd never imagined she would like it. She was discovering she was wrong on both counts.

"I used to dream about doing this," Ward said, his

lips still against her skin. "On nights when I couldn't sleep, I would imagine kissing every part of your body."

"But you were still angry with me."

"I tried to imagine other women, but it was always you."

She had been no more successful in banishing Ward from her thoughts. If she'd ever had any doubts about why she wanted to see Ward herself rather than send a lawyer, she didn't have any now. She had to see him again. She had to know it was over.

But it wasn't. It never had been. Seven years ago was just the beginning. Now it was up to them to decide the ending.

Ward leaned over and kissed her lips. "Have I told you how much I like kissing you?"

"You could tell me again." She could never hear it enough. The hunger was too deep.

"I think about kissing you even before I wake up," Ward said as he tugged gently at the corner of her mouth. "It's all I can do not to get out of bed and kiss you awake."

"I think I'd like that better than Mrs. Pruitt's rooster."

He smiled. "I think about it all during the day when I'm talking to other men's wives. I tell myself none of them are as pretty as you. None of them have such rich ebony hair or lovely white skin. Not a single one is nearly as shapely as you."

He placed a hand on her breast, then allowed it to move down her side and along her hip. Marina's body tensed so abruptly that it almost felt as if she'd flinched at his touch. His hand moved up her arm, trailed along her shoulder, cupped the side of her face, and turned her toward him until she looked into his eyes, their faces only inches apart.

"No one has your eyes or your smile. None of them are you."

Marina felt her eyes begin to water. She wanted to believe every word Ward said. She wanted to believe that she was the most important person in his life.

Because she loved him. She knew that now. She'd been a fool to deny it for so long, an even bigger fool to go on loving him after what he'd done. But she couldn't help that. If she loved him now, she supposed she would always love him. She might as well accept that and go on from there.

"For so many years I was sure I never wanted to see you again," he said. "But the moment I saw you, I knew I was wrong."

She'd known just as quickly that she'd never completely gotten over him. It took her a little longer to realize she still loved him. And now he loved her. She wondered how much of that love belonged to Tanner. Could Ward separate the two?

Ward was kissing her again, invading her mouth with his quicksilver tongue. His hand had returned to her breast. His touch caused tongues of flame to erupt all through her body. It was becoming increasingly difficult to think of anything except Ward and what he was doing to her body.

Feelings and sensations that had lain dormant her whole life suddenly sprang to life. Her body reacted in ways that were as new as they were unexpected. She might as well have been inhabiting the body of a stranger.

Even through the material of her dress, Ward's touch caused her breasts to become sensitive, her nipples to become hard. He caressed the tops of her breasts with his fingertips, dipping lower and lower into her bodice until he found her nipples. Though her mouth was held in a deep kiss, she gasped when he began to rub her nipple with gentle strokes. She had never experienced such sweet agony. She hadn't known it was possible.

She didn't object when Ward pushed her dress down to her waist. She didn't have the strength or the desire. She had been denied for too long. She wanted to experience in one night everything she'd missed in seven years.

When Ward's lips deserted her mouth for her breasts, she thought she wouldn't be able to stand it. The aching quality of the pleasurable sensations that flooded through her caused her to writhe against him. That seemed to ease the ache at the same time it increased the pleasure. Marina hardly knew what she was doing. She was barely aware that Ward had slipped her dress under her hips and off her body. She didn't care, a few minutes later, that she lay naked before him. She only cared about the sweet agony that was driving her wild.

Despite the chaotic sensations competing for her attention, Marina knew the moment Ward's hand left her side and moved down her body to cup her bottom and pull her hard against him. The feel of his bare skin against her own shocked her. She had no idea when he'd managed to shed his own clothes. The feel of his arousal, hot and hard against her, escalated the tension in her body to the point that she could hardly move. Every muscle was stretched tight.

Ward's hand moved between them, splayed over her abdomen. Heat, warm and liquid, seemed to flow through Marina until she felt hot and wet. The need growing in her was so insistent, so overpowering, she could think of nothing else. She pushed against Ward, forcing him to find her, enter her, take her to the fulfillment she knew only he could bring.

But Ward drew back. He was holding off or slowing down. She didn't know which. She didn't care. It only mattered that she was nearly going crazy and it was all his fault. He had to do something or she would begin screaming loud enough to wake Mrs. Pruitt.

"Help me," she groaned.

She pulled herself tightly against Ward, trying to force him to reach the center of her need, trying to crush the pleasurable agony within her that was turning her into a mass of unfulfilled, unsatisfied craving. Never had she wanted anything so much. Never had she needed it so badly.

"It's better if you go slow," Ward whispered.

But Marina couldn't tolerate the thought of slow. It had to be now. Ward started to enter her deliberately and carefully. In desperation, she threw herself against him, forcing him deep inside her, trying to make him reach the need that was growing more insistent with each movement of his body, each brushing of her breasts against his skin.

Ward started to move within her. The relief from the ache was brief and slight. Within seconds Marina felt she was about to explode. The feeling grew and grew until it encompassed her entire body. She felt consumed by it, suffocated by it. It had to end or she would go crazy.

She moved against Ward more quickly. He tried to slow her down, but she was having none of that. He'd started this. If he wouldn't finish it, she would.

She was the one being driven mad. He seemed to be in total control.

For a minute, he fought her for control. But when she dug her nails into his back, sank her teeth into the lobe of his ear, he seemed to catch the fire that raged within her. Instead of trying to hold her back, he quickly assumed command. The waves of pleasure started small, but quickly grew in size and force until she felt herself being washed away on a tumultuous sea.

Stifling a desire to release one long shriek, Marina sank her teeth into Ward's shoulder and let the waves wash over her. One after another they came, lifting, tossing, buffeting, until she thought she could stand no more.

Then she was carried to the crest and suddenly the tension broke and flowed from her body, leaving her limp and utterly satisfied. She had just enough concentration left to feel Ward tense and then shudder. His body bucked with the force of his release, and he collapsed beside her.

It took Marina several moments before her breathing slowed down enough so that she could begin to think again. She realized she'd just put another brick in the wall of her need for Ward. Nothing that had happened on their wedding night could compare to this. It didn't even seem to be the same thing. They had been two kids exploring their bodies, unaware there was anything to be gained but the ending of a taboo.

Tonight had been entirely different. They had come together in much more than body. She didn't know what Ward would say, but she felt even more pressure to make a decision she wasn't certain was right.

This time, however, the pressure came from within herself. She wanted to be Ward's wife.

"Ward, I'm not sure I can live with you. I've thought about it all night and most of the morning. I want to, but I'm not sure I can."

Marina and Ward were on their way back to the ranch. For nearly an hour she had listened to Ward talk about his plans for the three of them. Despite the wonders of making love to him the night before, despite the knowledge that she loved him and wanted to live with him, doubts and worries continually nagged at Marina until she could stand it no longer.

Ward spun around to stare at her. "But I thought . . . I was sure . . ."

"But you didn't ask," Marina told him. "It's just as well. I didn't know myself."

"Are you going to tell me why?"

It was so simple to say, yet so difficult to make him understand: She didn't believe he could do what he had to do for her to truly become his wife. And that was what she would have to be. There could be no half measures. She loved him too much for that.

"There was a time when I could have lived with you without needing your love. At least I think there was, but I couldn't do it anymore."

"I love you. I told you—"

"I know what you said, Ward, but I need more than your assurances. I need to feel it."

"What do you need to feel?"

"That you love me for myself, independent of Tanner."

"Marina, I—"

"Let me finish. This isn't easy to say. Don't make it any harder."

He looked about ready to burst with impatience, but he didn't interrupt her.

"I've fallen in love with you all over again. I don't mean I've been in love with you all these years and finally realized it. There was something left of what I used to feel, but the love I have for you now is something altogether different. I'm not picking up where I left off. I'm starting all over again. I love you quite desperately, and I've got to feel you love me just as desperately. Not Tanner, not being a father. Me, alone, all by myself. I can't come to you as Tanner's mother."

"But you aren't. I told you—"

"I know what you said, and I've tried to believe you."

"But you don't."

"I don't know. I'm not sure."

"What can I do to convince you?"

"You've made a good beginning." Marina gave an embarrassed little laugh. "I suppose I need time to learn to believe it."

"How much?"

"I don't know."

They rode in silence for a few minutes.

"There's something else." She had to tell him the rest. It was cowardly to wait.

"What?"

"I have to know you'll never leave me again."

Ward looked stunned by her words.

"When it came down to a choice between me or your family, you believed your family. I know you've told me you know now that they lied, but you still love them. You still want them to love you."

Ward didn't deny it. "I spent most of my life doing anything I could to make my parents give me the same kind of love they gave Ramon. At one time I would have done anything, sacrificed everything for—" He broke off. "I guess I did."

For a long moment he stared in front of him.

"I wouldn't do that again," he said, not looking at Marina.

Marina felt awful for even bringing up something that was so painful to Ward. Her family had disowned her, but she'd had Tanner and Bette. Bud, too. She'd never been without someone to love her and support her.

Ward had been alone.

She knew he hadn't forgotten his family. She didn't want him to. She just had to know she was more important to him than they were.

"What do you want me to say?" Ward asked.

"I don't know. I suppose I'm trying to tell you I need more time. I love you. Of that, I'm sure."

"But you don't believe I love you?"

That was what it sounded like, even though that was far from what she meant.

"No. It means I know you love me, but I need to know, *to feel*, you'd want me back even if we'd never had Tanner. It means I need to feel certain you'll never choose your family over me again."

"Why should I? They've turned their backs on both of us, even Tanner."

"Maybe it's because it's all so unexpected, like the first time."

"What you're saying is, you'd rather give up on a chance of love than risk my leaving you again."

"Not just for me. I don't think Tanner could stand it."

"You think I'd do that to either of you?"

"I didn't think you'd leave me the first time. Sorry, I didn't mean to say that. I've tried, but I can't just pretend it never happened. The years that followed were too horrible."

Ward didn't respond. She supposed he was angry with her. He had a right to be. She not only doubted his love, she doubted his character.

"Your mother hates me," Marina told Ward. "She's spent years telling everyone Tanner is somebody else's son. She's not going to smilingly accept that you want to claim me as your wife and Tanner as your son. That will tell everybody she and Ramon have been lying. She's going to try to force you to choose between her and us."

"I'd choose you and Tanner."

"She'll promise you anything."

"I won't believe her."

"She's your mother, Ward. You'll want to believe her."

"I made that mistake once. I won't make it again."

Marina wanted to believe him. She was so close, yet that sliver of doubt wouldn't go away. Luisa Dillon had never lost a battle yet. Marina didn't expect her to give up easily on this one.

They were within sight of the ranch. A piercing shriek from the direction of the barn told her Tanner had seen them. It was only a matter of seconds before he was running toward them, one hand holding on to his hat, the other waving frantically.

Drew and Will came running behind him. Marina felt happiness transform her face and her mood. She hadn't fully realized until now how much she had missed her son, how much she'd needed to see him to know he was all right. Neither had she had any conception of the feeling of completeness that would surround her. Her family was together at last—herself, her husband, and her son.

"We have to tell Tanner," Ward said. "I'm sorry you can't make up your mind about me, but we can't wait any longer."

"You've got to let me tell him," she begged him.

"Okay. When will you do it?" Ward asked.

"Tonight or tomorrow," she replied. "I don't know. I've got to choose the time carefully. It's going to upset him."

"It would be better if we could tell him together, as his mother and father," Ward said.

"No. I must tell him by myself," Marina insisted.

"Are you sure?"

Putting aside her worries for later, Marina slipped from the saddle in time to catch Tanner as he threw himself at her. He hit her with such force that she lost her balance. Next thing she knew, both of them had tumbled into the grass, laughing and talking at once.

"I thought you'd never come back," Tanner said, hugging his mother as hard as he could. "Pete said you'd probably got the cholera and would die."

"Drew beat him up for saying it," Will volunteered.

"Will helped her," Tanner said, still holding his mother tightly. "Jake had a terrible time getting them off him. You ought to see his shiner."

"I gave it to him," Drew said proudly.

"Isn't at least one of you glad to see *I* escaped the cholera?" Ward asked. He had dismounted and was standing over Marina and Tanner, smiling.

"I'm glad," Drew said, "but I don't go around hugging people."

"Me, too," Will said. "But I don't hug nobody neither."

"Except Isabelle," Drew reminded him.

"She doesn't count," Will said. "Everybody hugs their mama."

Tanner let go of his mother and stood up. He looked up at Ward, his eyes wide with the need he had for this man. "I'm glad you came back," he said. "I told Pete you wouldn't get the cholera. I told him you promised." He looked as though he wanted to fling himself at Ward, but he held back. He looked at Drew uncertainly.

"Go ahead," she said. "I won't tell nobody."

"Me neither," Will echoed.

Released from restraint, Tanner threw his arms around Ward's waist and hugged hard. Marina felt tears spring to her eyes. She couldn't see well enough to be sure, but she thought Ward's eyes were tearing as well. How could she even think Ward would leave them for a family that had never loved him as he deserved? She was a fool for even considering it.

As soon as she had a chance, she'd tell him. She'd also tell him she was sorry she'd doubted him, that she'd never doubt him again.

"There's a man here to see you," Will announced.

"Yeah," Drew said, "some flashy-looking dude who says he's your brother."

The warmth and happiness of their reunion was suddenly drenched with cold dread. She glanced up at Ward. He looked shocked, too.

"Where is he?" Ward asked.

"There," Drew said pointing to the house. "He's standing on the porch."

Marina and Ward turned in unison as Ramon Dillon walked down the steps and started toward them.

Chapter Twenty-five

"He showed up two days ago," Drew said. "I wanted to throw him out, but Isabelle said we had to let him stay until you got back."

"Is he really your brother?" Tanner asked.

"Sure he is," Will said. "Can't you see they look alike, just like me and Matt?"

"Matt and I," Ward said, automatically correcting Will. "And, yes, he is my brother."

Drew, never one to be shy about expressing her opinion, said, "I don't like him."

Marina got to her feet. "If I'd been as smart as you, I'd have saved myself a lot of trouble." She put her arm around Tanner and pulled him closer to her.

"Let's not stand here," Ward said. "Let's go meet him."

"You go ahead," Marina said.

Surprised, Ward looked at her.

"He won't want a lot of people crowding around just now."

"Especially if we don't like him," Drew added.

"You shouldn't say that," Ward said to Drew. "You don't know him."

"I won't like him when I do."

Ward had to give the girl credit. She was nothing if not consistent.

"You sure you don't want to greet him with me?" Ward asked Marina.

She shook her head.

Ward wasn't surprised. After what Ramon had done to her, he doubted she wanted to see him at all.

Ward couldn't straighten out his tangled emotions as he walked toward Ramon. Here was the brother he'd loved from the moment he was born, yet this man had tried to rape the woman who was now his wife and the mother of his son. Ramon had lied to him, told everyone he was missing in action. Was it possible to hate him as a man and still love him as a brother?

Ward couldn't look on Ramon dispassionately. Merely by being born, Ramon had shaped Ward's life more than Ward had himself. His smile was irresistible, his love of life infectious, his generosity, when it didn't cost him anything, admirable. Ward recognized Ramon's faults and forgave them. Everybody did.

As he drew closer, Ward saw that Ramon had grown older, more mature, even better looking. How could any woman prefer Ward to Ramon? Yet Marina did.

Ramon held out his arms in greeting. Ward hesitated only a moment before welcoming his brother with a warm embrace. He might distrust him, want to knock him down for what he'd done, but Ramon was still his own flesh and blood.

"Let me look at you," Ramon said when he released Ward and stepped back. "You're as tall and skinny as ever." He poked Ward in the ribs. "Don't they feed you here?"

"They feed me plenty, but they make we work it off."

Ramon had picked up about thirty pounds in the last seven years. Since he was five inches shorter than Ward, it showed.

"They tell me you've been trying to save the world," Ramon said. His smile was irresistible. Ward couldn't look at him and not smile in return.

"Only a tiny part of it."

Ramon put his arm around Ward's shoulders, as if nothing had ever happened. They walked toward the house side by side. "They tell me you're a miracle worker. If you move to San Antonio, you could soon be a rich man."

"I'm not planning to move anywhere. Now come over and speak to Marina." Ward glanced back over his shoulder. "Then we're going to sit down and you're going to tell me what you're doing here. After that we're going somewhere private and have a long talk."

Ward didn't expect the surprised look that flashed on Ramon's face. Then he understood. Not once when he was growing up had he ever told a member of his family what to do.

"I can say hello to Marina by myself," Ramon said. "You go on up to the house. They're eager to hear what you've been doing."

"They can wait. I've got things I want to know. A lot has happened that I don't understand."

Ramon flashed the dazzling smile that had gotten him what he wanted for so many years. "We can't do all that now. Your friends are so anxious to see you, they're all standing on the porch."

A quick glance told Ward they were all there. Not even Zeke and Hawk had been able to control their curiosity.

"The hero and heroine return."

Ward couldn't convince himself that Ramon's smile was without mockery.

Marina and the kids had caught up. She looked straight at Ward. Ramon might as well have been invisible. "You'd better get on up to the house before they burst with curiosity," Marina said to Ward.

"Aren't you coming?"

"Take the kids," she said, pushing Tanner toward Ward. "I'll be up in a minute."

"You sure?"

"Yes."

Marina wanted to be alone with Ramon. A sliver of fear arced through him. Then he told himself not to be a fool. He loved and trusted Marina. She would tell him what she said to Ramon. She just didn't want Tanner to hear.

And if she didn't tell him?

Then he didn't need to know. He had made the mistake of not trusting her once. He would never do that again.

"Come on," Ward said to Will and Drew. "I want everybody to ask me all their questions at one time. I don't want to have to go over this again."

"You'll have to tell Matt when he gets back," Will said. "He'll want to know."

"You can tell him," Ward said, roughing Will's hair. He looked back. "Don't stay out too long," he said to Marina. "As soon as she's through with me, Isabelle's going to want to hear all about it from a woman's perspective. I don't think she entirely trusts any male except Jake."

"She doesn't trust him all the time," Drew said. "He likes to play tricks."

"I guess that's only fair. We played the biggest trick of all on him," Ward said.

"What was that?" Will asked.

"Getting him to adopt all of us."

Marina wished she could think of an excuse for going inside without speaking to Ramon. She didn't know what he could hope to achieve by following her all the way to Jake and Isabelle's ranch. She didn't want to speak to him, but it would be easier to do it now and get it over.

"Hello, Ramon," she said. "I won't lie by saying I'm glad to see you. Frankly, I don't know why I should even speak to you now that I know everything you've done to Ward and me."

He didn't look guilty, embarrassed, or even uncomfortable. He just smiled at her, expecting her to forgive him everything.

"Mama thought it would be better all around."

"What did she plan to do when Ward came back?"

"She told him not to."

Marina had never liked Luisa Dillon. She believed she was an evil woman, but she couldn't understand how any mother could do something like that to her own son.

"She thought it would keep the scandal alive."

"Considering you and she caused the scandal, I consider that impertinent as well as heartless and cruel."

"Ward agreed to stay away."

"I rather think he didn't want to return to a home where he was unwelcome."

Marina didn't know how Ward had stood being part of his family. At least her family had pretended to love her.

"What are you doing here, Ramon? Why did you come?"

"I want to marry you. I want to raise Tanner as my son. I'll adopt him officially. It'll be just like none of this ever happened."

Marina decided Ramon was impervious to reason. Once he got an idea in his head, nothing could change his mind.

"And how do you plan to get around the fact that I'm Ward's wife and Tanner is his son?"

She didn't know why she asked the question. She was certain he had an answer that was just as incredible as everything else he'd said to her.

"You can divorce Ward and tell everyone we slept together before your marriage."

She was right. He was crazy. "You seriously think I'm going to brand myself a harlot so I can marry you?"

"No one will dare slander you if you're my wife."

It was impossible to reach him. He was impregnable within the ring of his own conceit.

"Ramon, listen to me. Don't hear what you want to hear. Listen to me. I'm not going to marry you. I love Ward, and he loves me. Tanner has a father. I have a husband. We don't need you. Go home to your mother. I'm sure she's worried sick about you."

Ramon acted as if he hadn't heard a word she said. "I'm rich, handsome, an accomplished lover. Marriage to me will make you the most envied woman in San Antonio."

Marina started toward the house, a hundred yards away now. She wished it were only ten feet.

"You know I've always wanted you," Ramon continued, following her closely. "I wanted you from the very first. That's why I wanted to make love to you. I knew that once I held you in my arms, you'd never want another man."

Marina could hardly believe what she was hearing, though she was rapidly learning she'd vastly underrated Ramon's conceit.

"So you thought if you raped me, I would suddenly fall madly in love with you. It would have been rape, Ramon. There was no love involved, not on your part or mine."

It was obvious to Marina that Ramon had started to believe his own rationalizations. He could mistake rape for seduction, confuse force with passion. Anything he did was okay simply because he did it. Or had Luisa put all this nonsense into his head? It didn't matter. He believed it.

Marina walked faster. The tall grass grabbed at the hem of her dress, whipping about her legs when she raised her skirt. She wished she hadn't let Ward take her horse.

"I know you were angry about the other women I slept with while I was courting you," Ramon said, "but they meant nothing. I loved only you."

Marina hadn't known about the women. If she had, she'd never have gone to the Rancho del Espada.

"Is that why you married?"

"Why shouldn't I marry after you refused me?"

Anger mottled his perfect skin. Even now he

couldn't accept that she had been the only woman ever to refuse him, to actually prefer someone else. The fact that the rival was his despised brother probably added to his anger.

"I must have an heir," Ramon said. "I'm the last of the Escalantes. That name must live on through my sons."

Marina stopped and turned to face him. "I'm not going to marry you—not now, not ever. I don't love you. I don't even like you. Tanner's not your son, he's Ward's. We're going to live together. Tanner will be with his father; I will be with the man I love."

He looked surprised, as though he didn't really believe her.

"You can't do that," Ramon said. "You belong to me, not Ward. I wanted you first."

"That's the difference, Ramon. You wanted me. You thought that was all it took. Ward loves me. Me, not my name or my father's connections, or my son. Me. He would want me if I came without any of those things."

"I want you, and I shall have you," Ramon said. "If I can't, no one shall."

"For the last time, you won't have me or Tanner. We belong to Ward. We always will."

"Why haven't you told Tanner that Ward is his father?"

Marina wasn't sure whether it was the question or the way Ramon looked at her when he asked it that made her sense danger. He couldn't do anything to her and Ward, but he could hurt Tanner. Marina knew he wouldn't hesitate if he thought it would help him get what he wanted.

"I came here meaning to divorce Ward and marry Bud. Tanner had already been told his father was missing in action. Knowing how important a father was to him, I didn't see any point in telling him he had a father he couldn't live with.

"But Ward and I started to feel differently about each other. We were waiting to tell Tanner until we were sure what we were going to do. Tanner adores Ward. He's already begged me to marry Ward so he can be his father."

"He's not going to be angry when he finds out?"

"He'll be delighted. You saw how he greeted Ward." She hoped Ramon believed her. It was essential he not say a word to Tanner until she talked to her son. "Now, I need to go talk to my hosts. After forcing them to keep my son for over a week, it would be rude if I put it off any longer."

Marina hoped that would be the end of Ramon's crazy idea, but she doubted it. She'd talk to Ward the minute she got a chance. Maybe he could help her convince Ramon to give up and go home. She'd also warn him to make sure Ramon didn't get Tanner off alone.

"Besides, I have a baby I haven't seen in more than a week."

She nearly laughed at the look of surprise on Ramon's face. She hoped that news would keep him off balance for a while. She certainly didn't mean to explain it to him.

Tanner was disappointed in Ramon. He'd never seen Ramon do anything more than ride up to Bud's ranch, but he'd expected Ward's brother to be an expert cowboy. It hadn't taken him long to realize Ramon was more show than substance. He rode a magnificent horse with thoroughbred and Morgan blood in him. He was an excellent rider with an excellent seat, but he couldn't *do* anything.

Ramon caught up with the kids about a mile from the ranch. He said he'd gotten bored taking a nap, that he was anxious for a good, long ride. Tanner didn't understand when Buck looked unbelieving and Drew made a rude noise.

Ramon, however, quickly became bored with Buck's work. When Tanner resisted his urging to ride on ahead alone, Ramon challenged him to a race.

"I've heard you've got the fastest horse in this part of Texas," Ramon said. "I wanted to buy him, but Bud got him first. That's okay, though. I think my Salvador is faster."

Tanner couldn't let a challenge to his horse's reputation go disputed. "He can beat that horse any day, can't he, Drew?"

"Don't know and don't care," Drew said.

Tanner didn't understand her. She'd been crabby from the minute Ramon showed up. Tanner didn't much like Ramon either, but he'd been nice, even offered to stay with them while Buck went hunting for a missing bull.

"Want to have a race and see?" Ramon asked.

"Sure. Come on, Drew."

"I ain't coming," Drew snapped. "I'm riding a cow pony, and I don't mean to cripple him by racing up and down like some fool."

"That's because you know he can't keep up," Ramon said. "Come on, Tanner, let's see which is faster."

"Go on," Drew said. "I'm tired of looking at you."

Tanner figured he probably shouldn't leave Drew by herself, but she was in a nasty mood. Besides, he couldn't refuse Ramon's challenge.

"First one to reach the head of the canyon," Tanner called.

"Let's make it a real race," Ramon said, his smile growing even more brilliant. "Let's make it the first one to reach that ridge over there."

"That's more than a mile away," Tanner said.

"You worried your horse can't last that long?"

That was it. Tanner couldn't take any more. "I know a ridge that's two miles away," he said. "I'll beat you there and back."

With a yell they were off.

Tanner loved the feel of a galloping horse between his legs. He loved the hills that rose on either side of him, the mountains that towered in the distance. It was warm and quiet and green, and he was beating his Uncle Ramon's horse.

But only by a neck.

Instead of turning around at the ridge, Ramon veered off into a side canyon. Tanner followed. They pounded down the little valley, scrambled up a narrow path, and raced down another canyon. Ramon was a couple of lengths ahead now. Tanner had a feeling Ramon's horse was truly faster, but he wasn't willing to give up. Both horses slowed as he followed Ramon up a rocky, twisting trail into another canyon. It ended in a sheer rise of nearly two thousand feet.

The two riders pounded down the little valley, neck and neck. Gradually, Tanner's horse pulled ahead. He won by half a length. Even as he whooped in victory, Tanner had the feeling Ramon hadn't ridden as hard as he could. If Drew had been riding Salvador, she'd have won.

"That's quite a horse you've got there," Ramon said, breathing heavily after his exertion. "I don't know another horse that could beat Salvador at two miles."

"That was nearly three," Tanner said.

"Even better," Ramon said, smiling as he pulled up to give his horse a rest. Then he looked around with a disapproving frown. "What a god forsaken place."

"I like it," Tanner said. He led the way up a steep, rocky trail. "Wait until you see the canyon up above."

"You mean there's another canyon?" Ramon asked.

But Tanner didn't wait. He pushed his horse through the narrow passage until it opened out into a little valley about a mile long and a hundred yards wide.

"See," he said proudly, "this is where we brought the yearlings we helped brand."

About two dozen yearlings grazed in a loosely scattered group alongside a shallow stream that started from water pouring through a crack in the rocks. Ramon didn't seem interested in the yearlings. He started to dismount.

"Ward says you ought to keep a horse moving when he's hot."

Ramon paused. "He's tired."

"Then walk him. Ward says a man who doesn't take as much care of his horse as he takes of himself is a fool. Ward says—"

"You seem to think a lot of Ward," Ramon said, sounding slightly irritated.

"I like him a lot. I want Mama to marry him. I like him better than Bud."

Tanner didn't know why Ramon should look so upset. He didn't think he was Bud's friend.

"Wouldn't you like me for a daddy instead?"

The question shocked Tanner. Though he'd seen

Ramon on numerous occasions, he didn't really know Ward's brother. He had no idea why he should want him as a father. He could ride mighty good, but he'd bet his best boots he couldn't rope a calf.

"I want Ward," Tanner said as they walked their horses slowly down the center of the little valley. "I like him best of all."

"You know I've always wanted you to live at my ranch," Ramon said. "It's bigger than this."

Ramon made a face as though Jake's was a poor excuse for a ranch. Tanner didn't like that. He loved Jake's ranch. He wanted to stay here forever.

"You could ride anywhere you want, have as many horses as you want. One day when you grow up, it would be yours."

"Mine?" Tanner had no idea why Ramon should want to give him a ranch.

"After I die," Ramon said, "which won't be for at least forty or fifty years."

For Tanner a year was a long time. He didn't believe in anything as far away as fifty years. He'd be a very old man then, probably dead himself.

"Thank you," Tanner said, remembering his manners, "but I'd rather stay here with Ward."

Ramon looked angry. Tanner didn't understand. He had said thank you. Mama had told him people wouldn't be mad at him if he was polite. They rode for a while in silence. Tanner started to feel uncomfortable. He wished he'd asked Will to come with them. Will was always showing off, but he didn't sulk the way Drew did. He'd have raced no matter what horse he was riding.

"There's something you ought to know about Ward," Ramon said, finally. "I wasn't going to tell you, but I can't stand to see a young boy admire a man who's so unworthy of veneration."

Tanner wasn't sure what Ramon was saying, but it didn't sound nice.

"What would you say if I told you Ward already had a son?"

Tanner jerked so hard on the reins, his horse threw up its head in protest. "I don't believe you," Tanner exploded. "He would have told me." Then he remembered. "Ward never got married. He was off fighting the war."

"You're wrong. Ward did get married, but he ran off and left his wife."

Tanner didn't believe that. Ward would never run off and leave anybody.

"Worse than that, when he found out his wife was going to have a baby, he didn't come back."

"Why are you saying these bad things about Ward?" Tanner asked. "He's your brother. Don't you like him?"

"He did worse than that," Ramon continued, not answering Tanner's question. "After his son was born, Ward said it wasn't his baby, that his wife had been bad, that he never wanted to see the little bastard brat."

Tanner was confused. "Had the mama been bad? Was it really a little bastard brat?"

"No, but when Ward wouldn't come home, that's what other people started to call it. They wouldn't talk to the mama. They wouldn't let their children play with the little brat."

Tanner couldn't believe Ward would do such a thing, but the thought of everybody turning their backs on the little boy caught his imagination.

"What happened?"

"The kind uncle tried to help. He lived in a big house and had lots of money. He wanted the little bastard brat to be his son. He promised him horses and anything else he wanted."

"Did the little boy go live with him?"

"No. Ward wouldn't let him. He said none of his kin was going to help that brat."

"That was mean! The uncle should have taken him anyway."

"He tried. But one day the little bastard brat found Ward. Not wanting to seem so terrible, Ward pretended to like the little bastard brat. He so fooled him that when the kind uncle tried to take the little boy to his big ranch, he didn't want to go."

Suddenly Tanner had a feeling something was wrong. This story wasn't about a little bastard brat. It was about him.

"What are you saying this for?" he demanded. "I'm not a little bastard brat. Ward's not my father!"

"I'm afraid he is."

"No, he's not!"

"Why do you think he's spent so much time with you?"

"Ward likes me. He told me so."

"Why did he and your mother go off together for such a long time?"

"They went to help all those sick people."

"Ward wanted to make you and your mother like him again. That way, when he told you he was your father, you wouldn't be angry at him for leaving you."

Tanner was furious at Ramon for saying these things about Ward. He was also angry at Ramon for making him confused and upset.

"That's not true," he shouted. He took his reins and

struck at Ramon's horse. The animal threw up his head and shied away.

"Stop that, you little brat!" Ramon shouted.

"I'm not a brat!" Tanner shouted back as he swung at the horse again. "I'm not!"

The end of the reins hit Ramon's horse on the nose. The animal reared and squealed in protest. Ramon had to struggle to stay on.

"Stop hitting my horse, you stupid bastard!" Ramon shouted.

"I'm not a bastard, either," Tanner shouted. "Mama told me my father was a famous doctor who was lost in the war."

"That's Ward, you idiot. Can't you understand that?"

Tanner wished Drew were here. She'd know how to stop Ramon from telling all these horrible lies. He kept striking at Ramon's horse. The more upset the animal became, the more trouble Ramon had staying in the saddle. That made Tanner happy. He wanted to see Ramon fall on the ground.

"Ward won't let you live on a ranch," Ramon shouted at Tanner. "He's going to be a doctor in San Antonio where you won't have a horse and won't be able to ride ever again."

"That's not true!" Tanner shouted. He turned his horse and started back down the canyon at a gallop.

"Slow down, you fool kid!" Ramon shouted when they reached the treacherous trail. "You'll break your neck."

They hit the winding trail at a gallop. Ramon kept shouting at Tanner to be careful, but Tanner wanted to get back to the ranch as fast as he could. Ward had to tell him Ramon was lying. He had to!

But all the while Tanner had a terrible suspicion

that what Ramon said might be true. Too many things fitted too well. He didn't want to be the little bastard brat. He didn't want a father who didn't want him. He wanted a hero who had been killed and couldn't come home to the little boy he loved.

The more upset he became, the faster he rode. He ignored Ramon's shouts that it was dangerous to ride so fast.

When the trail opened out into the valley below, Tanner's horse hit the canyon bottom and broke into a gallop. Tanner turned around just in time to see Ramon's horse stumble on some loose rocks. The horse fell to its knees. Ramon went flying over the horse's head onto the rocks below. His body bounced off the rocks and rolled to a stop on a piece of level ground.

Horrified at what had happened, Tanner pulled his horse up, turned around, and galloped back. He vaulted from the saddle and raced to where Ramon lay sprawled on the ground.

"Mr. Ramon, are you all right? Please say something! Don't just lie there."

Ramon didn't move. Tanner inched forward and peered at him. He couldn't tell if he was breathing. Gathering his courage, Tanner reached out and picked up a hand. When he let it go, it fell to the ground and didn't move.

Chapter Twenty-six

"Have you seen Tanner?" Ward asked Marina.

"He got tired of hearing about cholera and went off with Drew and Buck. I saw them ride off together about an hour ago."

Ward found Marina in the sitting room feeding Dale. He liked the picture she presented, only he wished it were their daughter. He decided to do something about that soon.

"I'd hoped he'd hang around," Ward said. "I've missed him."

"Me, too, but apparently we're not nearly so exciting as a ride with Buck and Drew."

Ward sat down next to Marina. He tickled the bottom of Dale's feet. She stopped eating and stared at him with deep blue eyes. "Not ticklish, huh?"

"Don't distract her," Marina said. "Isabelle said she hasn't been eating much."

"Eat up," Ward coaxed. "You've got to grow up

fast. I intend for Marina to have a baby of her own by mid-winter."

Marina blushed. "That's no way to talk. She might get the idea you don't want her."

"I want her, but I want more of my own."

They watched Dale kick her legs and wave her arms. Ward thought she almost smiled.

"Ward, would you be upset if we didn't keep Dale?"

"I thought you wanted her."

"I do, but we might find her family."

"I doubt it."

"Someone else might want to adopt her."

"Who?"

"Mrs. Pruitt."

"What in the world for? She's well past the age for having a baby."

"That's the whole reason. She can't have one of her own."

"You wouldn't mind?"

She blushed again. "Not if I had one of my own."

Ward put his arm around Marina. "Are you sure about this?"

"Yes. I'll miss her, but . . ."

"It's okay with me, but we'll have to tell somebody."

"Who?"

"The authorities."

Marina looked unusually meek. "Clyde is the only authority around here. I supposed we'll have to turn her over to him as soon as she's healthy."

Ward took hold of Marina's chin and turned her head until she was forced to look at him. "You had this all planned out, didn't you? You laid your trap and led me straight into it."

"Of course not," she protested, but the twinkle in

her eyes and the smile playing hide-and-seek with the corner of her mouth belied her words. "How soon do you think we can tell them?"

"Not until I'm certain there's no chance of another outbreak of cholera. I'd better flirt with you while I can," he said to the baby. "Looks like you won't be around very long."

He watched Marina try to interest Dale in eating some more. "Have you seen Ramon?" Ward asked.

"He said he was going to take a nap in the shade."

"Is he still there?"

"I don't know. To be quite honest, I hope to avoid him as much as possible." Marina paused. "You don't think he and Tanner could be together, do you?"

Ward hadn't considered it, but he wouldn't put it past Ramon to sneak off and find Tanner if he wanted something of the boy. "Did Ramon say anything in particular to you?"

"He thinks I ought to divorce you and marry him," Marina said, making a face. "He says he wants to raise Tanner as his son and heir."

Ward didn't put much past Ramon, but this was more than he'd expected. "What possible reason could he have for doing that?"

"I think he's gone a little crazy where I'm concerned. I'm the only woman who didn't fall at his feet."

Ward smiled. "Yes, that is something he wouldn't understand. Mother, either."

"Do you think he would try to kidnap Tanner?" Marina asked.

"No."

"Ramon will do anything he can to get his own way. I'm proof of that."

Ward vowed to himself he would find a way to help

Marina forget the past, but it seemed nearly everything that happened brought it up again.

"I'll look for him, but it wouldn't surprise me to find him still dozing. He's not fond of exercise."

But they couldn't find Ramon, and his horse was gone.

"Whistle for Will and Pete," Isabelle said as she came out to join them. "They'll know. You may as well come back inside and wait," she said to Marina. "You'll do nothing out here but get a sunburn and freckles."

Marina smiled. "I never get freckles."

"I do," Isabelle said. "Thousands of little tiny ones. I look like a brown speckled hen."

They had barely reached the door when they heard the sound of a horse coming at a gallop.

"That sounds like Will," Isabelle said. "Nobody else rides down the trail that fast."

It was Tanner. Even at a distance they could see him whipping his horse to wring the last bit of speed from him. The badly lathered condition of the horse's neck and flanks told Ward Tanner had come a long way. The boy practically fell out of the saddle into his mother's arms.

"I killed Mr. Ramon," he sobbed. "He's lying on the ground all dead."

Ward reached out to take him by the shoulders. "Take your time," he said. "Catch your breath and tell us what happened."

Tanner jerked away from Ward and pulled closer to Marina. "Get away from me!" he shouted. "I hate you. You called me a little bastard brat."

All three adults were stunned by this unexpected and vehement outburst.

"Tanner, what do you mean by that?" Marina asked.

The boy's eyes flashed with stubborn determination. Ward said, "Just tell me what happened to Ramon."

For a moment it looked as though Tanner wasn't going to speak at all. Then he broke down and started crying.

"What happened, Tanner?" Marina asked.

"He wouldn't stop saying mean things. He chased me down the trail, but he fell. I asked him over and over, but he wouldn't get up."

"Where?" Ward asked.

"Where Ward killed the lion," Tanner told his mother.

"Somebody saddle me a horse," Ward said as he turned and ran toward the house. "I'll be back as soon as I find where I put my medical bag."

"Do you think he's really dead?" Jake asked Ward. They had met on the trail.

"I don't know. He's a good rider but not over this kind of country. He doesn't know how to fall. Mother had a fit every time he rode faster than a canter."

"What do you think he told Tanner?"

"I don't know, but apparently I didn't come off looking good."

"Marina told me she didn't trust him."

"She has reason, but he's my brother. I thought I could."

They saw his horse first. Ramon was nearly a quarter of a mile away.

Once they reached Ramon's inert body, Ward's examination didn't take long.

Ward felt a great weight settle on his chest. There

was no question that he would have to operate despite the distance from the house, despite the primitive conditions. If he didn't, Ramon would bleed to death. Ward wouldn't know what was wrong until he could look inside. What if he couldn't fix it? What if Ramon died?

How could he face his mother? How could he live with himself knowing he couldn't save his own brother?

Maybe he shouldn't operate. Then no one could blame him if Ramon died. But he would blame himself. Despite what Ramon had done, he was Ward's brother and Ward loved him. He probably always would.

He'd run away when he went to study medicine. He'd run away when he married Marina in secret. He'd run away when he thought she didn't love him. Every time he'd been wrong. He wouldn't run away again. He might fail, but at least he would know he'd done what he could.

"I'm going to have to operate," he told Jake. "He's bleeding inside."

Jake's eyes widened in surprise. "You can't operate out here. Let me get the wagon and move him to the house."

"He'll never make it."

"Let me get Marina or Isabelle to help you. I don't know what to do."

"We don't have time. I'll do everything that's important. All you have to do is get a fire started and boil some water. And cut a few of those saplings to make splints."

"I can do that," Jake said, clearly relieved at not being required to assist in the operation. "You going to leave him lying there?" he asked. Ramon lay on his back, his arms outflung, a rock under one leg.

"At least until I finish operating. His back could be broken. I'm certain his left leg is. His arm as well."

"I can help you set his bones."

"First I have to stop the bleeding."

Marina closed the door to the bedroom she shared with Tanner. She put her arm around his shoulders and guided him over to the bed. They sat down side by side.

"Now I want you to tell me what Ramon said to you," she said. "Every word. Don't leave anything out."

"He said Ward called me a little bastard brat." The words burst from Tanner as though under pressure. Tears sprang to his eyes as he looked up at his mother. "Ward wouldn't do that, would he?"

"No," Marina said, hugging her son close. "Ward loves you. He would never do anything to hurt you."

"He said Ward was my daddy. I told him that he wasn't, that my daddy was lost in the war. Isn't that true, mama? That's what you said, isn't it?"

Marina had never expected there would be a good time to tell Tanner about his father, but she could hardly have imagined a worse situation.

"Yes, that's what I said." Tanner relaxed a little. "That's what Ramon told me, but I found out it's not true. Your father's not dead."

Tanner didn't look excited. He actually looked frightened. "Where is he? Was he captured like Benjy's father?"

Isabelle could tell he had little hope she'd give him the answer he wanted.

"No, he wasn't captured," she said. She felt like a coward for putting off the truth, but she couldn't figure out how to say it. "He's not very far away. He'll be here in a little while."

Tanner's face grew stiff.

"He'll be here as soon as he looks after your Uncle Ramon."

"Mr. Ramon is my uncle? Why?"

"Because Ward is your father, Tanner, your real father."

She saw disbelief, then anger, crumple his face. She grabbed him by his arms before he could back away.

"He didn't call you a little bastard brat," Marina hastened to assure him. "Your Uncle Ramon told lies to both of us. He told me your father was lost. He told Ward I had disappeared and never wanted to see him again. Ward didn't know about you until we came here."

She talked as fast as she could, trying to explain before the full impact of what she'd told him took hold. But no matter how fast she talked, no matter what she said, she could see she was losing ground. Ramon had planted a seed of doubt that Tanner, in his terrible need for a father, couldn't forget. Ward might not have called him a little bastard brat, but his absence had made Tanner one just the same.

Tanner tried to break away. "I don't believe you."

"I would never lie to you, certainly not about something as important as this."

Tanner broke Marina's grasp. When she stood up and reached for him, he backed away.

"I hate Ward. I don't want him for my father. I hate him! I hate him!"

He opened the door and ran out of the room. Marina followed, calling his name, but she wasn't nearly as fast. By the time she reached the bottom of the stairs, he'd disappeared through the front door. Isabelle came hurrying in from the direction of the kitchen.

"He ran off toward the barns," Isabelle told her. "Drew went after him."

"I've got to find him. I've got to explain."

"Did you tell him about Ward?" Isabelle asked.

"Yes." Marina sighed.

"I thought he'd be glad."

"He might have been if his uncle hadn't poisoned his mind first. Ramon told Tanner Ward never wanted to see him, had called him a little bastard brat."

"Why would he do that?" Isabelle asked, shocked.

"You would have to understand Ramon. He's sick, obsessed. He wants to marry me. He thinks if he sets Tanner against Ward, I'll have no choice." Marina started toward the door but turned back. "You have more experience with boys than I have. What do you think I ought to say to Tanner?"

"Nothing," Isabelle counseled. "Leave him alone for a while. Boys have a strange sense of right and wrong. I don't understand it. Fortunately, Drew does. You'd be surprised what I've learned from that child."

"Tanner feels betrayed. Even if he understood me when I said Ward didn't know about him, he still feels the loss of those six years. Even though it wasn't Ward's fault, he'll never be able to give them back. Tanner will always hold that against him," Marina worried.

"Maybe not. Boys are also surprisingly sensible sometimes. Now come into the kitchen and have some coffee. One thing I've learned from being surrounded by males is that you can't rush them—the big ones or the little ones. Given time, they sometimes act like the sensible creatures God intended them to be. Push them, and they'll settle on the absolutely worst possible choice and hold to it with their last breath."

"Do you really like men?" Marina asked.

Isabelle laughed. "I love them. I wouldn't trade a single one of them for any female God made. But there's no point in pretending they're what they're not. Now while we wait for Drew to bring Tanner to his senses, you can explain why that over-stuffed little peacock thinks you could possibly prefer him to Ward."

The operation had been long and messy, as bad as during the war. Ward hadn't rushed, but he had known he had to finish before the light began to fade.

"Did I look like that when you took that bullet out?" Jake asked. Once he'd started to help, he had been steady and dependable.

"I only had to make a hole large enough to get the bullet out."

"I never realized a person could get hurt like that from a fall."

"According to Tanner, Ramon hit those rocks at a hard gallop. He's lucky to be alive." Ward heaved a sigh of relief when he closed the incision. "Now it's up to God."

Half an hour later Buck rode up. Isabelle had sent him to check on them. "Is there anything I can do?"

"You can get Marina's tent," Ward said. "I can't move him yet."

"You ready to set his leg?" Jake asked after Buck left.

"I guess."

They set and splinted the broken bones. Ward checked Ramon every few minutes to make sure he was still breathing.

"When is he going to wake up?" Jake asked. He had built a fire now that night was starting to close in on them. It would be cold before morning. Ward would need the tent and plenty of blankets to keep Ramon warm.

"I'm not sure. I used a lot of chloroform. I didn't want him to wake up during the operation."

Ward heard the sounds of something moving in the dark beyond the fire. He turned to see the eyes of several cows glowing red in the dark.

"Is that the first time you've operated since the war?" Jake asked.

"Yes. I can't really count the bullet I dug out of you."

"Were you nervous?"

"I thought I would be, but I was calmer than I've ever been."

"Even knowing it was your brother?"

"Even knowing my mother would hold me responsible if he died."

"You think you've gotten over what it was that drove you away from medicine?"

Ward would have expected such a question to unsettle him. He was pleased to discover it didn't. "You trying to get rid of me? I thought I was carrying my weight."

"You do a lot more than that. But everybody knows something's been eating you. You hadn't been back from Cypress Bend five minutes before I knew something had changed. I was hoping you'd figured it out."

Ward had never gotten used to having Jake and

Isabelle practically see inside his head. He supposed it was a useful skill with so many troubled children, but it made him uneasy.

"I think I have. Not everything, yet, but I think I got most of it."

Jake tossed more wood on the fire. Sparks flew up into the night. "None of us would want to lose you, but if that's what it takes for you to find peace—well, then, we'll wish you the best."

"Sounds more like I'm being tossed out on my ear."

"I know I'm not good with words, but don't try to make out I didn't say it right."

Ward took hold of Jake's shoulder and squeezed hard. "You said it just fine. Isabelle couldn't have done any better."

Ward wished it had been lighter. He had the distinct impression that Jake was blushing.

"That's not true, but it's nice of you to say. I doubt I'll ever get the hang of it, but Isabelle says—"

Jake broke off at the sound of a galloping horse. Two horses. Ward was wondering what could have brought Buck back so soon when Tanner materialized out of the night. Drew followed close behind.

Tanner tumbled off his horse. He came to a halt in front of Ward, the fire between them. Ward could tell he'd been crying. The trail of the tears still stained his face.

"Mama says you're my daddy. Are you?"

He stood there, his fists clenched, his mouth set, his whole body wound as tight as a spring. Ward didn't know whether his answer would set off an explosion, but he had no choice.

"Yes."

Ward wouldn't have been surprised if Tanner had climbed back on his horse and disappeared. But he just stood there, waiting, anger and pain obviously boiling inside him. He glared at Ward, appearing not to know what to do.

Jake got up and moved quietly off, taking Drew with him.

"I hate you!" Tanner said. "You didn't want me. You called me a little bastard brat."

Ward could tell Tanner was just waiting for him to deny the accusation. He didn't know exactly what Ramon had said to him, but he had obviously put the worst possible complexion on what had happened.

"I never knew I had a son until you ran up to ask your mother if you could go riding with Monty," Ward said. "Do you remember that? You admired him so much. You wanted to be just like him."

"Monty's the best cowboy there is."

So he'd been relegated to second place. That was okay. At least Tanner was talking to him.

"I don't want you to be my father anymore. I want Bud."

"I know you like him. I'm sure he's a good cowboy, but he can't possibly love you as much as I do."

"Bud loves me more than anybody. He said so."

Ward could see some of Tanner's resolve to hate him weakening.

"From the first moment I knew you were my son, I made up my mind I'd never leave you again. I tried to make you like me so much you'd never want me to leave. Why do you think I spent so much time teaching you how to rope? Don't you remember Will complaining I wasn't spending any time with him anymore?"

"I guess so." Tanner was weakening even further. "Why didn't you tell me?"

"I wanted you and your mother to come live with me. But Ramon had lied to us, and we were very angry at each other. Your mother wanted to divorce me and marry Bud."

"That's what I want her to do."

It was obvious he didn't.

"Come sit next to me," Ward said.

Tanner didn't move.

"Come on. You must be cold. You forgot your coat." Still Tanner hung back. "What do you want me to say, Tanner? I'm more sorry than you'll ever know that I missed all those years with you. When I think of what Ramon did, I'm tempted to pull out all those stitches and let him bleed to death."

Tanner had forgotten Ramon. Looking shocked and frightened, he glanced over at his uncle. "Is he dead?"

"No. I had to operate on him, but I think he's going to be okay."

"Mama said he lied about me."

"He lied to all of us about a lot of things. Most importantly, he never told me about you. If he had, I'd have come home right away."

"They'd let you leave the war?"

"I'd have found a way. Now come over here before you catch a chill. Your mother would never forgive either of us."

Tanner came reluctantly. He allowed Ward to put his own coat over his shoulders, but he kept some distance between them.

"You really never called me a little bastard brat?"

"Never. Why would I call my own son something like that?"

"You really didn't know about me?"

"No."

"And you would have come home right away if you had?"

"Yes." As soon as possible was the more truthful answer, but Ward didn't figure Tanner would understand that.

"And you want Mama and me to live with you?"

"Always." Ward had already answered these questions. He figured Tanner was going down his list, checking one by one.

"Where?"

"I don't know. There are a few things I haven't worked out yet."

"What?"

"They have nothing to do with you or your mother. No matter where we live, I love you both very much and want us to be together forever."

Tanner thought for a bit. "Can Drew come with us?"

"Drew will want to stay with Jake and Isabelle. They're her family."

"Pete told me Indians killed her family."

Ward should have known Pete wouldn't miss a chance to spread his own hatred of Indians to anybody who would listen, even a child as young as Tanner.

"That's true. Isabelle and Jake adopted her just like they adopted Will and Pete."

"Can't you adopt her, too?"

"No, but maybe you could have a brother or a sister, maybe several of them."

That appeared to be an idea Tanner had never considered. "Would a sister be like Drew?"

"I doubt it," Ward said. He chuckled despite himself. "There's not another girl in the world like Drew."

"Then I'd rather have brothers," Tanner said.

Ward reached out and put his arm around Tanner's shoulders. When he didn't draw away, Ward pulled him closer. Tanner resisted at first. Then he scooted over until he was up against Ward.

"I don't really like Bud better than you," he said finally.

"I hoped you wouldn't," Ward said. "Fathers don't want their little boys to like anybody better than them."

"Not even Monty?"

"Especially Monty. I want you to like me better than anybody in the whole world. You're my favorite little boy."

"If I'm your favorite, can I have a new rope? Drew says nobody in San Antonio knows how to make a decent rope."

Chapter Twenty-seven

Ramon had been conscious for more than an hour. Ward had sent Tanner back to the ranch with Jake and Drew, so he was alone with his brother. Ramon didn't speak until Ward had fed him and changed his bandages. Using just his fingertips, Ward gently touched the long incision in Ramon's abdomen.

"What did you do to me?" Ramon asked.

"I had to stop some bleeding inside you."

"Would I have died?"

"Yes."

Ramon didn't speak after that. He went back to sleep, awoke and ate, went back to sleep again. Each time he woke he would stare at Ward, but he didn't speak. Ward waited through that night, the next day, and the following night. People came and went, bringing food and more blankets. Ward fed and cared for Ramon, and still he remained silent.

"How's he doing?" Jake had asked the second morning.

They stood outside the tent. The chill of night had given way to the warmth of midmorning. It was a glorious day.

"He's fine."

"You want somebody to stay with you or take your place?"

"No."

"You must be getting bored just sitting here."

"It gives me time to think."

"You think too much," Jake said. "It's going to addle your brain one of these days."

Ward grinned. "You're just bothered because you have to do your own roping."

"Could be," Jake said, climbing back into the saddle. "When can we bring him up to the house?"

"Not for two or three days yet."

"He was hurt right bad, wasn't he?"

"If he'd hit his head as hard as he hit his insides, it would have split wide open."

Jake made a face. "And I've fallen a hundred times and never hurt more than my pride."

"Lucky."

"Yeah. Well, you take it easy. Fire your rifle if you need anything. Marina's going to bring your dinner."

The next day, Jake stood on the steps watching Will and Pete ride as hard as they could, each trying to reach him first. They tumbled off their horses and broke into speech.

"There's a lady coming," Pete managed to say first.

"And she's got lots of people with her."

"She made Buck stay with her so she wouldn't miss the ranch," Pete said.

"I don't like her," Will said. "She looks mean."

Jake had no idea who this woman could be. Neither did Isabelle. No one ever visited them.

"Maybe it's somebody from Cypress Bend," Marina said. She was feeding Dale. The baby was fully recovered, but she still had to be coaxed to eat.

"You ought to see her," Will said, unable to keep quiet. "She's in this great big buggy. It's got red seats and real windows."

"And she's got four cowboys riding with her," Pete added. "And they're all wearing guns."

"It sounds like a coach," Isabelle said. "I haven't seen anything to fit that description since I left New Orleans."

They all moved out to the front porch. Pete and Will kept up a dialogue, each trying to rival the other in their description of this unexpectedly magnificent equipage.

They all watched as the coach drew closer. It was like a procession. A second and more modest coach followed the first.

"Oh, yeah," Pete said. "I forgot to mention that one."

Glancing at Marina, Jake noticed that her color had faded.

"Are you all right?" he asked.

Marina nodded, but she didn't take her eyes off the approaching caravan.

"Do you know who that is?"

"No."

But Jake was certain she had a very good idea and didn't like it one bit.

When they were about fifty yards from the house, Buck left the coach and rode up to the porch.

"There's a woman in that carriage who's come to see Ward. She says she's his mama."

Ward went inside the tent to check on Ramon. He was awake. He checked Ramon's scar. "You're healing nicely, but I'm afraid I've spoiled your perfect hide."

Ramon just looked at him.

"Your arm and leg will be fine. No scars, and you won't walk with a limp."

Still Ramon remained silent. Ward washed his face, fed him his lunch, and prepared to leave the tent.

"Why did you do it?" Ramon asked.

Ward looked up. "What?" he asked, relieved that Ramon had finally spoken.

"Why did you save my life?"

Ward felt a twinge of guilt. He wondered if Ramon knew that for a moment he'd considered not operating. "I'm a doctor."

"That's not it. Why did you do it?"

"For God's sake, Ramon, you're my brother. What else would you expect me to do?"

"Let me die."

"Why?"

"Because I'd have let you die."

Ward swallowed. Ramon must be delirious. He couldn't know what he was saying. "I don't believe you." Ramon's stare made Ward's skin crawl. Maybe he did believe him. "Why?" he asked.

"Because I hate you. I've hated you for years."

Ward found that impossible to believe. "Don't be ridiculous. You've got everything a man could want. Why should you hate me?"

"You've got Marina."

"You'd have let me die for that?"

"Yes. She's the only woman I ever wanted."

Ward decided not to respond to that. Ramon had wanted many women. Marina just happened to be the only one he didn't get.

"She said she despised me, that she would die before she would let me touch her."

That didn't surprise Ward. Marina never had been mealymouthed about her feelings.

After a period of silence, Ramon asked, "Do you really love Marina?"

"Yes. I don't think I ever stopped."

"Mama said that. She said we had to get an annulment. When we couldn't, she said we had to make you think we did."

"Why? What was wrong with my being married to Marina?"

"Papa would leave you his money."

"Mama was wrong. He didn't leave me anything."

"Yes, he did."

"What, a couple hundred dollars?"

"Forty-five thousand. It's in a bank in Austin."

Ward was speechless.

"I wasn't going to tell you. I was going to let it sit there. If you didn't claim it in ten years, it would come to me."

"Why did you change your mind?" Ward didn't understand. Ramon was always in need of money.

"You didn't let me die."

Ward would have preferred to hear that Ramon had discovered he had some brotherly feeling for him. But then, he'd always hoped for the impossible when it came to his family.

"Papa left Tanner half of the ranch."

Ward stared hard at Ramon, certain he was lying.

The money he might have believed. He wanted to believe his father hadn't forgotten him, but he didn't believe he'd left Tanner half of the ranch. Luisa wouldn't have let him.

"We told him you were dead, mother and I. We decided it between us so I'd get everything. He must have suspected we were lying."

"But why leave Tanner half the ranch?"

"Whether he was your child or mine, he was Papa's only grandson."

"Why Austin?" None of this made sense. It was getting more fantastic by the minute.

"He didn't trust Mama's friends in San Antonio."

"What do I have to do to get this money?" Ward didn't know why he asked when he didn't believe there was any money.

"Nothing. It's in your name."

"And Tanner's share of the ranch?"

"The bank controls that."

"How do you know this?"

"I found out when I tried to sell some stock."

"You could probably get around the trustees."

Ramon smiled, and this time it wasn't irresistible. "I did."

Ward was actually relieved to know Ramon had been stealing from the estate. That enabled Ward to believe about the money and the ranch.

He could hardly credit it. He felt lighter of spirit than he had in years. It wasn't the money. He could make all he needed. It was the knowledge that he hadn't been forgotten. That alone was worth the three miserable days he'd spent in this tent.

"Are you really going to take Marina back?" Ramon asked.

"Yes."

"Mama will be furious."

Ramon stared at Ward, and a look of wonder gradually came over Ramon's face.

"You don't care. She's going to hate you, but you're going to do it anyway."

Ramon lay back and closed his eyes. Ward crawled out of the tent. Blinded by the sunlight, he stumbled over to a log in the shade of a maple. He sat down. He had a lot of thinking to do.

"She followed Ramon here because she was furious he'd gone against her wishes. The moment she learned he was hurt, she insisted on being taken to him."

Marina had come to warn Ward his mother was on the way. He almost wished she hadn't. The surprise of her showing up unexpectedly couldn't have been worse than waiting an hour for her arrival.

"I had hoped we'd have a little more time before we had to face her, but I guess it's better not to put it off."

"I don't think I should be here," Marina said.

"You're my wife. Of course you should."

"Later. Not at first."

"Why?"

"You've something to settle with her. Maybe it'll be easier if I'm not here. At least, not visible. How is he?" Marina asked, indicating Ramon.

"Still in a good bit of pain."

"Good. I hope he's in agony for at least a month."

"Marina! He's my brother."

"He's also the man who lied to both of us, who did everything he could to destroy your life as well as mine and Tanner's."

"I think he's paid for what he did."

"No, he hasn't. He's only been here three days. We suffered for seven years. You can forgive him if you want, but I never will."

Marina had ignored Ward's protests and taken her horse to drink. She remained out of sight. He heated the venison stew she'd brought over the fire. Ramon would be hungry when he woke up. It probably wasn't the best thing for him, but a kitchen geared to feeding teenaged boys wasn't stocked with suitable food for convalescent patients.

Ward saw his mother long before she reached him. He had the whole length of the valley to figure out what he was going to say to her. In the end, he didn't get a chance to say anything.

The moment she was helped down from her horse—it would have been impossible to bring her carriage—she demanded, "Where is my son?"

"Inside the tent," Ward said.

She looked about her with such rage and disgust, Ward thought she was going to strike him right then. Instead she sailed into the tent without giving him a chance to speak.

Ward hadn't seen his mother in seven years. She hadn't changed much. She still dressed almost entirely in black and silver. Her skin seemed to have grown whiter, more like parchment, but her hair showed no hint of grey.

The remains of her great beauty could still be seen, but the poison in her soul had begun to show in her face and eyes; her expression was malevolent. She reminded Ward of a huge, black vulture. He was relieved she'd gone inside the tent.

"We'll wait out of sight," Jake said. He and Buck had accompanied her.

"You may as well join Marina at the creek," Ward said.

Jake grinned and winked. "We will." He mouthed the words *Good luck*.

Ward wondered what he should do and decided to stay outside. His mother obviously wanted this time alone with Ramon. Ward hadn't expected to be included in her greeting, or for her to be happy to see him again. Nevertheless, being ignored by her still had the power to hurt. He decided it always would.

He listened to her upraised voice and Ramon's muffled replies. He couldn't help smiling. She'd never wanted him to be a doctor, but she checked everything he'd done with a knowledge that was surprising in its depth.

She finally emerged. Again she gave him no chance to speak.

"You must move Ramon immediately. I will not have him recuperating out here like a wild animal."

"Not yet. It's more than six miles to the house. He can't ride a horse, and a wagon would shake him to bits."

"I would never take him to that house," Luisa Dillon said, as though Isabelle's home were some kind of verminous slum. "I shall take him to San Antonio where he can be cared for properly."

"He'll have to stay here for another three or four days," Ward said. "His injuries are mostly internal, but they are serious and extensive."

"Where is that boy who did this to him?" she demanded. "I demand that he be punished immediately."

"Ramon did this to himself. He was riding much too fast down a dangerous trail."

"Who lured him to such a place?"

379

"He challenged Tanner to a horse race. Ramon always did have to prove he had the fastest horse."

Stymied in that line of attack, his mother tried another.

"I will not have him kept here. I want him seen by a real doctor, one who knows what he is doing."

Trust his mother to find a knife to twist.

"I'm his doctor. He won't be moved until I say so. Then he will only go as far as the ranch until I decide it's safe to take him home."

His mother turned livid. Ward wasn't surprised. He'd never flatly refused to obey her before.

"I can hire enough men to take him by force."

"Would you remove him if you knew it would kill him?"

"I do not believe you."

"Are you prepared to take that chance?"

Luisa didn't reply immediately. She might not believe Ward was a competent doctor, but she wasn't willing to take a chance with Ramon's life. "I do not trust you. You have always been jealous of him."

"How can you say that, you spiteful old witch?"

Ward turned to see an infuriated Marina come round the tent. She'd obviously not stayed by the stream.

"Ward had to operate on your worthless son to save his life. He's spent almost three days without leaving Ramon's side for one minute. After the things the two of you have done to him, you ought to get down on your knees and be thankful he didn't leave him to die."

Luisa's skin turned pasty white. "How dare you speak to me, you hussy!"

"She's my wife, Mother," Ward said. "You'll speak to her properly, or you won't speak to her at all."

Luisa glared at both of them, rage flaming in her eyes. "So you have decided to take her up again, have you?"

"We're still in love," Ward said without waiting for Marina to speak. "We want to give Tanner brothers and sisters."

Something about that thought seemed to cause Luisa to seethe with fury.

"If you touch that woman, you will not come within a hundred miles of the Rancho del Espada," Luisa said to Ward. "I refuse to speak to her."

"Why? Ramon has been trying to get her to divorce me and marry him. You'd have to talk to her then."

"I would never let him do such a thing," Luisa declared. "She bewitched him. Ever since that day he saw her in San Antonio, he could think of no other woman. He even talked me into inviting her to stay at the rancho. I thought it would cure him of her. I was thankful when she married you."

"You didn't seem thankful," Marina said.

Luisa turned on Marina. "He married the finest woman in San Antonio, but do you think he gave her one half the attention he gave you? You bedeviled him, cast a spell on him—"

"The only thing I did was refuse him," Marina answered, hotly.

"It's time we forget all of that," Ward said, "and try to act like a family again. You have a daughter-in-law and a grandson. As soon as I—"

"I will not perpetuate such a lie," Luisa stated flatly.

"Mother, you might not like it, but—"

"I will never accept *that woman* as my daughter-in-law. However, I will accept Tanner as my grandson if she will let it be known she was bedded by Ramon."

Ward and Marina stared at Luisa in disbelief.

"Ramon needs an heir. His wife died without—"

"Tanner is not Ramon's son," Marina said, cutting Luisa off. "He's Ward's."

"I know you hope to repair your reputation by that lie, but I will not countenance it. Tanner is Ramon's son. I will accept him only if you admit you were willing to do anything you could to convince Ramon to marry you."

"You son is a liar and a libertine," Marina said. "You should be thankful you have at least one son you can be proud of. You ought to cut your losses. Send Ramon off to the Territories with an allowance and orders never to come back, and welcome Ward home with open arms."

Luisa looked at Marina as though she were in the process of growing three heads.

"You have to admit Ward is a much more admirable son. He's a doctor and a war hero. You don't have to be ashamed of Ramon, but I—"

"Ashamed of Ramon!" Luisa thundered.

"I know you're bound to be prouder of Ward, but you—"

"Never!" Luisa thundered. "Never would I be proud of a bastard!"

"What?" Marina exclaimed.

"Do you think I would be the mother of one such as him?" Luisa demanded, pointing at Ward, scorn written deep in her face. "Ramon is a son to be proud of. He"—she gestured at Ward again—"is nothing but the bastard son of a *puta*."

"I always knew you were a mean, spiteful, wicked old woman," Marina said, "but I never suspected you were crazy enough to call your own son a bastard."

"He is no son of mine!" Luisa screeched. "His mother was a little whore his father picked up in Austin. We thought I could have no children. When she swelled up like a melon, I agreed to accept her baby as my own. By a cruel twist of fate, I gave birth to a perfect son of my own three years later."

At last Ward understood—all the slights, the feeling of not being good enough. He understood everything.

"What happened to my mother?" he asked.

Luisa looked as though she would have liked to spit on Ward. "She was supposed to leave after you were born. She died instead."

"Where is she buried?"

She did spit. On the ground. "In the orchard. Your father wanted her buried in the family graveyard, but I would not allow it."

"Ward, I'm so sorry," Marina said, turning toward him.

"Don't be. Actually it's a great relief. Now I have the answer to my last question."

He meant it. Luisa's disclosure had lifted a huge burden from his shoulders. He didn't have to care about this woman any longer. She wasn't his mother. He didn't owe her any duty, any allegiance.

He didn't have to feel guilty because he couldn't love her.

"What question?" Marina asked.

"We're not going back to San Antonio or the Rancho del Espada. We're going to stay here. Mama . . . Luisa . . . was right. I may be trained as a doctor, but I'm a cowboy at heart. I'm going to buy up some of this riverfront land and start my own ranch."

"How can a pauper buy land?" Luisa said, the contempt in her tone thicker than her accent.

"You didn't convince my father to turn his back on me entirely. He left me over forty thousand dollars."

Eyes blazing, Luisa glanced toward the tent. The only person besides herself who knew that was Ramon.

"And though you don't want me at the rancho, you haven't seen the last of me. My father left half of the rancho to Tanner. He didn't know which of us was Tanner's father, but he was certain Tanner was his grandson. You knew that, but you weren't going to tell me. You wanted Ramon to get hold of Tanner so you could get control of the rancho. Now that my father and I aren't there to run it, it's not making enough money to support Ramon. He wants to sell the stock, even the land, to pay his bills."

Luisa didn't have to answer. It was obvious from her fury that Ward was right. "I do not care what Gardner said in that will." She was so enraged, she could hardly get the words out. "You set one foot on the rancho and I will shoot you myself."

"Don't worry. I don't want to see you anymore than you want to see me, but I won't let you waste Tanner's inheritance. I'm going to have the bank appoint a new foreman. Ramon will have to clear everything he does with the bank. If he sells any more stock without permission, I'll have him put in jail."

Luisa looked furious enough to kill Ward.

"You don't like it now, but one day you'll be thankful. You'll be able to live the rest of your life in luxury. Ramon would have paupered you in ten years."

"Get out of my sight. I do not wish to set eyes on you ever again."

Ward nearly sighed with relief. He felt the last of

the tension ebb from him. "Quite frankly, that will suit me just fine."

Luisa Dillon watched Ward and Marina walk away, and a new and bitter hatred began to fill her soul. It was not enough that she should have had to mix her pure Castilian blood with an Anglo's to regain the wealth and position her family had lost in two Texas wars. She must now see her husband's bastard claim her grandson.

She knew in her heart that Tanner was Ramon's son. Ward could never had sired such a perfect boy. That bitch lied when she said Ramon had not lain with her, that she had fought him off. No woman could deny her son. She merely wanted to hide her shame.

Luisa had no idea why Ramon had given up, but she would not. Never. Luisa Escalante would never let her grandson pass as Ward's son. One day she would get him back.

She turned and entered the tent. First, she must take care of her son. Once he was well again, she would plan her revenge.

"Don't you think it's about time you gave me your answer?" Ward said to Marina.

They were walking arm in arm toward the stream where Jake and Buck still waited. Luisa had insisted she be allowed to care for her son alone. Ward had given her a few instructions he hoped she wouldn't ignore and left her.

"You know what it's going to be."

"I'd rather hear you say it."

"You're a literalist, just like your son."

"Don't try to get around me with big words. Luisa

let the tutors teach me once they were done with Ramon."

"I love you, Ward Dillon, and I know you love me. I don't know how, considering what's happened to both of us. I'm no longer afraid you want me because of Tanner or that you love your family more than you love me. I want to be your wife and will follow you anywhere. Is that clear enough?"

"Even a cowboy can understand that," Ward said. He took Marina in his arms and kissed her.

"And even a cowgirl can understand that," Marina said when she'd recovered her breath.

"Good. Let's find Jake and Buck and get away from here. I've learned more about my family in the last two days than I ever wanted to know."

"Were you really relieved to learn Luisa wasn't your mother, even though it clouds your birth?"

Ward laughed. "Now Tanner can call *me* the little bastard brat."

"He wouldn't dare. I'd tan his backside."

Ward put his arm around her and kissed her again. "You were mighty fierce back there. I thought you were going to attack Mama. Oh, hell, I guess I'll always think of her like that."

"I'm glad she's not. Now I can dislike her and not feel guilty."

"Feisty little thing, aren't you!"

"Yes. I waited a long time and paid a big price to get what I want. Anybody who tries to take it away had better watch out."

Epilogue

"You mean we're going to have a ranch right next to Drew?" Tanner asked.

"As close as we can," Ward told him. "I'm going to buy all the land I can between here and Cypress Bend. It'll keep the town from expanding out this way. We'll save the hills for the boys."

"If they want to come back," Isabelle said. She looked at Buck, now a big, strapping young man of eighteen. "They so seldom do."

"We'll have plenty of room, just in case."

"Are you sure you want to be a rancher?" Jake asked.

"A cowboy," Ward corrected, glancing at Tanner. "Just like Monty Randolph. I'm going to have to start practicing. I mean to be better than Monty and Bud one day."

Tanner hung his head. "You're already better. I only said that because I was mad at you."

"You still mad?"

"Maybe a little."

"You stupid boy!" Drew exclaimed. "After all the time I spent explaining to you how—"

"Let it ride, Drew," Ward said. "He'll come around. Now Marina and I have to look for a place to build a house," Ward told Jake and Isabelle. "Do you think you could do something with this crew so we could have a little time to ourselves?"

"I'll take care of Tanner," Drew said. She marched him off, despite Tanner's protests.

"She's got to have somebody to mother," Isabelle said, laughing. "The others are too big."

"Maybe by the time Tanner's too big, she'll be interested in mothering slightly bigger boys!"

"God forbid!" Ward said.

"He won't have to," Isabelle said. "Jake will do it for Him."

"You sure this is where you want to build?" Ward asked. "It's only four miles from town."

"I don't mind. Are you sure you don't want to be a doctor? You don't have to stay here, you know. I'll go anywhere you want."

"I guess I'm a little too big to be an orphan, but that's what I feel like. Jake and his boys are more family to me than my own kin ever were. I want to stay here. You and Tanner are like orphans as well. It's time we all started over."

"And medicine?"

"I realized some time back that I became a doctor for all the wrong reasons. I worked till I was exhausted to make the Rancho del Espada the best ranch in Texas, but my family took it all for granted. I thought if I did something else, was a great success, they'd have to notice me. I didn't realize until later that it wasn't what I did or didn't do, it was me. They didn't love me. Now I understand why. I'll still help people when I can, but Luisa was right. I'm a cowboy at heart."

"And your son wants to be just like you."

"Maybe we can have another one who wants to be a doctor."

"Or a daughter?"

"A female doctor?"

"Why not?"

"She'll have to specialize in tonsils and hangnails. No man will let her examine him."

Marina looked ready to do battle.

"There's only one solution," Ward said, anxious for peace. "We'll have to have twins, a boy and a girl."

"Do you really want more children?" Marina asked, apparently more interested in babies than battle.

"Very much. But most of all I want you."

They were in the middle of what was turning into an exceptionally passionate kiss when they heard the sound of galloping hooves.

"It's a rotten thing when you can't find privacy in a deserted valley," Ward complained. "Maybe there're too many children here already."

"Jake says you got to come right away," Drew shouted the moment she came within earshot. "He says Isabelle is starting to have her baby."

Author's Note

Cholera was one of the most dreaded diseases of the 19th century. It spread rapidly and easily across continents and oceans. Able to kill in a matter of hours, it could sweep through whole army camps, towns, even countries, killing as many as 60% of its victims in a matter of days. Unfortunately, surviving cholera didn't give the victim immunity.

Cholera was probably endemic in India in remotest antiquity. It recurs there annually in epidemic form and with great loss of life. With increasing facilities for travel, it gradually spread to much of Asia. At least four pandemics occurred during the 19th century. The pandemic of 1863–66 reached Europe by overland routes via Mecca and Egypt and spread to North America, giving rise to the outbreak which started in 1867.

The cholera bacillus enters the body through the mouth, usually through contaminated water. The incubation period is between 12 and 48 hours. The onset of symptoms is sudden and violent. Through vomiting and diarrhea, the body loses its fluids. This loss could be as much as four gallons in a single day. This causes agonizing cramps in the muscles, especially the legs and feet. The patient will soon collapse or go into shock. With the cessation of vomiting and diarrhea, the patient enters the last stage. Either he will die, or, if the loss of fluids has not been severe, recover. The mortality rate was usually 40% to 60%.

Cholera outbreaks were terrifying because they were so quick, so deadly, and doctors knew neither how to prevent the disease nor how to cure the patient once the disease had struck. Doctors didn't know that people without symptoms could carry the disease. Too, mild cases were often diagnosed as simple diarrhea. The situation was further complicated by the near lack of personal hygiene.

An English physician proved in the 1850s that water contaminated with the feces of cholera victims transmitted cholera, but most doctors didn't recognize his work. The germ theory was present by the end of the Civil War, but most physicians rejected that as well. Progress was finally made when army doctors connected the disease with the filth that was prevalent in army camps.

After 1868, military doctors tended to quarantine patients. They showed great interest in keeping quarters scrupulously clean and latrines disinfected. They required that soiled bedding be burned. Unsoiled linen was disinfected and boiled before laundering. Civilian doctors gradually began to accept these practices.

The last major epidemic in the United States occurred in 1873.

AUTHOR'S NOTE

Cholera was one of the most dreaded diseases of the nineteenth century. It spread rapidly and easily across continents and oceans. Able to kill in a matter of hours, it could sweep through whole army camps, towns, even countries killing as many as 60 percent of its victims in a matter of days. Unfortunately, surviving cholera didn't give the victim immunity.

Cholera was probably endemic in India in remotest antiquity. It recurred there annually in epidemic form and with great loss of life. With increasing facilities for travel, it gradually spread to much of Asia. At least four pandemics occurred during the nineteenth century. The pandemic of 1863-66 reached Europe by overland routes via Mecca and Egypt and spread to North America, giving rise to the outbreak which started in 1867.

The cholera bacillus enters the body through the mouth, usually through contaminated water. The incubation period is between twelve and forty-eight hours. The onset of symptoms is sudden and violent. Through vomiting and diarrhea the body loses its fluids. This loss could be as much as four gallons in a single day. This causes agonizing cramps in the muscles, especially the legs and feet. The patient will soon collapse or go into shock. With the cessation of vomiting and diarrhea, the patient enters the last stage. Either he will die, or, if the loss of fluids has not been severe, recover. The mortality rate was usually 40 to 60 percent.

Cholera outbreaks were so terrifying because they were so quick, so deadly, and doctors neither knew how to prevent the disease nor cure the patient once the disease had struck. Doctors didn't know people without symptoms could carry the disease, and mild cases were often diagnosed as simple diarrhea. The situation was further complicated by the near lack of personal hygiene.

An English physician proved in the 1850s that water

contaminated with the feces of cholera victims transmitted cholera, but most doctors didn't recognize his work. The germ theory was present by the end of the Civil War, but most physicians rejected that as well. Progress was finally made when army doctors connected the disease with the filth that often accompanied army camps.

After 1868, military doctors tended to quarantine patients. They showed great interest in keeping quarters scrupulously clean, latrines disinfected. They required that soiled bedding be burned. Unsoiled linen was disinfected and boiled before laundering. Civilian doctors gradually began to accept these practices.

The last major epidemic in the United States occurred in 1873.

LEIGH GREENWOOD

**"I loved *Rose*, but I absolutely loved *Fern*!
She's fabulous! An incredible job!"**
—*Romantic Times*

A man of taste and culture, James Madison Randolph enjoyed the refined pleasures of life in Boston. It's been years since the suave lawyer abandoned the Randolphs' ramshackle ranch—and the dark secrets that haunted him there. But he is forced to return to the hated frontier when his brother is falsely accused of murder. What he doesn't expect is a sharp-tongued vixen who wants to gun down his entire family. As tough as any cowhand in Kansas, Fern Sproull will see her cousin's killer hang for his crime, and no smooth-talking city slicker will stop her from seeing justice done. But one look at James awakens a tender longing to taste heaven in his kiss. While the townsfolk of Abilene prepare for the trial of the century, Madison and Fern ready themselves for a knock-down, drag-out battle of the sexes that might just have two winners.

___4178-2 $5.99 US/$6.99 CAN

SEVEN BRIDES
VIOLET

LEIGH GREENWOOD

"Leigh Greenwood is a dynamo of a storyteller!"
—*Los Angeles Times*

Jefferson Randolph has never forgotten all he lost in the War Between The States—or forgiven those he has fought. Long after most of his six brothers find wedded bliss, the former Rebel soldier keeps himself buried in work, only dreaming of one day marrying a true daughter of the South. Then a run-in with a Yankee schoolteacher teaches him that he has a lot to learn about passion.

Violet Goodwin is too refined and genteel for an ornery bachelor like Jeff. Yet before he knows it, his disdain for Violet is blossoming into desire. But Jeff fears that love alone isn't enough to help him put his past behind him—or to convince a proper lady that she can find happiness as the newest bride in the rowdy Randolph clan.

_3995-8 $5.99 US/$7.99 CAN

LEIGH GREENWOOD'S

SEVEN BRIDES

Laurel

Although Hen Randolph is the perfect choice for a sheriff in the Arizona Territory, he is no one's idea of a model husband. After the trail-weary cowboy breaks free from his six rough-and-ready brothers, he isn't about to start a family of his own. Then a beauty with a tarnished reputation catches his eye and the thought of taking a wife arouses him as never before.

But Laurel Blackthorne has been hurt too often to trust any man—least of all one she considers a ruthless, coldhearted gunslinger. Not until Hen proves that drawing quickly and shooting true aren't his only assets will she give him her heart and take her place as the newest bride to tame a Randolph's heart.

_3744-0 $5.99 US/$6.99 CAN

BY LEIGH GREENWOOD

Seven Brothers Who Won the West—
And the Women Who Tamed Their Hearts.

The way Zac Randolph sees it, he is the luckiest man on earth. The handsome devil even owns his own Little Corner of Heaven, the best saloon in California. And with every temptress on the Barbary Coast yearning to take him to paradise, he certainly has no plans to be trapped by the so-called wedded bliss that has already claimed his six brothers.

Refusing to bet her future happiness on an arranged marriage, Lily Goodwin flees from her old Virginia home to the streets of San Francisco. Trusting and naive, she vows to help the needy, and despite Zac Randolph's wealth, she considers him the neediest man in town. When the scoundrel refuses Lily's kindness, she takes the biggest gamble of her life. And if she wins, she'll become the last—and luckiest—of the Randolph brides.

_4070-0 $5.99 US/$6.99 CAN

Dorchester Publishing Co., Inc.
P.O. Box 6640
Wayne, PA 19087-8640

Please add $1.75 for shipping and handling for the first book and $.50 for each book thereafter. NY, NYC, and PA residents, please add appropriate sales tax. No cash, stamps, or C.O.D.s. All orders shipped within 6 weeks via postal service book rate. Canadian orders require $2.00 extra postage and must be paid in U.S. dollars through a U.S. banking facility.

Name_____
Address_____
City_____State_____Zip_____
I have enclosed $_____ in payment for the checked book(s).
Payment <u>must</u> accompany all orders. ❑ Please send a free catalog.